Xu,
Thanks so much
for your
Support!
♡ Annie
xoxo

LAST TRAIN TO OMAHA

Front cover photo by Christian Lagereek, copyright permission obtained through warmpictures.com

Back cover photo by Mahathir Mohd Yasin, Malyasia, copyright permission obtained through amartimages.photodeck.com

Book design and development by WildElement.ca

Hardcover: ISBN 978-0-9918325-3-8
Paperback: ISBN 978-0-9918325-0-7
eBook: ISBN 978-0-9918325-1-4

LAST TRAIN TO OMAHA

Ann Whitely-Gillen

WWW.ANNGILLENBOOKS.COM

This book is dedicated to my mother, Danielle Galletta,
who always dreamed of writing a book one day
and
to my father, Tony Whitely,
for his courage and never ending creativity.

INTRODUCTION

A funny thing happens to you when you hear the words "you have cancer." Your inner and outer worlds change completely and stay forever in this new vein, never allowing you to return to what you once knew about yourself and your everyday life.

I recall years ago listening to an interview with award-winning actress after she had been recently diagnosed with breast cancer. She explained that even the simplest of things like a book on a shelf becomes sharper and more defined to the naked eye, as if its mere existence illuminated a more profound clarity. I was drawn into the wonder of what it would be like to face such a disease— one so powerful that your life would dangle in the balance.

While a part of me found the description of her experience quite haunting, there was an element of peace and beauty in the fact that she could see light under such dire circumstances. Little did I know that a few years later I would face the very same fate.

On January 13, 2012, I was diagnosed with ductal carcinoma in my left breast. At the age of forty eight and with four wonderful children and an amazing husband, the thought of having to fight for my life consumed me. Much like the famous actress had described, all things tangible and real began to pop out in front of me with more intensity and force. Fear and happiness constantly battled for my devoted attention, both winning a round or two during each match. Every day was a struggle to try and understand *why* this was happening to me. At same time, I fought relentlessly to remain faithful to all the blessings in my life, despite having cancer. My inconsistent emotional state started to wear me down as I withdrew from family and friends. I was alone in my newfound state and desperate for resolve.

My surgery occurred quite quickly after my diagnosis and with it came this unwarranted feeling of abandonment. Now that the cancer was out, I was forced to wait for more tests to see whether it had spread into my nodes and if I would require chemotherapy. The feeling of isolation became more intense, and I wanted more than anything to face my destiny but I wasn't sure how.

Shortly after, my niece and a friend, who is also a cancer survivor, recommended I read the book *Anticancer* by the amazing Dr. David Servan-Schreiber—a leading scientist in his expertise of mental health disease, and a cancer survivor of nearly twenty years. I devoured the information in this book and would spend hours going over several chapters and taking notes about nutrition for my mind and body. Despite the fact that I was determined to believe I would not die from this disease, I felt compelled to read the chapter on the passage towards death. It was oddly morbid and yet, in the same breath mesmerizing and enlightening.

In this particular chapter, Dr. Servan-Schreiber references another author by the name of Dr. Scott Peck known for his theories on the acceptance of death as an essential part of life and is often referenced as quoting the poem "Limited" by American poet Carl Sandburg, as a metaphor for his philosophy on the subject.

I went to bed after reading that chapter of the book and instantly began thinking about why death's looming presence is not independent of its inevitability. The more I thought about the one and only thing that no one can avoid, the closer I came to my own conclusion: Life and death are very much connected within each and every moment randomly captured and released within the realm of our mortal existence.

Before I fell asleep, I focused on the importance of living my life in the grander scheme and on the idea that *none* of us should merely schlep through only for the sake of enduring the daily demands and sometimes-onerous routines. I had, after all, succumbed to that very viewpoint for years and it was time to change direction.

When I woke up the next morning, I told my husband that I had a dream about a man who was afraid to live his life and make connections with others because of something traumatic that had occurred in his youth, and that his only release was during the hours in which he volunteered at a veterans' home. You can only imagine the look on my husband's face when I began to recount the names of the characters in my dream. When I stopped talking, he took me by my shoulders and said, "you must write this book."

With his encouragement, and the love and support of so many people, I did just that. This is my first novel and so I humbly present it to you as such.

Writing this story has been extremely cathartic. It allowed me to explore my own spiritual epiphanies and begin my physical and emotional healing. I hope that it inspires others to seek clarity in the simplest forms of life.

In closing, my story is not only about the characters that fill the pages, but also about all of us who share in this world of definite qualms and uncertainties. It is these very reservations in life that miraculously defines who we were meant to be during our journey here, and in the end summarizes what became of us.

I AM riding on a limited express, one of the crack trains
  of the nation.
Hurtling across the prairie into blue haze and dark air
  go fifteen all-steel coaches holding a thousand people.
(All the coaches shall be scrap and rust and all the men
  and women laughing in the diners and sleepers shall
  pass to ashes.)
I ask a man in the smoker where he is going and he
  answers: "Omaha."

- "Limited", Carl Sandburg

Lisle, Illinois – August 3, 1995

T he hot sun beats down on Saint Joan of Arc Catholic Church, illu-
minating its stained glass windows and causing beams of light to
crisscross above the dark oak benches inside. Stephen Pike, a once-
vibrant eighteen-year-old, is being laid to rest today in his hometown, a full
ten days after the bizarre accident that took his life and shocked the community. His family expected a smaller, more intimate service, but as hom-
age would dictate, the turnout is much larger than anyone imagined. Students and teachers from all grades of Lisle High School cram into the small
church, filling all of the pews and leaving nothing but standing room for
those who arrive close to the scheduled starting time. The heat accumulating inside is unbearable and amplifies the intensity of grief being shared
amongst the crowd.

James Milligan sits in the first pew, heavily sedated on Xanax and paralyzed
by the entire ordeal. He has been unable to process the accident since it happened. The images of Stephen's death burn behind his heavy eyes and continue to burrow into the depths of his memory like an aggressive carcinoma.
His mind and body float over the ceremony as it commences. A familiar voice
vibrates towards his ears in his semi-conscious state.

Stephen's Uncle Patrick is standing at the altar, hunched over the po-
dium and leading the eulogy. "He was a dynamic person with a golden
soul and a mischievous mind. He can never be replaced …" he recites, barely
maintaining his composure.

1

The sound of people weeping makes James agitated and he fantasizes about escaping somehow. Sweat pours down his temples, leaving him drenched in his own perspiration and sealing his claustrophobic skin into his dark suit. By the end of the service, nausea takes over and he cannot bear to attend the burial with the rest of his family. Instead, he breaks away from the milling crowd and makes his way to Stephen's house, now occupied only by Stephen's parents, Lynn and Dean Pike.

The Pikes' home has always been like a second home to James, and yet, as he enters the family room he is overtaken by a feeling of unfamiliar discomfort. A musty smell seeps out of the ten-year-old brown shag rug that covers the amber-stained maple floor. The pale beige drapes are hanging open slightly, allowing a beam of sunlight to pierce through and enticing streams of dust to glimmer around the room. As James sits down, the dark checkered couch sinks beneath his weight and has a damp feel that embraces him as he remembers the many times he and Stephen fell asleep on it. A large taupe pillow is placed on either end, and a small embroidered pillow is perched in the middle. He fingers the embroidery, recalling how he and Stephen used to toss it around football style. James allows himself a minute to hold it tightly in his hands, until the memory begins to plague him with more pain and forces him to move.

After pacing the floor for a few minutes, he finally rests in the most reasonable piece of furniture in the room—the dump, as the boys used to call the old rust-colored La-Z-Boy. He pictures Stephen blessing the chair with that name after a night of indulging in heavy weed and Russian vodka. Another wave of sadness delivers a blow to his chest. Without thinking, he gravitates to a pile of videos on the corner of the television stand and starts to rummage through them curiously. The one that stands out is labeled "Homeward Bound." He pops it into the video machine as he makes himself comfortable on the floor.

The video starts with a montage of early still shots of the Pike family, starting from before Stephen was even born. Close family members and friends stream across the television screen.

A sea of black surrounds James on the inside as he listens to the sounds of Simon and Garfunkel playing over the images. He recognizes his younger sister Kitty and his mother and father, Janice and Aaron Milligan, as the camera zooms in on them. The next images are of Stephen's mother and father, Lynn and Dean Pike, in the kitchen preparing for a barbeque. Suddenly, a very young version of himself and Stephen come running in with water bombs. Lynn starts chasing them out. The footage skips momentarily and reappears with images of Stephen and James at their high school graduation just a few weeks before. Stephen is roughing up James's hair and pulling out his bowtie. He flicks a cigarette at the camera. His mother Lynn chases him around the front porch and scolds him. Stephen is laughing as he imitates her. The video trails off into a turbulent flow of static. James waits for more visuals to appear, but like the void in his heart, there's nothing left.

ONE

Chicago, Illinois – September 2011

James is sitting peacefully at his kitchen table, sipping his coffee absently and staring out the window of his seventeenth-floor condominium in the heart of downtown Chicago. It's a beautiful fall morning with a clear blue sky and the weather channel is describing the day ahead to be a warm Indian summer-like day with blustery winds. Despite the good weather forecast, an overwhelming dread seizes him as he is reminded of his obligatory family celebration today. He turns to look at his BlackBerry to check his work schedule, but is interrupted by a phone call. Call display tells him it's his sister Kitty and he answers it reluctantly.

Her voice booms through the speakerphone. "Happy birthday, big brother!"

"Thanks." James tries to sound grateful, but his lack of enthusiasm gives him away.

"Okay, well, too bad for you," she scoffs, immediately taking control of the conversation. Kitty has always been a domineering person, but he loves her despite his intolerance.

"Mom is on for dinner tonight, and so is Jake. Seven o'clock at Madrid's Café."

"Uh huh," he replies, intentionally distracting himself by channel surfing.

She pushes on with the details and asks if he is planning to come by the hospital to see Rick Miesner. Rick is a Vietnam veteran and the best friend of their late father, Aaron. He has been in palliative care for over a year, and his health is steadily declining.

"He's been asking for you," Kitty announces, then pauses briefly to accompany the silence on the other end. "Stop channel surfing!" she barks, hoping to grab her brother's attention.

He instantly looks away from the television and takes her off speakerphone. "Got it."

"Lunch hour is a good time to come, especially since we're going out for your birthday dinner tonight," she states.

"Okay, I got it, Kitty!" he snaps, grabbing his jacket off the back of the kitchen chair. "I have to go now. I'm late."

"Good, so I'll see you this afternoon then. Try to be happy, Jimmy. You're thirty-five today," she sings with enthusiasm.

James ignores her advice as he tries to locate his keys and portfolio case. He stops suddenly and backs up to the living area, where he pinches some fish food between his fingers and drops it into the tank. A large Arabian angelfish swims to the surface. James heads towards the door and exits, barely paying attention to Kitty's persistent nagging on the other end of the line as they finish their conversation.

Morning rush hour is a painful experience for James. People are scrambling to get to their destinations on time, and it never ceases to amaze him how annoyed it makes him every single morning. He listens to a talk radio station as he deviates through the clogged traffic until he finally reaches the lineup to get into the underground parking garage of the Willis Tower on Wacker Drive, in the heart of Chicago's West Loop.

He takes a deep breath to ease his anxiety and seizes the opportunity to look over his agenda. Glancing at his BlackBerry, he sees that his day is loaded with meetings and his inbox is already filled with messages. Unlike his personal life, his professional life is well intact and nothing about the insanity of his daily work schedule fazes him. Leaving his car and his prime parking spot, he rushes over to the elevator and nods to a colleague. The man is on his cellphone, but acknowledges James with a quick smile. They both work for Barnes and Miller Architecture and Design on the twenty-first floor.

The office is posh and exudes grandeur and wealth. Passing the front desk, he is struck by the beauty of the young receptionist who happily acknowledges him.

"Good morning, Mr. Milligan," she says, trying to please.

"Morning." As usual, James is quick with a sparse response. He walks by several small cubicles occupied by colleagues and subordinates who all regurgitate the same morning salutation. His response to each is lame and repetitious.

He enters his stylish office and immediately notices the message light on his phone flashing. Before he can settle in, his assistant Jade saunters through the door to hand over four message slips and a revised agenda. She is a young and curvaceous Mediterranean woman in her early thirties and is most definitely in control of her job. Her daily duty is to faithfully and meticulously govern James's every working hour.

"You've got a hectic schedule today. You sure you've got time to go to the hospital?" she asks.

James smirks. "How do you know I'm going there today?" he asks, completely aware of Jade's insightfulness into his business.

She stands tall over his desk with her hands hugging her luscious hips. James notices how nicely her form squeezes into her gray pinstriped pencil skirt. "Because Kitty called here looking for you earlier, and it's never a quick and dirty conversation with her." She smiles at him playfully.

James notices how her eyes twinkle as the words quick and dirty roll off her plump ruby lips. Her long bronze hair is in a sleek ponytail that falls past her shoulder blades. James is almost mesmerized by her profound sexiness and can't help but stare at her.

"Hello? I said, 'do you want anything from the cafe?'" Jade asks, obviously repeating herself.

Embarrassed, James snaps out of his daze and shuffles around uncomfortably in his chair. "Oh. Yeah, uh … the usual coffee, please."

"Sure thing, boss," she says, turning to leave. He rests his eyes on her round behind as it passes through his doorway.

Glancing down at the small pile of phone messages in his hand, he sees that Lynn Pike has called to wish him a happy birthday. He rubs the palms of his hands over his face and stares out the window, trying to find a way to ignore the message. He looks at his other messages and scribbles down a few notes for Jade to act on when she returns.

When he flips on his computer, he sneers at the calendar invite that immediately pops up. Kitty has sent a reminder of the dreaded dinner plans for the evening.

"Nice look." His colleague and work friend, Ty Henderson, is leaning up against the doorframe. His slight athletic frame complements his perfectly sculpted face, and his ostentatious attire oozes confidence. Shades of pale pink and gray show off his dark brown skin.

"Wish I could say the same about yours," James jokes, looking his colleague over.

Ty pretends not to hear. "Listen, man, can you make the Deagan meeting with me? It starts in five, and I could really use your design expertise."

"Of course you need me there," James spouts, grinning for the first time that morning. "Your mother breastfed you until you were nine, hence the reason for your vexatious codependence issue."

"Screw you," Ty scoffs. "But I appreciate the observation so much that your next hooker is on me."

James serves up another shot. "You do have the pimp look about you today," he snorts, looking Ty up and down. "You're missing your fedora, though. Is it at mommy's brothel?"

Before Ty can strike back with another comment, Jade gently pushes him aside.

"Down, boys," she hisses, then places a tray of coffee on the round table in the corner of the spacious office.

As she bends and twists her hips, both men notice how lovely she is, with her beautiful shiny hair and skin the color of Milk Duds. Noticing Ty's stare, James makes an effort to look away. "Thanks, Jade," he says, passing her some of the phone messages. "Can you please call these two clients back to see what they want? And could you try to reschedule my meetings this afternoon?"

"Will do. I'll hold down the fort," she says confidently.

Ty interrupts their obvious connection. "Forgive me for interrupting this lovely scene, but Jimmy, do we not have a meeting to attend?"

"Papa Bear comin' to the rescue again, I see?" Jade asks, batting her eyes at him.

"It's a good thing I like you, girl," Ty responds, smiling, then turns to James. "Come on, my man, let's go."

The two men make their way past the window offices lined up against the south end of the floor and enter a very sleek and modern boardroom. The scenery through the floor-to-ceiling windows is spectacular, and the room is filled with bright sunlight. There are a dozen or so high-back black leather chairs around a long cherrywood table. Several businessmen in their late forties and early fifties are already sitting around the table. Some are chatting, while a few others wait quietly as Ty and James enter the room. Ty sits at the head of the table and James takes the chair on his right.

Ty introduces James as one of the firm's chief architectural design experts. He goes on to explain why theirs is the best firm to take on the project, and how Barnes and Miller fully understands the need to enhance the downtown's current transit lines. "The Bus Rapid Transit line will serve hubs like Union Station and the Ogilvie Transportation Center. And consider the potential for BRT lines along Western and Ashland," Ty continues, doing his best to pitch the proposal.

James steps in to discuss the firm's vision for the transit line's architectural design, citing that it would complement one of the country's most historically famous structures—Union Station.

His BlackBerry goes off in the middle of his presentation. He quickly looks down at the number and sees that it's the hospital. "I'm terribly sorry, but I have to take this," he says, looking at the irritated faces around the table. "Ty, please continue on my behalf." Ty gives him a dirty look, but James ignores it and excuses himself before stepping into the hall.

It's Kitty calling to explain that Rick's situation is getting worse. "We don't think he's going to make the day," she explains. "His blood pressure is dropping and his organs are shutting down. I'm sorry, Jimmy. I know how close the two of you are."

James takes a deep breath and tries to shrug off her sentiment. "It's fine. I'll be there. I'm leaving now." He finds Jade on his way out of the building. "Listen, tell Ty I'm really sorry but I had to leave on an urgent matter."

Jade acknowledges his request without asking any questions. He knows that Kitty's already told her about the veterans he sees at the hospital on a weekly basis.

The drive to the hospital is quick and easy. The usual big-city rush hour that plagues the main highway is at a lull for the time being, and James enjoys having the quiet time and space to himself. Twenty minutes later, he pulls into the parking lot of the Aaron Milligan Veterans' Hospital, a long-term and palliative care hospital for veterans that was built by his grandfather, Fionn Milligan, in 1942.

His grandfather was one of Chicago's most prominent architects and wartime combat engineers. He was summoned to France in 1944 to work with the United States Army and assist with the design and construction of bridges, particularly Bailey and portable steel bridges to enhance road access and transportation loads for the larger, more modern American tanks. His grandfather named the hospital after his firstborn son, Aaron, before he departed for Europe in the event he would not return to see him grow up. As it was, he would not. Just two days before he was due to return home, his truck hit a German mine north of Carentan and he died instantly.

James's frequent visits to the hospital are constant reminders of the grandfather he never met, but came to know and love through the endless stories about him and the legendary photographs that covered the walls of his home growing up. Unfortunately, the name of the hospital is also a cold reminder of the father he actually did have growing up, but whom he never really knew.

He approaches the elevator and notices a woman in her late seventies impatiently pushing the button. She appears frail and somber. Her wrists are small and delicate. James fears that if she pushes the button one more time her feeble wrist might snap. A small poppy-print purse dangles from the crook of her right arm. Blue veins and deep brown spots are visible on her weathered and worn skin. He quickly looks away, uncomfortable with the feeling of empathy that is filling up his insides.

The elevator arrives and James steps in to hold the door for the woman. She quietly mumbles her thanks, and he asks her which floor. She indicates the fourth, and he pushes the button to take them up to the palliative care wing. He suddenly recognizes the woman. She is related to one of the men dying there—Hans Webber is her older brother. She's been there several times over the past month, and although never formally introduced, James has seen her with Hans in the ward several times. As she steps off the elevator, James takes her arm to assist her.

"How is Hans doing today, ma'am?" he asks softly.

The small-framed woman looks up at James with her ancient gray eyes and a smile curls upwards. Her voice shakes out a rattling sound. "Oh, he's just fine, thank you, son."

An orderly is pushing her brother out of his room and down the hall to meet her. She unwraps her arm from James's and eagerly shuffles forward to meet him.

James watches her attempt to quicken her step and feels an ache in his stomach. He wonders yet again about the inevitable process of life moving towards death—the chance to age, which can be cruel and insufferable, versus not having the opportunity to do so. He's distracted by the sound of Kitty's voice nearby, and he turns to catch sight of her down the hall talking to a doctor.

Although he doesn't want to acknowledge it, she looks beautiful when she's pregnant. With one hand on her porpoise-like belly, she signals to James with the other that she'll be with him in a minute. The doctor hands over the chart and she commences the long waddle back towards the reception desk where James is standing. They embrace, but James pulls away much faster than she would like.

"Rick's lungs aren't able to take in enough oxygen to sustain him much longer," she says when they part. She's using her nurse voice. "We've taken him off the ventilator because all of his organs are shutting down quickly. I just spoke with his doctor. It's only a matter of time now—maybe less than an hour." She stops to take a breath and tries to keep her composure. She, too, is emotionally invested in this patient, given how he is more like family than a family friend. Her voice softens. "Thanks for coming as soon as you could."

James only nods his head in acceptance, as he has no words for what is about to occur and he does not relish the thought of upheaving his reticent emotions. They make their way to the semi-private room where Rick lies dying. As they enter, the frail man lying on the bed opens his eyes and manages a slight smile. Kitty walks to the other side of the room and pulls the curtain for privacy. She adjusts the morphine drip and then puts her hand on his cheek.

"Hey, Uncle Rick. Jimmy is here. I'm going to give you two a few minutes of alone time, and then I'm coming back, okay?"

Rick raises his index finger as if to say okay. She looks at James and puts her hand on his back, and then she turns towards the door and quietly leaves. James pulls up a chair and huddles in close to Rick's bedside. Rick has no other family outside of the Milligans. His wife Margaret was barren and they decided not to pursue any other options for children. She died ten years earlier from ovarian cancer.

James rests his hand on Rick's left leg, and he can feel the bones underneath several layers of blankets and sheets. The dying man's eyes remain closed, but regardless, James speaks to him about his childhood memories of them together with his sister and his parents. He weaves in details about the Milligans' rural home, asking Rick if he recalls certain quirky stories about their family gatherings there. "Remember how Aaron used to play the harmonica and you the spoons, despite the fact that neither of you knew how to play at all?"

James never referred to his father as anything other than Aaron, and nobody ever challenged him on that—not even Aaron himself.

"It didn't matter though," James continues. "You guys would bellow out songs for hours, and mom and Maggie used to beg you to stop because they were trying to crochet and watch their television show … What was it called again? God, I can't remember the name of it, but I do remember you both laughing so hard that Aaron would fall off his stool every time."

He pauses for a moment, trying to fight his emotions.

"I've always admired your friendship with Aaron. I looked up to you for being able to love him so much, despite his intolerance of others. You always managed to calm him down. It's just like how I was with Stephen. You and dad were kind of like the two of us boys. The ying and the yang." James feels an overwhelming need to cry but manages to hold it back.

Rick begins to cough momentarily and James instinctively moves closer to help him settle. His goal is to soothe the old man with his words, to sweep his soul of any fear that might trickle in.

"Rick, you're the luckiest man I know," James says lovingly. "Your life has had meaning and purpose. There was nothing you didn't do for the ones you loved and cared for. You never messed up, not even once. I've always envied that about you—how you mastered everything and treasured the time you spent working to perfect your relationships. You never wasted a moment."

Rick grunts and mumbles something that James cannot decipher. The old man's breathing slows, and from experience James is aware that death is about to enter the room. He squeezes Rick's hand tightly. "It's okay to let go. I'm here with you. I'm here, Uncle Rick. Thank you for looking out for me, and for not ever placing judgment on me."

Rick's mouth is wide open, but barely sucking in air. His hazed eyes open and look upward to the ceiling, and then suddenly roll back. One breath resists the force of exhalation. Ten seconds later, he labors for another. He struggles through the inhalation and resists the force of exhalation again. The thought comes to James that there are parallel patterns of breath during the birthing and dying processes.

Suddenly, the rattle of Rick's breath triggers the monitor, and it begins to hum loudly like a cicada. The sound brings the doctor rushing into the room with a nurse in tow. James rises from his chair and gives the medical staff space to do their jobs. After a few brief minutes, both the doctor and the nurse are resigned and give their condolences to James before he exits the room to find his sister.

Kitty is sitting at the desk with Rebecca, the nurse that has come in to replace her while she goes on maternity leave. Rebecca Doyle is a thirty-three-year-old single mother of an eight-year-old girl, Miesha. Rebecca is pretty, with a slight build, dark shoulder-length hair, and almond-shaped brown eyes. Her features are small and dainty, almost childlike. Rebecca may be petite, but her character is large, filled with gusto and determination. Today, however, these characteristics lie dormant while nerves take over.

Nurse Donna Braggen walks over with a stack of files and interrupts Kitty and Rebecca's conversation. She possesses the characteristics of a short and stocky bulldog and bears the couth of a laughing hyena. "Hey ladies, I hear The Shepherd is here today. Who died?"

"Donna! Mind yourself!" Kitty scolds, smacking her lightly on the hand.

Rebecca stands next to them, totally bewildered. Before Kitty can explain that Donna is referring to her brother James, Donna interjects, looking straight into Rebecca's eyes.

"James is her big brother. He's not bad on the eyes. Oh, you'll see. Anyway, he's a volunteer here and somehow is able to assist veterans through their passing. He just shows up and starts talking to them about anything—and then, poof! Lights out."

Kitty glares at her. "Honestly, Donna. You're talking about my brother, you know."

Donna ignores the rebuke. "I've had several conversations with patients who've witnessed his virtuous and calming effect by the deathbed." She marches over to the file cabinet and starts systematically putting away a pile of charts.

Rebecca seems impressed, and Kitty feels the need to further explain the situation to her. "Never mind her. Look, my brother is an introspective kind of person."

Donna pipes up again. "You mean emotionally handicapped."

"I mean—" Kitty snaps, "—he has insight into things that most people don't. He's a wealth of knowledge on all subjects, especially art and world travel, and sometimes he sits with the veterans and talks about these things because it gives them something positive to focus on. Besides, I actually think it helps *him* more than it helps the patients."

Donna totally ignores Kitty's comment. "I saw this story on the news a while back. It was about this cat that lived in a palliative care hospital, just like this one, and he could sense who was going to die next. He'd turn up at that person's door on the very same day."

"Donna, *please!*" Kitty demands.

Rebecca is somewhat disturbed and yet humored by this. The girls start to giggle when Rebecca is interrupted by James's obscure and unexpected presence. He is standing across from the reception desk, his eyes dull and void of expression. She and James look at each other for a few seconds with puzzlement until James cannot look any longer. Kitty sees her brother and struggles to rise from her chair to greet him. She looks into his eyes, where the emptiness says everything. She hugs him tightly. Tears start to stream down her face. Rick is gone.

Dr. Lewis approaches Kitty and James and they speak of the situation quietly. A pastor comes forward to join the conversation, and a minute later Kitty escorts him down the hall towards Rick's room. James slowly walks towards the elevator feeling drained of his unwanted emotions. A veteran named Gerry Robinson is walking past him towards Rick's room. He is a tall, thin man, balding at the crown, with shifty blue eyes. He putters by sporting a light blue housecoat with holes in the pockets and trolling an intravenous drip on a roller.

"Hello, Jimmy! You going back to the office now?"

James tries not to look him in the face. "Uh, yeah, Gerry, I am. Have a good day," he says, though most of the words catch under his breath.

Gerry's eyes follow him into the elevator. James knows that the old timer can sense that something isn't right.

"Okay, Jimmy, you too," Gerry says. "I'm off to see if Rick wants to watch the game with me tonight."

A quick wave goodbye is all that James can manage as he watches the elevator doors begin to close, separating him from the awkwardness of the situation.

TWO

"Hey dawg, you're in big shit for letting me play ball with those hard-asses all by my lonesome." Ty's voice is carrying its usual sarcastic ring. "You owe me *several* drinks, man."

James smiles at Ty's voice message and presses the button to hear the next one prior to finishing up the work he promised his boss by the end of the day. Janice Milligan's unsettled voice comes over the speakerphone.

"It's such a day of mixed emotion," she stammers. Her voice is meek and timid. "Rick's passing and your birthday … I just don't know what to say, Jimmy. Are you still up for dinner? I mean, we certainly are if you are. Anyway, I love you, dear. Call me back."

He deletes the message and goes back to rolling up the plans he had been working to finalize for the last three hours in his home office. He couldn't bear to return to the office after his visit to the hospital. He is shaken by Rick's death, and doesn't yet know how to manage it—let alone deal with Jade's attempt to do so on his behalf. It is bad enough that his mother and sister are waiting for him tonight. He pictures them like vultures swooping down on the smallest prey, picking it apart until each limb is painfully dismembered.

His watch alarm goes off and he sees that it's six o'clock. Dreading dinner, he knows of no escape other than to face the inevitable. Kitty could be a ruthless beast about changing plans, despite any life-altering events like Rick's death. To him, this fact is more torturous than the vicious and unforgiving vulture he just dreamed up.

He looks out the window to see St. James Cathedral standing strong and mysterious with its wrought-iron crown and meticulous design. He and Stephen used to visit it frequently with their parents to listen to the Chicago Symphony while

15

it performed underneath the jagged, sweeping beams and the golden interior. He closes his eyes and pictures himself with his best friend—a friend with whom he shared the same birthday. He tries hard not to absorb any more anguish, but still the intensity of his memories seeps through his skin, seemingly ripping it open in one slow and painful tear. Now Rick is dead, and his birthday would forever be marked with yet another blow. Was he cursed? Was this punishment for being a part of Stephen's demise?

His head starts to pound at the sound of his heart beating in his ears. On the walls of his home office hangs a picture of Rick, Aaron, and a few other soldiers in Vietnam. He wonders how they reacted to watching their friends and fellow comrades die. All the horror stories that were told time and time again float around in his memory and seed his guilt for having the luxury of his life despite being absent from it.

He walks into his kitchen and grabs a beer, then turns on the living room television in an attempt to distract himself from his own thoughts while he starts to get ready. Kitty has made reservations at a small pizzeria and wine bar in Roscoe Village, and while he is not looking forward to an evening of emotional interrogation with his family, he is looking forward to filling the void in his stomach with something other than his usual bland fare. Minutes later, he throws himself into proper attire and heads out the door.

The evening wind blows at his core, forcing James to quicken his pace down East Huron Street. He flags down a cab and jumps in, politely giving the driver his destination. He closes his eyes and takes a few deep breaths to prepare himself for the night's festivities. When the cab gets closer to the restaurant he asks to be let out a few blocks away so he can walk off his jitters. The cool, brisk night air reminds him of the coming of another long and unrelenting winter. He passes a group of teenage boys playing street hockey on Michigan Avenue. The sound of hockey sticks slamming the pavement ends with a puck in the back of a mesh net. This signals to James that hockey season is about to start. For a brief moment, it is a happy distraction from his perpetual anxiety.

The short walk does him good, and he is able to find peace following today's episode of loss. The sadness that overwhelmed his mood throughout the day is finally easing, and he feels satisfied that Rick's passage through life and death was good and meaningful.

By the time he reaches the restaurant his face is flush from the nip of the night air. He takes a deep breath before opening the door. A young man in his twenties, dressed in black dress pants and a form-fitting white shirt, greets him at the door and leads him towards a table in the back corner of the dimly lit room. Kitty is waving her arms like she's sending out an SOS signal. Within only seconds of being there, he already feels the intolerance creeping up his spine.

As he reaches the table he notices that Kitty is sitting beside the girl who was at the reception desk at the hospital earlier that day. He turns away, feeling the anxiety burn up his spine and settle in his neck. The only empty chair is across from the young woman, which Kitty intentionally planned.

"James, you sit right there," Kitty says in her usual way of ordering him to do something.

A feeling of nausea comes over him as he does what he is told. His mother Janice is sitting to his right, and his brother-in-law Jacob is to his left.

Janice immediately takes his arm and pulls him over to give him a kiss on the cheek and stroke his face. "I'm so happy you could meet us for dinner, love. Happy birthday."

He gently pulls away, giving a nervous smirk. He is feeling excruciatingly uncomfortable and wishes he had taken a double dose of his anxiety medication.

Jacob seems to be able to sense James's unease and tries to break the ice. "I wish there was a television around here," he whispers, leaning in towards James. "I think the Cubs are playing right now."

James nods with agreement but is immediately sidetracked by his sister, who is trying with all of her might to reach over the table and kiss him. It's clear that her pregnant belly won't pave the way, so he gets up to do the work for her and receives an adoring kiss.

Her eyes twinkle as he finds his way back to his seat. "So, Jimmy, do you remember Rebecca?" It seems to suddenly dawn on her that they were never officially introduced under the circumstances of Rick's passing. "Oh, I'm sorry. I was so devastated when you came by with the news about Rick. I didn't even think about introductions at that point." She looks down, clearly feeling the sting of the day's event.

Rebecca's eyes catch James off guard for the second time that day. "Hi. I'm Rebecca Doyle," she says confidently, extending her hand. "I'm so sorry for your loss."

He slowly reaches his hand towards Rebecca's, and she warmly embraces it. The sensation of her fingertips touching his startles him, and he feels his stomach muscles involuntarily contract. He barely manages a response.

"Thank you."

Rebecca seems to be able to sense the tension around the table but does not back away from it. Instead, she uses the power of her sincere charm and openness to connect everyone's thoughts in the moment. "Thank you for inviting me to share this day with you all," she says humbly.

"We're more than happy to have you join us," replies Janice sincerely. "It's our pleasure." She flags down the waiter to request another glass of Shiraz.

17

Kitty's eyes light up as they dart back and forth between James and Rebecca. "Rebecca's my replacement at work," she explains, patting her ample belly. "I asked her to join us because she's new to this part of the city. She finally has a night to herself, since her gorgeous little daughter is with her dad tonight."

James can feel the sweat flowing down the back of his neck. His palms are sweaty and he wishes he could be anywhere but here.

Kitty continues to orchestrate the conversation and bounces back to the topic of Rick again. "Mom, were you able to see Rick before he passed?"

"Oh yes, I did, love," Janice replies softly, searching for a tissue to wipe the corners of her eyes. "I sat with him most of the morning before your shift. My goodness, he was such a great person. Always there for us." She turns to James and places her hand on his. "Thank you again for being there for him." Her voice shakes with sadness as her eyes mist over. "You know, I always hated the fact that he spent most of his life alone. He was such a good person. Not afraid of anything—except dying alone. He once told me that if he'd died in the jungles of Vietnam he would have taken comfort in knowing he wouldn't be alone. His battalion was his family."

The server arrives with Janice's wine and asks if anyone else would like a drink. Janice orders a bottle of wine for everyone to share, and James asks for a scotch straight up. His mother looks at him and he knows that she recognizes his anxiety. She tries to ease his tension by announcing what's good on the menu.

"Well, I just love their wood oven pizzas!" she exclaims as her eyes scan the choices in front of her.

"Well, that does it then," James states, closing his menu and putting on a plastic smile. "I'm going to have the shrimp and artichoke Cajun-style pizza. Waiter!"

James's heart is racing now. There is no other option—he'll have to eat and run if he hopes to survive this evening without having some sort of emotional breakdown. The waiter must sense the urgency from one corner of the table, because he comes over and takes everyone's order. Kitty glares at her brother in disapproval, but doesn't say anything. Everyone takes their time asking the waiter particulars about their meal. Within twenty minutes the waiter returns, balancing loaded plates on a massive tray.

During dinner Janice asks Rebecca many questions, but Kitty answers most of them for her, as though she is the more skilled Q&A expert on Rebecca's life. "She has two brothers. One is a pediatrician in Toronto, and the other teaches in Australia."

James sits in silence, shoveling his food down between swigs of whiskey. His primary goal is to leave as soon as possible, unscathed and without guilt.

During a short lull in the conversation, Rebecca decides to take matters into her own hands and openly offers up details about her life. "I'm from Woodstock," she says after taking a sip of wine.

James's ears perk up. He puts his cutlery down and reaches for his drink. "Woodstock, New York?" he asks eagerly.

Rebecca chuckles. "No, sorry to disappoint. Woodstock, Illinois." Her perfectly shaped dark eyebrows accentuate her lovely face.

James tries not to notice her beauty and instead focuses on the information being put forth. "I love that town," he replies. "A bunch of us from college travelled there during first year to study the Victorian-style architecture. There's a lot of history in that little place."

Janice cuts in. "Do you know the Mortenbergs?" she asks, her words slurred slightly from the wine.

"Mother!" Kitty snaps. "As if she knows the Mortenbergs, whoever they are. I'm sure Woodstock isn't *that* small."

Rebecca's eyes beam across the table. "Oh, you'd be surprised, Kitty." She turns back to Janice and tries to ease her unwarranted humiliation. "There was a Hilda Mortenberg who taught at my high school, but I never had her."

"Oh my goodness, that's her!" Janice squeals with excitement. "We went to college together. My! What a small world." Janice is now intrigued and leans in towards Rebecca. "So, I understand you live close to the hospital?"

Kitty wipes her mouth with her napkin and rolls her eyes. "Mom, maybe we should try to let Rebecca finish her meal in peace."

James signals the waiter again for one last shot of whiskey to ease the pain caused by his sister's assertion for control.

Rebecca pipes up, "That's okay. I'm happy to share my story." She rests her elbows on the table and folds her delicate hands under her chin, then gives them a quick summary. "I live on Fourteenth Street, near the hospital, with my beautiful eight-year-old daughter, Miesha. I've been divorced from her father for about four years, and my parents still live in Woodstock. My mother runs the library there and my dad is a retired engineer. And as Kitty mentioned, my brother Kane lives in Toronto and Eric's in Australia."

Everyone's looking at her except for James, who is searching for the waiter to come with his drink.

"I received a scholarship to Aurora University for the nursing program," Rebecca explains. "I loved it, but I wanted more extensive experience. So I enrolled in the Master of Science in Nursing program as well, hoping it would open more doors for me."

Janice is intrigued. "How did you end up in Chicago?"

"I met my former husband here while I was visiting a friend after second year. I moved here after I graduated, and we got married two months later."

"Shotgun?" Kitty blurts out.

"Oh, for heaven's sake, Kitty. Do you have to unleash other people's private matters?" Janice scoffs in her disappointed mother's voice.

Jacob looks up from his iPhone after catching the fifth inning of the Cubs game. "She can't help it."

The waiter comes to the table to pour more wine and remove empty plates.

Rebecca seals her gaze on James. "So, James, Kitty tells me that you know a lot about architecture and history."

Barely able to make eye contact, he manages to nod yes.

Her eyes are deep and rich with confidence and intensity. "My dad is obsessed with that kind of stuff, too," she tells him. "He used to sit me down with his books on the history of architecture. He actually designed commercial aircraft for thirty years, but he always had a love for old buildings."

James's face lightens and he finds himself somewhat impressed.

Kitty breaks into the moment to explain that James's fascination with architecture dates back to when he was a kid. "He loved going to the library to look at anything he could find on architecture and the history of buildings and structures." She laughs heartily. "Of course, I had no interest at all."

"Yes, well, it's always about you, right Kit?" James smacks back.

"Please, let's not start this. Not today," Janice implores.

"I'm not saying that, Jimmy," Kitty swings back. "It's just that I liked Barbies and you liked building things for my Barbies with your Lego blocks."

Janice intervenes. "You and your father *did* spend hours working on things in the garage," she says, trying to redirect James's thoughts. "You never talked much to each other, but somehow you both found a way to communicate through your construction projects."

James feels his anxiety building up again at the mention of Aaron. He flags down the waitress and asks for an Irish coffee. The others at the table also request after-dinner coffees and teas.

James is trying not to shift his attention towards Rebecca, who is talking to Kitty about subjects he knows nothing about—pregnancy and childbirth. Rebecca laughs and his stomach drops. She glances at James and seems to immediately notice how uncomfortable he is.

She quickly finishes her wine and starts to gather up her coat and scarf for departure. "It's been so nice to spend time with you all. Thank you again for including me in your plans tonight."

There's the expected chorus of pleas urging her to stay for coffee.

Rebecca gracefully declines. "Unfortunately, I have to pick up Miesha at eight o'clock tomorrow morning from a friend's place and then take her to her dance class across town. So I'd better just—"

Kitty grabs her arm and pulls her back down hard on her seat. She nods over her shoulder to the waiter heading to the table with a birthday cake. Rebecca sits, embarrassed, which reignites James's angst about the whole evening. Within moments the entire staff is circled around the table to sing "Happy Birthday."

James is screaming inside. The fight-or-flight response is raging through his body. His hands are folded in front of his mouth, and although he's trying to smile and seem grateful, he can't help but feel contempt in his heart. *Why does Kitty always have to push?*

The birthday song finishes and Janice quickly cuts the cake and passes the first one to her son.

"No, thanks," he says politely.

"I'll take it!" Kitty calls from across the table. "I'm not the one obsessed with being thin right now," she says, chastising her brother.

All the while, Jacob continues watching the game on his iPhone. James makes a note of how everyone notices but says nothing, and he's envious.

"Listen, I want to thank you all for tonight, but it's been a long day and I'm going to head home," James says.

"Rebecca could use a drive home," Kitty asserts.

Rebecca shoots a shocked expression over to Kitty.

Kitty pays no attention to her new friend. "It's just that we'll be sticking around for a bit to eat more cake, and you both seem to be in a rush to get home. Besides, we have to drive mom home and it's the opposite direction." She looks over at Janice, whose eyes are closing every few minutes from the wine. "It's the gentlemanly thing to do, right?" she pushes.

"Yes," James agrees. "Except that I took a cab here and I planned to take a cab home."

Kitty's eyes almost cross with frustration. "Then cab home *with* her," she insists through gritted teeth.

Rebecca is looking embarrassed in the moment. "I appreciate your concern, Kitty, but I'm fine taking a cab home myself."

James looks at her small frame and innocent features and suddenly feels responsible for her safety. "Listen, maybe that's a good idea. How about we share a cab and I'll drop you off first?"

"Don't you live nearby?" she replies with doubt in her voice.

"It's all right," he assures her. "We can head your way first. It's only ten minutes or so difference."

At this point, Rebecca becomes resigned to the suggestion. She seems to want

21

to get out of the situation as badly as he does. The two say their rounds of good-nights with hugs and waves. Janice is barely awake but manages to stand up to see them both off.

Outside, a gust of wind almost knocks Rebecca off her gait, making James react quickly to stabilize her. She looks up at his face and mutters a soft thank you, exasperating James's already heightened anxiety from his unwanted attraction towards her. He tries to ignore it by making small talk about Woodstock and how well the nineteenth-century architecture in Woodstock Square has been preserved.

Rebecca agrees and expands on the conversation. "The town walks the talk about preservation. My father is a volunteer docent for tours of the historic buildings, including the 1890 Woodstock Opera House and the Italianate-style Old Court House built in 1857."

James hails an oncoming cab. "I'm impressed," he states sincerely. He opens the passenger door for Rebecca and scoots in beside her. The moment is clumsy and somewhat embarrassing.

"Fourteenth Street, please," Rebecca says sweetly to the old taxi driver. The song "Brandy" comes over the radio and Rebecca smiles. "God, I love this song," she says quietly, her eyes fixed on the dark night flashing by. "My mom and dad used to dance to it when I was a little girl." As the music surrounds them, Rebecca turns to James and continues reminiscing. "They used to have great parties with their friends." She chuckles softly. "They'd cook and eat this great big meal, drink wine all night, and dance."

James feels lighthearted. He notices Rebecca's face highlighted by the passing streetlights, and her eyes are shining with loveliness. As they pull up to her driveway, they see a man is standing there beside a car.

"That's my ex-husband," Rebecca explains, her voice sounding panicked. She quickly jumps out of the cab, leaving James confused in the back seat.

"Oh my God, Ben, what's wrong?" she asks, anxiously. She noticeably calms when she sees the form of a young girl sleeping in the back seat of the ex-husband's car.

"Look, I'm really sorry, Beck. I tried calling you a hundred times …"

Rebecca looks in her purse and realizes she forgot her cellphone at home.

"I'm such an idiot," she mutters. "Sorry, Ben. I didn't know my phone wasn't with me."

Ben is understanding but obviously frustrated. "She was insisting that she wanted to be home with you. She wouldn't go to bed. She must still be having a hard time dealing with me and Martina moving in together …" he trails off.

Rebecca sighs. "It's all right, I understand."

Ben reaches into the car and pulls out the sleepy eight-year-old. He starts to carry her up the steps towards the front entrance.

James discreetly observes the situation from afar. Rebecca shoots a look over to the cab and signals for James to roll down the window.

"It's okay," she tells him. "Miesha just wanted to be in her own bed."

James nods, not knowing how to engage in this particular conversation.

Her big eyes cast a hopeful display of affection, catching him off guard somewhat. "I really enjoyed tonight," she says. "Maybe I'll see you again?"

James can only muster up a hapless grin and a few curt words. "See you. Nice meeting you, too."

The taxi starts to back out of the driveway, but James's eyes continue to fixate on the three strange characters playing out a scene in the driveway. The images get smaller and smaller as the car pulls farther away towards the Lake Shore. The radio is now off, and silence has replaced Rebecca's recounted memories. He is left completely unsure of how he feels about the evening.

THREE

The sun peers through the thick clouds that are rapidly moving across the September sky. Rick Miesner is being laid to rest today, and just over a dozen people are gathered around his gravesite. A pile of fresh soil sits beside a silver-plated coffin that is draped in an American flag and perched over a hollow cavity in the earth.

Father Doherty is giving a speech about eternal life, but James can't stop his cynicism from creeping into his thoughts. Eternity is not something he subscribes to, especially in the context of any physical life form. Nevertheless, out of respect for Rick, he stands beside his mother and sister, trying to appear to be as much of a believer as they are. Kitty continuously wipes away tears with one hand, while her other arm is looped around his for support. Although she is only six months pregnant, James fears she might give birth on the spot due to her rapidly increasing size.

The priest blesses the casket with holy water. Despite being an atheist, James fights the sadness this ritual triggers. Janice looks at the grave with a soft smile, content that her husband now has another mate with him in the afterlife. James can see the peace residing within the lines in her expression.

He looks up into the small crowd and notices an unfamiliar face. An elderly African-American man is standing slightly behind the ceremony. He is tall, with broad shoulders and bright, heavy eyes that testify to his once being a handsome man. He appears frail, yet there is something incredibly strong about his presence. A young and attractive African-American woman is standing at his side with her arm wrapped around his waist.

Kitty notices that James is staring at something. She stands on her tippy toes to see what's caught his attention. She smiles as her eyes make contact, and the man gives a slight nod back to Kitty.

"Who is that?" James asks discretely under his breath.

Kitty leans in towards him to whisper. "His name is Martin Diggs, and that's his niece or something, Kendra. He's a new patient. He knew Rick from the war. They weren't in the same battalion, but they knew each other well. Mom said dad knew him, too."

Curiosity hangs over James like dread. Learning how Martin knew Rick is something he'd be interested in, but this connection with Aaron? He decides he doesn't want to know.

The ceremony is over and people start to disperse. James stands there for another moment, observing Martin. A train passes by in the distance. He closes his eyes and takes in several breaths to fight off the exhaustion brought on by his anxiety. The sound of his mother calling disrupts his headspace. When he opens his eyes, Martin Diggs is gone.

★★★

A week passes by quickly and James is overwhelmed with work deadlines and demanding clients. Today marks the first time since Rick's passing that he manages to get to the hospital to volunteer.

He exits the elevator on the palliative care floor and notices Donna sitting behind the reception desk. He instinctively tries not to make eye contact. She terrifies him, not because of her plump and obnoxiously cherublike face, but because of her insipid chattiness and gluttonous need to be social all the time. Her eyes twinkle and shift constantly, and this annoys him immensely. James finds his opportunity to try to scoot past her unnoticed while she is preoccupied with the printer behind the desk. It doesn't work.

"She's on the seventh floor helping with the transfer of a patient," Donna announces with her insincere chipper voice as he passes, her back still turned to him.

Shivers run up and down his spine as he walks down the corridor. He's convinced she has eyes in the back of her head. The image of an old porcelain doll with rolling eyes comes to mind. It was a doll given to Kitty when she was four years old, but it disturbed James so much that he buried it in the woods. He still claims to this very day that he was not responsible for its mysterious disappearance.

Worried that Donna might be following closely behind, he scurries past room three and takes a sharp right turn into room five. The room is divided into two areas by a curtain. Bed one is closest to the door, and bed two has the window view. He turns to see Robert Gainsborough, a fifty-year-old veteran of the Gulf War, lying in the first bed. Kitty has already told him that the man has brain cancer.

"It's about time, boy," the man says with a thick grumble.

"Nice to meet you, Mr. Gainsborough," James says politely. They shake hands.

"I didn't know your father, but I heard a lot about him so I've been waiting to meet the next best thing," says Robert. "They say you visit all the residents here, and I was getting a bit offended that you hadn't visited me yet." A gravelly chuckle seeps from his lungs. "Then again, they also call you The Shepherd and say you come around when somebody's about to kick the bucket, so maybe I should be worried."

James chooses to ignore Robert's last statement. "Do you mind if I pull up a chair?" James asks.

"Well, what else did you come here for, boy? Sit yourself down. And don't call me Mr. Gainsborough. Call me Robert, or Bob." His voice cracks with every word.

James drags the chair closer to the old man's bed, and Robert starts the conversation without hesitation.

"I've heard a lot about you, boy. I think it's mighty respectful, what you do around here, helping out all of us vets and all that shit. Sometimes I think dying would have been better out there in the desert or the jungle or wherever the fucking Nazis didn't play nice …" He pauses, waiting for a good solid breath. "Anyway, it's just that dying in a hospital bed isn't all it's cracked up to be, you know?"

James agrees. "I know what you mean. It can be very isolating. But at least you're warm here, and you have people around you who care. That's important, right?" James is always amazed at his ability to spew off the obvious song and dance, even though he can never find it within himself to conform to it personally. He leans forward to better engage. "So what's your condition, Bob?"

Robert starts to explain that he was diagnosed seven years ago with a malignant brain tumor. He managed to fight it off through various rounds of treatment over the years, but the cancer keeps returning. James listens intently as Robert carries on with his story.

"I'm damn sure that my cancer isn't a result of my time in battle like so many people talk about. That's all horseshit 'n gravy, if you ask me. Mine is directly related to genetics."

James leans in closer as Robert gets more fired up.

"My father and my grandfather died of cancer quite young, and they both led clean lives." His voice begins to wheeze. "I'm mighty proud of being a veteran and what I've done for my country and the world, and screw anybody who blames my sickness or anybody else's on the United States Army!"

The phlegm in the back of his throat initiates a small coughing fit. James passes Robert some water and he swallows it down.

"I'm a goddamn Republican, son, and I was just doing my duty is all," he grunts, handing the glass back to James.

They are silent for a moment before James asks about his family. "Do you have a wife and children?"

Robert's eyes soften as he speaks about his wife Marie. "She's a beauty," he says, grumbling out the words. "We've been married for twenty-six years and I've enjoyed every second of them. Of course, I'm not so sure she can say the same," he proclaims with a sly grin. "We have two boys," he says, his smile dissipating quickly. "Nineteen-year-old twins, but you'd only know it by looking at them because they couldn't be more different."

"What are their names?" James asks.

"Luke and Casey," Robert answers gruffly. He shifts around, uncomfortable in his own skin while he speaks of them. "Casey is some artsy-fartsy living in Manhattan with a bunch of faggots." His vile disapproval spews out of his mouth.

James instantly feels uncomfortable, but tries to remain objective towards Robert's ignorance. Still, his expression must be clear because Robert picks up on it immediately.

"I can see I've made you a bit jumpy," he says, softening up his tone.

James relaxes. "That's okay," he replies. "I'm not here to judge anyone."

Robert takes this as an opportunity to continue on with his unforgiving rant. "Don't you think boys should turn into men and do things that come naturally? Men should like women, son, don't you agree? That's the natural thing. God made us that way, didn't he?"

James just sits and listens, trying hard not to let his anxiety flare up. He pushes down thoughts of his own father's similar view on the subject by diverting the conversation. "So, what about your other son?"

Robert grunts proudly. "Luke? He's got a football scholarship at Notre Dame. That boy can play ball, Jimmy." He pauses. "I can call you Jimmy, right? I just assumed, because everyone around here calls you that."

James nods in agreement. "That's pretty impressive, Bob. You must be really proud of him," he says.

"Luke loves his football—and girls! Yep, that boy's just like his father."

Robert's face is alight with pride when he speaks of this particular son. James suddenly pictures Aaron's eyes lighting up at the mention of his sister Kitty.

"Shit, Jimmy, I was full of piss and vinegar in my day, too," Robert's voice wheezes on. "I was born and raised in North Carolina. After my father got back from fighting the Nazis, he started a soybean plant. We all worked like hell every day to build that business, but we sure knew how to play hard when the whistle blew."

James can see Robert's wheels starting to turn.

"Before I went off to war years later, I was sent here to Chicago to do some basic training sessions with some new recruits, and that's when I met Marie. She was working in a downtown watering hole—a classy joint. Well, I was hit by Cupid's arrow and it's been like that for over two decades now. For the most part—outside of my time overseas, that is—we've lived a quiet life near the west suburbs in Maywood." Robert suddenly stops talking and James can see some emotion behind his eyes.

"I can come back tomorrow, if you want," James offers. "You must be getting tired."

"Death is coming quick, Jimmy," Robert blurts out, "and I don't want Marie or anyone else by my bedside when it happens. I've seen too many people I care about die right before my eyes, and I don't want that for them. It's a goddamn ordeal, Jimmy, and it's nobody's business but my own."

James nods in acceptance. The sting of Robert's words rings true to his experience of watching his own best friend die. His pulse starts to quicken and his anxiety begins to escalate.

Kitty enters the room at that very moment and James can feel the weight of the world lift off his chest. *A perfect time to exit*, he thinks to himself.

"Hello, Bobby. How're you feeling today?" she asks, her voice full of pep as she prepares to check his blood pressure.

James can hear a spring of life forming in Robert's voice. "I'm feeling just fine, Miss Kitty. Those drugs you're loading me up with are some good."

Kitty chuckles. "Okay, well, take it easy there, my friend. You're on them for the pain, not for the fun of it." She grabs his arm and rubs it gently before wrapping it with the inflatable cuff.

Robert looks up at her with big eyes and smiles with each stroke. "Nothin' wrong with that," he says with a smirk.

"I'm happy you finally met my brother," she says, pumping up the cuff and then watching the meter drop.

Rebecca suddenly saunters into the room. "Hey, all! Sorry to disturb you, but Robert, I have to take you for a scan."

James jumps up immediately and fumbles around Robert's bed.

Robert's eyes light up at the sight of the pretty nurse. "Can't say I object to having a beautiful lady escort me to a private room and undress me."

"Okay now, Robert, mind your Ps and Qs—after all, there are ladies present," Kitty remarks.

Rebecca smiles and opens the door wider to make room for the young orderly who has come to assist with the transfer. The two nurses and the orderly manage to help Robert onto the gurney. James stands there feeling helpless, wondering why he's unraveling inside. Rebecca guides the orderly and Robert through the door and then follows along behind them.

Kitty shuts the door and concentrates hard on her brother's face. "It's time you let your guard down and let someone into your life."

James feels stunned and is unable to respond.

"Jimmy, she's a good person and a good mother. She's pretty, smart, caring, and available." Kitty stands with her hands on her bulging hips, waiting for a response. When none comes, she throws her arms up in the air in frustration and walks out of the room. James is left bewildered.

From the corner of the room behind the curtain comes a man's voice. The tone is soothing, almost hypnotizing as it recounts what James recognizes to be a Chinese proverb. "To attract good fortune, spend a new coin on an old friend, share an old pleasure with a new friend ..."

James slowly walks to the other side of the room and peers behind the curtain. Martin Diggs occupies the second bed.

FOUR

Ty is laughing as he puts his beer down on the wooden water-stained table at O'Malley's Pub. He and James are talking about a difficult client who insists on asking the company to do the impossible. A gorgeous blond waitress comes over and puts down two hearty club sandwiches with sides of coleslaw.

"Miss, I just want to compliment you on your impeccable timing and service," Ty says, eyeing the young waitress with a coy expression. She smiles and walks away, leaving both men fantasizing for a second before diving into their meals.

"You've been at the hospital a lot these days. What's going on?" Ty asks, arranging his sandwich before biting into it.

"There's just a lot going on there, that's all. Fall seems to be a busy time of year for some reason," James responds.

"No wonder you walk around so depressed all the time," Ty teases.

James puts his sandwich down and glares hard at his colleague.

"Listen, sorry, man. I just don't get it," Ty backtracks. "I mean, don't get me wrong. I get the whole 'kindness' and 'giving to your community' thing, but it has to be affecting your psyche, bro."

James shakes his head at Ty as if to say that he doesn't know what he's talking about. He doesn't want to disclose anything to Ty. He picks up his sandwich again before changing the subject. "I want to travel this summer," he says, grabbing his beer.

Ty's eyes widen as he gulps down his cold draft. "You serious?" he asks, surprised.

"I want to get away. I *need* to," James explains. "I've always wanted to go to Southeast Asia to experience the culture."

A sudden burst of feminine laughter trickles in from the main entrance of the pub. Two girls walk in, eyeing the venue for a prime seat. The waitress walks over, grabs menus, and sits them down at a table on the other side of the room. James and Ty watch them walk in and sit down.

"My, my, my, that is some round of hotness over there," Ty says like a sly fox.

James pushes his plate away with his hand. The rest of his body is frozen with fear. It's Rebecca with a girlfriend. James quickly signals to the waitress for the bill.

Ty is confused. "Jimmy, what the hell are you doing? We just started eating."

The waitress comes over with the bill and places it in front of James. Panic starts to surge through his body and he feels an attack coming on. He throws down the cash and hisses at Ty, "We're leaving. Now!"

He manages to escape the pub unseen. His heart is pumping heat through his veins, and the sweat starts to bead on his forehead despite the cool evening air hitting his skin.

Ty runs out behind him. "Jimmy! Slow down, man!"

James reaches his parked car and turns to Ty, who is trailing behind him, trying to catch his breath. "Ty, get in the car if you want a drive home."

Ty does what he's told and the two men fall silent as they peel out of the parking spot.

"You know those two?" Ty asks curiously.

James takes in a deep breath. "I know one of them from the hospital," he says quietly. "Which one?"

"The shorter one," he answers, making the distinction.

Ty shakes his head, perplexed and confused. He knows better than to take this inquisition any further. Instead, he asks about work. "Are you coming to the meeting in the morning?"

James's eyes are fixated on the road ahead. "Yes, but you're leading it this time."

"I'm okay with that, my friend," Ty says, reassuring James. "That's fine."

James grunts. He is not so sure that anything's fine.

That evening James is in bed trying desperately to fall asleep. He sees his father's face. He remembers the time when he and Kitty were trying to catch tadpoles in the lake near their cottage when she suddenly slipped under the water. James managed to pull her out, but Aaron scolded him for allowing it to happen in the first place. His parents fought loudly that evening about it, and his mother did her best to defend him. Kitty lay beside him that night in his bed, hugging him tightly.

James closes his eyes and remembers Stephen. He sees his face in detail. He recalls the first time they both slept with girls. It was at a weekend cottage party. Stephen bragged forever about his performance, but James always feared that he did not do as well.

He pictures Stephen laughing. He sees flashes of the train racing towards him. His body's memory is relentless and he starts to sweat. His heart beats out of control, making him bolt out of bed, whimpering and pushing the thoughts down towards his bowels.

He shakes it off and walks into the kitchen. He is wearing only his boxers. When he opens the fridge door, the light cuts through the darkness of the room and instantly soothes him. He chugs on a carton of orange juice and heads into the living area, where the view of the city seems endless. The lit-up structures and buildings put him in a state of tranquility. He turns to see Thatcher, his fish, swimming and he feels the guilt of forgetting to feed him yet again. He reaches for the food, opens the can, and sprinkles some on the top of the water. Thatcher swims towards it. James sulks as he recognizes himself in the fish—alone, encased in a tank with limited space and no way to escape.

He goes back to his bedroom, looks at his bed, and walks out into the living room again. He decides that the couch might be the best place to fall asleep, under the view of the skyline, the stars and the illuminated structures. He drifts off with Rebecca's face on his mind.

The sound of a phone ringing slowly shakes James out of his sleep. He squints against the daylight. It's Jade calling. She is wondering where he is.

"You've got a meeting in forty-five minutes and Ty is flipping out."

He gets up off the couch and looks at his BlackBerry. It's almost nine o'clock. "Jesus," he replies, still half asleep. "I'm on my way."

★★★

The office is buzzing with activity. Jade runs over to James and hands him the documents he needs for the meeting that's scheduled to start in two minutes. James walks into the boardroom and apologizes to Ty for cutting it so close. Those present quiet down and he immediately goes into the planning of the project, including the requirements, timelines, cost, and contingency planning. He warns that there will be a long road ahead for public consultation, but he goes on to say that the project is quite feasible and that he doesn't foresee any real issues with moving forward. Ty adds the fact that they have the city's most trusted architecture and design company on board, and provides heavy statistics on their proven record.

A few of the clients have questions, which are easily answered by the two men. Eventually everyone shakes hands on the deal. James excuses himself and heads towards his office, leaving Ty to deal with any loose ends.

"I don't know whether to kiss you or kick your skinny white ass," Ty says, sauntering into James's office a few minutes later. "Why do you look like shit?"

"Lack of sleep," James mutters.

"Oh yeah? Anything to do with that lovely brunette last night?" Ty asks, expecting a flippant response.

"Fuck off," James snarls instead. "And close the door behind you."

Ty shoots an imaginary gun at him. "Yeah, yeah buddy. Oh, and by the way, thanks for spending the coin on me last night."

James is immediately reminded of Martin Diggs and his strange little proverb. He goes back to his drafting table and puts his head in his hands. Jade walks in and hands him message slips. "Two from clients, one from your mother, and one from … a Rebecca Doyle?"

James stares at the messages as Jade hovers over him.

"Do you want me to follow up with any of them?" she asks.

"Uh, no thanks, Jade. I can do this," he says.

"You all right?" she asks, concerned. She is leaning on one hip with her arms folded across her tiny waist.

"I'm just really tired," he explains. "I didn't sleep well last night. In fact, I don't seem to sleep too well at all these days."

"I'm going to get you something to eat," she says, mothering him. "You need energy."

James doesn't dispute her logic and lets her go without argument. He decides to call the first client, who just wants confirmation that changes to the plans will be made by early next week. The second client has an easy question regarding a public consultation that's about to take place. It takes James all of ten minutes to satisfy them both.

He returns his mother's call, but she's not in so he leaves her a message. He takes a breath before picking up the phone again to dial Rebecca's number. *Why is she calling?* he wonders. His mouth is dry and his palms are sweaty. He feels his heart rate escalate in his chest. He quickly dials the number before he loses his nerve. She answers after one ring, startling him.

"Hello?" she says, her voice relaxed.

"Uh, hi, Rebecca? It's, um … it's James," he stammers into the receiver.

Rebecca doesn't hesitate to explain the reason for her call. "I hope you don't mind, but I asked Kitty for your number. She said your work would be the best place to reach you."

"Sure. No, not at all. Um … ah, yep, that's true," he responds, fumbling with that fact.

She seems to realize that the conversation is about to turn painfully awkward so she blurts out the reason for her call. "Listen, I just wanted to know if you would like to get together for a drink after work today," she says. The words fly out of her mouth, catching James completely off guard.

He is shaking on the other end. He stammers and starts to decline. "I, uh, I'm not sure I can, er, make it …"

But before he can finish, she makes things more difficult for him by insisting that it would be just for a few drinks. "It will be an early night. I promise," she states convincingly.

Without knowing how to decline politely, he agrees. "Oh. Um, okay then. I guess," he says, regretting the words even as they are being spoken.

"Great," she responds happily. "Let's meet at the Buckingham Pub at seven."

James can only grunt a response. He sets the phone down and struggles for air.

★★★

Rebecca hangs up her cellphone, feeling very proud of herself. Donna, who is paying for a coffee, catches Rebecca's eye. She walks over and sits down without invitation.

"Were you talking to The Shepherd?"

Rebecca straightens. "Explain to me again *why* people call him that?"

Donna sips her coffee and starts to explain. "Like I said when you just started, he has this ability to take veterans peacefully through their passing. I've never seen it firsthand, but I hear people talking about it all the time. For some reason, patients just feel connected to him. It's like they see a side of him that none of us are privy to."

She pauses to take a large bite of her apple fritter. She swallows her pastry down quickly, leaving Rebecca somewhat disgusted.

"Anyway, somehow he's able to reduce their fear and ease their suffering just by being by their bedside," Donna continues. "It's his presence, and his knowledge about places in the world. He talks to them about things they'll never get to experience or see, like the Taj Mahal or the works of some famous European artist."

Rebecca can feel her heart soar from the compassion Donna speaks of.

"The strangest part," Donna says, leaning in to whisper, "is that during their final hours, when they can't respond to anything, he opens up about himself. Intimate stuff. Personal, you know? Things that Kitty says he won't even talk to her about."

Rebecca is now one hundred percent intrigued. "And other patients overhear this?"

Donna nods her head. "A lot of the rooms have shared beds with only a curtain divider, so you can hear what's going on. The patients say they hear him talking about his dad and about his friend Stephen. Stephen was his best friend growing up. They'd known each other since they were kids, for Pete's sake. They lived down the street from one another and did everything together. Kitty says they were like bookends."

"Where's Stephen now?" Rebecca asks intently.

"Well," Donna ramps up for the big finale. "He died in a terrible accident when he was just eighteen years old. It happened a month before his birthday, which by the way *also* happens to be James's birthday."

35

Rebecca gasps, completely sucked in by the drama.

"Uh huh," Donna continues. "Apparently, Stephen was walking on some train tracks after hanging out with friends that night when the train came around the bend. Poor fella. Almost twenty years later, and James *still* hasn't recovered."

Rebecca sits quietly, stunned. She understands him now. Her heart pounds with sadness. She feels his pain and is drawn to him.

Donna examines her reaction. "Are you okay, honey?"

Rebecca shifts in her seat and prepares to head back up to the fourth floor. "Yeah, I'm fine. Thanks for the information. We should get back."

The nurses' station is quiet, with only Kitty occupying the desk. Kitty looks up from her chart and notices Rebecca standing there, looking solemn.

"Is it true what people say about your brother? That he seems to have a calming effect on dying veterans?"

Kitty sighs and puts down her pen. "Honestly, I don't know for sure what it's about, but he does have an excellent rapport with the veterans. His compassion for them is unexplainable."

Rebecca sits down beside her. "What about Stephen? Donna just told me—"

Kitty cuts her off. "Whatever you do, do *not* talk to him about Stephen. Ever!" she says explicitly. "Look, over the last year or so, I think I've managed to make some progress with my brother. I've been trying to get him to open up and face his fears and anxieties—which, by the way, were triggered by the accident and continue to totally consume him." Kitty rubs her eyes, looking exhausted. Then she suddenly looks up. "Wait a minute," she says, pausing with anticipation. "Did you call him? Is that why you're asking about him?"

Rebecca smiles. "Yeah. We're meeting for drinks tonight."

Kitty tries to get up, but is immediately reminded of her gigantic belly. She opts to give Rebecca a sitting high-five instead.

Shouting from the television room across the hall interrupts them. Gerry is coming out, shaking his head while dragging his intravenous pole. "Bloody Cubs are down nine-six to the Mets in the ninth."

Rebecca and Kitty smile, shaking their heads. "I'll go and investigate," Rebecca says, leaving Kitty to get back to her charts. She walks over to the television room and sits down beside Martin. She notices that he looks tired.

"Hey, Mr. Diggs. How are you feeling? You seem fatigued. Did you take your meds this morning?"

He pats her knee gently. "There's no way I could avoid my medication with mama Kitty-cat lurking about," he says, reassuring her. His eyes sparkle and his genuine smile makes her laugh.

"Well, as long as you're not overdoing it," she cautions.

"Why, Miss Rebecca, this is the most excitement I've had all week. Well, outside of moving here, of course."

"How are you adjusting?" she asks.

"I'm comfortable anywhere, my dear." His voice is smooth and exudes years of logic and wisdom. "It's always been that way for me, even in the jungle. My comrades couldn't understand how well I slept at night. I find peace in the strangest of places."

"Hum," Rebecca chortles. "I envy that about you. I wish I could do that."

Martin rhymes off a quote. "Let us train our minds to desire what the situation demands."

She tilts her head. "That's very insightful," she says, encouraged.

"Indeed," he says. "It's Seneca. He was a Stoic philosopher of the Silver Age of Latin literature. A very wise man indeed. He was an advisor to Nero, but was later forced to commit suicide for participating in a conspiracy to assassinate him, although it was never proven."

"Jesus H. Christ!" Robert is sitting half upright in a La-Z-Boy with plaid blankets flowing around him. His intravenous bag dances around the pole while he stirs and shifts from his outburst.

Rebecca jumps up to settle him down. "Try to behave, please," she says softly, "or I'll have to put you back in your room."

Robert grunts and obliges. Martin gets up and reaches for his cane. He has cancer in his hip, which is making the pain in his leg difficult to manage. Rebecca assists him to stand before turning back to Robert to make sure he's okay. "I'll be back in a bit to take you to your room, all right?"

"I'm not going anywhere anytime too soon, remember?" he calls out in his gruff voice.

Martin laughs out loud and shakes his head. "That man is feistier than a nest of angry hornets."

Donna and Kitty are at the nurses' station, busy with charts and medication containers, as Rebecca and Martin walk slowly by.

"Miss Kitty is much prettier than her brother," Martin remarks to Rebecca with a chuckle. "And she's far more chatty. In fact, she tells me everything—even things I don't want to know."

Rebecca laughs hard. A tall young orderly walks by, and Rebecca lets him know that Robert is in the television room. They reach Martin's bed and she gently helps him back into it. She fixes the covers to make him as comfortable as possible. He smiles graciously at her. His face is warm and familiar, and his deep brown skin is sprinkled with a mix of light and dark freckles that speckle his nose and cheeks. The deep shade of his eyes swims in the brightest of whites, making the contrast beautiful and stark.

"Thank you, my dear," he says sweetly to Rebecca.

She smiles and grabs his chart. "I'll be back in a few hours before I leave for the day to make sure you take your meds before dinner."

"And what's a pretty girl like you doing tonight?" he asks.

"Me? Oh, nothing much. I'm just going to meet a friend for a drink."

She leaves the room with a small wave. Something in Martin's grin makes her think that he knows exactly who she's meeting that evening.

As if the workday wasn't rushed enough, Rebecca finds herself racing the clock at home during the dinner hour. She frantically tries to finish getting ready for her get-together with James while the neighborhood babysitter, Ava, is attempting to make macaroni and cheese for Miesha's dinner.

Rebecca calls down from the top of the stairs, "Hey, Ava? Can you please add some of the cut-up broccoli in the fridge to the water?"

"Aw, Mom!" Miesha objects, her voice carrying through the house.

"Broccoli in or dessert out!" she calls back down, trying to balance on one shoe.

The phone rings and Ava answers it promptly. "Rebecca! It's Kitty!" she yells up the stairs.

"Shit," Rebecca swears under her breath.

Miesha's magic ears hear the word. "Mom! Language!" she reminds her mother.

Rebecca rolls her eyes and quickly picks up the phone. "Bad time, Kitty," she says, out of breath.

"Are you excited?" Kitty chats back.

"I would be if you'd stop calling."

Kitty brushes it off. "Remember to just be yourself and don't pry too much. Let him do the talking."

"You sound like you're prepping me to be a guest on the Oprah show," Rebecca snips. "We're only meeting for a drink."

"Fine," Kitty huffs. "But I'm so happy for you!"

"Whoa, Kitty, let's not get ahead of ourselves, okay? I have to go now, otherwise I'm going to be late." She hangs up before Kitty can say anything more.

Rebecca rushes downstairs to get her purse.

"You look nice, Mom, but your dress doesn't match your belt and shoes," informs the little girl as she walks past.

Rebecca looks down at her shoes, mortified. "What?"

Ava turns around from stirring the pasta and passes judgment. "I'd say she's right."

Rebecca swears again and runs back upstairs. She comes down with a different dress. This one is simple, black and sleeveless and perfectly tailored to Rebecca's small waist and hips. It falls just above the knee. She's lost the belt and added a small burgundy three-quarter length sweater as the accent. Her wavy brown hair naturally flows down to her shoulders. She's wearing four-inch black suede heels that elongate her tiny sculpted legs. Her makeup is very natural, but her lips pop with a light berry-colored lip gloss. The only jewelry she's got on is a fine silver bracelet she received from her parents on her thirtieth birthday. She feels good about the way she looks.

"Mom!" Miesha squeals. "You look like a famous model!"

Ava agrees. "You do. Oh, you'd better get going—I see the cab outside."

Rebecca kisses Miesha on the head. "Regular bedtime, and only one story," she asserts. "Oh, and Ava, I have my cellphone if there's any problem."

She grabs her black fall coat out of the closet, then looks around for her purse and cellphone. She scoops them up while checking for her keys. "I won't be late!" she says, running out the door and down the stairs towards the taxi.

The driver gets out of the car to open the back door for Rebecca. She glides into the clean-scented cab and feels soft leather underneath her.

"I'm going to Buckingham Pub on Lawrence Avenue, please," she says politely.

It's Friday night and Rebecca can feel the weight of the week leaving her body as the cab drives away from the house and proceeds into the busy streets of Chicago. It dawns on her that she's going to meet James—mysterious, compassionate, handsome James—and surges of nausea and excitement flood her insides.

The driver has both front windows cracked and Rebecca accepts the cool breeze gently pushing back her hair. *Don't be nervous*, she instructs. She reminds herself of all she's got going for her. She's worked hard to get to where she is today. She has a beautiful daughter and a good life. Memories of her brothers come to her mind as she sinks deep into the soft seat and watches the skyline passing by. A sudden pang hits her as she longs to see them. She smiles, knowing how much they love her. She is their baby sister, after all.

They are about ten minutes away from the restaurant when another surge of anxiety courses through her veins, initiating wild thoughts that start to attack her self-confidence. She begins to worry about what the night will be like, and whether she'll be able to carry a conversation with such an intelligent and successful man. A little voice enters her head, telling her to shut up and be still. Then she remembers Martin and tries to remember what he said to her earlier today. Something about desiring what the situation demands.

She takes a few deep breaths as the cab pulls up to the pub. She pays the driver and gives him a generous tip. Grateful, he hops out and walks around to open Rebecca's door.

She slowly makes her way up to the front door and reaches for the handle. She suddenly feels a strong presence around her as she hears a voice asking her to allow him to get the door. It's James.

Her body pulls towards his while his arm reaches across her chest for the door. The scent of his body ruptures her mind. As he pulls the door open she steps towards him and closes her eyes.

"After you," he says, his voice slightly wavering.

She waltzes in and suddenly remembers Martin's quote. *Now's the time to train the mind*, she thinks to herself.

FIVE

The Aaron Milligan Veterans' Hospital is hauntingly peaceful at night. The dim lights from the nurses' station hover over the hallways in silence, allowing for time to pass inconspicuously without movement or sound. The occasional whisper or cough usually interrupts the silence, but tonight, a gentle weeping moves in.

Gerry is sitting on his bed with his trusted intravenous pole standing upright against his body. He literally clings to it like a security blanket even though he doesn't physically require it to live. Some of the nurses on staff lovingly refer to him as Linus. He pretends not to care, but deep down he understands and hates the comparison to Charlie Brown's enfeebled friend.

He looks up and stares at the empty space across from him. The curtains are wide open to expose the second bed, freshly stripped of its coverings. His roommate Jonathan Davis is no longer there. He passed away forty-five minutes ago with Gerry at his bedside. Jonathan's wife Margaret didn't make it to the hospital in time, so he played the surrogate wife by holding Jonathan's hand while he took his last breath. Although death came and took his friend's soul, it left behind his vivid sky blue eyes, open wide. They burned through Gerry's heart.

Before he starts to weep again he quickly pulls himself together. He can hear Margaret out in the hallway speaking to the doctor. He cannot appear weak, for her sake. He goes into the small bathroom to clean up before she sees him. He looks at himself in the mirror for what seems like the first time in years. He sees a tall, thin man in his late sixties looking back at him. He has a full head of wavy gray hair and his complexion has a slight pinkish hue. Perhaps he was once a handsome man, but now his pale blue eyes seem to blend into his face and have become too small for the rest of his features.

41

Gerry has been told by women that his eyes are sad. He doesn't doubt it—seeing what he's seen, how could they ever look happy? He served in the Vietnam War between the ages of eighteen and twenty-one, and he knows that behind his back he is known mostly for being the lone survivor of a fatal helicopter crash that killed five of his close friends. He hates that distinction and a part of him wishes that he had died along with his comrades. And a part of him did. His parents called it shell shock. Nowadays, people say he has a mental health disease. Some acronym he can never remember, even if he wanted to. Now he's living in the Aaron Milligan hospital because of his congestive heart disease. *I'm here for my broken heart*, he likes to tell himself silently on his worst days.

Gerry hears Margaret's voice disappearing down the hall. A wave of relief fills his lungs, but a slight rap at the door quickly takes it away. Wiping his tears with his sleeve, he walks out of the bathroom to find Martin standing in the doorway. Martin's eyes focus on Gerry as he signals for him to follow. Gerry slowly gets up, grabs his pole, and shuffles down the hall, following Martin into his room.

Gerry and Martin got to know each other after spending time together in a military hospital in Vietnam in 1966. They kept in touch over the years since then by sharing various veterans' celebrations. Although they were not close friends, they had a sincere respect for each other.

Gerry looks down the hall and sees a few nurses in the main waiting area. All is quiet and most of the patients are asleep. He peers into Martin's room before stepping in. He notices how warm his friend's room is and spots a small portable heater at the side of Martin's bed, tucked away and hidden from the staff.

"You're not supposed to have that," Gerry remarks. "It's a fire hazard."

Martin waves his hand to dismiss the point. "It's the only thing that keeps me warm at night. Except for this," he says, pulling out a small flask from his housecoat pocket. "Come in and shut the door behind you," he whispers. "Now, sit down here," he instructs, pointing to the chair at the end of his bed.

Martin pulls the curtain around, blocking the view of the empty bed across the room and the door that might be opened by a night nurse at any given moment. He bends down to pull a small black duffel bag out from under his bed. Gerry hears the sound of glass clinking together. Martin pulls out two shot glasses in the shape of Hula dancers and cups them both in the palm of his left hand.

Gerry is nervous. "What are you doing? What are those?"

"They're shot glasses, my friend. What did you think they were?" Martin grins. "My lovely niece picked them up for me last year in Hawaii."

Gerry's eyes light up like a child at Christmastime. "Whoa!" he says, totally impressed. He leans in closer to study the details of the painted hula dancers with their protruding three-dimensional breasts.

"Hold them up," Martin orders as he prepares to fill the cone-breasted women with forty percent malt liquor.

Gerry obliges, grabbing the two shot glasses. "This is the closest I've ever come to touching two girls at the same time," he jokes. There is a tone of truth in his voice. His eyes widen with anticipation as he watches the liquid fill up the girls.

Martin hesitates for just a moment before completing the task. "Are you on any medication that might be interrupted with booze?"

"Not interrupted," Gerry says, then clears his throat, intending to clarify. "Just enhanced."

The men smile at each other and carefully grab a shot glass, trying not to spill a drop. As they raise the whiskey towards their lips, Martin makes a toast. "To our comrade and friend Jonathan. Tonight is his night to move out and move forward."

The men gently clink the girls together before tossing back the golden syrup in one swig.

"Whooo wee!" Gerry exclaims, trying not to be too loud. "That's good stuff, Marty!"

Martin reaches back into his bag and pulls out a pack of cigarettes.

Gerry's jaw drops. "You're not serious, Marty, are you? There's no way they won't smell that!"

Martin pops a cigarette between his lips and points his head towards the open window. He lights the stick of tobacco and takes a long haul before exhaling into the night air. Gerry looks around the room nervously before joining him. The two men quietly squat next to the window, sharing a cigarette and finding comfort in the fact that tonight they are not alone.

★★★

The evening is going fairly well for James, despite his frequent urges to leave due to his anxiety disorder. Nevertheless, Rebecca manages to ease his nerves by keeping the conversation on subjects that are safe and desirable for him, like art, architecture, and world travel.

A few hours pass before Rebecca says she feels it's time to close out the evening and head home. She steps out of the pub first and turns to James while she fiddles with the buttons on her jacket. "Thank you for your kind company and chivalry," she says, flashing him a sweet smile.

James can only smile and nod. His mind is muck and he has no means of communicating a decent response. He enjoyed the atmosphere tonight, and he finds

Rebecca quite attractive and charming. *She's nice*, he thinks to himself. *Simple. Pretty.* They walk down the street together, close enough to graze each other's shoulders, igniting an unexplained energy each time.

"Kitty looks like she's going to have the baby early," Rebecca states. "How do you feel about being an uncle?"

James thinks this is an odd question and isn't quite sure of himself in this new role. "I guess I don't really have any feeling towards it."

Rebecca seems puzzled by this answer and lets out a chuckle. "Well, that's a bizarre response."

"It's an honest one," he says, shrugging his shoulders.

She tilts her head, thinks about it, and seems to accept it. She immediately starts to talk about her daughter in this context.

"Having Miesha changed my life. Before her, life was simply a blip in time. She's given me so much perspective and strength. She just oozes unconditional love."

James's body shifts and he alters his walk so that he is not incidentally making physical contact with her anymore.

"Miesha is the one constant joy in my life," she goes on. "The one thing I can count on in this world. It's a love I've never felt before, for anyone or anything."

A rush of fear takes hold of James. He feels sick to his stomach, knowing he's on the verge of experiencing another panic attack. A surge of adrenalin strikes hard and he starts to panic. Rebecca is looking down, oblivious to his state, and continues to talk about her love for her daughter. "She's everything to me …"

Before she can say any more, James interrupts her. "I'm sorry, but, uh, how are you getting home?"

Looking stunned and disappointed at the interruption, she stammers her way to an answer. "Well … I, uh … I was probably going to take a cab."

"Me, too," replies James, holding his arms tight against his body and clenching his jaw. He proceeds to look around nervously for one.

"James," she says, trying to get his attention. He is whistling for a cab and her voice doesn't register. She calls his name again. "James!"

He turns abruptly and spews out what he feels is a polite way to end the evening. "It was a nice night, thank you. But I'm very tired and need to get home." His tone is quick and curt.

A cab pulls up and he hurries towards the door to open it for her. His heart is pounding so hard in his chest that he is convinced he will lose consciousness at any second. He fumbles for his wallet and finds forty dollars that he eagerly hands over to the driver.

Rebecca is standing four feet away, looking flabbergasted and upset at his cold and unexpected attitude. She runs over to the cab driver's window. "Give it back to him!" she orders.

Confused, the man does what he's told.

James insists that the cabbie keep the money. "Please, take her home."

"I don't want your money, James!" Rebecca seethes.

"Please take her home," he says again to the driver, pushing the money back towards him. The cab driver slowly pulls the money back towards his chest.

Rebecca storms over to the driver's side, then reaches in and snatches the money out of his hands. "I can pay for my own damn cab!" she sneers, tossing the money out the window. The cab driver watches the bills float to the street.

James scrambles to collect it and jumps into the back seat. "Call another cab for her please," he says, embarrassed and fatigued.

The cab driver is completely perplexed and watches through the window as Rebecca walks away angrily. Shaking his head, he calls for another cab.

James is mortified and, even more so, is absolutely terrified. His heart is pounding so hard that it's making his head feel like it's about to explode. He looks in the rear mirror to see Rebecca disappearing from his view.

★★★

Tears are welling up in Rebecca's eyes as she makes her way down the street. Frustrated and angry, she pulls her BlackBerry out of her purse and looks up the address listing for James Milligan. Thirteen potential addresses come up.

"Damn it!" she swears, passing an older couple on the street. She texts Kitty, hoping she's still awake, but there's no immediate response. She walks until she finds a bench where she sits quietly, trying to get a hold of herself for long enough to understand what just happened.

She recalls the conversations about James with Kitty and Donna and suddenly begins to understand his onslaught of actions towards her. Things were going so well until she started talking about babies and unconditional love.

Her phone beeps. It's Kitty. She decides texting is much better than talking to her right now.

R: What's your bro's address?
K: Y do u want it?
R: Need to c him, forgot my wallet in cab
K: U sure that's all? :0)
R: KITTY!

K: LOL! 2014 East Huron unit 1707

R: TXS

K: C U tomorrow!

Rebecca calls home to check in with the sitter.

"Miesha is in bed reading, but she's almost asleep," Ava reports.

"Okay, great. I'll be home shortly after midnight," Rebecca says. "Oh, and thank you, Ava."

Rebecca sees a cab coming towards her and hails it. She climbs in and looks at her phone to confirm the address again.

"Twenty-fourteen East Huron, please," she says to the driver.

Rebecca has no idea what she's doing, only that she must do something to make this evening turn out the way she wants it to—well. It was going that way until she started to get deep into the subject of emotional attachments and, God forbid, actual feelings. "God, I'm so stupid." she says out loud.

"Excuse me, miss? Did you say something?" the driver asks, concerned he might have missed something important.

"Oh, no, I'm so sorry. I was just talking to myself," she explains.

Within minutes they arrive at the address and she is amazed at how beautiful the structure is. The lower part of the condominium is made up of smooth white marble with a mix of Romanesque forms resembling a classical church, while the upper part is constructed like a modern luxury high-rise, with mirrored windows and shiny steel framing each unit. The top penthouse suites have expansive balconies that overlook the amazing views of the Lake Shore and the Loop.

Rebecca feels dizzy taking in all the detail. She notices a young man approaching the exit from the lobby, so she quickly pays the driver and takes advantage of the easy access into the building.

The young man exits through the large glass door and Rebecca grabs the handle before it locks behind him. He looks at her with an unassuming grin and she finds herself smiling back casually. She checks her phone for the apartment number as her heart continues to pound in her chest. She is nearly deaf from the sound of it. She steps across the beautiful marble foyer and walks gingerly over to the elevators. *What am I doing?* she thinks to herself, feeling too nervous to be reasonable.

The elevator doors open and she rushes in and looks at the control panel. All the numbers appear jumbled to her. She watches her shaking hand take an extra few seconds to locate seventeen. Without thinking, she presses the button and twitches at the instant sound of a motor pulling the cage upwards. When the doors open, she tentatively steps out and looks around.

"Shit," she says under her breath, trying to ignore her pounding heart. She's sure she is going to have a heart attack, but she somehow continues down the corridor. Looking at the numbers on the doors, she realizes that she's going the wrong way and turns around to sneak up to unit 1707. The bold numbers jump out at her, making her feel like she might vomit. She takes several deep breaths, wipes her mouth, and pushes her hair off her face. Without realizing it, she knocks rapidly on the door six times. She hears footsteps drawing closer.

Her mind goes into convulsions. *Oh my God, I'm going to be sick!* she thinks. She cups her mouth, then releases it and takes a deep breath. She can hear James on the other side of the door. There's a pause that feels like a lifetime.

She is just about to say something when the door swings open. James is standing there in his black boxers. His bare chest is cut with lean muscle and a fading golden brown suntan. His perfectly groomed brown hair is slightly tussled and his sweet and masculine features match the shape and intensity of his pale brown eyes.

They stare at each other without speaking. Her heart is pounding so loudly now that she's sure she is visibly vibrating. James is completely paralyzed.

What have I done? is all she can think.

★★★

As James looks into Rebecca's quivering features, he feels a sensation of betrayal brewing in his guts. *How could she invade my personal space like this? How could she come here without warning?* He can't think of anything to say.

Rebecca tries to speak, but the words aren't forming properly. "I … I just needed to …" She takes a deep breath. "Why did you … I mean, how did I offend you? Why didn't you …"

Before either of them can process another thought, Rebecca throws her arms around his neck. She presses her body against his warm flesh and her mouth covers his. Her warm tongue is slowly and gently swimming around his mouth, searching for his. He is stunned. He can't move.

Her tongue finally finds his. He is captivated by her taste. He can feel her warm breasts pushing up against his chest and her heart smashing up against him like a tsunami. He fears his chest might crack open and cause a flood of blood to rush out of him without warning. He loses control and grabs her round behind and pulls her groin into his hardness. His other hand has her head cupped gently while his tongue plunges deeper into the kiss.

They back into the apartment as one twisted form, causing the door to automatically slam shut behind them as they crash against the wall in each other's arms. He lifts her up and carries her down the hallway to his bedroom, where he sets her down softly on the bed to gently unwrap her. Tears he doesn't understand are streaming down her face. He cannot look at them. He cannot look at her, but it doesn't matter—he wants her with every ounce of his body. He tugs at her pumps while she pulls off her dress. He takes her panties off while she unhooks her bra. He's stunned by her beautiful curves and the way her hair falls onto her shoulders. Her body is soft and her skin is perfect shades of pink and white. He fears he might go off at any second.

He gently climbs on top of her while filling her mouth again with his tongue. He puts his left hand on her right breast and softly caresses it. She moans. He takes the time to glide his hand slowly down the accents of her womanly curves. He follows the lines with his eyes, as if admiring a great piece of art. She is shivering with anticipation and the chill of the night air that still clings to her.

He takes his hand and guides a finger inside her, making her gasp. He becomes one with her moisture and scent. He can feel her sensuality taking over her body, and this excites him even more. Without warning she wiggles out from underneath him and climbs onto his stomach, pressing herself against his hardness.

James throws his arm out from underneath her and quickly fumbles through his bedside table for protection. She quickly unwraps the shield and proceeds to pull it over his mass. He forgets he is embarrassed and closes his eyes in anticipation. She is about to climb on when he lifts his torso up off the bed and places his arms around her waist to regain control. She's on her back again, and the warm breath on his neck frees him of all restraint. With one hard motion he's inside her, knocking the wind out of his ribs. His body tingles with the promise of euphoria. She gasps and moans with every push of his body.

James is an open wound, bleeding with the anticipation of being healed. The feeling of being inside Rebecca is almost too much for him. His mind and body are suspended, and he sees a bright light behind his eyes flowing down into his cavity and filling his entire being. Shots of intense pleasure sweep away all his pain and angst. He is temporarily severed from the person he has known to be himself for most of his life. With every thrust he becomes more suspended inside of this woman. He opens his eyes to see her arching neck and he bites it softly to taste her sweat. She pulls on his shoulders, making him blind with aggressive passion. He pushes harder and spears her with a final euphoric blow. She climaxes and he follows.

His body collapses on top of her. Her delicate hands start to gently massage his head. She kisses his cheek softy and he returns the gesture. When he rolls off he feels exhausted and relaxed. His eyes are heavy and start to close as he drifts off into a semi-dreamlike state for the first time in months. In a moment he is under sleep's spell.

In his dream, his mother Janice is caressing his face. She is younger, yet he is his current age. He looks around his apartment and sees Stephen on the couch smiling at him. A noise comes from the kitchen. A man resembling Martin Diggs is leaning up against the counter, smoking a long black cigarette. James looks back at Stephen and notices he's dressed in army fatigues.

Janice wipes James's brow with a cloth, mothering him like a child. He swats her hand away, completely annoyed with the gesture. He asks Stephen what he's doing and why he's wearing army gear. The Martin Diggs character turns to James as if to say something, but the man's cigarette is smoldering so much that James can barely see. When the smoke clears, Aaron is standing in Martin's place. James suddenly feels the ground vibrating. The loud, distorted sound of grinding metal pierces the apartment. Janice eagerly pulls him towards her and says his name over and over again, stroking his face.

James jolts awake. He feels the sweat sticking to his body.

"James," says Rebecca in a whisper. "I'm sorry if I startled you. I've been trying to wake you for a few minutes, but you were right out of it."

James is disjointed and confused. He feels Rebecca's hand on his face and immediately removes it.

He sees pain course behind her eyes as she pulls her hand into herself, as if his touch has just burned her. She lies motionless for a moment, curling away from him.

"I have to go," she mutters, unwinding the sheets from her legs.

"I'm sorry," James proclaims, feeling ashamed of his inexcusable behavior. "I can drive you home."

She seems to be contemplating him as she hastily pulls her underwear back on. "That's okay, thank you," she replies, obviously uncomfortable in the situation. "Could you please call me a cab though?"

He tries to refute. "Please, don't. I'm sorry I … I'm sorry I wasn't …"

Rebecca cuts him off, assuring him that she really would prefer taking a cab. "It's probably better this way," she says.

He fumbles around looking for his boxers. He finds them and climbs awkwardly out of bed to reach for his BlackBerry. He speed dials the number for the taxi company and mumbles his request for a cab.

Rebecca is getting dressed as quickly as she can. James feels his heart breaking and unconsciously takes her tiny wrist and pulls her towards him. He cannot look into her eyes, even though he wants to desperately.

She hugs him and thanks him for a lovely evening. "It turned out better than I expected," she says, forcing a smile.

He feels some of the tension release. He leans his head on hers. "Thank you for coming over," he whispers.

They walk out of the room towards the front door. "Let me at least walk you down to the lobby," he says.

"No, please," she insists. "I'm fine. Let's just say goodnight from here."

She grabs her jacket and purse, then turns to him and flashes a smile before shutting the door behind her. James stands unmoving, unable to respond to his emotions. He hears the elevator doors open and close. He walks over to his window, lurching forward to see if he can spot the cab. He manages to catch a glimpse of it pulling away with a small figure sitting in the back seat.

A heavy sadness creeps over him. He crosses his arms and stares at the night sky. Eventually he slowly lowers himself onto the couch and turns onto his side. The warm glow of light from the fish tank behind him settles his tension, as do the outlines and shadows of the structures outside his front window, towering above and beyond his own tiny personal space. He is completely alone.

★★★

Rebecca clutches her purse in the back seat of the taxi as it cruises down Lake Shore Drive towards Fourteenth Street. Crouched down with her head leaning up against the seat in front of her, she can't help but cry.

For a short time, she experienced the inception of James's person. Inside, she found floating pieces of love and tenderness, bludgeoned and shattered by the growing mass of his dark pain.

She carefully wipes the tears off her chin and tries to put on a brave face, but she cannot seem to keep it together for more than a few seconds. *What have I done?* she wonders as she watches the city pass by the taxicab window.

SIX

Kitty calls at nine-thirty on Saturday morning and leaves a message on Rebecca's voicemail. Her voice sounds annoyed.

"Becky, it's me. Call me as soon as you get this. Bye."

Rebecca's phone buzzes, indicating a message, but she is in the middle of a conversation with the receptionist at Miesha's dance studio about fees and a payment plan for the year. She finds herself multi-tasking her thoughts and emotions today, carefully putting them in their respective compartments in order for things to run smoothly. Flashes of James invade her mind like a kick in the gut as she struggles to soak in the information that the receptionist is giving her. She thanks her, shakes off her thoughts, and turns to Miesha to assist with her ballet bun. She kisses her daughter on the forehead.

"Don't forget!" she calls out to Miesha, who is running towards her dance class. "Your dad is picking you up after class!"

"I know, Mom!" Miesha replies, rolling her eyes. But before she can say anything more, two of her friends swoop in and pounce on her. Their little black ballet suits, pastel pink tights, and matching slippers swarm around her like happy bees to a perfect flower. The girls squeal and giggle as they drag Miesha off to class.

"Bye, Mom!" she hollers.

"Bye, sweetie. I love you!" Rebecca smiles along with the receptionist. "Thank you for your help today," she says to the friendly woman behind the desk.

On her way out to the car, she remembers that she has a few voicemail messages to check before getting on the road. The first one is from Ben, confirming that he will be picking up Miesha after dance and that he plans to return her after dinner at around eight o'clock. Rebecca anxiously waits for the second message to play.

51

Regrettably, it's Kitty, who's calling to see how last night went. She closes her eyes in disappointment as she listens. She deletes both messages, drops her BlackBerry into her purse, and looks quickly at her watch. She runs over to the parking lot and jumps into her car. She heads towards the hospital, alone in her thoughts.

"I'm Not in Love" by 10CC comes over the radio and she immediately pushes the buttons to change stations. "Cherish" by Madonna plays instead, and it eases her anxiety by sparking memories of Miesha's dance recital last year. The little girl looked so precious on that stage in her emerald green sequined dress and cherry red lipstick. She drives on with a smile.

Rebecca arrives at the hospital a few minutes later and pulls into the busy parking lot. Weekends are not her usual shift, but one of the part-time nurses called in sick and she agreed to take it because she really needs the extra money. She thinks about getting some takeout sushi for dinner later and relishes the idea of having time to soak in a nice hot bath before Miesha returns home from her dad's. Life is good for Rebecca and she knows it. Every minute is a gift, and she is reminded many times a day of how lucky she truly is.

Thoughts of James start to seep back in, deflecting her positive energy. She suddenly finds herself holding her breath. She lets go of the tension by pushing the air out of her lungs and filling them up again with another fresh breath.

She can see now that James is clearly not in the same frame of mind. He has a darkness about him that frightens her. It's an intense sadness—a bottomless sorrow—and yet she did feel the potential of his light last night. He has an incredible aura about him, and she believes that others can see this mysterious quality too. True, everyone is initially drawn in by his good looks, but there is something else about him that raises their antennas. Despite his personal emptiness, he is filled with a certain spirit that feels anything but empty—if only he would let it show more often.

She starts to dissect his character in depth. She wonders if he is even aware of his inhibitions, and if so, if he has tried to rectify them. If not, would he ever be able to move forward? As she grabs a soda from the vending machine on her way to the main doors, James is still on her mind. She finds herself questioning if he knows of his abilities to help people, especially the veterans at the hospital. *Is that why he volunteers to sit with them? Or is there something in it for him?*

"Everyone here seems to be under his spell—and now I'm one of them!" Rebecca catches herself saying out loud. The unexpected words force her to seal her lips as she approaches the entrance to the hospital.

Up ahead at the elevator stands a beautiful young African-American girl. She is absolutely stunning, and Rebecca cannot help but stare.

"Hello," says the beauty queen.

"Oh, hello," replies Rebecca, trying hard to decipher where she knows this person from.

The girl senses that Rebecca is unsure of her identity and takes the opportunity to introduce herself. "I'm Kendra Diggs, Martin Diggs's niece," she says, reaching her elegant hand out to shake Rebecca's. "I recognize you. You're one of the nurses on my uncle's floor."

"Of course," Rebecca jumps in. "Yes, Martin! I'm so pleased to meet you."

"Likewise," Kendra says, flashing her gorgeous white smile. They ride up to the fourth floor while chatting about the hospital's excellent quality of care.

"I'm so grateful for how wonderful the facility and staff are," Kendra says sincerely.

They step off onto the floor together and wave to each other as they go in separate directions. Rebecca's phone goes off again and she sees that it's Kitty calling for the second time this morning. She answers the question abruptly before Kitty even asks. "It was a nice evening and no, I have not heard from your brother."

"Wow, for a *nice* evening you sure are snippy," Kitty gripes.

Rebecca nods to Linda, one of the weekend nurses. She walks behind the nurses' station. "Kitty, I'm sorry. Listen, I can't really talk right now. I'm at work."

"What? Why are you there? You're not supposed to be in on the weekends."

"One of the part-time nurses called in sick, so Janice phoned to see if I wouldn't mind taking her shift. I could use the money, and since Miesha is at dance for most of the day and with Ben later on …" she trails off.

"Well, thanks for helping, Becky. I know my mom really appreciates this," Kitty says, sounding grateful. "Now, to change the subject …" she deflects. "I tried to call Jimmy several times but he's not answering."

Rebecca scoffs. "And you're surprised because?"

There's a pause.

"Okay, something obviously happened from the sounds of it," remarks Kitty.

Rebecca sighs heavily. "Kitty, I can't talk right now. I'll call you later, okay?"

"Promise?" Kitty asks, practically begging.

"Yes," Rebecca asserts. "Goodbye." She places her phone in her purse and straightens out her scrubs. She's dodged Kitty's questioning for the time being.

Linda asks if she wants to go over the patients' charts and the day's routines and she agrees. Dr. Lewis comes over to the desk to update them on Martin's medication and asks that further scans be scheduled for next week. He also hands over Robert's charts and asks that they look into some dietary substitutions to help ease his abdominal pain and cramping. They both look over the chart and comply.

After a few minutes, Rebecca prepares to make her rounds. Her first stop is Hans Webber. "So there's a big birthday party happening soon!" Rebecca announces as she enters his room. Hans is turning ninety in a few weeks. He is a happy permanent resident at the hospital who suffers from Parkinson's disease. Rebecca is always amazed at how sharp and intact his mind is despite his feeble and restricted body.

"Oh yes, and my daughters and grandchildren are going to be here," he says, voice warbling. "I wish my Gina could be here, too. She was Italian, you know. A real beauty. I met her in Naples when I was posted there, and I somehow convinced her to marry a fool like me and come back to the United States. Must have been the officer's uniform." His eyes are misting over. Rebecca doesn't tell him that she's heard this story before. "And boy, did we ever have a great go of it together," he continues. "All the dancing, and laughing. Everybody loved Gina. She used to light up a room. When she got sick …" Hans trails off. Rebecca knows that Gina lost her battle with Alzheimer's over ten years ago and that Hans has never gotten over the loss. "It was like watching her drift away as though she was having an ominous affair with the great unknown."

Rebecca feels the sting of his words but knows exactly how to cheer him up. "I know for a fact that the old movie channels are playing Danny Kaye movies. Would you like me to find one for you?"

Hans wiggles in his bed with excitement. "Oh, would you, my dear?"

"It would be my pleasure." She turns on his small television and switches to the exact channel before helping him put on his headphones. His face lights up as the sound fills his ears and he doesn't even notice Rebecca slip out of the room.

Her next stop is Gerry. Linda advised her earlier that Jonathan Davis passed away and that Gerry has been quite affected by it. Rebecca walks into the room with Gerry's medication and a few magazines she's found lying around. Gerry loves gossip magazines. He argues that there is a defined purpose for them. He says it keeps old people's adrenalin going because it's easy reading and allows for escapism.

Rebecca likes Gerry a lot. She sees him like a taller, thinner version of Mr. Magoo. She also feels the loneliness that surrounds him. He never married and doesn't have children, but many of his friends' children come around to see him. Rebecca thinks this is one of the special perks of being in the military—everyone is treated like family.

Gerry is lying on his bed with his arms behind his head and legs crossed. He appears to be in deep thought.

"Look what I have," Rebecca announces.

His eyes light up. "New editions of the daily rags? Aw, you're a good egg, Miss Doyle!"

"Did you see how much weight she's gained?" Rebecca says, jumping into gossip land with both feet.

Gerry looks at the famous actress on the cover. "I think she looks better. She was too skinny before. Women aren't supposed to be so skinny. Marilyn ought to have shown you all that!"

"Ha!" Rebecca scoffs loudly. "I always knew I liked you a lot! Why can't there be more of you?"

"You should eat a sandwich or two as well, Miss Doyle. No offense, of course."

Rebecca laughs. "None taken. Speaking of which, I think I may do just that. Lunch is just around the corner for you, too. We'll talk later and you can bring me up to speed on what's happening in Hollywood."

"Sure thing, Miss Doyle." He winks at her as she leaves.

She moves down the hallway towards room five. Robert is lying in bed, watching his mini television with his earphones. He grunts at Rebecca and signals her over. She hovers over him with a smile. He points to the water jug on the side table, and she picks it up and fills his glass. He gives her the thumbs up sign and goes back to watching television.

She pulls the curtain to see Martin reading in his bed. Some disco-era grand funk is coming from his CD player. He looks up and sees her, and then places the book on his lap, gently folding his hands over it. He is smiling from ear to ear.

"Good morning, Mr. Diggs," she says cheerfully.

"You're feeling fine, I see," he states.

She ignores him momentarily while she lifts his arm and prepares to take his blood pressure. It is slightly low, which isn't surprising given that he is on a steady diet of morphine. He is hooked up to an intravenous drip for ongoing pain relief. She looks at the bag and adjusts the drip to slow its flow. She takes his temperature with an electronic ear thermometer and scribbles a few notes in his chart.

When she's finished, she tilts her head and smirks at him. "Okay, Mr. Diggs, I'll bite. What's behind that Cheshire cat grin of yours?" she asks, sitting down on the corner of his bed.

He evades her question, but that morning Rebecca finds out all about Mr. Martin Joseph Diggs.

He was born in Omaha, Nebraska, in 1941. His earliest memories are growing up on North Twenty-Fourth Street, where Blacks and Jews learned to coexist in peace. His father's name was Joseph Louie Carter Diggs, but everybody called him Big Joe. He was a tall man who worked as a meat packer for the neighborhood deli and fruit market, which was owned by a Jewish family. He was a proud man, a strict man who didn't like it when Martin and his brother Moe Carter started stirring up ruckus. He was a church-going man who believed in God and the Devil and who made no neverminds about threatening the boys with his theories of heaven and hell. But deep down Big Joe was a sensitive man who adored his family. Every

Sunday and Tuesday night he would head down to the church to sing in the choir. When he sang, his face was transformed into that of a lighter being. He would even sing at work sometimes. People would come into the store and ask him to hum a few bars, and he would happily oblige.

Martin's mother's name was Ester Wen Jackson Diggs. She was a beautiful, tough woman. She was fairly tall for women back then, and she had a sturdy, almost athletic, build. She was fierce and loving, and if she didn't like what her boys were up to, she would chase them down with a rolled-up newspaper, yelling at the top of her generous lungs. But when she laughed, the earth moved and the skies opened up to pour down all the warmth and love in the world. She worked feverishly for her family around the house. She provided them with a loving home and did everything she could to make sure that they were all properly dressed and that their bellies were full when food was available. Ester worked part time as a nanny for a jeweler and his wife, and she was absolutely loved and respected by all.

Moe Carter was Martin's younger brother. They were born exactly four years and one month apart. They were very close growing up, and they remained that way until Moe Carter's death fifteen years ago. He died suddenly from a heart attack on his way to visit his daughter Kendra in Chicago. He'd been a good man his whole life, and had worked hard as a Union Pacific employee for over forty years, cleaning trains and eventually working his way up to the dispatch center in downtown Omaha, where he remained until his death.

As for Martin, he had dreams of becoming a history professor. He received his bachelor's degree in art history in 1965 at the University of Nebraska, after many years of working hard to save up money for college. At the age of twenty-four he was finally accepted into teacher's college when he received notice from the government that he had been drafted to Vietnam. Moe Carter, too, had been drafted, but had a heart murmur and didn't pass the physical. Martin would go on to call him a lucky bastard.

In many respects, the war brought Martin things both good and bad. He found a deep love and respect for his comrades over the years. They learned to follow and look up to him. He would ease their pain at night in the wet jungle, describing works of art from across the globe and reciting poems from memory. Moe Carter would send books to Martin, and Martin would carry them around like a literary crutch. One good phrase from a story by D.H. Lawrence or Tolstoy or maybe a poem by E.E. Cummings—it didn't matter; it was enough to bring a ray of light into those dark nights. It still is.

The war also brought Martin much pain.

"The horrors of war cannot be fully described or explained. They can only be experienced," he explains to Rebecca, who is being swept up by his vast and descriptive words. For her, they take on images of places and people's faces and of times past. He suddenly stops talking and stares at her intensely. She realizes she's drifted off into the details of his stories when she notices her grip on the corner of his bed sheets.

"Mr. Diggs," she says sweetly, "thank you for sharing your incredible journey with me." She remembers the part where his brother died on his way to visit his daughter. "Is Kendra Moe Carter's daughter? I just met her this morning. She's so lovely," Rebecca gushes.

Martin smiles. "Yes," he answers. "That's her. And now we're the only close family we have left." Pain comes over his face.

Concerned, Rebecca reaches out to him. "Are you all right? Do you need me to adjust the morphine?"

"No, child," he responds. "I'm just a bit tired, that's all. Would you mind shutting off my stereo before you leave?"

"Oh, I'm so sorry. I've overstayed my welcome." Rebecca gets up and shuts off the music.

"Please don't apologize," he says. "I've very much enjoyed our time together."

She feels his forehead and double-checks his intravenous drip. Everything is as expected. "Have a good day, Mr. Diggs," she says softly. "Linda will be checking in with you later."

He nods. "Next time," he announces, "it's *your* turn to spill the beans."

She just smiles and pulls the curtain across the rod.

SEVEN

The weekend went by unusually quickly for James. He spent most of the time over the past few days in a state of complete confusion and wonderment, but he managed to eventually distract himself by reading as much as he possibly could. He finished *Philosophy and Religion: Six Lectures Delivered at Cambridge* by Hasting Rashdall, an English philosopher who lived at the turn of the century and expanded on utilitarianism, claiming that an action is morally right if the consequences of that action are more favorable than unfavorable to everyone.

James knew about Rashdall from a professor in college who quoted him quite often. He recommended that his students read *The Theory of Good and Evil* so that they would be more likely to make the effort to find the answer to the practical question: What should a man do? The answer, according to Rashdall, was that a man's actions should produce the best possible consequences.

The problem, James thinks, is that no man can actually *trust* what the right answer might be—especially since a person never really knows what the outcome of his actions will be until it's happened. His mind bandied about this concept for days until Sunday evening arrived and he could no longer think about it.

Monday morning finally comes to mark the start of a new workweek. James prepares for his daily morning run and decides to shut out all of the things in life that he has no control over. His focus over the next few months will be to plan his escape to Southeast Asia. He'll leave in early March in order to be back in time for the commencement of the expansion of the rapid transit lines in May.

He looks up from tying his runners only to see Thatcher, tail sagging, hiding in the bottom corner of the tank. James immediately approaches the aquarium and swishes his finger around to stir the fish, but it doesn't move. He straightens up slowly to assess the situation when the phone rings. The call display reads Kitty.

He debates whether or not to get it, and his mind lands on Rashdall yet again. He decides to make the decision for the greater good and picks up the phone. Without taking a breath, Kitty starts in with her interrogation regarding Friday night's date with Rebecca. He is immediately filled with regret. *Screw Rashdall*, he thinks to himself.

"I can't seem to get anything out of her, so I thought I'd try you—not that I'm expecting anything different," she scoffs. It sounds like she is eating something. "You know I hate mothering you," she says, filling her mouth again. "But you really have to start dealing with your intimacy issues and get on with your life. I mean, my baby is on the way, Jimmy, and I'm counting on you to be a source of support. I want my baby to actually *know* his or her uncle, and that won't happen if you won't start learning to draw yourself out."

James says nothing, knowing that this will annoy her terribly.

"Jimmy, are you listening? You *have* to stop pushing away the people who care about you most." Then she asks the unthinkable question. "Why is it that you are so comfortable speaking to a bunch of dying old men who you hardly know, and yet you cannot seem to open up to Mom or me or anyone else who tries to get close to you?"

The deadly silence continues. James is incensed that she's referred to the veterans in such a flippant manner.

It must dawn on Kitty that she's said something inappropriate and hurtful. "Look, I'm sorry," she says. "I didn't mean it in that way ... I'm just really frustrated with you. Rebecca seems to really like you, and yet you don't seem to be capable of handling it at all. Come on, Jimmy. Mom and I have tried endlessly for years to support you."

James is pained. A wave of anger flows over his body. He wants to lash out at her but can't. He simply clicks the phone off. It's all he knows how to do.

★★★

Kitty remains on the other end of the line, listening to the dial tone. She tosses the phone onto the armchair across from the couch and her eyes immediately brim with tears. She turns onto her side and places a pillow between her legs for support. She reaches for the blanket sprawled halfway down her legs and pulls it up over her shoulders. She closes her eyes. She is exhausted from the baby's aggressive behavior and from work. She can't think about her brother today without tears forming. She aches for him, but mostly she longs for his companionship.

Growing up, James and Kitty were the best of friends. Despite their six-year age gap, they were closely bonded. James was a kind and gentle big brother who had the patience of Job. He would build things for them to play with, in, on, and under. Every week he built them a new structure of some kind—a tree house, an igloo, a bridge, and a baseball diamond, to name a few. She loved him wildly as a child. She would hug and kiss him every chance she could, and he would oblige. He was quiet and gentle. Kitty idolized his genius. There wasn't anything he couldn't do, and he certainly could not do any wrong in her eyes.

Aaron had a different view of James, however. He was harsh and often made comments regarding Kitty's relationship with him, citing that it just wasn't normal. Janice and Aaron didn't argue much, but when they did, it was always about James. Kitty felt she needed to protect her big brother and often found herself screaming at her father in James's defense. Aaron would look down at the little girl with his hands on his hips and laugh with amazement at how feisty his little blond-haired lamb was. Kitty would stick her tongue out at him and run off, and Janice would chase after her, reminding her not to be so disrespectful towards her father.

James nearly drowned in his own shame when his father would show his disapproval of James's relationship with his sister. Aaron wanted him to have more friends his own age. *And that's when Stephen Pike came into the picture,* she thinks begrudgingly.

Kitty can still remember seeing the big white moving truck travel down Tall Tree Crescent, where they all lived in Lisle. She was skipping rope in their driveway when the two men in the truck waved at her. She just turned six that week, and James was about to turn twelve in the fall. She watched the truck rumble away and stop at the bottom of their street. Janice came out to announce that it must be the Pikes. She heard that they had bought the Lindens' house last month and were scheduled to move in any day.

Janice took Kitty by the hand and walked to the bottom of the street to welcome the new family to the neighborhood. A woman and a young boy came to the door to greet the driver of the truck and the moving crew. The woman was slim and beautiful, with sandy blond hair that fell to her shoulders and bounced and swayed as she moved. The gregarious young boy ran over towards them and proudly introduced himself as Stephen. Janice smiled graciously and told him that it was a pleasure.

The beautiful woman turned away from the movers and walked towards Kitty and Janice. She introduced herself as Lynn Pike and bent down to say hello to Kitty, commenting on her beautiful hair. Kitty remembers hiding behind her mother's legs. The women chatted for a while before Janice mentioned that she had a son who looked to be the same age as Stephen. Before she could say anything more, Stephen zipped by on his bike and raced towards the hill at the end of the street. Lynn called out for him to be careful of cars. She remarked upon Stephen's daredevil tactics and how it might just turn her hair white one day. The women laughed. Kitty was horrified to think of this lady with white hair—almost as though she might turn into a witch of some kind.

James came out of their house to see what all of the fuss was about just as Stephen barreled towards him on his bike. When he stopped in front of James, Kitty could see the two figures conversing in the distance. She noticed James walking around Stephen's bike, staring at it. Stephen jumped off and offered his bike to James. Kitty can still recall James's reaction and how his body moved with excitement at the chance to ride the bike.

That day changed her relationship with her brother forever.

The sunlight retracts from her living room and she can feel fatigue taking over. She closes her eyes and tells herself to rest. The baby's feet are grinding up against her rib cage. She would give anything to give birth in that moment.

★★★

The office is busy with a mix of people getting ready to leave for the day and those who are planning on working into the evening. Despite the recession, projects seem to be moving along.

James is finishing up a meeting with a client when his BlackBerry calendar reminds him of a four o'clock volunteer session at the hospital. Jade arrives to do the same, but he intercepts by holding up his BlackBerry to let her know that he's already aware. She smiles at him and heads back towards her desk. James can't help but notice how attractive Jade is, despite the fact that he has seen her walk with her fantastic swagger so many times before. He suddenly thinks about Rebecca and a flush comes over his face. Embarrassed, he lowers his eyes and walks towards his office to retrieve his things.

"See you tomorrow," he mumbles to Jade.

"Don't forget, you're meeting Ty at nine a.m. tomorrow for squash," she calls out as he steps onto the elevator.

He stops for a second and throws his head back. "Shit," he grumbles, hitting the button to take him to the garage. He had forgotten. "Thanks."

She flashes him a sarcastic look. "It's a good thing you have a woman like me in your life," she heckles as the elevator doors start to close. "Even if it's only on a professional level."

Outside, James considers the sensation of the hot sun like a gift from God. Rays of light along Lake Shore Drive bounce off the car roofs as he speeds towards the hospital. He is happy to note that the traffic isn't too bad. He hates being trapped in traffic, as he becomes claustrophobic after only a few minutes.

He remembers how, back in early February, Lake Shore Drive became paralyzed by a massive snowfall, leaving about nine hundred cars trapped in the early morning rush hour. James's car was one of them. After thirty minutes of pure panic, he got out of his car and trudged through nearly two feet of snow. People tried to stop him, but he walked right through their words of concern and found his way through the blizzard to a tiny coffee shop. He returned the next day after work to find that hundreds of cars were still stuck. It took him two hours to dig his own abandoned car out of the drifts and slowly move along Lake Shore.

He listens to the DJ from his favorite radio station give his opinion about the Cubs' performance the previous night before segueing into a classic Peter Gabriel song. James mumbles a curse under his breath, knowing full well how the Cubs performed the night before. He turns up the radio as the song fills the car. He feels a tingle of anxiety and anticipation as he thinks about Rebecca. A wave of relief comes over him when he realizes the time. *It's close to the end of her shift*, he thinks to himself, feeling safe inside.

He parks his car in the hospital parking lot and then makes his way into the building and up to the fourth floor. The elevator doors open and he instinctively steps out without looking up.

As the doors close behind him, he sees that the unit is bustling with activity. "What's going on?" he asks Donna, who is manning the desk.

"There's a new patient in today," she tells him. "She just arrived from the military hospital in Germany. Anna McBain. Hit by a roadside bomb in Afghanistan."

"Is she going to be okay?" James asks, not sure of what else to say.

Donna shakes her head. "Her parents moved her here for palliative. The bleeding on her brain put her in a coma, and there's just too much damage. I hear the other two patrolmen she was with died. Not even any remains to send home to their families." Donna clucks her tongue sadly. "Shame, though. She's just a young thing."

He starts to make a move to escape when Donna fixes her eyes on his.

"I'll be watching you today to make sure you behave," she adds, glaring directly at him. She releases him and starts to walk away backwards, pointing her two index fingers towards her eyes and then at his, repeating this motion twice as she moves away.

James sees Rebecca at the nurses' station, but her back is turned as she speaks into the phone. He feels a sense of relief. He's not ready to see her—not yet. She appears deep in conversation and is speaking softly so as not to be heard. His nerves bend and twist as he walks feverishly past the station.

In that moment, Gerry comes out of the television room and hollers at him down the hallway. "Jimmy! Did you catch the game last night?"

Rebecca spins around, making the phone cord twist and coil around her forearm like a wild sea serpent. She pauses mid-sentence and stares at James.

He looks back at her sheepishly and offers a meager salutation. "Hey …"

The look she gives him is one that shoots directly into his corneas, piercing his brain. A blinding pain sears his head and crashes into his chest where his heart violently pounds.

She resumes speaking quietly into the phone, still maintaining her death stare.

He turns and walks away, jutting into the first room he sees. Hans is there, curled up on his side, asleep. He sneaks back out into the hallway and is making his way across the hall to another room when he hears his name being spoken. He freezes on the spot.

Closing his eyes, he turns around, knowing full well that he cannot escape her any longer. He feels awkward and uncertain as Rebecca steps towards him. He holds his breath, unable to move.

"How are you?" she asks quietly.

He is about to respond when a few nurses and an orderly wheel an unconscious woman on a gurney around the corner towards them. Her head is wrapped in extensive white bandages and tubes are coming out of her everywhere. She can't be more than twenty-five years old. It must be Anna McBain.

Rebecca quickly moves out of the way to assist the other nurses in moving Anna into the room. James takes a few steps backwards and presses his shoulders up against the wall. He watches intently as the four nurses and the orderly move carefully around Anna. They arrange her tubes and attach her monitor and intravenous drip before transferring her onto the bed from the gurney.

"One, two, three, lift!" the orderly grunts. James gasps lightly under his breath and is relieved when he sees that they've managed to make the transition smooth for Anna. The orderly scurries out of the room while the nurses convene at the right side of the bed to go over her chart. Dr. Lewis comes around the corner and passes James, swiftly shutting the door behind him as though James was an unnoticeable fly on the wall.

James suddenly feels like an outcast and is ashamed for inadvertently intruding on the situation. He feels his face flush.

"Don't make this about you, Mr. Jimmy," comes a voice, deep and low, vibrating down the hall.

Surprised, James clears his throat and looks up to see Martin Diggs standing a few doors down.

"Come here, son," Martin instructs.

James stands there, confused. Although he hasn't yet officially met Martin, there is a sentiment about him that seems oddly familiar.

"Are you waiting for any particular shade of green to move forward?" Martin asks facetiously.

James tucks his hands into the pockets of his dark overcoat and walks over to Martin, who is standing in the doorway of his room. "I'm supposed to be sitting with Hans," he says nervously.

Martin shuffles slowly towards his bed. "Well, we can plainly see that he's asleep, so come sit with me."

James reluctantly follows behind him, passing Robert on the way. As usual, Robert is watching television with his official Chicago Cubs mini earphones on. James looks at Robert and raises his hand in greeting. In his usual fashion, Robert grunts in response. He momentarily pulls out his earphones. "Hey, Jimmy, it's about time you started the hockey pool!"

James turns back and gives him a thumbs-up. "For sure, Bob. I'll get Ty to set up an online pool this week."

"Goddamn it!" Robert yelps, startling him. "Don't you know that I'm no good at that electronic shit? I mean, can't y'all do it like normal, with a goddamn piece of paper and a pen?"

"Careful, Bob," warns Martin. "You may hurt yourself picking your players."

Robert is quick to come back. "What do you know about the Cubs, old man? Stick to your basketball. This isn't the NBA we're talkin' about over here, ya know?"

"Well, lookie here, Mr. Jimmy," Martin responds with a coy grin. "Bob over there is real good at reciting the letters of the alphabet."

All three men laugh in sync.

"Hell, Marty, you're gonna make me wet the bed!" Robert proclaims. He manages to catch his wind and settle down to watch his television in peace.

Martin discreetly motions to James to draw the curtain. Without hesitating, James does what he's asked. Meanwhile, Martin is busy getting something out of his black bag under his bed. He pulls out a small, aged black and white photograph in a thin silver frame. It is the image of a couple, and James assumes they are Martin's parents. Martin sits on the edge of his bed and beams a smile at the picture in his hands. James has no idea where Martin is going with any of this.

"This picture was taken in 1946," states Martin. "It was the day my parents decided to renew their wedding vows at the St. John African Methodist Episcopal Church. Lord, we were so happy that year. So much had gone right for the Diggs," Martin continues. "Money was steady, although we certainly weren't rich, and we lived in a decent neighborhood and had the good fortune of receiving a good education."

He sets the photo down beside him on his bed. "I remember that day so well. In fact, I sometimes wonder, with all of the memories I have, what it is exactly about that day that keeps it so rich and vivid in my mind. It's grounded deep in my soul, you know?"

He turns to James, who is feeling incredibly lost. Martin looks him in the eye before saying anything more. James tries to look elsewhere, but before he can, Martin starts to speak again.

"I'll tell you why, Mr. Jimmy. What makes it so memorable is that it was the day when, for the first time as a family, we had all accepted that the happiness that we collectively felt in our hearts was truly ours to own. It was no longer somebody else's gift or privilege. It was *ours*."

James sighs. For a moment, he forgets that he's in a hospital listening to a complete stranger. He slides over to the edge of Martin's bed and looks out the window. Gray clouds fill the sky. He turns to the old man and asks about his life. "Where are you from? How did you end up here?"

Even before Martin begins to speak, James knows that the man has the ability to suck people into his realm. He is magnetic, charming, eccentric, intelligent, warm, and seems to be genuinely interested in people. James is completely unaware that he himself holds the same power. Martin, however, is fully aware and feels the connection.

Martin begins to share a history of a rambunctious boy from Omaha who turned into an art history major, and who eventually ended up a soldier for the United States of America. James considers this recount to be the typical standard roll call of historical facts that people rhyme off in order to accommodate small talk. But something about Mr. Martin Diggs leaves him feeling intrigued.

Without thinking, he asks Martin to reveal more. "Tell me one interesting fact about yourself," he asks.

"All right," Martin agrees. After a brief pause, he straightens his back and relaxes his hands. "My maternal great-grandfather was a Chinese immigrant who worked on the Transcontinental Railroad's Central Pacific Line in the mid-eighteen hundreds. He worked for peanuts under the most grueling of conditions. And they were responsible for providing their own food and tents. That's some kind of set-up, isn't it?"

James shakes his head in disbelief. "So, you have Chinese blood in you?" he asks, taking a closer look at the woman in the black and white photograph. The fact that the Chinese worked on the Transcontinental Railroad starts to fill James's memory. He remembers something about this from high school. Perhaps he can see a bit of Martin's heritage in his eyes. He studies Martin's face further.

Martin closes his eyes and begins to recite. "The lack of light brings the frost to my home, But when the Moon begins to burn bright, Frost begins to melt at night, And soon the sun will rise in good faith." Martin opens his eyes and smiles.

James looks out the window and reveals the author's name. "Chin Lu," he says. He recalls the art exhibition inspired by Lu's work that was held at the University of Chicago's Oriental Gardens during the summer.

Impressed, Martin turns to him with a grin. "Of course."

"Did you ever learn to speak the language?" James asks, still curious about Martin's heritage.

"No, I didn't, but my mother knew some Mandarin and she loved everything about that part of her life. She became an expert at Chinese art and history and it inspired me to research everything about the culture. I loved looking at pictures of the landscapes as a child. When I landed in Vietnam for the first time, I recognized the same type of plush forests and greenery. It always reminded me of my mother and that gave me comfort."

James listens intently and wishes he could carry his own mother in his heart in the same way.

It's half past five and the nurse Darlene has come to tell Martin that she has to check his blood pressure before dinner arrives. James gets up and turns to Martin to say goodbye.

Before he can speak, Martin places his hands on James's arms. "It's nice to be reacquainted with you, son."

James's eyes move from side to side. "Uh, yeah. Nice to meet you, too," he says.

Just as he leaves Martin, he hears a commotion coming from coming from Anna McBain's room. The small glass window in the door is an open invitation for him to peek through and appease his curiosity. He notices what appear to be her family members standing around her bed. A man and a woman in their mid-fifties hover over her, exchanging heated words while a young man, perhaps her brother, stands in the corner, looking distressed with his arms crossed over his chest.

James suddenly remembers that it's past Rebecca's quitting time. She's most likely left the hospital, and he's unsure if he's relieved or bothered by this fact.

The young man who could be Anna's brother suddenly sees James looking through the window. Before James can flee, the brother opens the door and steps out. After closing the door quietly behind him, he approaches James, aggression clearly coursing through his veins. "Can I help you?" he seethes.

"No, no, I'm uh … I'm sorry," answers James. The words stumble out of his mouth. "I'm just a volunteer here at the hospital. I was here earlier when they brought this patient in. I … I just wanted to check to see how she's doing."

The young man's eyes go to James's hospital volunteer tag. His shoulders relax and he sighs heavily. "Sorry," he says. "Listen, we're just a bit on edge here."

"I understand." James replies. "I'm James Milligan. My family runs the hospital."

"Oh yeah?" the man says, a new respect coming into his eyes. "I'm Connor."

The men shake hands.

"How old is she?" James inquires.

Connor looks back through the window and crosses his arms. "Twenty-seven." He sighs heavily. "She's not just my big sister, she's my best friend. She'd do anything for me," he states. "It was like that even when we were kids."

James smiles, hoping to encourage Connor to say more. It works.

Connor laughs and goes into detail. "When we were young, she used to chase around the guys that picked on me in the school yard and kick them all in the groin if they didn't promise to stop. One year she ended up in the principal's office nine times." He chuckles and James joins in. "She sent Donny Hadler to the hospital that year, too. They weren't sure if his balls were ever going to drop back down out of his asshole." Connor shakes his head, smiling like he's the biggest brother this side of New York.

The hallways are getting busy as the dinner carts start their rotation.

"So, your family runs this place?" Connor asks, changing the subject.

James nods. "I come here a few times a week to sit with the vets in the absence of their family. It's hard for people to be here around the clock. It can be exhausting for loved ones. Are you okay if I sit with Anna sometimes in your absence?"

Connor looks at James, surprised. "Yeah, sure," he replies. "We'd be grateful knowing she isn't here alone. We'll try to get here every day, but it'll be difficult, you know? Dad's going through chemo for prostate cancer. He's going to be fine, but Mom needs to take him because he's blind in one eye, so he can't drive himself. That's what all the ruckus was about in there—Dad threatened to stop his chemo to stay with Anna, and Mom won't hear of it."

James suddenly feels as though this boy will never stop talking. To his dismay, he appears to be right. Connor goes on to talk about his football scholarship and how lucky he is to have received one because his parents don't have the money to support his degree.

James is pretending to be interested, all the while looking over Connor's shoulder at Anna through the window. Connor's voice becomes distant static to James, who focuses on the side of Anna's face that is revealed. He can tell that she's pretty, despite the white bandage covering most of her head. Her features are small and delicate and her skin is golden peach. She has a tiny nose and round cheeks. Her strawberry blond eyebrows are the perfect shape. She has a small frame that makes her appear almost childlike.

James can see Anna's mother sitting beside the bed now. She looks fragile and worn. She is smaller than Anna, with shoulder-length red hair that looks brushed, but not very well. Her eyes emit too much sadness for James to note their color.

He hears Connor repeat a question. "Do you think the Bears have a chance this year?"

James snaps out of his own world. "I think it's too early to tell right now. Listen, man, I have to go visit another patient, but it was nice to meet you."

Connor reciprocates the sentiment. They shake hands and go their separate ways.

The distant sound of Gerry singing in his room is followed by that of a group of people laughing. James suddenly feels overcome with ease—a rare feeling for him.

★★★

Later that night, Rebecca helps Miesha with last-minute bedtime prep. Miesha is brushing her teeth while Rebecca is brushing her daughter's long, wavy brown hair.

"Do you think I have your hair or Dad's?" she asks her mother.

Without thinking, Rebecca replies, "Mine."

"I know we have the same color, mom, but I'm talking about the *texture*." She's talking and brushing at the same time.

Rebecca spins her around to look directly into her eyes. "Mine," she repeats.

Miesha smiles and puts her toothbrush in the holder. "Done. Now get out—I have to pee!"

Rebecca closes the bathroom door behind her and takes clothes out of Miesha's dresser for the next day. She hears the toilet flush, and then the sound of water running in the background as she turns down Miesha's sheets and duvet. Miesha dances back into her room, making Rebecca beam with pride.

"Come here, little monkey," she says lovingly.

Miesha happily hops onto the bed and slides under her sheets.

Rebecca leans over and kisses her fondly on her little round nose. "Good night," she whispers in her ear.

"Don't let the bed bugs bite," Miesha echoes back. Rebecca gives her one last tuck in and leaves the little girl's room, shutting off the light behind her. She walks into her own bedroom and turns on the lamp. Emptiness hovers and she understands that it's loneliness that weighs on her heart.

★★★

Across the city, James is having a similar revelation. Hoping to escape the void, he downloads some books and indulges in their promise to provide him with a distraction from his cyclical and analytical thoughts. By midnight, the lullabies of literature prevail and sleep comes with more ease than usual.

In his dreams, he is hovering over Anna's bed in a medical unit in Afghanistan. She is lying motionless on her makeshift cot with her head tilted to one side. He gently adjusts her head so he can see her entire face. She has long, flowing red hair. He bends down to touch it, but before he can, she opens her eyes and grabs his wrists. His heart pounds at the surprise of seeing her vibrant green eyes.

She pulls him down towards her and starts to kiss him. Her mouth is sweet and wet. She is wearing a black summer dress with slight spaghetti straps. Her shoulders are creamy and delicate. Freckles cover her clavicle bones. His hands move down her body to where he can feel her hipbones protruding, accentuating her flat stomach and tiny waistline. He becomes nervous and excited at the same time. Her breasts are small but full, and he wants nothing else but to put his mouth on them. He does, and the sound of her whimper melts his insides. When he looks up to see her face, he finds Rebecca running her hands through his hair, smiling lovingly at him. He looks around in a panic and realizes he's in his bedroom with Kitty standing in the doorway. She is wearing a pink flannel housecoat that cannot mask her pronounced belly.

"I need you to help me with something," she says calmly.

James looks back to the spot where Anna and Rebecca lie. The bed is empty. He turns back towards Kitty, completely out of sorts. "What?" he asks.

Kitty's water breaks and spills around her feet. Startled, she looks down at the floor. Her head slowly moves back up until her gaze finds James. Her voice is quiet and almost monotone when she replies, "It hurts."

James wakes abruptly and jumps out of bed. He spins around to get his bearings and accidently knocks over a glass of water on his bedside table. He stares at the puddle on the floor and his mind flashes to Kitty standing in her baby's amniotic fluid. He rubs his head and pats his face with his hands.

He takes a breath. He bends over to pick up the glass and sets it back on the side table. Stepping over the puddle, he reaches for the t-shirt on his bed to mop up the mess. He lies back down on his bed and stares up at the ceiling. The terror in his heart eats away at his sensibility. *It's just a dream*, he thinks, trying to convince himself.

Pulling the blanket over his head, he can't wait for the night to pass.

EIGHT

In the morning the sun is battling the clouds outside, and bright rays randomly jet in and out of the bedroom window. James is completely tangled up in his comforter, holding a pillow over the right side of his head to combat the light. His BlackBerry has been going off for over an hour, and his home phone continues to ring on what feels like a fifteen-minute cycle.

James can hear these noises in the background, but sheer exhaustion has anchored him in a state of peace. He can't move, so he decides he won't even try. He's comforted by the thought of a new day with the horror of the previous night behind him—for now, at least.

By nine a.m. the phones stop harassing him. James opens his eyes and tries to assess his surroundings through his haze. He lies still in his bed and the silence in his apartment assures him no one else is around. When he sits up, he is seized by a raging throb in his right temple. A nauseous wave forces him back down. He figures that Jade and Ty must be wondering where he is so he rolls over gingerly and reaches for his BlackBerry. There are seven voicemails.

"Ty," he gripes out loud to himself. He dials into his voicemail. He puts his BlackBerry on hands-free so he can get out of bed and listen at the same time. The first one is from Jade, asking his whereabouts and wondering whether he's forgotten his squash date with Ty.

The second message is from Ty. "You know, you're a real bitch. Why do you always have to play hard to get? If you can get your finger out of your ass for one second, then try using it to dial and let me know what the hell is up with you and where the fuck you are!"

James smirks and waits for the next message. It's Janice telling him to call her

71

back right away because it's urgent. The rest of the messages are all hang-ups. Curious as to why, he checks his call log and sees Kitty's cell number listed several times. He immediately speed dials his mother but there's no answer. He tries Kitty's cell and hears his mother's voice on the other end. James is slightly confused.

"Mom?"

"Jimmy, thank God! Where have you been, honey? We've been trying to reach you!"

James's heart starts to race. "What's wrong?"

Janice tries to contain her worry. "Your sister is in emergency at Mercy. Her blood pressure spiked in the middle of the night. She was on the verge of going toxic. Jacob rushed her to the hospital around four this morning. They've stabilized her and the baby too."

His mind scrambles. "What? What happened?"

"The doctors said …" Janice pauses, trying to remember. "They said she's suffering from preeclampsia. Jimmy, she's been asking for you over and over. Can you please come?"

James can feel his throat tightening up. "Yes, I'm on my way now."

He works through the pain in his head and quickly emails Jade to let her know what's going on and to ask if she can reschedule his meetings. He scrambles to the washroom, brushes his teeth, and hurries back to his bedroom to grab his clothes. He searches for his keys and finds them on the table next to the aquarium. He notices that Thatcher is still at the bottom of the tank and quickly tosses in some food before heading out the door. He can't worry about that now.

Suddenly, his dream flashes before him. "I'm sorry," he says out loud to Kitty and to himself.

★★★★

Rebecca is at work, trying to manage the floor in Kitty's absence. Janice called very early in the morning to let her know what was happening. Rebecca's trying to remain calm about the situation. After all, Kitty is in great hands and preeclampsia can be managed if diagnosed in time.

The doctors on staff agreed to allow Rebecca to run the schedules full-time from now on.

"She's ready," proclaimed Dr. Lewis at the morning meeting. "As of today, Kitty is officially on maternity leave and Rebecca is in charge of handling the job."

Donna is on the phone with a patient's family member, giving them an update on the patient's status. Rebecca is on the other line, trying to arrange for another nurse and orderly to come in to work. A flu bug is plaguing the staff and they're running short on help. Patients are up and about today and family members are filling up the hallways.

Why is it always like this here? Rebecca thinks to herself. *As soon as we're short-staffed, things get crazy.*

In between rounds and consults with patients and families, Rebecca thinks about Kitty and how afraid she must be. She is thankful that her friend's going to be all right, but when James enters her mind, her stomach tenses up and aches. She wants so badly to talk to him, but she doesn't know how to reach him—to get through to him. The sound of men bellowing down the hall interrupts her thoughts, so she moves swiftly towards the noise.

When she opens the door to room one she finds Hans and Martin sitting across from each other, fire in their eyes.

"Gentlemen, what's going on?" she asks, sounding just like a grade-school teacher. "Do I have to remind you that this is a hospital?"

Both of them hang their heads like little boys being scolded by the head schoolmaster.

"We're having a difference of opinion," states Martin.

Not impressed, Rebecca looks sternly at them both. "Clearly."

"He doesn't seem to understand the evolution of war," Martin explains. His voice is shaky from age, disease, and absolute frustration. "All I did was try to explain to our friend here that man has always been preoccupied by the idea of war, and that this preoccupation hasn't always been about the preservation of mankind."

"Poppycock!" Hans grumbles. "Men lose their lives in order to protect mankind and their freedom."

"Ah, yes," agrees Martin. "But one can also say that the preoccupation with war has been a fabrication of ours since the beginning of mankind. In the last two thousand years, on the whole, there have been thirteen years of war for every year of peace!"

Hans huffs. "Oh, for Pete's sake. Where did you get that?"

Martin glares at him. "From a book."

"Geez, I must have missed that Spider Man edition," Hans mumbles under his breath.

Rebecca takes the opportunity to adjust Hans's saline drip.

Martin goes on, "Hans, think about it. It's never really been about preserving mankind. No, it's about the preservation of man's desires and beliefs. World War II was only a carry-over of the unresolved political issues that fueled the First World War, right? In the end, we have won civilization as we know it by drudgery, sacrifice, and a lot of blood."

Hans is starting to quiver so Rebecca decides to take charge. "All right, boys, that's enough." She settles Hans back into his bed. "I ought to make you two kiss and make up."

Martin blows Hans a kiss while struggling to get up from his chair. Hans returns the gesture by giving him the finger. Martin laughs and Hans cracks a smile.

"You'll get yours at the game in a few hours," Hans says.

Rebecca looks impressed. "Wow, you guys got over that pretty fast. So there's a game tonight?" she asks.

"Yes, and the Cardinals are going to give the Cubs a licking," assures Hans.

Martin shakes his head as he makes his way towards the door. "We'll see about that, old man."

Rebecca is concerned about how slowly Martin is walking. His last bloodwork indicated a rise in his white blood cell count. She sees that the disease is starting to take over and feels heaviness in her heart. "Come on, Mr. Diggs," she says softly as she takes his arm and escorts him down the hallway to his room.

He wraps his arm around hers and cups her hand. "You're a mighty soul, Miss Rebecca."

Back in his room, she settles Martin into bed and then scribbles some notes on his chart. She tells herself that she will speak with Dr. Lewis and Dr. Monty regarding Martin's latest test result. Before she leaves, she checks to see if Martin needs anything to make him more comfortable. "Can I get you anything? Some tea?"

Martin politely declines. "I think I'll just tuck myself in and read. Maybe even grab some shut-eye," he says, hopeful.

She rubs his arm. "A nap is always a great idea." Rebecca leaves the room and quietly shuts the door behind her. She checks her BlackBerry to see if there is any word about Kitty, but there's nothing.

Disappointed, she makes her way down the hall and veers into Anna McBain's room. The room has only one bed and is quite small compared to most of the others. Anna's parents placed a small radio on her bedside table and set it to a classical station with the hope that Anna can hear the beauty of the rhythms and notes. Rebecca looks at Anna and notices how pretty her face is. She is overwhelmed with sadness at Anna's prospects. She sees the girl as being far too young to have witnessed so much pain and destruction. Now, her life will soon come to an end and there's nothing anyone can do to change its course.

A slight smell of urine perforates the room. Rebecca thinks about how strange it is that the body can continue with its daily functions even though the spirit has gone on to master bigger and better things. She checks Anna's chart and then replaces her intravenous bag before going into the washroom to prepare water and soap for Anna's sponge bath. Clean hospital gowns are folded neatly on a rack above the toilet.

The door to the room opens and she hears Donna's voice. "Rebecca?"

Rebecca answers in a whisper, "In here."

Donna enters the room. "Listen, Janice just called to say that Kitty is doing well. Jacob and Jimmy are there, too."

Rebecca's heart skips a beat. "Oh, thank God." She sighs heavily. "Did she mention the baby at all?"

Donna heads into the washroom to grab washcloths and a towel to assist Rebecca with Anna's bath. "She said the baby's fine, not to worry," she replies. "Doin' just fine."

Donna grabs the portable table and pulls it towards the right side of Anna's bed. She efficiently places the bath items on it in preparation. She passes Rebecca protective gloves and then gently rolls down the sheets.

Both ladies work in between Anna's thin white legs. Donna holds the tube of the indwelling catheter while Rebecca takes away the drainage bag to dispose of it in the biohazard bin. Donna passes her a new drainage bag from the table, and Rebecca carefully hooks it up to the tube. Urine starts to flow.

The nurses dispose of their gloves and immediately start preparing Anna for her sponge bath. With skill, they remove the hospital gown from the young woman's limp body. Rebecca tosses the dirty gown into the soiled linen basket in the corner of the room. She then dips a washcloth into a bowl of warm, soapy water and starts to bathe Anna lightly. Donna immediately pats the area dry with a warm towel so Anna won't feel any chill.

The women are completely silent throughout the entire procedure. They have the utmost respect for their patients, and Anna is no exception. Rebecca grabs a quilted mattress mat for underneath Anna's bottom. Donna steadies her with her two hands while Rebecca gently rolls her over and pulls the old, soiled liner out, then replaces it with the fresh one.

Donna grabs two clean hospital gowns and starts to dress her patient. Her technique is precise because she's done it a thousand times before. Rebecca assists by maneuvering Anna's body into the proper positions.

When they are done, Rebecca pulls some white socks out of the drawer next to Anna's bed. "Her mother asked me to put these on her to keep her feet warm."

Donna smiles at her as if to say she understands completely. Rebecca tucks the girl's feet into the socks. Donna grabs fresh linen from the hallway closet and swaddles Anna into crisp new sheets. Extra blankets are placed with care.

Dr. Lewis enters the room. "Hello, ladies." He notices that his patient has been cleaned and changed. "You girls sure know how to take care of people. Thank you." He flashes a smile at them both, but his smile happens to linger a little longer on Rebecca. "You sure have caught on quick around here," he compliments her.

She blushes. "Thank you, Doctor. I'm happy to have Donna working with me. She's the real pro."

Donna waves her hand at Rebecca to slough off the comment. "Ack. I could do it with my eyes closed, and with pleasure. No biggie!" She turns to look at Anna. "I just wish there was something more I could do for this young'un." Her voice is filled with sincerity and love. She exits the room, leaving Rebecca and Dr. Lewis alone.

"I've looked at her latest test results," Dr. Lewis says. "I'm afraid we're going to have to prepare the family sooner rather than later. The scans have revealed that the hemorrhage is about to completely consume both sides of her brain." He looks at Rebecca's face. Her eyes are welling up. He puts his hand on her shoulder and tries to console her. "I promise you, Rebecca, she's not feeling any pain or suffering." He then leaves the room.

Rebecca pulls up a chair beside Anna and looks again at her young, pretty face. Her eyelashes are thick and orange. Rebecca wishes she could see the color of her eyes. She puts her hand on Anna's and marvels at how rugged they are for such a small, delicate young woman.

There is something about this girl that is captivating, and in a way Rebecca envies her. *She is so beautiful. So flower-like*, Rebecca thinks. The creamy golden color of her skin, the hearty strawberry blond shade of her hair, and her sweet apple-red cheeks flood Rebecca with a strange feeling of happiness. *Storybook pretty*, she thinks, then quickly removes her hand, feeling ashamed. How can she find so much joy in this person whose life is about to end?

"What's wrong with me?" she says out loud. She immediately gets up and leaves the room. She looks at her watch; it's slightly past eleven in the morning. She feels like she's been at work all day long despite having only started a few hours ago.

Neil the orderly is coming out of room three.

"Hey!" she calls out to him.

Neil turns to her and sets aside the gurney he's moving. "Hi, Becky. How's it going?"

Rebecca is about to answer honestly but then realizes what Neil just called her. "Becky?" she repeats in disbelief.

Neil is embarrassed. "Oh, sorry," he says. "I just figured Becky would be all right."

Rebecca giggles. "Yeah, of course. It's just that I haven't heard that in a while, that's all. My brothers call me Becky or Beck, but they both live out of the country and we don't see or talk to each other as much as we'd like."

Neil pushes the gurney forward as they walk together. "Yeah, I know how that is," he replies. "I have three brothers. One younger, who is teaching English in Japan, and two older ones who live here, but they're both bankers so touching base with family isn't much of a priority for them, you know?"

Rebecca shakes her head. "Actually, no. I don't get it." She goes on to expand on her opinion. "Here's how I see it. We're here for such a short time, so we really do need to appreciate our loved ones while we can. It sounds so cliché and trivial, but I think working in this business …" She shrugs. "It becomes far too clear to me."

Neil looks at her and nods. "I know. If people only experienced what we do on a regular basis, then maybe things would be different."

She looks up at Neil, noticing for the first time that he's rather tall. She also notices his broad shoulders and bulging biceps as he pushes along the gurney. Why hasn't she noticed how good-looking he is before? Maybe because of his age? He seems to be younger, and she wonders by how much. She looks down at his left hand. No ring.

Neil catches her. "Nope, not married."

Rebecca blushes. "Oh my God, I'm sorry."

He smiles at her and stops at the elevator. "Don't be."

"Well, um, I'll see you later, then?" she blurts out.

"Yeah," says Neil. "Maybe we can go for a drink some time."

Rebecca responds quickly. "Sure!" But before the elevator doors shut, a feeling of guilt and regret seizes her, and she knows the reason has something to do with her feelings for James.

Feeling exhausted, she decides to go to the cafeteria to rejuvenate with a quick coffee and muffin. On her way down, her cellphone vibrates. She picks it up and says hello, and is immediately gratified to hear Kitty's voice on the other end.

"Kitty, thank God you're okay! How's the baby?" she asks.

"He's fine," Kitty replies.

"*He?* Really?" Rebecca squeals.

"Nah, just kidding," responds Kitty. "We still have no idea what the sex is. They offered to tell us, yet again, but I insisted on not knowing. Jake isn't too happy about that, but you know, we women have our prerogatives."

Rebecca starts to agree, but Kitty continues to speak before Rebecca can expand on her thoughts.

"So, James spent the past hour with me here at Mercy. He seemed relieved when he left the hospital knowing that his baby sister and his future niece or nephew are going to be okay," she happily proclaims.

Rebecca is happy to hear any mention of James. She is about to jump into the conversation, but Kitty keeps going.

"He told me that I was going to have a hard time staying here for God knows how long. I don't do well sitting still for too long, you know."

"Really?" Rebecca sarcastically responds.

Kitty ignores her and moves on. "So, do you think you'll get a chance to visit me?"

"Of course! I'll try to get over sometime tomorrow."

"Bring Miesha!" Kitty demands.

A few minutes later, Rebecca hangs up the phone and stares at her stale muffin and coffee. She laughs under her breath as thoughts about Kitty's boundless energy bounce around in her mind. *James is right—she's going to have a hard time lying in bed for the next two months.*

She recalls the story that James told her over dinner the night of their date. Kitty was grounded at the age of eight for telling their father Aaron to piss off. She wasn't allowed out of her room for two days except to go to school. But what was supposed to be reprehension for her behavior turned out to be a very productive and enjoyable time for Kitty. She completely redesigned her room and wrote an extensive book of poems about her life that was loaded with happy, colorful illustrations. When Aaron passed away, Kitty's poetry book was laid out as a part of his memorial display at the funeral parlor. It was one of his most cherished possessions.

James said he felt happy for Kitty about her relationship with Aaron. He summarized the story by saying that at least one of them had the benefit of having a loving father. Rebecca remembers trying to get him to expand on that point, but he quickly went on to talk about movies and how German Expressionism was one of his all-time favorite film genres. She's annoyed at herself for not having had the guts to investigate further that night, but immediately rolls her eyes for even attempting the thought. "Disaster," she says under her breath.

Two pretty teenage girls scamper by and appear to be gossiping. Rebecca recognizes them as part-time volunteers. One girl has striking red hair pulled back into a slick ponytail. She has big brown eyes and a wide smile with freckles on her nose and lips.

She studies the girls standing by the cash with chocolate milk containers and cookies in their hands. They represent life at its richest. They have infinite room to grow and can find ways to change the world if they want to. Then it dawns on her—shouldn't everyone have the opportunity in youth to possess the freedom and right to be who they *want* to be and not what they *should* be?

Seeing the girls makes Rebecca think of Anna again. She sees Anna as an incredibly spirited girl—one who found her calling and lived it to the fullest. She went out into the world to shine light on those who needed it the most, especially the children in the villages of Afghanistan. She is a beautiful flower sprouting life from within—so much so that even on her deathbed, her aura continues to exude a certain warmth and energy.

Rebecca breaks her train of thought and realizes the time. She gets up and passes the two girls sitting at a table. She smiles at them and they wave back at her. She sees everything clearly now. With thirty-three years of life behind her, she is still waiting to fully blossom as Anna has.

The long hours of the day shift have finally passed and staff is preparing to transition over to the evening shift. Rebecca has one more stop to make before she heads out to pick up her daughter. Miesha just started an afterschool program, and Rebecca is looking forward to having a little extra time to run errands prior to picking her up.

She turns down the hall and sees Gerry hobbling along with his intravenous pole. His hair is in tufts and he's wearing a battered old smoking jacket over his pajamas. "Gerry!" she calls out to him.

He turns around and she sees that he has a stack of papers in his hand. "Oh, hi, Rebecca. I'm glad I caught you. I'm hoping that you and the rest of the staff will let me put up some of these posters."

Rebecca takes one from his hand. *Saturday Night Big Band Birthday. Please join us in the hospital lounge to celebrate Captain Hans Webber's ninetieth birthday. Saturday, September 24 from 5:30 to 7:30.* Beside the text, set off by a beautiful penned frame, is a black and white photo of Hans in his twenties. His face is fresh and handsome and his military suit looks neat and pressed.

Rebecca is pleased. "Wow, Gerry, this is so great. Who came up with the idea?"

Gerry points down the hall to Martin's room. "That one over there," he says. "He's the party planner around here. You didn't know that?"

Rebecca chuckles. "Okay, well, I do now." She admires the poster again and points to the artwork around the photo. "And did Martin do this, too?"

Gerry shakes his head. "Nope. That would be on account of Jimmy over there." He is pointing over to Anna's room. "His ass-clown—er, excuse my language, Miss Rebecca—his so-called friend at work … Ty? I think that's who did it up for us. We gave Jimmy the picture, and the details, and presto! All these posters arrived the next morning. Goddamn technology, eh? Oops! Pardon me again, Miss Rebecca. I guess I'm a little bit excited over here."

Rebecca doesn't even hear what he is saying. She is still stuck on the words 'Jimmy over there.' She snaps out of it.

"Oh, um, Gerry, no worries. Listen, you can count on me to be there with Miesha. Has anyone ordered a cake?"

Gerry takes a second to recall. "I think his daughter Madge is going to make one."

"Well, it's all covered then," Rebecca says with a smile.

"You can keep one, Miss Rebecca," Gerry insists, handing her a paper invitation.

"Thanks, Gerry. Please, go ahead and ask the volunteer girls at the reception desk to help put the rest of those up. I don't want you overexerting yourself anymore today, okay?"

He wheels off down the hallway, shuffling one foot at a time. "Yes, Miss Rebecca. Have a good night."

Just then, Rebecca gets an eerie feeling in the hallway as she creeps towards Anna's room. Her heart starts to pound as she anticipates seeing James inside. When she sees him through the small window in the door, her stomach immediately turns inside out. She looks down and notices Gerry's poster shaking in her hand.

James's back is turned to her while she peers through the window. He is speaking softly to Anna with his hand placed on hers. Rebecca feels a twinge of jealousy. She looks away and places her back up against the wall and closes her eyes. A feeling of guilt overwhelms her as she realizes the inappropriateness of the feelings she's directing towards this young, dying girl. She slowly returns to peer through the small window again. She would give anything to hear what he's saying.

She sighs heavily and turns around to find Martin directly behind her. "Oh!" she gasps, covering her mouth with her hand. "God, Martin!" she says firmly, but in a whisper. "Do you always sneak up on people like that?" She brushes the hair away from her face nervously.

"Funny," he exclaims. "I was just about to ask you the same question."

Rebecca feels her face turn red. "Martin, you're right. How totally unprofessional of me."

Martin takes Rebecca's hand and leads her towards the small sitting room around the corner. Confused, but too ashamed to think, she doesn't resist. They reach the two powder blue armchairs outside the small kitchen. Martin gestures to Rebecca to sit down, and they both make themselves comfortable. Rebecca doesn't know what to say. Martin brushes the remaining crumbs from an earlier snack off his pants. He looks into Rebecca's eyes while she fidgets in her seat.

"He goes to see her sometimes in the middle of the night when he thinks nobody is around," Martin says. "He goes to see her because she, and all of us here who are dying, provides him with a certain sense of power and security."

Rebecca feels as though she may be sick to her stomach. "What are you saying?" she asks.

"I knew Aaron Milligan from my days in Vietnam. After the war we made an effort to see each other whenever the opportunity came along and we'd get together for a few drinks. He talked to me about this place a lot. He also told me a story about Jimmy that may help explain things to you. I can see that you have a vested interest in him."

Rebecca blushes. "I know about Stephen," she interjects.

"Oh, but I don't think you do, Miss Rebecca. You see, Kitty was sworn to secrecy by her parents not to exploit the situation by spreading details about the incident, and, most of all, not to talk to anyone about it—including Jimmy."

Rebecca is surprised. "What? That seems almost cruel."

Martin looks straight ahead as he continues. "Jimmy has suffered emotional and psychological trauma as a result of an extraordinarily stressful event in his life. He's lost his inner sense of security. He feels helpless and vulnerable, and he sees the world as a dangerous place. To feel less vulnerable, he surrounds himself with those far more so."

He turns towards Rebecca, but waits for two people to walk past before continuing the discussion.

"And what better way than to find intimacy with someone who is not able to respond to him on an emotional level," he says, folding his hands in his lap. "We veterans can't hurt him if we're dying. He's been working this way for close to twenty years now. He is very damaged, Miss Rebecca. You need to be very careful."

Rebecca takes a deep breath and exhales. She feels scared. She doesn't know what to say, so she responds with a question. "How do you know him so well, Martin? I mean, you may have known his father years ago, but it's my understanding that you two just met." She's almost defensive on this point.

Martin shrugs his shoulders. "Because, Rebecca, I *was* Jimmy for over twenty years of my life. But that, my good girl, is a story for another day. Right now, take my advice. Be good to yourself. Focus on your own life, including your beautiful daughter. Maybe, in time, Mr. Jimmy will heal."

Rebecca resents the tears that are about to stream down from her eyes. "Thank you, Martin. Now I really need you to get back into bed, because the night nurse will be around soon to check on you and I can smell food, which means that the dinner trays are coming."

"You mean you can smell dog shit," Martin growls.

Rebecca lets out a giggle as she wipes the corner of her eyes. She gets up and extends her hand to help the old man stand. He accepts. She says goodnight, but before turning to leave, she asks him one more question. "You said that you knew Aaron Milligan and that he told you about this place and about James and the accident. You're obviously here for decent long-term care, but did you also come here for James?"

Martin waves to her. "Good night, Miss Rebecca. You take care now."

Rebecca takes his evasion in stride and heads back down the hallway towards Anna's room. James is no longer there. She opens the door and checks Anna's tubes and support system. Her family will be in shortly, and this time they may be spending the night, since soon Anna will be taking her last breath.

She touches the young woman's face. "I just want to thank you, Anna," she says gently. "Thank you for making me see that I need to do more with my life. Thank you for your strength and courage, and most of all, thank you for spreading unconditional love to those who needed it most."

Anna's face is thinning, which Rebecca recognizes as a true sign that death is coming. With a heavy heart she leaves the room. She catches a glimpse of the clock and realizes she's almost done her shift. At that very moment her cellphone vibrates. She knows the name on the call display—Patricia Ogilvie, the mother of Miesha's best friend.

"Hi Pat, what's up?" The voice on the other end suggests that the girls work on their project together and is offering to take Miesha for dinner. "Yes, sure! Fantastic. Thank you. I'll pick her up at eight, okay?"

Relieved and ready for some quiet time, Rebecca makes her way to the front desk to check out. Julie and Mark are on the night shift and have already set out on their rounds. She leaves them a quick note before grabbing her belongings and heading downstairs to the parking lot.

The outdoor air soothes her aching muscles and she looks forward to a glass of wine and a nice hot bath. A man appears in the near distance, preoccupied by his smartphone as he walks slowly towards his car. What feels like a hard punch to her stomach makes her stop suddenly in her tracks. It's James. She wants to call out his name, but she fears he might run. She decides to walk towards him calmly instead.

His back is turned to her and he doesn't hear her approaching until it's too late.

★★★

He turns around and is startled to see Rebecca standing directly in front of him.

"Hello," she says softly.

James looks down at the ground, not wanting to make eye contact. "Hi."

"James, are you okay?"

"Yeah. Yeah, sure. You?"

"I'm good," Rebecca replies shyly. "I'm … I'm actually really tired," she adds.

"Yeah, I know what you mean."

Rebecca moves closer, making him step back slightly. "Would you like to come over to my place for a drink?" she asks. "You look like you could use one. I know I could."

He looks directly at her, overwhelmed by her loveliness and intoxicating scent. His body stiffens as he searches for the right thing to say. "I'm not sure."

"Listen, Miesha is out for a few hours so we could just hang out over a bottle of wine. If you're hungry, I could make us some pasta."

James is silent. A nearby car starts up and the sound breaks the tension.

"It's okay," says Rebecca, obviously interpreting his silence as a rejection of her offer. "Maybe some other time?"

Say something, dammit, James chastises himself. "No, it's fine. Sure. I could really use a drink."

Rebecca smiles.

James is still trying to grasp the situation. "So ... I'll just follow you there, then?"

Rebecca nods yes. "Do you remember where it is?"

"I do," he replies.

She walks towards her car, but turns back around to recite her house number out loud just in case James has forgotten. "1985 Fourteenth Street."

He hadn't forgotten but he doesn't reveal this fact. As he follows her small sedan, James can't believe what he is doing. *What will I say? What did I just agree to? Will it be easier than the last dinner?* "Of course, that particular night didn't end up badly," he reminds himself out loud. Flashes of Rebecca's naked body fill his mind, and her taste and smell have already invaded his senses. He feels his heart rate escalate to an uncomfortable level. Anxiety has plagued him for so long that he forgets what it was like before it started so many years ago.

He takes advantage of the red light and reaches over to the back seat to grab his portfolio. Inside the side pocket is a little box of pills. He fumbles with it quickly, nervous that the light might change before he can organize himself. He pops a little blue oval-shaped pill into his mouth and swallows it down. Xanax always manages to take the edge off.

The light changes just as Ty calls his cell. James turns on his hands-free device. "Ty, what can I do for you?"

Ty is his usual sarcastic, belligerent self. "Come on, man. You really think I was going to let you go through the day without calling you just to tell you how much I miss you?"

James laughs. "No, actually. What the hell took you so long?"

"Well, those nasty suits from the rapid transit project are insisting that the time-lines aren't realistic for the completion of the project. They're worried that they might need to get more funding if the work extends past our proposal."

James is trying to listen and pay attention to the traffic at the same time. He can't see Rebecca's car anymore. "It's *not* going to go on any longer than what we've proposed. We've already factored in a sizable contingency and it's been approved by City Council, so I don't see a problem."

"*I* know that and *you* know that, but somewhere along the gig *they* aren't lining up for the same parade. We have a face-to-face with them tomorrow. Please tell me that you'll be getting your not-so-fine ass into the office tomorrow?"

James is turning into Rebecca's neighborhood, looking around for the street name. "Yes, Ty, I'll be in. Did I not mention that in my last email?"

"Yeah, but I can never be one hundred percent sure where you're going to end up on a day-to-day basis, man. You're like …" he trails off, struggling to find an appropriate comparison. "You're like fucking Where's Waldo, man."

James chuckles. "Well, I did own a shirt like that once."

Ty snorts. "I have no doubt. And speaking of—can you at least *try* to dress like a businessman from *this* century tomorrow?"

James shakes his head. "Right. Okay, see ya."

Ty hangs up just as James turns into Rebecca's driveway. Her car is parked and she's already made her way inside the house. He takes a deep breath and allows the Xanax to take over. He makes his way up the stairs, but before he can ring the bell, Rebecca opens the door. She's even more beautiful than he remembers, standing in front of him in designer jeans and a fitted Bob Marley t-shirt. He's sure the wind has just been knocked out of his lungs.

"Come in," she says happily. "I thought you'd changed your mind."

James enters the house. "Sorry. I must have lost you for a minute." An overwhelming urge to sprint back to his car comes over him, but the Xanax pushes his shoulders down, making it easier to relax.

Rebecca's home is simple and sparse, but neatly decorated with good taste. Original artwork hangs on several of the walls, including in the living room and entranceway. James doesn't recognize the artist, but he is impressed with the use of color and the contemporary style. She has several pieces of IKEA furniture that match the lightness and functionality of each room. It's a comfortable space with a minimalist feel to it. He recognizes the paint color by Benjamin Moore. Midnight Safari. *Nice.*

The phone rings and Rebecca answers. "Hi, Patricia," he hears her say. There's a pause. "Of course Miesha can stay longer. No, nine's fine," she says before thanking the caller and hanging up.

She signals to James to join her in the kitchen. "Beer or wine?" she asks.

James points to her glass. "Wine would be great, thanks."

Rebecca's kitchen is very bright and modern. She has maple cabinets with black granite countertops and stainless steel appliances. The kitchen floors are a beautiful natural stone with streaks of gray and brown marble. They merge nicely with the hardwood that is covering the rest of the downstairs area. *Classy.*

She sees him checking out her place. "I really wish I had a big kitchen with a huge island in the middle," she says.

James sips his wine. "It's really quite nice here. Who's the painter?"

"Oh, that's my dad," she says with pride in her voice.

They simultaneously move into the entranceway, where a three-foot square painting of an Aboriginal woman's face covers the canvass. The dark browns, blues, and reds are absolutely stunning. James is completely drawn to the face. He studies the brush strokes and overall technique. Her eyes captivate him. "This is really good."

Rebecca beams. "My dad's always been a painter, but he never had the opportunity to paint as much as he would have liked in his earlier years." She goes into the kitchen and he hears her topping up her glass. "I must get three paintings a year from him now."

The wine is slowly hitting James. He suddenly remembers that the anti-anxiety meds increase the effects of alcohol. He walks over to the couch to examine the large painting hanging over the opposite wall. The painting is so dark it's almost black, but there are splashes of a rich, velvety red with a hint of burnt orange and cool ocean blue. The more James stares at the painting, the more the image starts to form. He steps backwards as his eyes widen, bumping the sofa table behind him. The wine spills onto the area rug. "Shit," he grumbles.

Rebecca comes out of the kitchen to see James struggling with the mess. "It's okay," she says, trying to reassure him. "It's Scotchgarded. Here, let me …" She moves in front of James. He paces behind her, trying to fight off his embarrassment. His eyes catch the painting again and the image forms clearly now, making him hold his breath.

"This old rug …" Rebecca starts, and then stops. She looks at the painting and her eyes immediately fill with understanding. "It's the old railroad that once ran between Illinois and Georgia and Nebraska," she says quietly.

She sets the damp cloth on the table and walks over to him, taking the glass of wine from his grip. He flinches as she touches him. The sadness he feels puts him at a loss for words. She pulls him in closely and wraps her arms around his neck. He fights the urge to run because she feels so good, but when he closes his eyes, he can feel panic surging through his veins, trying to overtake his mind and body.

Rebecca says nothing and instead strokes the back of his head. She draws herself closer to his face and starts to kiss his cheek. James is electrified, causing his senses to collapse into a pool of weightlessness. His eyes close as she slips inside of his soul, but still his demons try to resist her. A vision of Stephen flashes in his mind. Without thinking, he grabs Rebecca tighter and doesn't let go. The visual of the train speeding down the track crashes into his mind's eye.

"Please," James begs, whispering into her ear. He gasps for air before he buries his face in the cradle of her warm, soft neck. Tears are streaming down her cheeks and James can taste them.

He lifts her body and carries her up the stairs and into a bedroom with a double bed. He has no clue of his surroundings, but is navigating instinctively—driven by desperation and lust. He sets her gently down on the bed and presses against her. Their shirts come off simultaneously. She sits up to take charge, straddling his waist with her legs and leaning down over his body to reciprocate the heavy kissing. He rolls back on top of her and starts to claw at her bra, fumbling around and finally unhooking the center closure. He feels the release of her breasts into his large hands. James slowly goes down her torso and assists in the removal of her jeans and panties. He lingers at her hips for a moment to savor her scent.

He feels the tension and anxiety of the beast inside his body and soul losing the battle. Rebecca pulls him back on top of her, taking his face in her hands and anchoring her gaze into his eyes. It feels like he's finally seeing her for the first time. There are no surprises. Her warmth reveals a nurturing, kind, and loving person.

She kisses him again and undoes the buttons of his jeans. She gently pulls them down to just above his knees and then makes her way to his underwear, which she slides down so that she can take his large muscle into her mouth. He breaks away to position himself on top of her so that he can find his place inside her. When he does, she climaxes instantly. He can sense something light, pure, and powerful floating around the room. This feeling of tenderness is something he knows nothing about.

★★★

At that moment, Anna Louise McBain takes her last breath. With her family by her side, she leaves her body behind, never to return. Her parents hold each other closely and weep over her tiny body while her brother stands outside her room, punching the wall with his fist over and over again until the blood streaks down to his feet. Mark, the night nurse on staff, grips his shoulders generously until he eventually calms down.

Martin hears the commotion and enters the hallway to see what is happening. A few other patients pop their heads out their doors as well to catch a glimpse of the unfolding drama. When word gets around that Anna is gone, many of the veterans gather in the chapel to honor the loss of their fallen young comrade. Candles are lit as the men discreetly pass around a flask of brandy from pew to pew.

Martin raises his flask up in the air. "I'll be seeing you, McBain."

NINE

"You did not! Shut up!" Kitty yells, trying to climb out of her hospital bed. "Whoa, whoa, whoa, woman. No way! Get back in there!" instructs Rebecca.

"Seriously, you think you can fight a three-ton beluga whale like me, do you?" protests Kitty.

"I'm thinking killer whale," Rebecca says, adjusting Kitty's bed sheets.

Kitty sighs. "Fine. But I have to pee—what a surprise," she says, rolling her eyes in frustration.

Rebecca pulls down the sheets. "Okay. Let's go. But no funny business."

Kitty waddles over to the bathroom, hanging onto Rebecca for extra support. Kitty crouches down over the toilet. Rebecca releases her gently and steps outside the bathroom.

Kitty calls out to her, "So you guys actually made out twice and I'm only hearing about it for the first time?"

"Look, it's not an easy thing to talk about, because honestly, I don't think either of us knows what's going on," Rebecca replies. "At least I sure as hell don't."

The toilet flushes and Rebecca walks back into the bathroom to help her friend. Kitty is huffing as she tries to stand. Rebecca scoots over to help her up.

"Thanks, hun," Kitty says graciously before redirecting the subject back to James. "Well, I warned you that he was going to be a tough nut to crack. I mean, I grew up with the guy my whole life and even *I* haven't been able to get into his head since I was six, which was around the time that Stephen came into his life. When Stephen was killed, Jimmy totally shut down. His emotional connection with everyone shut off—just like that," she says, snapping her fingers.

Rebecca listens intently as she tucks Kitty back into bed. "So, Kitty," she begins, then pauses to get her thoughts together before going on. "Um, what exactly happened the day Stephen died? I know he was killed by a train, but that's all I know." Traces of her conversation with Martin are floating around in her head.

Kitty's broad shoulders droop downwards after taking in a deep breath. "Nobody really knows, Rebecca, except that it was an accident. They were drunk coming home from a party and heading back to Stephen's aunt and uncle's place in Edelstein. Somehow Stephen ended up on the tracks at the same time a train was coming around the bend. My dad said that the police report mentioned that Stephen had his back to the train and was listening to his walkman. He didn't even see or hear the train coming, but Jimmy saw the whole thing. He hasn't been the same ever since, and it's been almost twenty years now."

Rebecca thinks about it for a minute. She shudders at the horrible visual painted in her mind. "You would think that someone would be able to feel the vibrations on the track."

Kitty huffs. "You didn't know Stephen Pike. I'm sure the only thing he was feeling was high." She clears her throat. "No disrespect to the dead or anything."

Jacob enters the room. "Hey, how's my girl?"

Kitty squeals. "Baby! Come give me some of that fine sugar. Wait—did you bring me some Arby's?"

Jacob pulls a greasy bag out from around his back like a magician pulling a rabbit out of a hat.

"Bring it on!" Kitty exclaims with anticipation.

Jacob and Rebecca exchange salutations and Rebecca prepares to leave. "Okay, Kitty, I guess I'll head out. Sorry Miesha couldn't make it. She's been working on this school project that's had her out until past nine the last two nights. Thank God tonight's the last night for it."

Kitty starts talking with her mouth full of cheeseburger. "That's okay, hun. You give that girl a great big kiss for me, okay? I hope to see you Saturday night for Hans's party. The doctor says they'll let me out just for a few hours if I take it easy." She wipes her greasy chin with the back of her hand and Jacob digs into the bag for a napkin.

"Oh, thanks, babe," Kitty says to him while shoving fries into her mouth.

Rebecca takes this as her cue to leave and kisses Kitty on the cheek. "Okay, well then make sure you *do* take it easy so that you can at least come for cake. Bye Mama and Papa Bear," she says, leaving the room.

As she makes her way across Mercy's parking lot, she spots Janice trying to juggle a few packages in her hands. She scurries over. "Janice! Here, let me help you."

"Oh, thank you, dear," Janice says, slightly frazzled. "How are you? Are you liking the job?" she asks sincerely. Rebecca knows that the running of the Aaron Milligan Veterans' Hospital is never far from Janice's mind.

Rebecca nods, then points to the parcels she's holding. "Can I help bring these upstairs?" asks Rebecca.

"Oh no, dear, but thank you so much. I'm fine. How's Kitty today?"

"She's her usual firecracker self," replies Rebecca.

Janice smiles, seeming to know exactly what Rebecca means. She turns her head towards the hospital entrance, hesitating. "And how is Jimmy? Kitty mentioned that you've spent some time with him recently."

In that moment, Janice's face seems older to Rebecca. She hesitates before answering. "Well, to tell you the truth …" She clears her throat. "I've only seen him a few times over the last few weeks. I'm quickly discovering that he's not easy to reach."

"He's not easy to reach," Janice repeats as though she's repeating a mantra. She shakes her head in disappointment. "I'm sorry, dear," she says. "I know what it's like to try to get close to him, only to find yourself further away than you were when you started."

A tall, elegant elderly woman is briskly walking towards them. She has beautifully styled hair with streaks of gold and gray. Her eyes are a piercing green and her makeup is meticulous, as is her choice of fashion. "Sorry about that, Janice," she calls out, slightly out of breath. She is carrying a large fruit basket. "The parking here is ridiculous. I tried to get a spot closer to the door, but there's just no finding one. With all the donations this hospital receives, one would think they could expand it." She notices Rebecca as if for the first time. "Oh, I'm sorry for interrupting, love," she says politely.

"This is Rebecca Doyle," Janice says, introducing her. "Rebecca works at the hospital with Kitty. Rebecca, this is Lynn Pike, an old family friend," Janice proudly announces.

"Pleased to meet you," Rebecca says, rolling the surname Pike around in her head. *Why is that name so familiar?* she wonders. "Are you sure I can't help you both inside?"

"No, dear, that's fine," Janice insists. "You go on and enjoy the rest of your afternoon. It was good to see you. Will we be seeing each other at the birthday bash on Saturday?"

"Yes, I really hope to make it. I think Miesha will enjoy it, too." She looks at Lynn and smiles. "It was nice to meet you, Mrs. Pike." Suddenly Rebecca remembers. Not ten minutes before, Kitty had mentioned that Pike was Stephen's last name. *This must be Stephen's mother.* She can't help but feel curious about this woman, given the tragedy that struck her family many years ago. It is almost as though Rebecca can finally sneak a peek at the mystery that surrounds the ghost of Stephen.

"Likewise, my dear girl," Lynn replies.

Rebecca skips off the curb and walks towards the center of the parking lot where her car is parked. She feels both women watching her as she goes. They are still standing there in the parking lot as she drives past them on her way to pick up Miesha. She waves and they both wave back. She thinks she sees a shadow of sadness in both of their eyes as she passes.

When Rebecca finally arrives home after picking up Miesha and running some errands, she feels like the weight of the world is on her shoulders. Miesha is busy finishing up homework at the dining room table, patiently waiting for dinner while Rebecca folds and puts away this morning's loads of laundry.

As she reaches the top of the stairs with her final load, she stops for a second and looks into the spare room—the room she and James were in last night. It has an empty feeling to it, as though it belongs to no one. There's an old oak dresser in the corner with a few doilies and candles resting on top. A few paintings from her father give the room some character, and the small window allows a little light to shine through a sheer blind. A smoky gray comforter covers the old oak-framed double bed, and matching light gray and white sheets give it a fresh, clean appearance.

She stares at the pillows where she and James lay their heads together not even twenty-four hours earlier. She gravitates to the bed and sits down, oblivious to the heavy laundry basket still in her arms.

Her mind drifts off to yesterday's events, and to how sweet he was to her after they made love. He lay perfectly still with her and drifted off. He seemed to be at peace. Rebecca recalls his fingers softly moving up and down her shoulders as if to say, I'm here with you. His body was warm and damp, and she remembers his scent being sweet and salty. Butterflies take over her stomach, forcing her to shut her eyes momentarily until they pass. Her smile turns to sadness when she recalls the way panic had completely seized James before their encounter.

"What are you doing, Mom?" Miesha asks, breaking the spell.

Rebecca snaps out of it in a blink. "Oh, nothing, hun. I was just thinking that I should redecorate this room."

"I'm hungry," Miesha whines.

Rebecca sighs. "All right, sweetie. Dinner should be just about ready. Go wash up and I'll fix your plate." She looks at Miesha and notices how tall she's getting. "But come here first," she says in a funny growl.

Miesha giggles and runs over to her mother's arms. Rebecca's heart soars as her little girl puts her arms around her neck and kisses her cheek. "I love you, baby," she says softy to her daughter.

"I love you too, Mom," Miesha says in her little girl voice, and then scoots off.

Rebecca looks around the room one more time and thinks about how bad she felt having to wake James up to leave before Miesha got home. He was so gracious about it. They ended the evening with an embrace and a kiss that made Rebecca's insides feel as though she was being hit by a wrecking ball. She knew James was feeling the same sensation, too. She was certain they had become one last night.

★★★

Saturday came so quickly, James thinks. Friday was a blur, as the issues with the bus rapid transit project seem to be consuming ninety percent of his time. He spent most of Friday with Ty going over Chicago's Planning Council report and looking at maps of Central Loop and full-scale transit plans to see where they can respond to complaints about their proposed use of road space. He isn't looking forward to going on site next week to identify where changes can be made to the plans. *There are too many people involved in this project*, James thinks, *and all with opposing views.* Money, power, and stress are all driving forces.

James shakes it off. He continues to prepare for his six-mile morning run. The sun is shining into his apartment and the light bounces off the aquarium. Thatcher seems to be over whatever was bothering him, and James is pleased to see that he is going to stick around a little longer after all.

James runs down the pathway that leads to the Lake Shore. The wind is blowing in off the water and a chill runs up his sweaty back. He starts to run faster to elevate his heart rate and body temperature. Wakes are rippling in the gray-blue water and sea gulls are gliding about, searching for something to scavenge.

This morning he is struggling through the first few minutes of his run and is anxiously waiting for the moment when his runners' high will take over. Some days it never comes, but he hopes that it will today. A female reserve officer is approaching at a jog and they exchange the usual runners' nod as they pass. James immediately thinks about Anna, and his stomach knots at the thought of her passing. He found out through the usual hospital administration grapevine that she died just a few hours after his last visit with her.

He feels his blood flow increasing as his strides lengthen. Breathing steadier, his mind starts to float. A clean slate slides across his psyche. He rewinds to Thursday and to his one-way conversation with Anna.

I wish I could see your eyes. I imagine them to be beautiful. I've seen pictures of you before the accident, and I know that you could stop men in their tracks. I'm not sure, but I feel that you can hear me, Anna. My God, your hand is so tiny and warm. It's hard to imagine you being anything but sweet.

91

You're so fragile and pretty as you lie there in your bed, dreaming. I hope they are good dreams, and not bad ones about the horrors you've experienced. I know all about what you've seen, Anna. I know what it's like to have nightmares. I feel your pain, every day. It's unbearable, isn't it? You feel as though you might crumble from the inside out. I can't explain it, but I know you understand. You've watched your friends die. You've seen innocent people being blown up and murdered in ways too sad to say out loud. You went through all of that, and you were still able to see the grace and beauty in your life. How did you do it?

Every time I think about Stephen, I feel like I'm being physically tortured and psychologically raped by some disgusting demon. I want to just disappear, to become invisible. But you—you are the epitome of purity and the essence of everything that is good. I want you to know that you are not like me, not at all. You never let your family and friends down. You fought bravely for them and for freedom all around the world. When I think about all of the people you've helped, it makes me feel good. You've saved so many people, Anna. Me? I couldn't even save one. Not even my best friend, my other self. I let him die alone and afraid, all because I was a coward. I still am. And that's why I have no peace.

I hope to God there is peace for you somewhere, Anna. I'd like to say that you'll find it in heaven, but I don't really buy into that. But you have energy, and that energy has to go somewhere when you leave this earth. I hope to feel you around me sometime. If you ever do see me from wherever you are out there, just let me know you're around. Maybe then I won't feel so alone. Goodbye, beautiful Anna. Goodbye.

James is suddenly tumbling through the air. The sound of bicycle wheels screeching and skidding fill his ears.

"Jesus Christ, you fucking idiot!" a man shouts. He is lying on his twisted bike by the side of the path.

James is shaking his head, trying to make out where he is at that moment. He, too, is lying beside the path. He has blood trickling from his right knee and there is an intense pain in his elbow. He looks up at the man, who is taking off his helmet. "Fucking Christ, man!"

"Shit!" James says. "I mean, I'm so sorry! Are you okay?" He gets up, ignoring his own pain.

The man exhales firmly. "Yes, I'm okay. But what the hell? Are you on fucking drugs or something? You totally ran right into me—and I do mean directly into me!"

James extends his hand to the man, who is still lying on top of his mangled road bike. The man grabs it and James pulls him to his feet. "I'm so, so sorry. Do you need me to call an ambulance?" James asks, hoping the answer is no.

"No," he says through a clenched jaw. "I think I'm okay."

James silently thanks the gods above. He looks at the man's twisted bike. The front tire is completely bent. "Listen, I'll pay for the repairs. Do you have a phone on you?"

"Yeah, in my backpack," he responds.

"Take down my name and number, and when your bike is fixed I'll go to the shop and pay for it, okay?"

The man looks skeptical, but accepts his offer. James spouts off his coordinates—name, email, and phone number. The man slowly types the information into his smartphone and saves it. James goes to shake his hand, but the man just waves him off. He hoists his bike over his shoulder and begins to walk in the direction he came from.

James stands motionless on the path, trying to catch his breath. He looks to his right and sees an old woman sitting on a nearby bench with a little dog at her feet.

"I saw what you did," she calls over to him, petting the white-haired dog. "You did the right thing."

Totally bewildered, he watches the woman and her dog get up and walk off. With his hands on his hips and his body slightly bent over, his breathing finally returns to normal.

★★★

The veterans' lounge is situated on the third floor on the west side of the building, where the sunlight lingers through the rooms before going down for the day. That evening, the cloud cover carries in the cold wind off the lake into the heart of the city but the residents of the Aaron Milligan Veterans' Hospital don't seem to be bothered by the sound of it whipping around their windows. Tonight, Hans is the center of attention, along with little Miesha, who seems to have adoring fans all around her. Martin is busy setting up the sound system for the music and Gerry is assisting him, although it's clear to anyone watching that Martin would prefer that he didn't. Both men are getting more fragile as the days go on. The combination of disease and age isn't working in their favor.

James is lurking around the corner of the lounge, occasionally glancing through the doorway and trying to muster the nerve to enter the room. A balloon pops and the sound makes him jump. He can see that Miesha is laughing as she runs around the room with Kristen, one of Hans's great-granddaughters. She's three years older than Miesha and has three times the energy. Rebecca is trying to rein them in by having them help her set up the buffet table with the standard party plates, cups, hats, and plastic cutlery. With his eyes closed James fights the urge to disappear. He hears a tiny voice from below.

"Why are you closing your eyes in the hallway?" Miesha is standing by his feet looking up at him. She's grinning a semi-toothless grin.

James can't answer. He just stands there observing Rebecca's daughter.

"Are you sad?" she asks him, twirling the frills of her burgundy party dress.

James barely chokes out his response. "Um, no. I'm not sad. It's a party, after all," he says sarcastically.

Miesha sticks her tongue out at him and runs off. James can't help but smile. He sees both Rebecca and Ben in Miesha, although he is certain that Miesha has her mother's feisty spirit.

Kitty slowly waddles out the door and gives her brother a look of disapproval. "You haven't even come in yet. Do I have to tell Mom on you?" she asks in her tattletale voice.

James shakes his head and smiles with a heavy sigh. "No, please don't. You know she'll kick my ass."

She grabs his arm and pulls him closer. "I'm happy you're here. You know how much Hans loves you. This'll mean a lot to him."

James understands that he has to follow through with this responsibility. He can see Hans in the center of the room, enjoying the children dancing around him. He thinks about how Hans was a difficult patient to connect with at the beginning of their visits. Hans seemed to resent James's intellect at first, and was hesitant to believe that James could ever fully sympathize with his time at war. After all, as Hans pointed out more than once, he had *lived* the war and James had only read about it. After a time, however, the two men stopped focusing on their opposing views during their visits. James started to talk more about his own life experiences. Hans never spoke, but he always listened. Sometimes he would make small gestures, like a nod of his head or a twist of his hand, to let James know that he understood.

Hans soon seemed to take a certain comfort in their visits. If James visited him at night, he would drift off into a deep sleep that seemed peaceful. Similarly, James would fall asleep those nights without dreaming about his last experience with Stephen. It became a mutually soothing, if somewhat uneasy, friendship.

Within seconds of following Kitty inside the lounge, Robert wheels himself over to where James is standing.

"Bob," says James, nodding his head.

"Jimmy," grunts Bob in acknowledgement.

James knows that in about ten seconds Robert is going to start complaining about something. He starts the countdown in his head. *Ten, nine, eight, seven, six, five, four, three …*

Robert starts his rant a few seconds early. "Can you believe they aren't showin' the game in here? I mean, for Pete's sake, don't they know it's close to the goddamn play-offs? An old man like me doesn't have much to live for nowadays, except for maybe baseball and football and the occasional shit hockey game, and even at that it has to be the NHL, none of that local kid crap. I've been here for three stinkin' years now and I've never seen anythin' like this before. I'm sure as shit not gonna want somethin' like this for my ninetieth." He clears his throat and fidgets in his chair.

James doesn't have the heart to tell him that the Cubs won't be making the playoffs this year. Still, he wants to appease him. He looks down at Robert and whispers, "It's four-nil for the Cubs, top of the second."

"Quit pullin' my pin, boy!" Robert snaps, but his eyes are hopeful. "How do you know that?"

James pulls out his smartphone, which happens to be streaming the ball game. He hands it to Robert. "All you have to do is look at it. Do you have your headphones with you?"

Robert is awestruck "No, but I sure as hell can wheel myself back down to the room to get them."

James starts to back up. "Not to worry, I'll get them for you. But don't tell anyone that I'm doing this, okay? Especially not the women. You know how they are about proper etiquette."

"I wasn't born yesterday, son. But I'm pretty sure you know that," says Robert sarcastically. The tiny machine in his hands continues to mesmerize him.

James exhales and leaves the lounge. He can now breathe for a second. He heads up the stairwell and discovers that the fourth floor is like a tomb—quiet and still with an ominous presence hovering around, like ghosts lingering.

The stillness of the empty hallway makes him feel anxious about nothing. He passes the room where Anna used to be, and a deep sadness fills his chest. The vacant room has been stripped clean of her personal belongings and the naked bed seems to beckon him. Reluctantly, he enters the room and sits down on the bed, hoping to find some answers—and an excuse for not returning to the party where he's supposed to be.

The wind rustles through the trees outside just as a doctor is being paged over the intercom, and the two sounds seem to contradict each other in the moment. The paradox immediately reminds James of his relationship with his father. Although he knows that Aaron loved him by default, the two of them never really connected despite their common blood. Aaron was a distant father whose preference towards Kitty was all too obvious to everyone around them, most of all James. Janice overcompensated by smothering her son with her mother's grip—infusing her love into his nervous system to form a symbiotic bond. She too had suffered from Aaron's passive-aggressive behavior towards her, and therefore when James was born she seized the opportunity to find some new form of unconditional love and acceptance in life.

When James met Stephen, he felt instantly alleviated from the strain of having to measure up to his parents' expectations. However, over time, that strain seemed to blossom into a lifelong barrier. His father felt that the boys had an unhealthy relationship and continually tried to make James feel ashamed about it. Although his mother loved Stephen, she too had some form of resentment towards the boy for having taken away her son's attention. She never dared speak of this, but James could feel it in his heart. He was grateful for the fact that Janice, despite her envy towards his love for Stephen, honored their special connection.

As the years went by, the boys became more inseparable and therefore more complex. When they became teenagers, their interests and desires naturally started to differ. At the time of the accident, both James and Stephen had just graduated from high school and James was finally starting to get excited about his future. Stephen, on the other hand, was becoming more cynical in his philosophies and more rambunctious in his approach to living them out. James thought this divergence to be the natural progression of things given their vastly different characteristics; after all, throughout their relationship, Stephen was the reactor and James the equalizer, and it was that way right up until the moment of Stephen's death.

After the accident, James spent the following eight years burying himself in books, lectures, and museums. He travelled alone to Europe for six months after receiving a scholarship to an exchange program. He enrolled for a semester at St. Paul University in Rome to study anthropology, the origins of art, and politics. He loved being there, far removed from his past and personal hell. He dreamed of starting a new life in Italy. It was a captivating country that held a playful and mischievous place in world history—an enigma that had achieved Axis power against the Allies and yet remained non-belligerent at the beginning of World War II. James loved to dig deeper into the complexities of the men and women who had driven their communities into the realms of idealism and fear. The history of these perils allowed James to search for meaning in his own life. He needed answers—not simple ones, but complex and meaningful ones that he could fully digest. Intellectually he was thriving in Italy. On the emotional front, however, he carried around a heaviness that immobilized him and he knew it. It was a feeling he could neither get used to nor expel.

His semester at the university had just ended when he received the phone call from his mother about Aaron. She told him that he needed to return home because his father was ill and needed to be admitted to his own Veterans' Hospital for palliative care. Shortly after his father passed, James became a hospital volunteer at the request of his mother. Eventually, the veterans' palliative care wing became his sanctuary.

The silence on the floor is broken by footsteps shuffling down the hall. "Damn," he says, cursing out loud. "The headphones." Someone else must have been sent there to retrieve them for Robert.

"There is nothing new except what has been forgotten." Martin's voice is unmistakable.

James slumps down further onto Anna's bed and throws back his head. "Marie Antoinette."

"You are impressive, Mr. Jimmy," Martin replies, stepping into the room.

James straightens up and runs his hands through his thick dark hair. "So, let me guess. Kitty asked you to look for me?"

"No," Marin answers. "Bob started barking about you getting lost on your way to get his headphones. Apparently it's four-one for the Cubs at the bottom of the fourth inning. He says you've been gone for almost forty-five minutes. What are you doing here?"

James looks around. "I'm not entirely sure."

Martin waves him over. "Come on, I'd better get you back downstairs before the cavalry comes a calling."

"Yeah," sighs James. "I just gotta grab the headphones."

Martin pulls them out from his housecoat pocket. "No need."

The lounge is humming with people. Popular war-era songs are coming from the CD player, and Johnny Mercer and the Andrews sisters get everyone moving. Hans is sitting in his chair, looking overwhelmed with joy and love. His left hand shakes mildly from his Parkinson's. His daughters are fussing over him and photographs are being organized with different groups of people. Hans's younger sister, who must be nearing ninety herself, is standing nearby grinning and tapping her fingers to the music.

Janice, Lynn, and Donna are arranging the cake while chatting over the music. Miesha and Kristen are still dancing, while the other veterans are enjoying the buffet. Kitty slowly waddles over to one corner of the room where the vets are all huddled near the window ledge with their coffee cups. James sees them shush each other when they notice Kitty's approach. Kitty's face turns from curious to condemning as she nears. She puts her left hand on her hip before extending her right hand out.

"Give it here," she says sternly. The veterans look scared. "Now!" she insists.

Gerry walks over with a small bottle of Jack Daniel's and hands it over. James, watching from a distance, bursts out laughing.

Miesha runs up to Martin and grabs him to dance, and Rebecca rushes over to rescue the sore veteran from the wrath of her little one. As Miesha retreats, Martin signals to her with his hands. "Come back over here." She does. He says something into her ear before passing her a CD and pointing a long, bony finger at James, who is standing by the boom box examining the CD case entitled *Songs from WWII*.

Miesha runs up to James and hands him a CD. "That old man wants you to put this on, but I can do it if you want. My dance teacher gets me to change the CD in class all the time."

"I'd better handle this one," James says. "This CD player is pretty expensive."

"Okay," she says before prancing off.

James looks down at the CD, then glances across the room to locate Martin. He shakes his head in disbelief but does what the girl has asked him to do. In a minute, a song by Three Dog Night comes over the speakers.

The crowd instantly starts singing along. The women jump up and grab the men and start dancing. Hans is laughing in his chair. James is witnessing something he hasn't seen since he was a young child, when his parents held their famous summer parties and danced until four o'clock in the morning. His toe taps without his knowing it and his eyes scan the room, subconsciously looking to find more happiness. The next song comes on and people start to exchange partners for the slow dance. Rebecca walks over to James.

"Wanna dance?" she asks in a saucy voice.

He feels frozen and isn't able to react to her proposal. "Um … uh …" He looks across the room and sees Kitty glaring at him. He looks to the other side of the room and notices Donna giving him the death stare. Sweat is running down his back.

Without waiting for an answer, Rebecca takes James's hand and pulls him into the center of the room. Just the touch of her hand makes him anxious, and this makes his hunger for happiness vanish.

They move slowly in a circular motion with their bodies pressed together. He can feel both of their hearts beating fast. He asks himself, *How can this be?*

When the song ends they slowly part. The music is being turned down so that Gerry can say a few words.

"Everyone! Thank you so much for coming tonight. It's an honor to be standing—or barely standing—here." There are good-natured titters of laughter around the room. "I'll ask you to raise a toast to our good friend Hans Weber. Hans is not only a great American soldier, but he's the kindest, most respectful person I know." Gerry turns heartfelt eyes to Hans. "Hans, we thank you for your dedication to this country, but mostly for showing us what it means to be dedicated to love, first and foremost. So everyone, please raise a glass to a great father, husband, grandfather, uncle, friend, and comrade. Happy ninetieth, buddy!" The crowd cheers.

Hans starts to speak, but tears catch in his throat. His daughters rub his shoulders and hover over him with pride. He continues, "Thank you, thank you all. You are all so wonderful for coming tonight. For my ninetieth birthday, I ask you all for one thing—and that is to cherish the ones you love. There is so much wickedness and sadness in this world, but our need to love and be loved makes all the suffering bearable." Hans beams up at his daughters and his eyes mist over again. "I've been so blessed. I ask that you do your best to feel your own blessings deep within yourselves. That's the one thing that got me through losing my beautiful wife, Gina."

Hans starts to weep again and hastily raises his glass in thanks. His daughters smother him with kisses and his great-granddaughter Kristen hugs his legs. The crowd applauds his speech for longer than James expects. The music of Benny Goodman plays softly in the background as the party-goers wait for cake to be served. The room empties quickly after the cake is eaten, leaving the veterans tired and content. James slips away without saying goodbye to his mother, Kitty, or Rebecca.

A week later, Hans is floating in and out of consciousness in his hospital bed after suffering a stroke the day before. His daughters sit with him for twenty-four hours straight and are exhausted. James offers to relieve them so they can rest a while. He watches over Hans, as does Martin. Both men sit very still and quiet. Hans makes random speech sounds with his throat. Only one word is clear—*Gina.*

At 8:02 p.m., on September 13, Hans Webber takes his last breath.

TEN

The fall colors mark the trees and the city is suddenly awash with autumn activities. Today is the Bank of America Chicago Marathon run, and James is one of forty-five thousand runners participating in the race. Janice attends to watch James like she does every year; she is amazed at how he can be such a social phobic and yet partake in this massive social event. When she calls him at home before the run and asks him this, James tells her that she doesn't know what it means to be a runner.

"The space in your head is all the space you need," he says.

Janice has no problem challenging him on his point. "Need I remind you that there are an additional million and a half spectators who will be sharing your space today?"

James ignores her statement and tries to focus on his running strategy. He realizes he won't be breaking any world records, but that's not his goal. He simply enjoys the challenge and finds the city's flat terrain most accommodating. Best of all, it's an opportunity to hide inside himself for four straight hours without distraction while appeasing his mother and sister that he hasn't totally dropped out from society.

Janice asks him about Rebecca. "Is she coming today?"

He avoids the question. "Mom, it's six o'clock in the morning. I really need to get going if you're planning to come with me." He hasn't spoken to Rebecca since Hans's birthday party, and she finally stopped calling and leaving messages. *It's about time she gave up on me*, he muses.

Janice seems not to want to pry today, which makes it easy on him. "Okay, dear, I'm on my way. Do you need anything?"

"Just for you to be on time if you want to walk over with me, please," he says nervously. "And don't forget the street closures."

The start and finish lines are at Grant Park on Columbus Drive near Bucking-ham Fountain, which is a twenty-minute walk from James's condominium on East Huron Street. James has already made arrangements for his mother to park in his neighbor's vacant spot.

Janice finally pulls up at 6:40 a.m. James juts over to the driver's side door and opens it. "I'll park it, mom."

Janice steps out cradling a thermos of what he assumes to be tea in her thin-gloved hands. The wind is blowing hard this morning. "Sorry I'm late, dear. The streets are shut down everywhere and I had a hard time finding an alternative route …"

"It's fine, Mom. Don't worry. Just wait here." James jumps into the driver's seat and peels down into the garage. James exits the building sporting navy blue Columbia shorts and a windbreaker. He knows he can't overdress, but he needs to warm up before the run.

"Won't you be cold?" Janice asks, concerned.

"Mom, you ask me this every year. I'm thirty-five years old, not ten." He sud-denly feels bad for snapping at her. "Besides, I have an undershirt underneath my t-shirt," he reassures her.

They walk along the street together towards the starting line. Not a word is spoken until they get there. There is a sea of people, so James tries to find that 'space' inside his head. He starts jogging on the spot. Some of his fellow participants are doing the same, while others are stretching out their legs. Janice is smiling. The excitement replaces the chill in the air. James takes off his jacket and hands it to his mother. His red and white bib number is already pinned onto his gray cotton t-shirt. B5520.

He scans the massive crowd of people with all of their colorful attire. A sea of lime green, yellow, blue, red, and orange fills the starting area. James tries to remain focused and on point. The announcer comes over the loudspeakers to indicate five minutes to race time, and also that medical stations are set up along the route and that volunteers will be handing out food, water, and Gatorade along the way.

Runners are lining up. People are cheering for their friends and family. Media and cameras are everywhere. The crowd is electric with shouts of encouragement and the sound of clappers and whistles.

Janice looks nervous. She moves in closer to give him a hug and a kiss. "I guess I'll see you in a few hours then," she says, rubbing his back.

James nods. "Thanks, Mom."

He puts his head down and wades into the crowd.

★★★★

The pain in Martin's hip keeps him up almost all night. Nurse Julie consults Dr. Sarin, who suggests that they increase his morphine slightly and alternate extra-strength acetaminophen and ibuprofen every two hours. This appears to do the trick, and by seven o'clock the next morning, Martin finally falls asleep. The morphine entices his memories to unfold into a deep and fluid stream of unconsciousness.

It's 1966, and the Viet Cong are becoming increasingly aggressive in their offense and continue to threaten the U.S. air bases stationed across South Vietnam. Martin and his comrades are part of a U.S. Marine platoon sent in to the province of Quang Nam to search out and destroy a large insurgent barracks approximately four thousand yards away from their holding area. This is an important siege for the team, as the barracks is one of the key weapons' facilities for the Viet Cong in this part of the region.

In Martin's dream, nightfall is settling in. The bugs are overwhelming the troops just as much as the onslaught of fatigue and the three straight weeks of stifling heat and humidity. Martin is draped over a small stump in the heart of the hot jungle. His best friend, Lance Corporal Frank Kenney, a Canadian from Newfoundland, is across from him, tucked away behind an eight-inch patch of elephant grass. Frank is teasing Martin under his breath as they wait for the command from Staff Sergeant John Michaels to move in towards their target.

"Listen, you southern prick," whispers Frank, a cigarette dangling from his crooked mouth. His Newfoundland accent is thick and raw. "I don't wanna hear you cryin' yer rawny nish off behind me that you want yer mama. Because garteed, by, this ain't no time to shule."

Martin shrugs with a chuckle. He's already picked up the Newfie lingo.

"Shut up yer prate," he scoffs under his breath. "Stay where yer at and I'll come where yer to." They're both tucked down with their semi-automatics ready and in position to lead them into battle.

"Seriously, Frank," Martin says under his breath. "Don't do anything *stupid*. Just listen to Michaels."

"Mm hmm, get yer panties out of a twist there, Diggers," retorts Frank, tossing his cigarette into the moist forest.

Within seconds, Michaels gives the signal to move in. Martin's heart is pounding with fear and tension. He spits to the side and refocuses. Night has fallen. Approximately a dozen other team members rush over towards the barracks incognito. Everyone is equipped with night vision devices. Warrant Officer Roy Lukas is scouting out the enemy's position and communicating to his platoon brothers with tactical hand signals. Three team members quickly move to the south end of the barracks, while another six disperse to the north and west sides. Martin, Frank, and

Staff Sergeant Michaels are holding the east side main entrance.

Michaels signals a command that is relayed behind the barracks. All of the men leap forward, away from the structure, to seek temporary protection as a grenade flies towards the back end of the building. The explosion pierces the humid air. Viet Cong soldiers come running out, shouting in their native tongue and blindly spraying gunshots into the night.

Martin and Frank are covering their colleagues. They've been designated the sharp shooters of the group because of their mastery.

"Frank, oh-one hundred to the left!" Martin is yelling.

Frank instantly kills two insurgents with two quick shots.

They can hear Michaels calling over the mass of gunfire and shouts. "Pull out! Pull out!"

"Jesus H. Christ!" screams Frank. "We're gettin' hammered, Diggers!"

A voice cries out in the distance, "Medic! Medic!" There's another explosion.

Martin looks up to see Private First Class Peter Smyth being speared with a machete through his throat. Martin aims his M60 and shoots, killing the culprit. He crawls over to Peter and knows immediately from his eyes that he's dead.

"Petie," he moans. Peter was just a boy.

He quickly unwraps the dog tags from around Petie's bloodied neck and puts them in his pocket. Bullets are flying all around him. Another bullet hits Petie in the head. Blood splatters on Martin's face.

"Fuck you, motherfucker!" Martin yells, running towards the barracks, shooting madly and hitting everything in sight.

Frank is running behind him. "Got yer back Diggers, got yer back!"

Michaels is running alongside Frank. "Move everyone up north over the banks! I'll cover you!" He digs his body down over the side of a bush and anchors fire, covering his men as they seek protection on the other side.

"Yes, sir!" yells Frank.

Bullets are ricocheting off the dense jungle terrain. Suddenly, Martin is on the wet ground. There's an intense pain in his right femur. His pants feel wet and sticky.

Frank calls out to him. "Diggs! Diggers! Motherfucker, where you at?" Frank swears under his labored breath. Bullets fly past his head, forcing him to dive onto the moist ground.

Martin lies across the jungle floor in shock. He looks down at himself to see the surreal imagery of blood pumping through his fatigues like a fire hydrant gushing with water. He can feel his heart slowly beating along to the stinging pulse in his shattered leg.

Frank is screaming in the distance. "Son of a bitch! Diggers?! Diggs, man!" He finally reaches Martin's side and anxiously looks around for the medic. "Medic! Son of a bitch, Medic!"

Corpsman Shaun Grimes comes running over. His hands are covered with red blood and black dirt. They are shaking so much from adrenalin that he can't unwrap the morphine pack.

"Here," Frank says anxiously, grabbing the tube and pulling off the wrapper. He hands it back to the medic.

Grimes thanks him and then quickly shoots off instructions for Frank. "Take this." He pulls a long piece of cloth out of his side pocket. "Wrap his leg *above* the wound, got it?"

Frank is panting. "Yeah, yeah, got it, by."

In a daze, Martin smiles at the Newfie form of address. By. He can't see much of anything now.

Grimes jabs the morphine needle into Martin's hip and Martin experiences instant release. Holding Martin's head in his lap, Frank comforts his teammate. "It's okay, by, it's okay. Yer gonna be fine, just fine."

Martin reaches for Frank's hand. He can barely talk, but he manages to get his message through. "Go. Leave. Go to the banks. Michaels gave the order. Go."

Frank looks at Grimes. "They need you on the north side of the barracks. I'm gonna carry Diggers over 'ere and we're gonna run together. You got a grenade?"

Grimes nods. "Yeah, one left."

"Well, use it. As soon as we cross over to the left side of what's left of that piece of shit barracks. That's where they're gettin' us, by. There's a sniper there. Just follow me. I know where he's at. When I say so, toss it and then run yer nish off. You got that, by?"

Grimes pulls himself together. "Got it."

Martin knows he is in shock. The morphine is allowing his mind to float away from his body.

Frank gives the signal. "Let's git 'er."

Martin feels Frank's arms circle behind his back, and with a grunt he is thrown over Frank's left shoulder. The three men make their way up the path through the bush, over a few of the silent, unmoving fallen. "Nothin' can be done for them now, by," he says to Grimes.

Martin knows he is dead weight, but Frank is still making his way through the path and up around to the banks towards safety. It's a good two kilometer hike. The thorn-like bamboo branches are scratching Martin's face as he's dragged along through the thick damp bush. The blood is pooling in his face, which is rubbing against Frank's grenade belt with every step.

The shooting continues in the distance, but there are longer periods of silence between shots now.

"They're tapering off," says Grimes.

Frank snaps back. "I don't give a rat's arse! That one bastard over *dere* might very well be the last shooter alive, and we need to git 'em!"

They stop moving when they come to an opening in the bush. From around Frank's waist he can see the north corner of the barracks. It's one of the only pieces of the structure left standing.

"See that?" Frank is out of breath, trying to point his gun in the direction of the structure. He shifts the weight of his friend with a grunt. "The fucker is in dere. I'm sure as hell tellin' ya, by," he growls in disgust. "I'm gonna spot you right 'ere. Cut through the point dere and cover yer nish behind that bush over to the right. I'm gonna take a shot to bring the sucker out, and when he comes, you toss that thing right into the crook of the building, okay?"

Grimes takes a breath. "Got it."

"As soon as you do that, run like hell over the banks and I'll be behind you. Now go on, by—I'll wave you the signal."

Grimes nods his head and moves slowly down through the path to the point. Frank lets out a breath as he squats down to his knees. Martin is wrapped around Frank's left side. Frank balances him so that both of his hands are free. Everything swims in front of Martin's eyes as Frank puts out a shot into the night. The Viet Cong solider comes out in full view. Martin's eyes suddenly focus. The soldier is clearly panicked and sprays gunfire randomly in their general vicinity.

"Come to papa," Frank pleads under his breath. He immediately gives Grimes the signal. Grimes looks up and unhooks the grenade, tossing it with precision directly into the north corner of the broken building. It erupts with a loud bang. An insurgent pops up with half of his arm blown off. Martin feels himself being picked up again and jolted down the path. Frank pauses to take another deadly shot. Another loud pop erupts in the near distance. "By Jesus, by," he says, and Martin knows that the Viet Cong soldier is dead. "We're almost there, buddy." He sounds winded and relieved.

Suddenly Martin hears a shot and feels Frank's knees buckle. They both crumble slowly to the ground, and Martin rolls off Frank's shoulders into the mud.

"Frank?" Martin wheezes, sensing immediately that something is wrong. He can see Grimes, a shadowed figure in the distance, firing at the enemy. "Frank?"

Frank's body suddenly rolls next to Martin's. His breathing is shallow and sporadic. Martin clutches for his hand and pulls himself on top of his dying friend. He can see Frank's eyes starting to glaze over and he can barely hear him muttering.

"Let me see yer face," says Frank, breathless. Blood starts to rush out from behind his back.

Martin feels the sensation of his own body floating away from the shock and morphine and wonders if Frank is feeling the same thing. "Don't be afraid Frank," Martin whispers. "I see you by, I see you, he cries softly." Within seconds, Frank's eyes release all signs of life. Martin lays his head down into the crook of his arm and starts moaning and clawing at his dead friend. Grimes and two other comrades are running towards them. He hears a voice. "Diggs! Diggs! Diggs …"

"Mr. Diggs?" Lynn Pike is gently caressing his arm. Martin opens his eyes slowly. He's lightheaded and confused by the random thoughts that keep swimming in and out of the past and present.

"Mr. Diggs, are you all right?" Lynn asks. "I'm sorry to wake you, but you appeared to be having a bad dream and I felt so helpless watching you go through it."

He remembers Lynn from Hans's party. "Missus Pike," he manages.

She smiles. "I was actually coming in to see how you're doing. I'm volunteering today, as Jimmy is running the marathon this morning."

She grabs the jug of water and pours some into a plastic cup. She starts to peel open a straw when Martin interrupts her, barely whispering. "No thanks. No straw."

She moves closer to the bed and helps Martin sit up, adjusting his pillows behind him and pulling up his covers. She hands Martin the water and he takes it graciously. The water flows over his lips and feels good going down his tight dry throat. Lynn notices that Martin's hand is shaking.

"Mr. Diggs," she starts, but Martin cuts in.

"Please call me Martin, or Marty," he says with a grin.

She smiles back at him. "Are you hungry, Martin? I can get you some food from the cafeteria. The lunch trays were delivered about half an hour ago while you were sleeping."

He shakes his head no. His eyes feel heavy.

"I understand from the nurse that you didn't sleep well last night," Lynn says. "How is your pain now?"

Martin looks at Lynn and sees her kind soul shining through her mesmerizing green eyes. She is caring and gentle. A warm feeling washes over him. It is the same sensation he got when his mother fussed over him. "It seems to be under control, as far as I can tell," he says in reference to his pain. "It was quite bad last night. I'm finding that nighttime is getting worse for me. Maybe lying down for seven straight hours isn't the best thing for a bad hip. Nonetheless, I'm doing fine, my good lady. Thank you."

"That's why I'm here," she says in return. "I'll go see if I can get the nurse over to check on you."

She is about to leave the room when Martin calls her back. "Lynn?"

She stops inside the doorway.

"Where's Robert?" he asks, worried he might not like the answer.

She comes back over to his bedside and passes him more water. "My under-standing is that Robert had surgery early this morning. He's recovering well, but he won't be back for a few days. They're keeping him in intensive care for observation over at Mercy."

"Mercy?" Martin is perplexed.

"Yes. We don't have the capacity for this type of extensive surgery on the brain, so he was transferred to Mercy last night after dinner," she explains. "You don't remember?"

Martin is afraid for a minute, but then reasons that he must have had a lot of morphine over the last twenty-four hours, not to mention his ongoing consumption of Jack Daniel's. "Oh yes, of course. Good Lord, what's happening to my memory?" he replies with a chuckle. "Would you mind keeping me posted on his recovery? I miss the grumpy old man."

Lynn smiles sweetly at him. "Of course."

As she steps out of the room, Martin takes a deep breath and looks outside the window. The sky is gray, casting dark, bland shadows over the building. He turns on the radio beside his bed. Simon and Garfunkel's classic "Old Friends/Bookends" is playing.

Martin closes his eyes and sees his friend Frank's face in front of him. He can picture his chiseled features—strong and angular. His dark, feathered hair is tousled with grease, dirt, and sweat. He is laughing so hard at something Martin has said that his eyes are welling up with tears. He takes a haul off his cigarette and then his smile turns somber. He wants to tell Martin not to be afraid or sad for him or for anything in life. Frank can't speak, but his expressions relay the message. He reaches over and offers Martin a drag of his cigarette.

Martin is haunted by these images juxtaposed against the sound of the beauti-ful music. His heart aches and the pain in his hip sears through his weathered skin.

"Soon," he says softly to the empty room. "Soon."

★★★

James expects to run the entire twenty-six miles of the marathon in his usual time of just over three hours. It is a grueling run—not because of his physical condition, which is outstanding as usual, but because of his mental state. Every now and then he can feel his arrogant father's presence in his chest, compelling him to go forward and to stop complaining. Sometimes he just focuses on his breathing, and other times he allows the scenery to distract him from his body's resistance to comply. The faces of strangers keep him preoccupied as he trudges his way through twenty-nine neighborhoods and countless historical landmarks around Chicago, and with every step, people cheer along the way. Volunteers hand him water and Gatorade while he pushes himself through the various stations along the route.

As he runs, his mind drifts in and out of events over the past few weeks; first Kitty, then Anna, and of course, the situation with Rebecca. It has been nearly two weeks since he last spoke with her. She tried to reach him a few times, but James could not allow himself to meet her halfway. She is knocking everything off-kilter, and it is shaking up his anxiety levels. What he desperately needs first and foremost is to preserve himself.

He is halfway through his run when he reaches deep for another mental diversion and starts to plan solutions for the rapid transit project. He is supposed to meet Ty for dinner later tonight to finalize the proposal. He thinks long and hard about the different angles and approaches to solving the problems. *How can we strengthen the north-south connections to the CTA and Metra's rail network? What's the best design to boost the job connectivity for the region's communities?* These thoughts keep him company as he runs the mid-section of the race.

The last hour of the race is particularly tough. He doesn't think he can go on. He forces himself to focus on anything but his sheer pain and exhaustion. Somehow he manages to finish.

Janice is there to grab him at the finish line. She wraps him in a warm blanket to keep his body heat from escaping too quickly. All he wants to do is lie down and collapse. This is his fifth marathon, and he wonders how many more he has left in him. Janice hails a taxi and she and James go back to his condominium. He insists that she doesn't need to come up, and he crawls into bed and falls into a deep sleep as she retrieves her car from the underground parking and heads home.

The phone rings and James stirs. When he tries to turn over, his body will not cooperate. He knows that his leg cramps are a sign of dehydration, so he forces himself out of bed and stumbles to the bathroom to get some water and use the toilet. Although he has no idea what time it is, he assumes by the dark color of the late afternoon sky that it must be close to five o'clock.

He jumps into the shower and embraces the hot water washing over his body. The phone is ringing again in the background. "Jesus!" he says out loud. He closes his eyes again and feels the warmth of the shower encase his whole being. He sees Rebecca's body in his mind's eye. Heat starts to pool around his groin. He opens his eyes and tries to distract himself, but the hardness won't escape him.

The phone rings again just as James is getting out of the shower. He's worn out from the day's run, and even more so now after achieving his self-induced elation. He searches for his cellphone in his bedroom and curses when he can't find it. He walks into the living room and finds it on the coffee table. He has four messages. The first message is from Rebecca's call last week. For some reason, he cannot bring himself to erase it even though he has no intention of responding. It isn't a happy message by any stretch.

James, it's Rebecca. Of course you know that. Um, okay, well … here goes. I can't seem to get you to talk to me. This is my second and final message. I have no idea what I did or said to make you act this way.

You're … well, you are the most curious, frustrating, suppressed person I have ever met. You're also the most interesting, charismatic, and … well, broken *person I've ever met. All I ever wanted to do is get to know you and learn more about you. I mean, is it so wrong of me to care? I care about the person you are deep down inside, James. I do. I really care, more than I want to, and I don't know why, because you're not exactly Mr. Right. You slept with me twice, and during those two times I know we connected. It wasn't just about sex. That's not who either of us is.*

Or maybe I'm just completely delusional and it was *all about sex for you. After all, you're a grown man and you're not attached to anyone and you've never been married, so come to think of it … maybe you* are *like that, and if so, well, you're … you're a child.*

Anyway, I just wanted to say that I'm not going to try to figure any of this out any more. I've got my life and my daughter to look forward to. I really hope you can find your way back to the person everyone says you once were. I see glimpses of that person sometimes, James. And maybe you can't do it for me, but for God's sake, you should at least try *to make an effort for your sister and mother, who've done nothing but* love *you despite your selfish indifference. Take care of them, James. I'd say take care of yourself, but you seem to be doing a pretty good job of that already. Goodbye, Jimmy.*

Listening to the message terrifies James this time, so he erases it. He realizes just afterwards that she called him Jimmy for the first time, and the way she said it was as though she had known him his whole life.

The next message is his mother checking in with him after the marathon. The third one is Kitty. She's been trying to get a hold of him and wants him to come see her tonight before dinner. The fourth one is Ty, giving him hell for not having his cellphone turned on and confirming dinner plans for that evening.

James looks over at Thatcher, who seems to be looking back at him disapprovingly. "Don't look at me like that," he says sternly to the fish. Thatcher swims to the opposite side of the tank. James is reminded that he forgot, yet again, to feed him today. "I know, I know," he sighs, acknowledging his own dysfunction.

"Calm yourself, Ty," James says into his cellphone. He is trying to talk his colleague off a ledge as he is spewing on about the issues pertaining to the design of the bus rapid transit line. "Look, would you just give me two goddamn minutes to find a parking spot so I can get to the restaurant?" James is on his Bluetooth, looking for a parking spot close to the pub. He tells himself he should have walked from his place, but he couldn't bear the thought of another twenty-five minutes of physical movement after the run today.

There's a spot on the opposite side of the street just half a block from the pub so he quickly claims it. Getting out of his car, he sees Rebecca and a young man walking down the other side of the street. He studies the man's familiar face. Rebecca starts to laugh, and the man puts his arm around her and kisses her near the ear as they walk along, obviously enjoying themselves.

James feels his stomach twist. His heart starts to beat hard and he has difficulty swallowing. The happy couple is about to turn and face the west side of the street, where James is standing. He quickly dodges across the street in time for them to miss him. He crouches behind a parked car and gets a clear view of the young man, whom he recognizes from the hospital. "Neil," he mumbles, gritting his teeth.

James always thought of Neil as an insipid kind of guy. He likes really bad nineties music and says 'excellent' and 'dude' so much that James is convinced he is the manifestation of a character from *Bill and Ted's Excellent Adventure*. "Ted Logan doesn't have anything on this guy," he once said to Kitty.

Rebecca is holding Neil's hand as they walk across the street. James stands up and jumps onto the curb, looking back at the happy couple before passing the window of the pub, where he sees Ty scowling inside.

When he approaches the table, Ty gets up and pops him on the shoulder with his fist. "Come on, man, did you or did you *not* say seven o'clock?"

James sits down and signals to the waitress. "Two beers and two shots of tequila." The waitress acknowledges the order with a smile.

"Shit. This ain't gonna be no business meetin', is it, partner?" asks Ty as he registers the look on James's face.

"Yes and no, Ty. We *are* going to nail this sucker down tonight, and then we're gonna get drunk."

ELEVEN

The following morning is bittersweet for James. Alcohol vapors are oozing from his pores, and as a result, he can't escape the looks of disappointment from his clients, whom he is meeting with in the enclosed boardroom. However, the disappointment appears to dissipate as the presentation goes on. His charm and intellect are excellent distractions, and the group appears smitten by his talent and capability to resolve the issues brought forth by the rapid transit project without compromising the design component.

Ty is sitting at the front end of the boardroom table, assisting with the computer-generated images being projected on the screen. It looks like death has come for Ty that morning. Still, James knows that once the project's proposed new plans are approved, Ty will finally be able to relax.

After a few questions, the group accepts the new proposal as final. Everything is on track and James finally gets around to commencing his second task of the day—visiting Kitty. It's been a few days since she's called, and he's fully aware of the fury that she's about to unleash. He heads to his office before leaving to ask Jade to process the revised contract and to inquire about his schedule for the rest of the day.

"By the way, do you have anything for a raging headache?" he asks, wincing. The combination of alcohol and marathon run is really doing a number on him. Jade pulls open a drawer and tosses a small bottle of pills over to him, then walks over with a bottle of water. James shakes out two pills and pops them into his mouth. He chases them with a sip of water. "Thanks," he says.

"What the hell did you two do last night, anyway?" she asks. "Ty looks like shit and you look like ... well, prettier shit."

He chooses to ignore Jade's inquiry. "Later," is all he says with a wave of his hand. He leaves the office for the day still feeling like hell.

The ride to Mercy Hospital sparks the anxiety that's been lurking inside of James for most of the day. He knows how Kitty is going to react to his absence, and somehow he has to find a way to get over it before he sees her. He reaches for his portfolio and blindly searches for his stash of Xanax. "Just get through it," he says out loud to himself.

Thankfully, Lake Shore Drive is reasonably quiet, leaving James the headspace to think about the morning's events and what might have happened had his client not supported the proposed changes to the project. He is thankful that Ty is on board with his plan. Despite their night of gluttony, they pulled off the impossible in the aftermath that followed.

His thoughts immediately drift away to his plans to travel to Southeast Asia. A nervous excitement floods his entire torso. Going away would bring him clarity and peace, and the antagonizing feeling of being needed or wanted would not follow him there. A part of him anticipates being expelled from the emotional demands of his loved ones, while another part hides behind his persistent shame.

He takes a ticket from the parking dispenser and heads over to a spot midway across the lot, not far from the front entrance. *Brace yourself,* he thinks.

Mercy is an active place. There are people chatting and moving about everywhere and the scent of leftover soup in the stale air makes James want to gag. The elevator doesn't smell much better. The only other passenger is an old man in a wheelchair who reeks of musk and feces. James rushes off the elevator, holding his breath, and makes his way down the maze of corridors, trying to remember the number of his sister's room. He peeks his head into the room he believes to be hers.

Kitty is sitting upright in her bed, watching television. She notices her brother and squeals. "Oh my *God!*" she cries, extending her arms outward. The weight of an elephant is clamping around his chest as they embrace. She hugs him so hard that he feels like his neck might break, and he can't help but wonder if that's her intent. He marvels at the size of her.

"You look like the Michelin Man," he says, laughing.

Kitty punches him. "Shut up." But she can't help but laugh herself. "Where have you been? I've been calling you over and over for the last three days!"

"Kitty, I just ran a marathon, and things are heating up big time at work," he explains. "I don't seem to have any time to do *anything.*"

"Even call Rebecca back?" Kitty zings.

He feels a surge of fear stirring. He does *not* want to talk about this. "Please, I didn't come here to talk about Rebecca," he says calmly. "I came to see *you* and to check in on the baby."

Kitty backs off slightly. "James, you're my big brother and I love you. But I *worry* about you. You really need to see what's right in front of you. You can't keep living like a caveman."

"Is that how you see me?" James fires back. "So I'm a caveman now?"

"No, no, it's not like that. It's just … I want you to find love and happiness."

"What if I don't want love and happiness the way you think of it, Kitty? Have you ever considered what *I* want?"

Kitty is startled. "Well, good. At least you're expressing some emotion."

James is angry now. He's feeling weak from the combination of yesterday's exhaustion, last night's self-debauchery, and the pressure of the current confrontation. "Kitty, please. Can we just talk about you and the baby?"

"Of course we can, but can't I express my love and concern for you without having you push me away?"

James feels his head pound and his stomach turn. Instinctively he turns towards the door. He is so intent on getting out of the hospital quickly that he doesn't hear the sound of his keys hitting the linoleum floor behind him. Kitty's voice is trailing in the distance, calling his name.

He makes it into the elevator before the door closes. Sweat trickles down his forehead and his chest is so tight that he can't catch a breath. When the elevator doors open on the main level, people start to get on before James can make his way off. He fights his way through the throng and runs to the main entrance, where he tries to make sense of the revolving doors but can't.

A deep pain stabs his heart and he's terrified he'll collapse in public. The florescent lights are creating a warped perception of the walls and floors; they appear uneven and crooked. He places his hands on the handicapped door to the right. It swings open. It takes everything in him to move his legs forward. When he manages to exit the building, the air outside rushes into his lungs and bowls him over onto his knees.

He gets up and makes his way across the parking lot, confused and disoriented as he looks for his car. When he turns around to get his bearings, he sees Rebecca walking towards him. His gut churns. He is almost convinced he's hallucinating. *Why do I keep running into her?* he wants to shout at the sky. Chicago suddenly feels like a very tiny city and he can't wait to get out of it.

Rebecca's carrying gifts for Kitty—magazines and flowers. He tries to walk around her, but she immediately blocks him with her small frame.

"Seriously?" she asks, incensed. "You're going to try to avoid me in person, too, even though we're right in front of each other?"

He's trying not to hyperventilate in front of her. "I … I can't do this right now,

Rebecca," he tries to explain, panting. As he starts to run towards his car, he can hear his name being called from a distance. He reluctantly turns his head to see Kitty heavily striding across the parking lot. Her face is puffy and red, and her eyes are wild with tears spilling out of them. Panic seizes him.

"Kitty? What on God's green earth are you doing out here?" Rebecca calls, running over to her friend.

"What am I doing? I'm trying to give my stone-cold brother his fucking keys, that's what I'm doing!" she screams. Her nightgown is blowing upward, exposing her bare swollen legs and flimsy white socks.

Rebecca places her bags down and gently grabs a hold of Kitty's shoulders and tries to calm her. "Kitty, please, you can't do this to yourself and the baby. Please, *please* take some deep breaths. Your blood pressure, Kitty … you need to think of your blood pressure, so *please* calm down."

It's no good – Kitty unleashes her wrath. She doesn't pause once between words and sentences. "You have never, *ever* loved me like I love you! And now look at you! You are *broken*, brother. Do you see yourself? Do you? You're lost. You've been lost to us ever since Stephen Pike moved in over twenty years ago. And you decided to go further into your childish emotional cubby hole when he died. Look at you! You toss away any chance you have for love in your life. Me, Mom, and now Rebecca!"

Rebecca cuts in, "Kitty, please stop."

James stands bewildered, trying to put together the collage of accusations. A man and woman walk slowly by, curious about the drama unfolding before them.

"What are you looking at?" Kitty yells at them, exasperated. Her hands are like balloons and her cheeks are like giant purple beets. Her pupils have completely dilated.

Rebecca reaches for her cellphone. "I'm going to call Jacob," she says quietly to James.

Kitty knocks the phone out of her hands and moves in closer to James. She punches his chest and starts to sob. "Get out of my life!" She's beating on him now. James is trying to grab her arms and console her, but she's like a machine. "Get out of my life! Get out—"

She stops suddenly. James sees a red spot appear on her nightgown by her pelvic region. The tiny dot starts to expand rapidly into a larger, more saturated blot. Blood starts to flow down her legs and onto the gray pavement. Kitty collapses in his arms. Her eyes are rolled back into her head and a white froth starts to foam at the corners of her mouth.

Rebecca has retrieved her phone and starts yelling to a 9-1-1 operator. She turns her attention to James, who has completely shut down. "James! Snap out of it and help your sister! Try to elevate her legs! Do you hear me? James!"

He feels a million miles away. He surrenders to his shock and tells himself that he is no longer anything to anyone.

★★★

Rebecca is terrified. Her voice is trembling as she tries to describe the situation to the emergency center. "We're in the parking lot at Mercy. We're already right here." Her voice is breaking into fragments. She finds her breath and lets out a howl. "Can't somebody there see us? Jesus!"

Kitty starts convulsing in James's arms. He finally seems to snap out of whatever spell overtook him. He gently lowers her to the ground and places her head on his lap. He watches a reddish-yellow liquid flow from between her swollen legs onto the pavement.

A man comes running over. "What's going on? Did someone go for a doctor from the hospital?"

Before she has a chance to answer, she spots the ambulance rushing out of the ambulance bay. Rebecca runs into the middle of the parking lot and frantically flags them down. The sound of the siren makes the cars in the lot seize. The paramedics pull up, jump out of their vehicle, and run towards them. "Sir, please step away," one of the paramedics orders James. "We need to assess her and get her into the hospital ASAP." James continues to cradle his sister. "Sir!" she insists. "We *have* to take her now!"

Rebecca and the bystander try to pull James away, but his arms are locked around his baby sister. His eyes are vacant. The second paramedic is a large man who is able to pry him away from Kitty. At first James resists, but then vomit starts to expel from his mouth, forcing him to release her and roll onto his knees.

Two more paramedics come rushing over and are instructed by the female in charge to assess James. "He's in shock," she says to her two colleagues.

Rebecca is out of her mind with angst towards James. She can't help yelling at him over the sounds of his own retching. "This is all your fault! Are you happy now?"

A police car arrives carrying two young officers. One of them rushes over to Rebecca, trying to assure her that Kitty is in good hands and offering to drive her home. The other asks the male bystander questions.

Rebecca begins to sob. "She has to be okay," she weeps.

Kitty is being lifted onto a stretcher and into the ambulance. A paramedic calls the hospital with her vitals. They take off across the parking lot to the emergency entrance. Another paramedic helps James to his feet as he watches his sister being whisked away. Rebecca feels her rage evaporate as she watches James being enveloped in grief.

The Aaron Milligan Veterans' Hospital is busy with people who are mingling about during visiting hours. Patients are busy spending time with their families, while the staff carries on with the usual morning routine. Lynn Pike is now volunteering on a regular basis on behalf of Janice, who is occupied by the situation with Kitty and her unborn child. Lynn has always been eager to take her place beside Janice in caring for the veterans, and now that her friend needs her, she is motivated to make the time. Another one of the volunteers has agreed to temporarily replace Janice on the board doing administrative sorts of things, and Lynn is happy to fill the vacant visitor role.

Lynn looks out the window of the tiny fourth-floor coffee room, her thoughts whirling as she arranges snacks on a plate for the veterans. Her eyes are drawn to the parking lot. Kitty collapsed from eclampsia, and although stabilized, she is still in a coma as a result of her condition. The baby survived the ordeal, though only barely. After she first collapsed, the fetus's vitals were terrible, so they rushed Kitty in an emergency C-section. The baby wasn't breathing, but the doctors and nurses at Mercy managed to get the blood and fluid out of his lungs. Within a few minutes, the oxygen was flowing and the preemie was finally able to take his first breath. Aaron Junior Milligan Khalid was born on October 13, at only thirty-two weeks, weighing five pounds and seven ounces. Jacob calls him A.J.

Lynn can't help but think about what Janice must be experiencing. It was seventeen years ago that she lost her son Stephen, and the upheaval that comes with such devastation can never be truly understood by anyone except those who have had the misfortune of experiencing the loss of a child themselves.

Lynn prays for Kitty's recovery and gives thanks for the blessing of Janice's new grandson. As the grace of God would have it, A.J. is an excellent baby who rarely fusses and has been sleeping through the night. He is a wonderful distraction for Janice, who is exhausted from the stress of her daughter's condition and her son's mysterious disappearance.

As Lynn makes her way down the hall with a tray of cookies and fudge, she sees Gerry coming out of his room in sweat pants and a faded Chicago Blackhawks t-shirt. Something about his attire looks unusual this morning. "Gerry?" she asks, happily raising an eyebrow at his new look.

"Bona fide, ma'am," he replies, taking a bow.

She laughs. "Gerry, I'm really impressed. Where is your pole?"

"That ol' thing?" he says with a shrug. "Ack. I left it in my room, where it's going to stay from now on."

"What's gotten into you? You're like a new man," Lynn asks curiously, checking him out. "Spin around, why don't you?"

Gerry proudly spins around with his arms open. "Ta-da!"

They both laugh out loud. A young man in a wheelchair comes whirling out of the Gerry's room. "Maxwell Emmerson, at your service," he says with confidence, wheeling his way over to Lynn. He's a handsome Native American young man in his early thirties, and is extremely muscular from the waist up.

He extends his hand towards her and she graciously accepts. "Mr. Emmerson, it's a pleasure to make your acquaintance," she says sincerely.

"The pleasure is all mine," he replies after kissing her hand.

"Let me guess. Massachusetts?" she asks, taking a gamble based on his accent.

"Yes ma'am. Boston, and darn proud of it."

"I am too," she replies. "My father was from Boston, and I spent the first twelve years of my life there before moving to Chicago," she explains. "I go back every summer. We have a family cottage in Scituate, just south of the big city."

"I know it well. It's a beautiful little historical town."

Lynn agrees and looks over at Gerry, who is flexing his muscles. "So what did you do to our friend Gerry?" she asks.

"I've been taking him to rehab with me," Max replies, grinning. "Next thing I knew, he's in the gym more than me!"

Gerry grins. "Our boy Max lost his legs in Afghanistan, and he doesn't let it get *him* down. Least I can do is get my own measly stems in order." Gerry swings an imaginary bat. "I'm back in the game even though the Cubs didn't get into the playoffs. Which reminds me ... somebody really should tell Bob that."

Lynn sighs. "Yes, I know. There are many unhappy Cubs fans around here. But you two should grab some treats here. I need to get these off my tray!"

Max and Gerry both oblige, pondering over the baked goods on the tray.

"Go on, take two!" she exclaims.

The men grab two treats each, thank her, and head down the hall together. Gerry is saying that he'll have to extend today's workout after the fudge. She smiles as she watches them walk away, feeling good that they are happy and healthy today.

She can hear voices coming from Martin and Robert's room. When she passes through the doorway she sees Martin tinkering with Robert's television set. Robert is grumbling at him in short bursts of syllables. Robert appears frail today—thinner than the last time she saw him. His head is bandaged up and the dark circles under his eyes make his face appear gaunt.

Martin is persistent. "Listen, ol' man. I told you to give me a few minutes so I can see what the problem is!" He studies a small plug on the television set and listens intently through the headphones. After jiggling the cord around a few times, he takes off the headphones. "They're fried," he announces.

Robert frowns in disbelief. He tries to take back his headphones, but is struggling to get his arm up to do it. His words are not coming out right.

"Calm down," snorts Martin. "I have an extra set you can have."

Lynn decides this is her cue to pipe up. "Hello, gentlemen. How are we today?"

Both men turn towards her, standing in their doorway. Two sets of eyes light up as they land on her tray.

Martin is the first to acknowledge her presence. "Why hello, Mrs. Pike. You're looking as lovely as usual today."

She smiles. "Something sweet?" she offers, holding up her tray.

"Don't mind if we do," Martin says, eyeing the goodies. He snatches the last two cookies and hands one to Robert. Robert holds his up as if to say cheers.

"I see you're having an issue with the television," Lynn remarks. "I know Janice mentioned the idea of replacing some of these old sets at the last board meeting. I'll remind myself to see where they're at with that. In the meantime, I can get you another set of headphones, Robert." She moves in closer to his bedside and checks his water supply. "And I'm going to fill this up for you, too," she says, taking the small blue jug into her delicate hands. "I'll be back in a jiffy."

Both men smile at her, looks of intense appreciation on their faces. She feels overwhelmed by the response she's been getting from the men since she began volunteering. *I should have started doing this a long time ago*, she thinks as she leaves the room with a cheerful wave. *Oh well, better late than never.*

★★★

The men watch Lynn's perfectly round behind leave the room. Robert's leg starts shaking as he muffles out a comment.

"Pig," Martin huffs back. Both men start to laugh, but Robert's chuckle soon turns into a wheeze. Martin walks over to Robert's bedside, concerned about his friend's current state.

"Here," he says softly. "You can have mine. I have a few spares." He gently places a set of headphones over his friend's bandaged head and plugs them into the television set. Robert gives the thumbs-up as sound streams into his ears. He shoves Martin out of the way and mumbles that he's blocking his view. The local sports station is on and Robert is now completely focused.

Martin pats him on the shoulder and shuffles back to his bed. Looking out the window, he notices how the sky is filling up with rain clouds. He hates days like this. The cold dampness is a catalyst for the nagging pain in his bones. He sits on his bed and gingerly raises his legs, then slips them underneath the crisp sheets. He wonders if Robert isn't in a better situation despite his brain cancer. *At least his pain isn't incessant*, Martin thinks to himself. He grits his teeth and reaches for his CD player, then presses play.

Martin closes his eyes and feels sleep trying to take over. He thinks back to a time in the Vietnam jungle with Frank and his other comrades. In his mind he sees Frank smiling his goofy smile. According to him, all the girls back home in Bay Bulls, Newfoundland, were suckers for it. Martin remembers when Frank was telling the boys about his first attempt to get into a girl's pants when he was just fifteen years old. Martin smiles at the memory as he drifts into a semi-sleep state.

"You should've seen er be, bys. I'm tellin' ya, er hair was all mops 'n brooms and er makeup was all done up like a raccoon. Da Lard tunder'n Jesus! She had a face only a mudder could love, 'n er arse, whoa! You'd tink she was up in the wind."

The men around Frank all laugh at his description and inch closer.

"I didn't get me nar fish, though, as er dad came in and grabbed me by the arse and kicked it out the door o' the barn. Said he didn't wanna see me again, otherwise he'd smack the gob off a dat."

The men laugh so hard they literally cry. Martin is among them and wipes his tear-streaked face.

Frank just smiles and breaks out into song. "We gotta get out of this place before the jigs up and we're sure to face the devil ..." It is his mantra—his armor. Music is everything to Frank, and he has passed this gift along to Martin.

When Martin wakes up, Lynn is knitting in the chair across from his bed. The bright red and blue yarn brightens up the room. He notices that she's studying a picture of a Cubs player.

"He doesn't have the greatest batting average this year, you know," he tells her.

Lynn's eyes are fixed on the picture as she speaks. "Yes, I know, dear. But I like this particular picture because the logo is very clear." She gives him a quick glance and then continues to work on her knots. "How did you sleep, Martin? You were out for about an hour." She looks up at him and places her yarn and needles on the window ledge. She stands up and makes her way towards the water jug. "You don't look so well, Martin. Are you feeling okay?"

He grunts in response. His joints are aching.

"Here, drink some. You're probably dehydrated. It's so dry in this hospital. It's a shame it's so cold out, otherwise we could open some windows."

Martin gladly accepts the water. It seems to be the only thing that goes down well for him these days. Even his trusted Jack Daniel's is rebelling.

"How is Kitty doing?" Martin asks, changing the subject from his health and the weather. "I haven't heard anything since the incident."

Lynn fills his glass back up with the water. "She's slowly coming around. She opened her eyes today, and the doctors are very happy about that. She's still not completely lucid, but there's hope that she's going to pull out of this all right. I do know that the road to recovery isn't going to be quick or easy, but you know our girl Kitty ... she's just one big ball of fire and sunshine."

He tries to smile but winces instead.

Lynn notices and looks at Martin with concern. "I'm going to get the nurse to come back in, Martin. She was here earlier to check on you, but she didn't want to wake you. She mentioned you were in a lot of pain these days. I wish there was something I could do to help you."

Martin doesn't think it would be appropriate to articulate his thoughts on that—that what would really help him would be just one squeeze of her perfectly round buttocks. Instead, he offers a more typical response. "I really appreciate that, Mrs. Pike, but really, the doctors are doing everything they can to manage it. I'm very grateful for your company, though."

Lynn gets flushed. "Can you please stop calling me Mrs. Pike? It makes me feel like I'm a hundred years old." She laughs and shrugs her shoulders.

Martin's thoughts shoot right back to her figure. *Oh, you are anything but a hundred years old, lady.* Her beautiful blond hair with its natural gray streaks frames her soft and elegant face. Her cheekbones are refined and her eyes still sparkle, despite the accumulation of six decades. He clears his throat. "All right, then. Lynn it is."

"You know, my husband's been dead for six years now, and Mrs. Pike is a person from my past now, I believe." She pauses for a moment. "At least I feel that way, anyway. So much of my life was spent as Mrs. Pike, but now that's behind me—so much so that I can't remember much of it, quite frankly. Especially after my son died. It makes me lonely to feel this way. It's almost as though the woman I was and knew so well isn't here anymore. I'm someone else now ..." Her voice tapers off as a look of sadness comes over her pretty face. "I'm someone new and old all at the same time."

Martin is focused on her perfectly shaped raspberry-colored lips. *Dairy Queen Lips*, he thinks to himself.

"... don't you think?" she asks Martin, then waits for a response.

Martin is mortified. He got lost in his thoughts and didn't catch her last point. "Um, what's that?"

"Life is so clever, isn't it?" Lynn says. "It tricks you by giving you all of this supposed time, but in actual fact, time isn't exactly reliable, is it? It's not tangible or real. It's just *there*, carrying on second by mere second, moment by mere moment. It moves too quickly to feel like it's accumulating, or to feel the actual motion of it moving forward into the future—and so we're just left dumbfounded, trying to figure it all out before it's too late." She looks out the window with her arms crossed. She seems unaware that she is shivering. "And to complicate things, everybody's time is completely different and unique from one another's, even though we may all be travelling in the same universe. I guess it's like DNA—we all have arms and legs, a heart and a mind and so on, but each of us is terribly alone in our own separate biological makeup." She suddenly snaps out of her one-way conversation. "Oh, listen to me! I've never been very good at science."

Martin is stunned by the words coming out of Lynn's mouth. They are poetry to his ears. He wants to tell her that he completely understands and feels instantly connected to her but she suddenly interrupts his attempt to do so.

"Martin …" Lynn says with curiosity in her tone. She hesitates before asking the question. "Were you ever married?"

Martin is a little surprised by the question but knows it's a reasonable one to ask. "No, I was never married," he says as a matter of fact. "But I did have one long-term relationship upon my return from Vietnam. It lasted about six years or so, but that was it. We weren't compatible by any stretch of the imagination. I think we stayed together out of false loyalty or maybe we were suffering from an acute state of complacency, I'm not quite sure. She was a nice lady, but I don't think she really understood me and, to be fair, I don't think I fully understood her either. We parted ways on good terms and that was that. I'm pretty sure she married the mailman directly after I moved out, if you know what I mean," Martin concludes, winking at Lynn.

"Oh, I see," replies Lynn grinning. "I think I know exactly what you mean." She walks up to Martin and takes his hand. *There is so much to see and explore behind those eyes,* she thinks to herself.

Martin looks at her and smiles with a quiet mutual sentiment. He can sense the pain leaving his body in exchange for the fierce endorphins pumping through his veins. Whatever time he has pending just stood still.

TWELVE

James walks out of the travel agency on North Slater Street carrying a large envelope containing airline tickets and a few Southeast Asia brochures. Despite the weightlessness of the package, he considers the magnitude of its contents. Excited by the prospects of leaving Chicago, he recaps the last few days leading up to this moment.

His bosses threatened to fire him after his initial request for an eight-week leave of absence. He made it clear to them that he didn't care should they decide to terminate his employment because he had already decided he was going regardless. In the end, they decided to grant him the time away even though the office would suffer in his absence. They assumed that his request for extended leave had something to do with Kitty's condition, and he never corrected them.

James outlined his plan for the office during his absence with careful consideration. Ty would carry on with their joint projects, and his other clients would have to deal with the junior designer, who was now under Ty's direction and had full access to Jade's support. Management was in full—if reluctant—support of his plan.

The walk home is taking less time than expected as his overall plan loops in him mind. The stores are busily preparing for Halloween, and shopkeepers are working diligently on festive displays of all shapes and sizes. Orange pumpkins and candles in the shape of goblins grace every store window he passes. Peering in, he can see the eclectic ensembles of scary witches and black cats lurking in store corners, and silly looking skeletons dangling from various shelves and countertops.

James is overwhelmed with skepticism and is reminded of the true purpose of these cute little displays—to generate revenue. Christmas, too, is just another scam that terrifies him. There are always too many unrealistic expectations put on him by family members and colleagues. *And Lord knows how I've already let them all down lately,* James muses, and the familiar acidic feeling attacks his insides once again at the thought.

He tries hard not to think about it anymore and lets the sensation of the warm sun soothe him. He closes his eyes for a second and pictures a Christmas away from home—a Christmas somewhere hot, filled with people he's never seen before in his life. People he can't disappoint.

James sighs. He resents the onslaught of perpetual drama into his life. He can't wait to dump it all behind him, along with his budding self-loathing, in just a few weeks' time.

He folds up his collar against the wind and turns the last corner before he reaches home.

★★★

Kitty is lying in her bed at Mercy, trying to move her mouth to speak. Jacob hovers over her, encouraging every attempt she makes.

"Hey, baby, look here," he says sweetly to his wife.

The sounds she makes are audible, but it's her eyes that are trying hardest to communicate with her husband. She refuses to allow her stroke to take her away from her family.

Jacob is holding Aaron Junior on Kitty's chest. Kitty manages to move her arms well enough to caress her baby. She can feel her husband's love for her, and their love for their son. She is so happy she could burst. She won't give in to her physical ailments. Her spirit will champion her healing process. She *will* recover—fully and completely. She's sure of it.

The baby is swaddled in a blue checkered receiving blanket and is sporting a white one-piece jumper with snaps at the bottom for easy access. Lynn has knit him a little Cubs cap that accentuates his dark blue eyes and coffee-toned skin. The fresh-cut flowers that sit on Kitty's windowsill are from Martin. He also sent along a homemade CD for the baby with all of his favorite songs from the sixties and seventies. The card reads, *Someone special passed these songs on to me. Now it's my turn to pass them on to someone very special. Love, Martin Diggs.*

A nurse enters the room and Jacob asks whether or not Kitty can attempt to breastfeed. Kitty feels her breasts becoming engorged, and it is painful. The nurses have been attempting to express milk using a pump and are having some luck. The nurse explains that the limited use of Kitty's arms will be an obstacle to natural feeding, as the positioning of the baby is crucial to the success of milk flow and

126

technique. Janice enters the room and asks her usual battery of questions. The nurse tells her it's good news that the baby has been accepting formula in between expressed milk bottles without issue.

The nurse leaves the room and returns momentarily with a specially designed nursing pillow and shows both Kitty and Jacob how to prop up the baby. Jacob is stabilizing A.J. while the nurse tries to bring him directly to the nipple. She pries his little mouth open with one hand and gently pinches Kitty's breast into a C-shape and brings the baby's mouth to it. A.J. instinctively opens his mouth and latches onto his mother's nipple. It hurts and Kitty winces in discomfort.

"He's not quite latched on properly," Janice says, peering down at her daughter and grandson. The nurse adjusts the baby so that he is tummy to tummy with Kitty, and then gets him to latch on a second time. The baby starts to suckle frantically and Kitty can feel a strange tingling in her breast. At first it's a prickly warm sensation, but then a hot rushing feeling takes over. Milk starts to drip down the baby's chin.

Janice claps with excitement and Kitty rests her head on her pillow and closes her eyes. Tears are streaming down her cheeks. Jacob kisses them away as he holds the baby and feeding pillow securely on Kitty's tender round stomach.

Kitty's feeling of happiness is interrupted by thoughts of her brother. Her heart beat quickens as she chokes back her emotions. She opens her eyes to see her baby happily suckling on her breast and releases her brother from her mind.

★★★

Rebecca is getting ready to leave work. She's just finished a twelve-hour shift and is beginning to feel cranky and tired. Thankful that Miesha is with her dad this evening, she looks forward to finally getting some down time to herself for the first time this week. She's supposed to see a movie with Neil, but she's contemplating cancelling the date and going home alone to a nice hot bath and a glass of merlot.

Her last stop for the day is to check in on Gerry. His health has been improving since he hooked up with his new roommate Max, the young paraplegic who seems to have a positive effect on him. As she heads down the hallway she notices Martin in his room, trying to get out of his bed with some difficulty.

"Mr. Diggs!" she calls out in a stage whisper. Robert is sleeping in the next bed. "Please, let me help you." She makes her way over to Martin's bedside and helps him shift his legs around so that his feet are touching the floor. His hospital nightgown is open in the back. "Where's your housecoat?" she asks, looking around his side of the room for the tan-colored robe he's always seen in.

Martin coughs and catches his breath. "I threw it out," he replies. "My niece

127

bought me a new one because she said my other one wasn't fit to wipe my …" He stops, realizing that his manners need to be checked. "She bought me a new one, and it's over there next to the chair." He points to a large department store bag.

Rebecca reaches over the chair and pulls the housecoat out of the bag. Tissue paper falls around her feet. "Super!" she says, her eyes wide with approval. "It's a really nice one. I love the deep navy color." She quickly picks the tissue up off the floor and shoves it back into the bag. "Okay, let me help you with it."

She directs Martin to wrap his arm around her neck while she lifts him upright by his waist and underarm. She closes the gap in the back of his hospital gown and stretches his right arm out to glide the new housecoat over it. She then pulls it over the left arm and ties the belt into an easy knot in the front.

"Thanks, Mom," Martin says with a cheeky smile.

Rebecca chuckles. "Sure thing. You all right now? You didn't seem to have too much pain or trouble moving earlier in the day when I saw you. I'd like to check your blood pressure and temperature again. Were you about to head to the washroom?"

Something about the way Martin sighs makes her think that he had been going to dig out his Jack Daniels again. Instead he says, "Yes, I was, and it might take me a few minutes if you catch my drift."

"Of course," Rebecca says. "But I'd like to take a quick second to check your blood pressure first. You're not due for more morphine until tonight. Donna says you've been off the drip for a few days. That's great news. Does it have anything to do with your new visitor these days?" she asks with a twinkle in her eye. She's referring to Lynn Pike. It's clear to her that Martin and Lynn have formed a special connection, and that it's been helping Martin immensely.

He doesn't answer and stands patiently while Rebecca uses the vinyl wrap to squeeze a reading out of his arm.

She unwraps it quickly. "All right, it's the same as before. A little low, but that seems to be your shtick. I'll help you to the washroom, then I'll come back and help you into bed."

A gentle look comes into his eyes. "Miss Rebecca, I love your dedication to my health and wellbeing, but I'm quite capable of getting myself to and from bed. In fact, I may just walk over to the lounge to watch some news and I certainly don't need assistance, as nice as your offer is." He places his hand on her shoulder and she feels like he is seeing through her loneliness into her soul.

Rebecca nods her head in acceptance. "All right then," she says, trying to sound perky.

"Miss Rebecca, thank you for your kindness and for your hard work. You are unmistakably the most efficient and thorough nurse there is in this place—but don't tell Miss Donna I said that."

She mouths the words 'thank you' as she turns to leave the room.

"Miss Rebecca," Martin says softly. "I want to know how you're doing. Are you okay? We haven't had a chat since … well, in a long while."

Rebecca's shoulders pull down. "I'm fine." She pauses. "Well, I *think* I'm fine." She pauses again. "Okay, maybe I'm not fine." She tilts her head and sighs heavily. "Actually, I really don't know."

Martin puts his hand over his heart. "I'm here to listen if you need someone."

"What I need is a drink," Rebecca says.

"Then how about you and me take a stroll around the premises?" he whispers.

She hesitates. "Well, all right—but just for ten minutes or so. I really do have to get home so it'll have to be short. I'll be back in two minutes, right after I check on Mr. Robinson."

"Who?" Martin grunts. "You mean Gerry? You really do need to let go of the formality," he suggests.

I think I need to let go of a lot of things, she thinks as she heads towards Gerry's room.

★★★

With the support of the chair next to his bed, Martin is able to crouch down and pull the black duffel bag out from under his bed. He opens it up and fishes for the sterling silver flask that has been recently topped up with Jack Daniel's. "Thank God for old man Packer," he says softly, referring to the janitor who diligently supplies him with his weekly juice. He looks around and moves to his closet as quickly as he can and grabs his long wool coat. He puts it on with some difficulty, and then discretely puts the flask deep in the pocket. He reaches for his military beret and dark brown leather gloves and slips on his rubber boots.

Rebecca bounces back in with her jacket and purse. "Mr. Robinson is happily tucked into his bed," she announces. Martin can't help but laugh at her use of the formal address. They pass the main desk, where Donna has already left for the day. Tina and Mark are working tonight. Rebecca calls Mark over and whispers something in his ear. Mark runs off and comes back with a wheelchair.

Martin is annoyed. "Miss Rebecca, is this really necessary? I'm perfectly capable of managing on my own."

"Who says it's for you?" she asks, laughing. He joins in. Her beautiful wide eyes suddenly make his knees weak.

"I gotta hand it to you, Miss Rebecca," he confesses. "You are mighty wicked … and I like that." He raises his eyebrows and winks at her.

The cool evening air sweeps into his lungs as they pass through the exit. It feels good on his face as he takes a few deep breaths to exchange the recycled hospital air for the natural kind. There is a scent of autumn around them. The leaves are a mix of orange, red, and green, and the sky is a majestic dark blue with a streak of bright violet near the horizon.

As Rebecca pushes along the empty wheelchair, Martin is so happy to be outside that he forgets to be annoyed that she brought it out with them. "My, my, my," he says, marveling at the early evening sky and fresh air. "Life is beautiful." His legs are aching but his stride is strong this evening.

He can see Rebecca's tired body resting against the wheelchair as she walks along. She flashes a big smile in response to Martin's comment, then takes him by surprise. "Martin, were you afraid in the war?"

He considers this is an odd question, but it's not the first time he's been asked. Silence comes between them momentarily.

"Yes, I was afraid," Martin explains. "I'm human and fear is a very instinctual and human part of our existence. But was I afraid for *my* life? Well, I can't say that I was, because my life was where I existed in those exact moments in time. That journey was where I was meant to be—with those men and under those specific circumstances. To be afraid would have been a betrayal of my personal destiny. What would be the point of fear? At the end of the day we're all headed to the same place, and I take comfort in that."

They stop at a bench along the path. She sits down first and folds her arms across her torso for extra warmth. Martin hangs onto the wheelchair and slowly lowers himself onto the bench beside her.

"I feel the same way, Martin. I mean, I've always felt different growing up. I never felt fear or anguish or anxiety. I instinctively went with the flow. My dad taught me that," she reflects quietly. "He is such a quiet and strong person inside. He went through a really hard stretch once—he'd just lost his job so he was drinking a lot. My mom and dad were fighting a lot, and my two brothers and I had no idea what to think. We were much more accustomed to seeing them laughing and holding hands. Anyway, my mom threatened to leave him. I was home from school that day and I overheard them talking about it. The weird thing is that I wasn't worried, but I felt like a bit of a freak because of it. My two brothers got wind of the potential breakup and both of them went off the rails."

Rebecca pauses to take a breath before continuing.

"For some reason, I just knew that I was going to be okay. About two weeks later, I walked out into the back yard and my dad was sitting at the picnic table with his head down, just staring at the lines and grooves in the wood. I walked over and asked him what he was looking at. He said that his perception had shifted and that he knew what he needed to do. After that, he started to run marathons."

Martin lets out a chuckle.

"Yeah!" spouts Rebecca, releasing a small laugh herself. "Freaking marathons! Not just a five-mile or ten-mile race, but twenty-six-mile marathons! Years later, he explained it to me when I was going through my separation with my ex-husband Ben. I felt like I was losing my way for the first time in my life. He said that it was the continuous flow of the horizontal grains in the wood that day that gave him the sign to just keep moving down his path—his trail, his road, whatever. And at the end of it, he was sure he would find meaning."

Martin is feeling happy. The urge for Jack Daniel's creeps up on him like it always does when he feels happy. He pulls the flask out of his pocket.

Rebecca looks down at his hands. "Martin!" she gasps.

"You said you needed a drink. So drink."

"But I can't. I …" she tries to explain.

Martin jumps in. "You're off duty, my dear, and I'm a grown man with no need for a chaperone. Now get into the *line* of being and drink up."

Rebecca looks closely at his face. He can see her wrestling with herself. "All right, but you have to swear to me that you won't say a word to anyone. I could lose my job," she finally says.

"I thought you said you weren't afraid of anything," Martin rebuts.

Rebecca purses her lips. "Well, I'm not." She grabs the flask and takes a great big swallow. She moves to hand it back to Martin, but retracts and takes another swig.

Martin gently takes the flask from her lips. "Whoa there, Joan of Arc! Save some for the ol' man here!"

She giggles. "You have such a way with people, Martin. What is it about you?"

Martin shrugs. "I'm not sure, but I'm hoping to find out one day." A moment passes before he carefully broaches the untouchable subject of James. "I've seen you around with that hulk of a boy, Neil."

He takes another swig from the flask before passing it back to Rebecca. She gladly accepts and takes two herself.

He notices that she is evading his question and decides to make an assumption. "I take it you haven't been in touch with Jimmy?"

Rebecca chugs some more whiskey before passing the flask back to Martin. "God!" she cries, shaking her head. "I have *no* clue about that man. If there is one thing that scares the bejesus out of me, it's *that* guy," she says, clearly tipsy now.

Two staff members walk by and say hello. Rebecca and Martin wave politely.

"I've been getting some scoop on our boy Jimmy over the past few days," Martin says, thinking of what Lynn has told him.

Rebecca doesn't respond, but her body language gives her away.

"I think I understand," commiserates Martin. "But like I said to you before, it's best that you just stand idly by until we unleash the beast."

Rebecca huffs. "I don't care, Martin. I don't. I thought we had a connection. It felt more real to me than anything I've ever felt before. But I will *not* let him use me. I'm not his pet. I'm not his experiment. I'm not his—"

"Savior?" Martin interjects.

"I don't even know what that might be," replies Rebecca.

"Everybody needs a savior, Miss Rebecca," Martin says, reaching for another drink. "Even you. We're all missing links to one another. I hate to disappoint you, but we all need to get our hooks into *some*body."

Rebecca is insistent. "I do have my hooks in somebody. My daughter, Miesha."

"Not in those terms, darlin'. Miesha is an extension of yourself and the very seed of your soul, but she's not a significant other."

The look that crosses Rebecca's face lets on that she knows exactly what Martin is getting at.

Martin stretches his arms. "Shall we walk back?"

"Yes, of course. I can't have you getting sick on me," she says.

"Too late," Martin replies with his sly grin. Now it's his turn to push the wheelchair.

Rebecca puts her arm around his waist to help him up. The ground seems to slant a bit under his feet after the whiskey.

"It's a good thing I didn't drive into work today," Rebecca muses.

"How are you getting home?" he asks.

"I guess I'll ask Neil to come pick me up. He's already offered. We're supposed to go for dinner." She doesn't sound overly enthused.

"I don't know about him, girl. He doesn't seem to possess too many funds in the proverbial bank, if you know what I'm saying."

"No, I don't. What do you mean?" It's clear to him that Rebecca is slightly drunk.

"Girl, I say hi to him in the hallway and he's stumped for an answer."

Rebecca roars with laughter. "That's because you're an intellect and you intimidate him."

"My point exactly, dear."

"You don't like Neil? Is that what you're telling me?"

Martin thinks about this for a moment and comes up with an answer. "Whoever eats chili gets burned," he recites.

Rebecca stays quiet as they walk along towards the main entrance.

In his mind Martin can hear James responding, *Malay.*

THIRTEEN

The evening temperature drops to thirty-five degrees Fahrenheit, an unusual low for Chicago in late October. Martin can feel the draft coming from his window despite the light flow of heat blowing from his small portable heater. Robert is fast asleep across the room. He's been sleeping a lot these days, and Martin wonders if this is a sign of things coming to an end. Although Robert is recovering fairly well from his latest brain surgery, this is his third operation and it was undeniably taxing on his body and overall spirit.

Mark, the night nurse, comes to look in on the two men. He briefly checks Robert's intravenous drip to ensure that it is functioning properly. He seems surprised to find that Martin is still awake. "How's your pain, Martin?" he asks, retrieving an extra blanket from the small linen closet.

"It's manageable for now, son. Thank you."

Mark spreads the powder blue blanket over Martin's bed. He turns to the window and shuts the curtains to try to block some of the draft. He notices the small heater but chooses to ignore it for Martin's sake.

Martin is wearing a pair of black flannel pajamas layered with his housecoat. "That's better," he sighs, melting into the warmth.

Mark takes Martin's temperature and checks his heart rate. "Did Robert end up watching any baseball tonight?" he asks while he calculates the number of heartbeats per minute with his wristwatch.

"He was watching something that made him mad as hell," replies Martin, shaking his head. "I'm not sure about that man. He really does love to hate his team."

Mark smiles in agreement. "He sure is a character." The nurse's expression suddenly gets serious. "So, Martin, you've got a bit of a temperature going on here. I'm going to bring you something to help with that, and in the meantime I want you to remove your housecoat. We need your body temperature to cool down a bit. Can you manage without it?"

Martin rolls his eyes. "I suppose," he says, reluctant to remove anything.

When Mark leaves the room to get the medicine, Martin takes off his housecoat and tosses it towards the end of the bed. "Easy access for later," he says out loud to himself. Moments later, Mark returns with some water and two pills. Martin swallows them down and slides back into his warm bed. Mark gives a nod of approval.

As soon as the nurse leaves, Martin grabs his housecoat and wraps it around his torso and neck. He's feeling tired tonight. His date with Rebecca and Jack Daniel's earlier has left him feeling groggy and weak. He closes his eyes, and within moments sleep sets in and a vivid dream replaces his consciousness.

Martin is holding Lynn above water in the Mekong River Delta. The steam from the wicked heat hovers over the murky water, making it difficult to breathe. Through the dense humidity comes a small motorboat slowly making its way towards them. They see a young man in the boat waving at them.

Lynn recognizes him and calls out his name. "Stephen!"

The boat is now moving towards them at high speed and doesn't seem to be slowing down. Martin pushes himself and Lynn underneath the surface while the sound of the boat roars above their heads. Lynn is fighting Martin for air. He pulls her back up for oxygen and they watch the boat disappear down the river. Lynn is gasping for breath and holds onto Martin for support. He swims towards the bush, floating her in his arms. When they get to shore, Frank is waiting for them and James is standing next to him. Frank and James pull them out of the water one at a time.

Martin is confused and weary from the swim, and Lynn asks James where Stephen is. James doesn't answer—he just stands there in his form-fitting army fatigues, looking at her suspiciously. The fear in his eyes makes Martin uneasy. The boat's motor is humming again in the distance. Nervous, they all duck behind the plush green bush off the shore. As the sound of the motor nears, James positions himself for battle. He lines his rifle up, preparing to shoot his target. Martin tries to persuade him to remain calm, but Frank interrupts and tells Martin to leave James alone.

The boat finally approaches. Stephen is standing on the hull dressed in Viet Cong fatigues. James starts calling out to him frantically, and although Stephen doesn't seem to hear him, he clearly sees him. He aims his gun directly at James and pulls the trigger.

The shot rings out and James goes down on the muddied grass. Blood is seeping everywhere. Lynn starts swimming towards the boat while Martin runs over to James. He presses down on the wound in his chest and tells him he's going to be fine. Martin can feel the thickness of blood seeping through his fingers. He looks into the younger man's eyes. They are open and vacant. He's dead.

Martin's heart begins to break. He feels Frank's hand on his shoulder. "It's not your fault," Frank says somberly. "Here, read this." He hands Martin a small white envelope. Lynn slinks back to the shore and calls out to Stephen in the distance. "Goodbye, Stephen!"

Martin jolts out of his sleep covered in sweat. His fever breaks, leaving him damp all over with the exception of his dry mouth. He can feel his heart pumping in his chest. He tries to shake off the dream by grabbing his legs to check in with himself in the moment. He reaches for the glass of water on his bedside table and takes a swallow. He needs to prop himself upright in order to get a better handle on his thoughts. He takes a deep breath and prepares to recall the dream in detail. The clock on the wall reads 5:00 a.m. *Not bad*, he thinks to himself. *Seven hours of sleep without morphine is an accomplishment.*

He decides that a cup of tea would help him relax through the dissection of his dream. Slowly and carefully, he plucks himself out of bed and puts on his housecoat and slippers. Although a little wobbly, he believes he can manage to make his way to the kitchenette without assistance.

As he is coming out of the room, Mark is making his final rounds before heading home after his long night shift.

"Hey, Martin. You're up early," he says, looking tired. "Can I get you something before I go?"

"No, son, but thank you. I'm just stretching out my legs by going for a cup of tea."

Mark places his hands on his hips. "All right then, sir. Just try to go slow and easy. And oh, I almost forgot—Lynn left you all some muffins yesterday. They're in a plastic container on the counter, so help yourself. They're cornbread and blueberry."

"Don't mind if I do, son," Martin says. "Now you go on and get some sleep. You look like hell."

Mark laughs and waves as he passes through the corridor.

Martin heads into the kitchenette. The florescent lights are blinding and he can feel their sting behind his eyes. He plugs in the kettle and parks himself on the tiny white chair next to the table for two. He's curious about the meaning of his dream and attempts to replay each segment in his mind.

Water can be a symbol of libido—motherhood and amniotic life and all that. So that part of the dream must be my connection with Lynn the woman, who tragically lost her son. Water is a habitual element that man cannot live without—much like love. It makes sense. Lynn and I are building a connection. So what are Frank and James doing there? And why are we all in Vietnam?

The whistle from the kettle startles Martin, breaking his train of thought. He gets up and pours his tea, then sits back down at the table. The hot liquid warms his insides as he continues to map out his analysis.

Okay, so Frank and I were best friends in Vietnam. James and Stephen were best friends growing up. Lynn is Stephen's mother, and a woman whom I happen to be developing a personal and intimate rapport with. Vietnam seems to be the connection with all of us, because it's my dream and it was a significant time in my life, and in Frank's life, too.

Martin is satisfied with his analogy. *Right! Now, what about James? Let's see … James is afraid of love. The last time he loved somebody so deeply it ended up basically killing him, hence Stephen being responsible for James's death. But James was prepared to shoot Stephen first … Why?*

Martin gets up again to grab one of Lynn's muffins. When the container opens, the sweet smell of corn and blueberry comes into the air. He takes a bite and closes his eyes in pleasure. His thoughts resume.

James is afraid of connecting to another soul, hence why he was prepared to shoot Stephen. Classic self-preservation. I'm surprised Rebecca didn't pop into my dream, too, he thinks, his train of thought drifting. *Where was I? Oh yes, now let me see. James yelled at Stephen before Stephen took the shot. Why would he do that? If James wanted to kill him, surely he would have tried to catch him off guard. Hmmm …*

He thinks back to one of his intimate conversations with Lynn about the accident. *Lynn did tell me that the police report included a statement from James saying that he tried to call out to Stephen to warn him, but that Stephen couldn't hear him because he was listening to music through his headphones at the time.*

Martin takes another bite of his muffin, his mind still flowing. *So the pain of witnessing the horrible accidental death of his best friend and the loss of that connection is prohibiting him from connecting with anyone else in his life. Sounds like guilt. But why would James feel guilty? Does he feel that he should've risked his life by running onto the tracks to save Stephen? And by not doing so, does he feel responsible for his friend's death? I felt responsible for Frank's death …* He stops chewing and recalls his own experience. *For a long time I wasn't able to let go of that pain and guilt—not until years later, when I met Frank's brother Sloan and he gave me the letter that Frank had written to him. That letter changed my life.*

Putting his teacup down, Martin can hear his voice speaking his thoughts out loud. "I need to get a hold of that police report."

It's closing in on 6:00 a.m., and the halls will soon start filling up with breakfast trays and nurses making their morning rounds. Martin wants to get back into bed to rest his sore hip for an hour or so before tackling his mission for the day. Lynn would be up in another hour, and he is looking forward to calling her. He rinses his tea cup and wipes his hands on a dish towel. As he approaches the door to his room, Donna intercepts him.

"I'd give him a few more minutes in there if I were you," she says. "He's decided to bless us all with his *worldly* presence this morning." Donna is not a big fan of James and she isn't afraid to show it.

Martin stops in his tracks and watches Donna move past him in her usual bulldozer-like way. He shuffles closer to the door of his room and, through the small inset window, sees the backside of James, who is sitting in a chair facing Robert. Robert's eyes are closed and he's nodding his head ever so slightly, as if to acknowledge James's words. Martin is curious. *What in the world is that boy saying?* He asks himself. He puts his ear closer to the door but he can't hear anything.

Donna makes her way back around the corner with a meal trolley. "He's not doing so well, Mr. Diggs," she says with certainty in her voice.

Martin assumes she is referring to Robert. "Is it approaching that time?" he asks somberly.

"I'm afraid so, dear," she replies. "Mr. Gainsborough took a bit of a turn for the worse last night while you were fast asleep. His family should be arriving any time now. He asked to see James first thing. I honestly didn't think he'd come, but as Mark said, nobody's that heartless as to deny a dying man's request." She shakes her head and starts to move forward with the meal trolley. "I'll be back in ten minutes with yours, Mr. Diggs. Hope you have an appetite this morning. Cook made porridge."

Martin shivers. He looks back through the small window. Robert is clutching James's hand. Martin feels death looming over his friend. He opens the door slightly so he can hear a bit of what James is saying.

"Go easy on yourself, Bob. You've done everything for your family. Don't be ashamed of anything—you're a hero."

Martin shuts the door quietly, his thoughts running at full speed. *Well, I'll be damned.* He stands in the hallway for another few minutes until the sound of a chair scraping against the floor entices him to peek through the small window again.

James is getting up to say his goodbyes to Robert. He puts his hand on Robert's scarred, bald head and whispers something. He turns to leave and sees Martin through the window. He's doesn't look surprised to see him, but he doesn't look overly enthused either. He looks tired.

"Martin. Hello."

"Hello, Mr. Jimmy. It's been a long time since I last saw you. Are you doing all right, son? Where have you been hiding?" James is about to answer, but Martin jumps back in. "You *have* been hiding, haven't you, Mr. Jimmy?"

"Do we have to do this today?" he asks, his eyes averting.

"You may delay, but time will not."

James smirks. "Ben Franklin."

"You're good, son, you're good," Martin says, patting his arm. "How is my buddy doing in there?"

"I'm afraid he's very weak," James tells him. "His family is on their way over now. That's all I know. I'm not a doctor so I can't really say what's happening to him." James looks uncomfortable saying even that much.

"I see. I'll inquire when I see a doctor, then," Martin says.

"All right then, Martin. I'd better head off now. Have a good day." James turns to leave.

"James!" Martin calls out quietly. A thought has just occurred to him.

James turns around.

"I'm wondering if you wouldn't mind escorting me to the Veterans Day celebration" Martin asks.

James looks stunned at the request. "Um …" he begins, unsure. "Okay."

Martin smiles. "Good. Pick me up here at ten o'clock sharp, two weeks from Thursday," he orders before he walks into his room.

The room is quiet. Only Robert's shallow breathing fills the airspace. Martin wants to sit with him while he waits for his family to arrive. Dr. Lewis and Donna were in a half hour earlier to adjust Robert's medication so he can remain comfortable.

Robert mumbles, "Is Marie here?" He takes a few more breaths. "Is that you, Luke? Is your brother Casey here?"

Martin's chest is heavy with remorse. "Bobby, it's Marty. Your family is on their way."

Robert's eyes open. "I told him that I didn't want them to come. I didn't want them to see me like this." His eyes shut. His trembling hand reaches up to signal to Martin. Martin sees a cup of ice chips sitting on the side table. He takes the cue and passes the cup under Robert's chin. With Martin's help, Robert extends his mouth over the rim and sucks in the ice chips. Martin gently helps Robert's head back down on the pillow.

Robert continues talking. "… but he said that they needed to be here and that I should be doing this for them."

"Who's *he*?" Martin asks softly.

Robert coughs. "That Bozo the Clown," he grunts, making Martin laugh. "Clown boy. Jimmy," he replies gruffly.

Martin sighs. He's always known there was something about that boy that wanted to reach out. "Well, I'm glad he was able to talk some sense into you, my friend," Martin whispers in his ear.

Robert opens his eyes and stares into Martin's. "I'm not afraid," he explains. "I'm just not sure of any of this."

Martin knows exactly what his friend means. He moves in closer and leans down to his ear. "It's the bottom of the ninth and the Cardinals are up five-two. Carpenter is pitching like wild fire, and Carlos Peña is up at bat. The bases are loaded. A fastball comes whippin' in. Peña fouls it off. The crowd is electric. Byrd is on first. Ramirez is eyeing' home plate and signaling to Johnson on second to watch out for the pop-up. Carpenter winds up ..."

Robert interjects with a weak growl. "Carpenter's a pussy."

Martin smiles and continues, "Carpenter winds up. It's a knuckleball. The umpire calls it. St-rike! The fans are callin' out for their man. Peña! Peña! Carpenter throws a curve ball. Peña smashes it. The ball sails high and far. In comes Ramirez, soon to be followed by Johnson. Byrd is sprinting around the bases. Rasmus is running towards the wall at full tilt. Byrd rounds third base and heads for home. Rasmus leaps into the air. His thick mitt is like a hungry shark goin' for the prey. The ball just nips the top of the glove and then rolls over to the other side of the wall. The stadium erupts. Fans are going crazy. The clubhouse is running out onto the field. The Cubs have won the World Series!"

Martin looks down at Robert. His eyes are closed and peace has evaporated the lifelong lines of pain and anguish from his face. He is gone. The door opens. Marie, Luke, and Casey file in, one inning too late.

FOURTEEN

Rebecca finds herself still pulling down orange and black Halloween decorations from the hospital corridors, despite it being the second week of November. For her, every day of this particular month feels like a Monday—long, tedious, and drawn out. She enters the television room expecting to collect paper and plastic pumpkins and witches, only to find a quiet and somber space with no joy in it. Robert has died, just two weeks short of Veterans Day, and his comrades are still feeling the loss. She pauses to reflect on the service that was held for him.

It was a beautiful funeral filled with laughter and stories. Marie seemed to be holding up well. Rebecca couldn't get over how much Casey looked like his father. She had made her way to the ceremony with Neil, but insisted that they sit in the very back corner in order to avoid being seen by James, who was sitting in the fifth row of pews beside Janice, Lynn, and Martin.

Rebecca can't stand the feeling she gets when she sees James now. It's like a kick in her gut every time. A full-body ache consumes her at the mere thought of him. At the funeral, she was having an especially hard time letting go of what could have been between them. She found herself staring at him from the back pew during the entire service, wondering what if.

"Howdy," comes a voice from behind Rebecca. She jumps, dropping some of the Halloween decorations from the box in her hands.

"Good grief!" she replies, panting. She looks up to see a fine-looking man in his late thirties with short blond hair, ocean blue eyes, and a gregarious smile.

"Sorry, ma'am. Here, let me get those for you," the man says, crouching down to help retrieve the decorations. He picks up each article carefully and helps her arrange the items until they overflow the small box she's carrying.

"Name's Stan. Stanley Jordan," he announces to fill the awkward space. His voice sounds Southern. "I just stopped by the lounge here to catch the score of the game," he says cheerfully. "I don't have a TV by my bed yet."

Rebecca is lost, looking at his handsome face. "Oh, hi. It's, uh, nice to meet you." In a moment she realizes that he must be the new patient who was admitted last Friday after her shift. She recalls Donna's debrief with her earlier this morning. ... *Stanley Jordan is a 38-year old man diagnosed with kidney disease six months ago. He's on the transplant donor list and requires dialysis three times a week in the interim. He's extremely healthy otherwise but will be a patient here under long-term care until a donor match becomes available. He'll be bunking with Martin until the time of the transplant and for sometime afterwards. We want to make be sure his body doesn't reject the new organ and that he's healthy enough to be discharged...*

Rebecca realizes Stan is staring at her. "Oh, so you're our new patient!" she says, breaking the ice. The two start walking out of the room and down the corridor. "I hear you're rooming with Martin," she says with false cheer. She tries not to think about Robert.

"Hell ya," Stan says enthusiastically. "He's such a smart man, I tell ya. He's always quotin' somethin' or other. Heck, I don't think I've even heard of half the people he goes on about. Guess I'm just not that good with worldly stuff."

Rebecca laughs. "Listen, Stan, you're in good company. I only know of one other person who can keep up with Martin's intellect ..." She stops herself. She can't bear to bring up James. She doesn't even want to think about him, but somehow her body still manages to carry him around inside her like a disease.

Stan senses something and drops the subject. "It's mighty quiet around this place," he says, looking around.

Rebecca recognizes the truth in his statement. "It's been a rough few months. We've had three deaths. It can take its toll because we're family to each other, you know?" They reach his room, where Martin is listening to music in the corner and reading his book of poems.

"I'd best be getting ready for Donna," says Stan. "It's almost time for my dialysis."

Rebecca nods. "You're in good hands, she really knows what she's doing."

"Oh, ya. She's a real firecracker, ain't she?" he says with a goofy grin.

"You have no idea, Stan," Rebecca replies. "No idea."

Martin looks up just then. "Well hello there, Miss Rebecca. How are you, my dear?"

Rebecca smiles as she places the box of decorations on the food trolley in between the beds. She grabs Martin's chart from the end of his bed and looks it over. Donna has been in, and everything seems to be in check.

"I'm fine, Martin," she says, holding her head up high and smiling brightly at him. "And it looks like you're good, too," she adds, motioning towards his chart.

"It was a good service for Bob, wasn't it?" he asks.

"Yes, it was. But wait a minute ... How did you know I was there? I was way in the back, and I left the church when you were up front with Bob's family talking to the pastor." Rebecca is puzzled. "I didn't see you turn around."

Martin looks her straight in the eye. "I have my ways," he says mysteriously.

"Okay, I'll just have to trust that," she says with a smile. "Can I get you something?"

"Nothing right now," he says. "But thank you, dear."

Rebecca gives a small wave as she heads out of the room. "Bye, Stan. It was good to meet you. I'll see you at lunch time."

"Good day, Miss Rebecca," Stan replies.

She smiles at his use of the word 'miss.' *Only a few days with Martin and already he's picking up on the lingo*, she muses. *Trust Martin to show the new guy the ropes.*

★★★

As soon as the nurse is out of sight, Stan jumps out of his bed and scoots over to Martin's side of the room.

"I've been locked up here all weekend," whispers Stan. "Whaddaya say we go for a little joyride?"

Martin looks surprised, yet intrigued by the idea. "Go on," he says, folding his book and dropping it on his lap.

"I know a nice little spot by the Lake Shore where we can hang out for a while and catch us some fresh breeze," Stan explains, excited at the prospects of getting out.

Martin is careful to comply. "And how do you propose we go for a joyride when we don't have a ride to enjoy?"

"I checked myself in here, man. My Lexus is sitting in the parking lot. My mom is supposed to come and pick it up later this week on account of the expensive parking, but it's here as we speak. Might as well use it before it's gone."

Gerry and Max enter the room. "Hey, Marty, Stan," Gerry says with enthusiasm, nodding at each in turn.

Martin can't help but notice how good Gerry looks. He's been working out regularly with Max, and he is most definitely reaping the benefits. His congestive heart disease has completely stabilized and the doctors think he may no longer need long-term care. Gerry isn't happy about this, though. He enjoys living at the Veterans' Hospital and he loves the company he shares—especially Max's.

Stan hops onto Martin's bed. "Listen, how do y'all feel about goin' for a spin in

143

my hot rod?"

"I hate to break it to you, Einstein," Martin says with a chuckle. "But a Lexus isn't a hot rod. Hot rods are typically American cars with large engines built for speed."

"It don't matter, roomie," Stan says with excitement. "What matters is that it goes like the wind!"

Gerry looks nervous. He's not adventurous by any means. "Uh, I dunno, Stan," he mutters, shuffling his feet.

"I say let's do it," Max says eagerly. "It'll be fine, Gerry. Don't worry. We're muscle machines now. We can do anything."

Stan looks to Martin to seal the deal.

"All right. I'm in," Martin says, with a twinkle in his eye. "But we need an escape plan. Not all of us here have the ability to leave the premises without some type of authorization."

"Not to worry, roomie. I've got it all worked out," Stan replies.

"Great. And I'm supposed to feel confident about that?" Martin snips.

Stan puts his arm around Martin's shoulders. "Come over here, y'all," he says, gathering up the rest of his teammates in a huddle where he secretly reveals the plan.

A minute later, Martin pushes himself away from the circle and smiles shaking his head. "If my mother could see me now."

Max laughs with anticipation and slaps the arms of his wheelchair. Gerry continues shuffling his feet and starts rubbing his hands together. Martin pulls Jack Daniel's out of his duffel bag and takes two big swigs. He passes the flask around the circle.

"No, thanks. Can't touch the stuff," says Stan. The other two happily oblige. "Are we ready then?" Stan asks.

"Ten-four," Max answers, saluting his comrades.

Stan runs out the door and starts the plan. Gerry heads to one of the empty rooms around the other side of the floor. Max goes to the physiotherapy room while Martin stays put. At exactly three minutes past ten, Martin, Gerry, and Max simultaneously push their respective buttons to the nurses' station, forcing a momentarily vacant reception desk and enabling a clear run at the elevators. After pushing his button, Martin rushes out of his room and ducks into the men's public washroom. He waits for Donna to pass by, and when she does, he heads for the elevators where Max and Gerry are already waiting. They hit the button for the ground floor and hold their breath as the elevator doors close. At eight minutes past ten, Martin, Gerry, and Max come flying out the revolving doors. In the meantime, Stan has pulled his car up to the hospital's main entrance. He is waiting there, idling the engine.

"Shit! Shit!" Gerry is yelling. People coming towards the front entrance look concerned.

"Keep it down, Gerry, you're attracting attention," Martin gripes.

Stan leaps out of the front seat and secures Max's wheelchair. "On the count of three, lift him up and toss him into the back seat."

Max looks like he is loving the attention.

Gerry counts, "One, two, three!"

On cue, the three men lift Max and roll him into the car.

Just then Martin sees Neil coming out of the elevator and yells, "Mother of God, move it, boys!" He pushes the wheelchair up onto the curb. It spins out and glides backwards down the pathway, devoid of its passenger.

The other three men scramble into the car and Stan peels out of the parking lot with Martin's door hanging wide open. Martin leans towards the center console to keep from falling out of the passenger seat and yells to Stan, "The door, boy!"

Stan reaches over and pulls the door shut. He swerves and speeds towards the parking lot exit. The tires squeal, and the piercing sound makes people stop in their tracks to observe the nuisance. Max is laughing hard, promising that he's going to wet himself from laughter.

Gerry screams behind Stan, "Watch it!" There's a brown car stopped in front of them at the exit to the parking lot. An old man is fumbling for his ticket to feed the automatic parking machine. He drops his ticket and has to step out of his car to retrieve it.

"Come on, old man," Stan says under his breath. "Come on!"

"Houston, we have a problem," Martin drones loudly. He can see Neil in the side mirror; he's barreling across the parking lot towards the Lexus.

The old man gets back into his car. "Jesus Jehovah, move it!" Stan yells.

Neil is fast approaching and Gerry starts whimpering in the back seat. The white arm of the parking gate lifts up and the old man advances with his car.

"Hang onto yer hookers!" Stan warns. He presses the gas pedal to the floor and the tires smoke and squeal around the brown 2008 Chevy. They dart off down the road, leaving the dust swirling around Neil's head.

"Whoo hoo!" Stan screams out.

Martin finds himself grinning. He feels alive inside for the first time in a long time. He fishes around for a reasonable radio station. Stan reaches over and grabs a CD from the glovebox. Martin opens the case and slides it into the player. A heavy drumbeat and raunchy guitar fill the car. *Get your motor running ...*

"I honestly think I pissed myself," Max calls out over the music. Martin passes him the flask of Jack Daniel's.

Gerry's head bobs to the music while Stan drives towards the highway, one hand on the wheel and the other hanging out the open window, tapping the outside of the car door. The four men bellow along with the music at the top of their lungs.

Back at the hospital, the nurses are frantic wondering how this happened. The doctors are unaware of the situation for now and Rebecca feels they should keep it that way just for a little while longer. She automatically thinks about her cousin Douglas—a patrol officer with the city's police department. She decides to call and ask him to informally investigate the situation. In the meantime, she instructs Donna to call Janice. Surely the head of the Board of Directors would know what to do. Rebecca paces anxiously at the nurses' station and can't help but wonder what Kitty would do in this situation. "Oh my God, why is this happening?" she shouts to Neil and Donna who are standing close by, consoling her.

★★★★

After driving for half an hour or so, the four men find a secluded area just off Highway 22 with a clear view of Lake Michigan. Martin finishes off his flask and places it in his pants' waistband. It's a clear day, and the veterans are all basking in the warmth of the sun around the car. Gerry has Max propped up on the hood. They're taking in the fresh air, examining the exquisite fall colors painted throughout the landscape.

Stan's dark blue eyes are looking across the water. His thoughts suddenly break the tranquility of the moment. "When I went to Iraq for the first time, I couldn't get over the beauty of the countryside. It was hotter than a whore in Texas—just like my hometown in Jefferson County in Mississippi. Only it was dry, you know? Bone dry."

Martin can almost see the desert scenery flashing before Stan's eyes.

"When you got into the villages, though, that beauty seemed to disappear," Stan continues. "Houses and roads are built out of sand and mud and clay there. When the winds would pick up, well, you just knew you'd be spittin' dust for days." He pauses and scans the surrounding scenery. "I missed seeing the greenery everywhere. I missed the color. Everything about my life at that time was either black or white. Nothin' else—nothin' in between."

Martin can guess where Stan is going with this. He understands the importance of being able to talk it out, and for people to just listen without judgment. Stan's voice sounds muffled, as if he's buried underneath someplace inside of himself.

"The house raids were particularly difficult. But not at first, when you'd get onto the ground with your troop and it's all beginnin', you know? It's just black and white then. You go in, you get what you need, and it makes no nevermind who you rough up to get it. But after a while your humanity takes over—and if you don't let it take over, then you just go crazy fightin' it all the time, is all."

Martin looks to Max and Gerry. They're nodding along with young Stan's words.

"After about half a dozen house raids, I just couldn't stay black and white no more. I mean, here I was, kickin' in doors of houses that belonged to innocent people. Babies and mothers screamin' in the corners. It was like chaos gone mad. There we were, separatin' these people—these *families*—from each other, and for what? We were lookin' for some kind of *intelligence*. Yeah, right. All I ever found was normal, everyday people tryin' to look after their kids. Funny thing is, once we started the raids, we would get to the fourth or fifth house or so and the families would already be awake with the lights on, just ready to be taken by us. It was like they'd gotten used to it, you know? I never got used to it, that's for sure—I never got used to seein' the fear and sadness on their faces when we took away their loved ones. Never. I prayed some nights for me to just die because I couldn't stand the guilt no more."

Stan looks around and catches Martin's eye. The sudden silence feels heavy to Martin so he quietly motions to the younger man to continue, but he doesn't.

"Anyway ..." Stan finishes.

Nobody says anything for a while. Max finally breaks the seal. "How'd you end up in Chicago, man?"

"I got me a big ol' job here at head office," Stan replies proudly. "I was also shacked up with a girl here that I met during the tour and we were together for a while, but that didn't work out so well in the end. Turns out she likes other girls."

The four men break up laughing. They hear a car rolling up slowly.

"Shit, it's the cops," Gerry says nervously.

"Let me handle this," says Martin.

A policeman gets out of the patrol car and approaches them. "Afternoon, gentleman," he says in a professional way. "Which one of you is the owner of this vehicle?"

Martin hikes a thumb at Stan. "That'd be this young buck, officer."

"I see. Can I see some documents, please? And in the meantime, may I ask what brings you so far from the Veterans' Hospital?" the officer says. His question is loaded. Someone from the hospital must have called them in. *Damn Neil*, Martin curses.

As Stan is fishing around for his license and ownership, Martin pulls the policeman aside to explain. "My good man," he begins, "our friend here is suffering from post-traumatic stress disorder. I'm wondering if you would please consider going easy on him."

"I understand," says the officer. "But that doesn't explain why the rest of you participated in this little getaway."

Stan hands the officer his driver's license and ownership. "Sir, I apologize for this. It's my fault. I talked my friends here into sneakin' out for a wee bit. I certainly didn't mean no harm by it all."

The policeman asks a few other questions about their escape and then radios into the station to verify the location of the missing men. "I'm willing to play nice this time and not file any charges. However, if a situation like this *ever* happens again, Mr. Jordan, you and the rest of your motley crew will have a few other disorders to deal with, namely my-foot-in-your-ass syndrome."

The policeman insists that he will be escorting their return. "All right, men, you're all going to follow me back to the hospital."

Stan winces.

"Don't say a word and do what you're told," scolds Martin.

Stan nods. "Yes sir, roomie sir." He cracks a sideways grin.

They lift Max up and place him in the back seat of the car. The ride home is quiet, but all four men are content with their own thoughts. *A valiant effort*, decides Martin. *And a worthy cause, too.*

★★★

That evening turns out to be a bust for the men, as they are confined to their beds due to the stress they put on their already compromised immune systems, not to mention the nursing staff.

At the dinner hour, Martin contemplates trying the contents of his dinner tray for a second time but ultimately decides against it. He starts to initiate a conversation with Stan but realizes he's napping, so he puts his head down on the pillow and opens a book of poems by an American poet, Carl Sandburg. Just as he starts to read, Lynn comes into the room carrying a casserole dish still warm from the oven.

"Hello, dear," Martin says, his mood lifted at the sight of her.

"Oh, Martin, what on earth did you get yourself into today?" She removes the meal tray from the trolley and replaces it with her own version of tonight's dinner. She stacks his tray over Stan's used picked-over one on his cart and starts to remove her jacket.

Martin is watching her every move. She is elegant and sexy—poised and in control of her life. His mind wanders from the immediate conversation. He feels drunk in her presence. *In all my years of trying to find the right woman, I think I may have finally done just that. From the moment we met we were bonded instantly without time or history behind us. Funny how time can be irrelevant when it comes to love, and yet timing is everything.*

Lynn's voice breaks his stream of thoughts. "Martin?'

Martin instantly returns to the point. "Listen, doll face, sometimes a man's gotta do what a man's gotta do to get his blood coursing through his veins," he explains.

Lynn rolls her eyes. "Martin, really. I understand, but you gave poor Rebecca,

Donna, and the entire staff quite a scare. They care about you guys!" She gets up and uncovers his dinner. It smells delicious.

Martin peers over to take a look. "Mmm, Chicken Kiev—my favorite."

Lynn pulls the curtain so not to disturb Stan's nap and quietly moves the trolley over Martin's bed so he can access the food. He grabs a fork and digs in, smiling as he swallows. "Delicious, my dear. Thank you."

"You are welcome. Now tell me about today," she demands with a mischievous smile.

Martin recounts the escape for his new lady friend, making her giggle generously at the tale while she fusses over him during his mealtime. When she steps out to place the leftovers in the fridge and make some tea, Martin sifts through the pages of Sandburg poems. He glances over the first few lines of a poem and is immediately intrigued, but Lynn returns quickly with tea and dessert, diverting his attention.

"Thank you again, dear, for such a great meal—and for coming to see me," Martin says.

Lynn blushes. "I know it's been a few days, but I was helping Janice with the baby. Gracious, Martin, what a beautiful boy he is." She takes the teabag out of her cup. "Oh, and I have some wonderful news!" she exclaims. "Kitty is going home in a few days. Isn't that great?"

Martin's heart fills with joy. "My, my, Lynn. That's the best news I've heard in a long time."

"It's a miracle, Martin. I'm so happy for all of them."

"What about Jimmy? Has he made himself known yet?" Martin asks.

"No, not yet, unfortunately," Lynn admits. "I don't know about him. He seems to have sunk further and further into a depression or something. I really do believe that he has never really recovered from losing Stephen all those years ago." Her eyes darken with sadness. "Not that I've really recovered, either. I mean, who could after losing their child? But I just felt that to throw my life away would be such a disservice to my son. He was, without question, the most charismatic and alive person in the world." The pain in her heart makes her face suddenly look older to Martin. "But I didn't just lose one son that day, Martin," she says with clarity in her voice. "Jimmy has always been like a second son to me, and I lost him that day, too. We all did."

Martin sips his tea, contemplating.

"James and Stephen were like twins from another mother, honestly," states Lynn. "You could see the love and connection between them. It was like there was this invisible wire holding them together all the time." She pauses to reflect. "James was so unlike the James you know today, Martin—he was so funny and sweet. He'd hug and kiss you all the time. He brought in so many stray animals, it nearly drove Aaron mad." She laughs fondly. "Once he actually tried to rescue a baby skunk from underneath their porch. When Aaron threatened to snare it, James ran after him screaming, and when he caught up to him, well that boy just bit his daddy right on the behind. Kitty just stood there yelling at her father, saying that if he touched that skunk, she'd never forgive him. Janice and I didn't know what to do. Eventually that little skunk got so scared from all the shouting that it took off like a shot!"

Lynn doesn't realize she has tears streaming down her cheeks until it's too late. "Oh my word!" she says sweetly, reaching for the box of tissues beside Martin's bed.

Martin grabs her hand. "It's all right, darlin'. It'll be all right." He wipes the tears with his hand.

"I know," she sobs softly. "I just wish that he could start living his life again. It's so hard on him … and it's so hard on his mother and sister, too. It's hard on *all* of us—on everyone who loves him."

"Rebecca included?" asks Martin, knowing full well the answer.

"Yes, I suppose so."

Martin pulls Lynn over to the side of his bed. He embraces her and gives her a kiss on her lips. She wraps her arms around his neck and kisses him back.

"What would you say if I told you I think I can break through to that boy?"

Lynn looks into his eyes. "What do you mean?"

"As you know, I've experienced a similar situation with my best friend, Frank."

"Yes, you told me," Lynn says, wiping her nose with a tissue. "I really wish I'd met Frank. He seems like someone I really would have enjoyed hanging around with."

"He would have really enjoyed you, too. As do I," Martin adds fondly. "We were soldiers who shared the same soul, and when I hear stories of James and Stephen … well, I completely understand that connection."

"What do you have in mind?"

Martin braces himself. "I … I'm wondering if you would be willing to get me a copy of the police report on Stephen's accident."

Silence slices the air. Martin can see that Lynn is struggling for breath. He slowly reaches onto his bedside table and takes hold of his volume of Sandburg poems. He removes a stained brown envelope from between the pages and hands it to Lynn. "Here. Read this and you'll understand."

Lynn reluctantly takes the envelope from Martin's hand and looks at it. When she turns it over, she sees it's addressed to a Sloan Kenney. She pulls out a piece of faded, flimsy paper. The writing is barely legible, but is still just dark enough to be able to make out the sentences.

Quang Nam, Vietnam, February 1966

Sloan,

How you getting on? I'm sittin' in the middle of nowhere thinkin' about having some fish n' chips with the old gang back home. Got a hankerin for somethin bad right now. Can't remember the last time I was blowed up like a sculpin! I miss you all very much. How's ma? I reckon she's holding up. Things are bad here Sloan. Got myself a good drop, though, thanks to my American boy Diggers. He's a good egg. I can't say that I could do any of this without him. Saves my arse every day. He's a bit of a pelt of a tripe, but every goddamn day when I can't get my shit together he's there to get me through it. I owe my life to him, I really do. Shite, the things that you see here and those Viet Cong are rimmed and warped and all but I'm all right with the way things are Sloan. I'm not scared see? You tell ma that too. I gotta go now. We're headin' back out in to the mess of it all. I'll be seeing you soon.
Yer's lovingly, Frank.

Lynn finishes reading the letter and gently places it back into the tarnished envelope. She looks up at Martin. "You really do understand, don't you?"

Martin closes his eyes.

"Martin, I'm just so sorry for what you had to go through. I'm so sorry you lost your friend."

"That's okay, Lynn. I'll see him again one day."

She hands the letter back to him and takes his hand. "Martin, I have to tell you something. I have never, *ever* read that report. Stephen was killed by a train, and I didn't want to know the details. We didn't even get to see his body. His remains were cremated." The muscles in her face are holding back the tears and anguish.

Martin pulls her in close to his side. "If you don't want me to read it, I won't either." They sit still, holding each other in complete silence.

★★★

The days of the week hurry along as celebrations are planned across the city for Veterans Day. The hospital is organizing an event in the chapel for the palliative care patients who are not able to leave the premises, and many other long-term care veterans are looking forward to attending the city's main event at Soldier Field Stadium. Martin, Gerry, Max, and Stan were among those taking part in the outing.

Rebecca is speaking to a patient's family member when she sees Janice out of the corner of her eye. Janice is standing at the nurses' station holding a file folder in her hand. No doubt it contains plans for the V Day celebrations at the stadium. It's well known among the nurses that Janice's father-in-law helped to engineer the stadium, and that Janice has been helping to plan the V Day celebrations there for years.

Moments later Rebecca walks over to the nurses' station to greet Janice.

"Janice! It's so good to see you," she says earnestly.

Janice gets a concerned look in her eye. "Are you all right, dear?" she mothers. "You look like you've lost weight, and you really didn't have anything to lose in the first place."

Rebecca looks down and observes the scrubs hanging off her small frame. She hasn't given her body a thought in weeks and is a little surprised by what she sees. "Um, I guess I must have lost a pound or two, but I don't know how. I'm eating normally—which means I'm eating a lot," she jokes. "I suppose I *am* a bit tired, though. Ben has been out of town all month, and I really haven't had much of a break with Miesha. She's getting busier now with dance and math tutoring and birthday parties and all that."

"Yes, I remember those days well," Janice replies with a slight laugh. "Well, you know I would love to take Miesha shopping or to a movie or something to help out. She's such a lovely girl and we get along well."

Rebecca is heartfelt. "Thank you, Janice. I know she would enjoy that very much."

Janice hesitates but asks the question anyways. "Rebecca, have you seen James at all?"

Donna comes up behind them. "No way, ma'am," she interjects. "But ask her where Neil is and she'll be able to tell you."

"Donna, cut it out," Rebecca snips. *That woman can be as insolent as a four-year-old*, she thinks as Donna waddles towards the lounge with a satisfied look on her face.

"I'm so sorry, Janice," Rebecca says sincerely. "I haven't seen or heard from James in weeks." She feels tears threatening to brim at the thought of James and scolds herself to keep it together.

The look on Janice's face says she understands. Rebecca has done exactly what James has done—made herself unavailable. "It's quite all right, dear. I know how it is," replies Janice. She pauses, as if choosing her words carefully. "But I can also see that you still care about him. Oh, I so wish that things were different between the two of you. You're such a beautiful person, inside and out, and …" she trails off. Her expression looks lost. "It's just that Jimmy's become so … so unable to care for anyone anymore. Ever since—" She stops herself short as Donna returns to the nurses' station.

Janice gives Rebecca a knowing smile and then starts to go over the documents in the file she's holding. Some of it is arrangements for getting the veterans down to the stadium, while the rest is minutes of the last board meeting and decisions made regarding an increase in required staff and funding to keep the social programs going. Janice also asks Rebecca to set up a meeting with the chief of staff and the doctors and nurses on new protocols for patient outings and security.

The elevator doors swing open and Lynn walks out, bringing with her the smell of hazelnut and vanilla. "Hello, ladies!" she says, smiling. There's a stack of Tupperware containers full of baked goods in her arms. Donna rushes over to help her.

"Lynn, thank goodness," Janice says in greeting. "I tried calling you all day yesterday on both your lines and never got an answer—not even voice mail. I was starting to get worried."

Rebecca finds herself smiling. She thinks of Lynn and Martin's budding friendship and how engrossed the two have been in each other lately.

"I'm so sorry," Lynn tells her friend. "My stupid home phone line went down yesterday on account of that pesky red squirrel in my yard—who, thank the Lord, finally met his maker on the cable after tripping it," she huffs, unloading her containers at the nurses' station. "And on top of that I took a trip to visit my brother in Edelstein and forgot my damn cellphone. I'm sorry to have worried you, Jan."

Janice stands still. "You went to Edelstein?"

"Yes, I did. I'll explain later. Are we still having dinner tonight?"

"Absolutely," Janice answers. "I'll pick you up at six."

"Sounds great," Lynn replies as she searches for something amid the baked goods. "My word. I know I had an envelope when I left the car ..."

"I've got it here," Donna pipes up.

"Oh, thank goodness. Thank you, Donna." Lynn takes the envelope and starts down the hall towards Martin's room. "See you tonight, Jan!"

Donna starts humming a few bars from 'Love Is in the Air.' Rebecca catches Janice's eye and they share a smile. *At least some people can break through all the crap,* she thinks as she reaches for a hazelnut fritter.

★★★

Martin is listening to music and resting when Lynn walks in. A smile breaks out across his face at the sight of her. Stan has company, and she stops briefly to admire the attractive young lady sitting at his bedside. The pair smiles at her. "Good day, ma'am," says Stan. "This is my friend, Cody Ann."

"Oh hello, Stan dear." Lynn extends her hand over to the beautiful young girl. "And hello, Cody Ann. I'm Lynn. Very pleased to meet you."

"Likewise," says the shy girl.

Lynn excuses herself and walks over to Martin's side of the room, pulling the curtain closed behind her. Martin reaches out his hand towards her. The black freckles on his nose and cheeks are amplified by the obvious weight loss from his face.

"Martin, are you okay?" Lynn asks, rushing to his side.

"I'm perfectly fine now that you're here, my dear." He is struggling to sit upright in his bed. Lynn adjusts his pillow and helps him along.

"You need to eat more, Martin," she scolds, worried. "Is your pain bad today?"

"I'm feeling tired, that's all. It's this bloody damp weather. My old bones don't seem to want to accept it." He shuffles himself into position. "Stop fussin', woman, and get over here. I need sugar."

Lynn giggles and moves to the edge of his bed to bend down and kiss him gently on his lips. Electricity flows between them, making Martin's toes curl up.

She runs her fingers through his thick blackish hair. "I brought you something."

Martin's energy lifts. "Chocolate mousse pie?"

"Actually, I do have some of that, too. But here's what I really want you to have at the moment."

She pulls a manila envelope from underneath her long black jacket and hands it to him. He immediately knows what it is. It's a copy of the police report from the night Stephen died.

"I'm sorry if the quality isn't great," she says. "They warned me that it might not be. But they say it's legible. Apparently anything over fifteen years old is now digitized, so I had them print it all out from scanned copies."

Martin is both nervous and excited all in the same breath. He looks at Lynn and realizes that this must have been a very difficult decision for her to make. He places his hand on hers. "Are you sure you're okay if I look into this?"

Lynn lowers her voice so that Stan and his girlfriend won't hear. "Martin, the Milligans have been like family to me for over twenty years now. I don't believe friendships like ours come along too often, and I want to do everything I can to finally help them move on from what happened to Stephen—and to James. Even though the whole terrible thing was pretty black and white, maybe you'll find something in here to help James. It should have happened years ago, and it's taking someone like you to put the pieces together. I know Aaron wanted to, but he was scared about what opening up the case might do to his family. And besides, he was always so hard on that boy ..." She shakes her head as she remembers.

"I know, Lynn, I know. I met the man, remember?"

She gives him a weak smile. "It's seems you've met *everybody*, mortal and immortal alike," she tries to joke.

"I won't tell you anything I find unless you ask me, all right?" he tells her seriously.

She nods. She places her head on his shoulder and he holds her tight.

"All right, darlin' girl?" he repeats in her ear.

"Okay, old man," she replies, making him laugh.

An hour later, Lynn is scooting out the door to get ready for her dinner with Janice. Martin is sad to see her go, but is anxious to commence the investigation.

He starts his initial scan of the documents. The first few pages are from the state police. Names of officers who arrived on the scene are noted. He finds the location, time, and weather conditions of the accident. There is information about the train and its operators, including their statements. James is listed as the main eyewitness. There are several diagrams of the crash site indicating the exact location where Stephen was struck by the train and depicting several angles. Attached to the police report is an accident investigation report from the State of Illinois Transportation Safety Board. It all appears to be as Lynn called it. *Black and white.*

"Black and white," Martin says, repeating those words again out loud. He places the documents on his lap momentarily and remembers Stan using that expression during their excursion. *I just couldn't stay black and white no more ... Babies and mothers screamin' in the corners. It was like chaos gone mad.* Martin shifts closer to the edge of his bed. Chaos gone mad. *Of course it was*, he thinks to himself. *There's no way that this situation wasn't anything but chaotic, and therefore there has to be something in this report that's going to point to exactly what caused it.*

Martin decides he needs a good cup of coffee and some of Lynn's baking to get his blood going. He slowly gets up and manages to put his housecoat and slippers on. Grabbing the files, he heads off to the small kitchen. When he passes Stan, he sees that he is lying on the bed with his pretty young woman curled up beside him. They are both watching Stan's new television set and sharing headphones. Martin waves and they wave back.

As he approaches the kitchen, he hears a familiar voice behind him. "You taking off again, Martin?" Rebecca is walking towards him with her arms crossed and a sly grin on her face.

Martin stops shuffling in his tracks. "Now, Miss Rebecca, if I remember correctly you were part of the dress rehearsal for that getaway," he replies, his sly grin outdoing hers.

She shakes her head with a smile. He knows he's got her beat. "You going for some of Lynn's goodies, huh?"

Martin nods his head yes, and as he does he loses control of the documents. Two of them fall to the ground. He panics. He's too slow to get down to retrieve them first. Just as he's about to stop her, she's already on the floor gathering them up. She slowly stands, staring at one of the papers in her hand. A look of confusion comes over her face.

"What's this?" she asks, sounding afraid to hear the answer.

"Rebecca, it's not for your eyes," Martin says sternly. "Please, just pass them back to me."

Rebecca does what she's asked and politely excuses her behavior. "Of course. I'm … I'm sorry, Martin. I just thought I saw something about Stephen Pike. But that can't be right, right?"

Martin sighs. He's not going to get out of this easily. He looks at the clock in the kitchenette. It's already past four o'clock. "Aren't you supposed to be going home shortly?"

Rebecca shakes her head no. "Miesha's best friend's mother is picking her up. She's taking the girls for dinner before dance class, so I have some down time," she explains.

Martin smiles at the mention of Miesha's name. "She's such a magical little girl," he says fondly, trying to change the subject. "She reminds me of my niece in some ways."

Rebecca nods and agrees. "I saw Kendra this morning. I haven't seen her in a while. It's good to know that she's here for you."

Martin pulls out the chocolate mousse pie and starts cutting it into slices. He notices the coffee pot is filled with what he hopes to be fresh coffee.

"Kendra's been away in London for the last month," he says proudly. "She's working on a story about some famous designer. I think it's one of the Beatles' kids," he says.

"Wow, Stella McCartney?" Rebecca has completely forgotten about the papers she wasn't supposed to see.

"Yes, I believe that's it," Martin replies, putting two slices of pie on the table. "Join me."

Rebecca looks at the pie and shrugs. "Janice told me I looked like I've lost weight, so I guess I should eat this, right?"

Martin nods. He knows why she's lost weight. "Enjoy it, dear. Besides, a man doesn't like a girl that's all skin and bones. We enjoy the curves."

"So you've told me," she reminds him. "So then why are ninety-nine percent of women obsessed with their bodies?"

"Don't know," says Martin, chewing his pie. "But I do know that ninety-nine percent of men are obsessed with women's bodies, too."

Rebecca laughs and jumps up to grab coffee.

"Speaking of men," he ventures. "How are things going with Neil?"

"Fine, I guess," Rebecca says, pulling a carton of milk out of the fridge and checking its expiration date. "I mean, it's easy, you know? It's cut and dry."

"You mean black and white," Martin says, correcting her.

"Doesn't that mean kind of the same thing?" Rebecca replies, setting a cup of coffee down in front of him.

"Never mind. I've just been hearing that a lot lately, that's all. Though I'm not so sure anything is either of those things—cut and dry or black and white."

"Well, as far as Neil goes, there are no surprises. We get together, have a good time, and then he goes back to his world and I go back to mine."

Martin puts his fork down. "So there's no real attachment? No real sentimental value to the relationship, then?" She's about to reply but he forges on. "Your heart and soul aren't being exercised? There isn't any self-exploration or mutual growth happening? No exchanging of morals and values or good and bad habits? You're simply just planted there in time, without any expectation of who the other person really is or, more importantly, what they can rise up to be?"

Rebecca's mouth is still partially open. "Uh, yeah. Isn't that cut and dry, or, uh … black and white?"

Martin huffs. "Sounds more like chaos gone mad to me."

Rebecca laughs. "What on earth are you getting at, Martin?"

"I heard that quote not long ago and it struck me as very profound," he replies.

"And what do you think it means?" she asks.

"In order for one to feel life, shouldn't one *experience* life and not just go *through* it?" he asks.

"I don't think anyone wants to go through life experiencing chaos," she states skeptically.

Martin's eyes widen. "Have you ever seen the famous Charles Allen Gilbert black and white illustration, *All Is Vanity?*" he asks.

Rebecca looks completely dumbfounded. "It sounds vaguely familiar."

Martin describes the image to her. "It depicts a grinning skull, but when you look at it closely, you can see a beautiful young girl gazing at her own reflection in the mirror."

"Yes, of course!" Rebecca recalls. "I remember being mesmerized by that drawing as a kid. It was in one of my dad's art books."

"It became one of the most commercially successful marketing images of its time," explains Martin.

Rebecca laughs. "So now that we've established that, what's your point?"

Martin tries to be patient. "The point is that the illustration is merely an optical illusion. From one perspective you find the symbol of youth and beauty, but from another, you're warned of life's brevity and looming death."

Rebecca shrugs her shoulders. "So?"

"So what I'm trying to get at is that sometimes the elements in life that appear simple and obvious turn out to be the most difficult and complex ones to accept. And in the case of this particular illustration, it all depends on how you look at it."

"Is this about James?" she asks suspiciously.

Martin looks straight into her eyes. "I don't know. Is it?"

Rebecca's eyes narrow. "Why do you have a document with Stephen Pike's name on it, Martin?"

"Because, Miss Rebecca, I'm looking to have a similar chat with our mutual friend James."

"Why do you care so much about him?" she asks.

"Don't be exclusive, my dear. I also care about you and his mother and Kitty and Lynn. You're all affected by his inability to see himself as he truly is. When he sees himself, it's like he's looking at the vanity illustration. He is, in a sense, chaos gone mad. And nobody knows how that feels more than I do."

A brief silence settles over the small kitchen table. "Lynn told me about your friend Frank," Rebecca finally says. "I can't even imagine …"

"No, you can't. But Jimmy can. He not only imagines it, he lives it in his heart every day, and the older he gets, the closer to the perpetual darkness he gets."

"What do those papers have to do with it?"

Rebecca waits for Martin to explain, but he chooses to remain silent.

"I want to help, Martin. Please."

Martin looks up from his empty plate. "If you want to help, don't turn your back on him. Give him time." Martin knows this is not the response she's looking for. "I know this is hard on you, Rebecca, but you have to trust me on this. When the time comes, I'll tell you everything."

"Sure," she replies sadly. "Until then, I'll just keep waiting." She sighs. "I have to go now, Martin. Thanks for the mousse and the chat. I'll be waiting to hear from you."

She leaves the room with tears in her eyes. Martin cannot help but feel bad for turning her help away. He has to figure this out in private in order to protect Lynn. In time, all will be well.

It starts to rain as Rebecca leaves the hospital, and her thoughts are churning in her head. How could she have any feelings left for James after the way he's treated her? And is Martin right—is she only seeing what she wants to see in her relationship with Neil in order to avoid having to look at the darkness attached to James and her feelings for him?

"Shoot." She smacks her lips as she remembers that she has to stop at the library to get a book on Russian ballet for Miesha's art class project. It's at moments like this when Rebecca resents being a single mother. The exhaustion is sometimes overwhelming, and there just doesn't seem to be enough moments for her, the woman. Most of the time these thoughts don't even enter her mind because she loves being a mother and considers Miesha to be her grounding life force. But on days like today, there are fleeting moments when exhaustion overrides everything.

Rebecca enters the city's central library for the first time since moving to this part of the city. The building seems foreign and strange. She is oddly uncomfortable, but at the same time she is enjoying the sense of academia filling the quiet space. She wanders around, finds a computer, and types in the name of the book. Miraculously, the information pops right up—*The History of Russian Ballet* by Mikela Balk. Beside the name is the location indicator. Rebecca scribbles it down on a small square of paper and turns to look for the section.

She's walking down the aisles of the performance arts section, marveling at all the beautiful and fascinating books. *Why don't I ever come here?* She proceeds to the next aisle and sees a row of Asian art and dance books. Before she can advance, however, she finds herself nose to nose with a familiar face coming around the corner. They are both caught completely off guard.

Rebecca swallows hard. "Hello, James." She is stupefied and feels the need to explain why she's there. "I have to pick up a book for Miesha," she says, her voice shaking. "On ballet."

James doesn't seem to know what to do or say, either. He catches her eye but immediately looks away. Rebecca looks down, feeling defeated. *He can't even look at me,* she realizes. "Well, goodbye. It was nice to see you again," she manages. And then she turns to walk away.

"The Ballerina!" James suddenly calls after her.

Rebecca turns around. "Pardon?"

"I said, *The Ballerina*. It's a book by Richard Austin. It's about the greatest dancers of all time. Um … Pavlova, Spessivtzeva, Fonteyn, Makarova—you know, all the famous ones."

"Really?" A light goes on in Rebecca's heart. She shows James the scribble on the paper. "She told me to get this one."

He moves in to read the title. He smells of exotic woods and orchids mixed together. "Yeah, that's a good one too, if you want more of a history of the art. But *The Ballerina* will give her some really good insight into the actual dancers themselves. Maybe you could get both." He begins to look more comfortable in her presence as he takes on the professorial role. "Come on, it's over here."

Rebecca trails behind as he walks down the row, running his fingers along the spines of the books. Rebecca's heart melts as she watches his hands. He suddenly stops and pulls a hardcover off the shelf to show her. "See? Take a look at the table of contents. This is more of a living history than an encyclopedia of facts."

Rebecca reaches out to take the book and her hand graces his. Instantly she notices a flutter in her stomach and remembers Martin's words. *If you want to help, don't turn your back on him.* She moves closer and finds herself kissing him in the quietness of the performing arts section of the library. She wraps her arms around his neck and, for that moment, she knows nothing else except that she loves him.

He slowly pulls away from her. She opens her eyes and sees his mouth open to say something, but no words come out. He hands her the book and moves quickly out of her space, then disappears through the maze of library rows.

Chaos gone mad, Rebecca thinks to herself.

FIFTEEN

"Today is November 11, and it's the day to honor and remember," says Miesha. "And no school!"

Rebecca looks in the rear-view mirror at her daughter with love and pride. "Are you looking forward to your celebration at dance camp today?"

"Yeah, it's going to be really cool. We have some soldiers coming in to read poems to us, and we're going to sing a few songs and then we get to do a ballet for them. Oh, and after that, we get to watch the ceremony at Soldier Field on a big television screen!"

Rebecca smiles into the mirror. Miesha is wearing a red and white tweed jacket, a red bonnet, white tights, and black leather ankle boots. Her wavy hair is falling around her beautiful round face, and her perfect cherry lips make her look adorable. "You look really pretty, girl," says Rebecca.

"Thanks, Mom. You too." She looks out the car window. "Mom, I don't know why, but I always feel sad on this day."

Rebecca sighs with empathy. "I know, baby girl. That's normal though. It's because we feel for those brave men and women who died and suffered so much in all the wars so we could have a good life."

"Why do we even have to have war, Mom?"

"Honey, I'm not really sure if anyone has the answer to that question." As soon as the words are out of her mouth, she thinks of at least two people who actually would have an answer to it—James and Martin.

"People fight each other over God sometimes, and I think that's just really dumb," says Miesha, taking a bite of her cereal bar.

Rebecca embraces her daughter's astute comment. "The most important thing

161

is that *you* don't fight, honey. I believe if we each do our own little part and learn to respect each other's beliefs within our own circle of friends and family, then in the end, the world will be a more peaceful place."

"So war is kind of like … like bullying?"

"Hmmm … Yes, I think it's kind of like that."

"I'll never be a bully!" announces Miesha.

"I know, and I'm *very* proud of you."

Rebecca stops in front of Miesha's dance school and helps her out of her booster seat. She runs after her with her dance bag and gives her the usual goodbye hug and kiss—only this time, she takes an extra minute to do it. "Thank you, love."

"For what, Mom?"

"For being my precious angel and for making my day." Rebecca rubs her daughter's chin with her thumb and pats her on the back. Miesha shoulders the big bag and runs up the steps to the front entrance of the school, where four other girls from her class scream with excitement at her arrival.

Miesha's head pops out of the circle and she yells goodbye to Rebecca through the squeals of eight- and nine-year-old laughter. Rebecca laughs and gets back into her car. *Okay, time to face the day.*

She's feeling nervous at the prospect of seeing James today. It's been two days since their little encounter in the library, and she hasn't been able to stop thinking about it ever since. She's given up on trying to make sense of it, but still it continues to fill her mind every waking moment.

The hospital is only a short drive away and she has lots of time, so she decides to swing by the coffee shop around the corner to grab a decent cup and maybe a quick muffin. As she's pulling into the parking lot she sees Olivia, one of the young hospital volunteers, running out of the place laughing. A second later Neil is behind her, smacking her behind. Olivia turns around, beaming a perfect smile and giggling as he pulls her in close to his chest and kisses her.

"Damn," Rebecca says under her breath and with inflection. She immediately thinks of Martin's cryptic proverb. *Whoever eats chili gets burned.*

She quickly steps out of the car in order to intercept the pair. "Say, hi there you two lovebirds!" Rebecca shouts from across the parking lot.

Olivia's jaw drops. Neil knows he's been caught. He starts to walk towards Rebecca, but she puts her hand up to stop him. "You know what, Neil? No explanation needed. And quite frankly, if I hear any stupid excuses, I will very likely throw up all over your stupid white boat shoes. I mean really, Neil. Boat shoes?" She storms off into the coffee shop trying hard not to laugh, but she can't help herself.

By ten o'clock, Rebecca and the rest of the staff is busy organizing the majority of the hospital's palliative veterans inside the small chapel for the on-site ceremony. The walls are pasted with poppy drawings from local school children, and the vets like looking at them. There is extra staff on board including Janice and Kitty. Kitty has managed to escape home for a few hours to help out with this special event, which she insisted on celebrating on behalf of her own personal war heroes—her father and grandfather. The veterans are excited to see her. She's managing with a cane now, and although she walks and talks a little slower than she used to, she's still a wildcat.

Martin and Stan have wartime music playing in their room, and it floats through the hallways of the fourth floor. Stan is helping Martin get dressed, as Martin is feeling particularly feeble today. His hipbone is throbbing, shooting pain down into his femur. Stan is talking too much, as usual, and Martin keeps thinking about the railway investigation report he's read three times in the last forty-eight hours. He's exhausted from his snooping, but it hasn't been without cause.

The envelope with the report lies on his bed, and Martin looks at it while he goes over the information in his mind one more time before seeing James. All of the factual information in the report is divided into sections, making it easier to look through: accident description, injuries, weather, recorded information, train and crew information, engine and whistle, regulations. The report goes on in full detail, including photos from every angle of the accident scene.

Freight train travelling eastward on the south main track … Pedestrian walking westward on the south main track when struck by train 102 … At the time of the accident, warning lights and bells were activated when the train entered the crossing's approach track circuit … All mechanicals in accordance with American Railway Engineering and Maintenance Association standards …

Martin interrupts Stan's ministrations. "My friend, can you go easy on the tie, please? You tryin' to choke me or something?"

"Oh, sorry, man," says Stan as he loosens the knot.

Martin's mind returns to the folder. *The crew of 102 consisted of a locomotive engineer and a conductor. Both were qualified for their respective positions and met all fitness and rest standards …* Something trips his mind back to the police accident report. *Engineer says the man was walking eastward, with his back to the oncoming train …* But according to the railway report, *Pedestrian walking westward…*

"Conflicting statements in each report," Martin says out load.

"You goin' on about that report again, roomie?" Stan's voice interrupts his

163

revelation. "Cheese whiz on a corn dog, am I ever gonna get the real juice on that story?" Stan gripes. He puts the finishing touches on Martin's military attire. "There, you look like a million-dollar man!" He spins his friend around to face the mirror that hangs beside the closet.

Martin sees himself looking distinguished in his naval uniform and decorative metals. He smiles at Stan's reflection. "You look mighty good yourself …" Stan straightens his shoulders at the compliment before Martin finishes, "… for a southern girl." The two men laugh out loud.

Just then Lynn comes into the room. "Oh my Lord, would you look at you two!" she says, gushing at the handsome pair. "Let me take a picture." She positions them together and tells them both to smile before snapping the shot. "Fabulous," she says.

Stan takes the camera from her. "Here, let me take a picture of y'all."

Martin puts his arm around Lynn's waist and pulls her in close. He feels like he's on his way to the prom.

"Smitten," remarks Stan with his goofy grin.

Lynn smirks. "Well, my dear Martin, James is waiting downstairs for you in his car by the front door. Oh, and don't forget this." She grabs the envelope off his bed and hands it to him. "Shall I walk you?"

"No, that's quite all right, love. I can manage. Besides, I know you have to help get the rest of the oldies onto the bus. Stan, you're helping too, right?"

"Yes, sir. I promised Janice."

Martin kisses Lynn on the cheek. "By the way, you look stunning," he says into her ear.

"I'll see you over there, bro," says Stan. Martin shakes his friend's hand and heads out the door. He passes Max, Gerry, and four other comrades in the lobby. Gerry whistles out a cat call as Martin steps onto the elevator. The doors start to shut. "I salute you, my friends," he shouts as he raises his middle finger. The doors close and all the men burst out laughing, Martin included.

On November 11, at eleven o'clock, Soldier Field Stadium hosts the best-attended Veterans Day celebration in the history of Chicago. The wreath-laying ceremony and gun salute silence the crowd as the cool gray sky embellishes the atmosphere. The keynote speaker is a Purple Heart recipient who lost his legs in Korea in a grenade explosion. He managed to save a convoy of troops ahead of him by intercepting the launch with his armored utility vehicle. He wrote a book about his recovery and now mentors other veterans through their healing process and integration back into civilian life. Martin knows exactly who he is; he's met him at several charity functions over the years, including a few times at the Aaron Milligan Veterans' Hospital.

James is his usual quiet self throughout the ceremony, but Martin can tell that he's listening carefully to all the speakers and that he is profoundly aware of the importance of this particular day. When the ceremony ends, James becomes clearly agitated by the sea of people swarming around the stadium, trying to make their way towards the various exits. Martin knows that his growing anxiety will not help the situation that's about to transpire between them. However, in his heart, he knows that there is no other way and that time is running out. James is planning to leave for Southeast Asia in a few days, and Martin wants to help him leave his past baggage behind him.

The walk to the car is too much for Martin to take today so James directs him to stay put while he fetches the car. A group of active African-American soldiers from the morning's parade walk over to Martin for a chat. Seeing them lifts his spirits and he feels a boost of energy surge through his body.

After a few minutes, James appears with the car and Martin salutes his new friends. *It's going to be a long ride*, he thinks to himself.

★★★

James has no idea he is about to be ambushed. The silence between him and Martin is so uncomfortable that James has no choice but to finally muster the courage to ask the question he's been holding close to his chest for days. "Okay, Martin, I'll bite. Why did you want *me* specifically to take you to the ceremony?" Agitation is evident in his tone.

The old soldier takes a deep breath. "Before I tell you, I'd like you to take me to one last stop."

James feels his hands gripping the steering wheel more aggressively now. "Martin, with all due respect, I'm really not enjoying these types of games that you like to play. As you probably know, I'm leaving for Asia the day after tomorrow and I have a lot of loose ends to tie up beforehand."

"Mr. Jimmy." Martin's voice is surprisingly firm. "You know I respect you, too, and that's why I need you to take me to one more place today and then I'm gone. I'm out of your hair."

Martin's words make James feel extremely uneasy. He decides the path of least resistance is his best game plan. "Fine. Where to? And will you at least tell me why?"

"I need you to cut an old man some slack, boy. *Crescat scientia; vita excolatur.*"

"*Let knowledge grow and thereby enrich human life*," James translates easily. "It's the motto of the University of Chicago."

"Yes, and I'd like to go there if you don't mind."

"I *do* mind, but obviously I'm not getting out of this." Tension is building inside the car. James is feeling completely in the dark. He's sorry he forgot his Xanax.

165

"I knew your father," says Martin softly.

James looks away from the road momentarily to stare at Martin. "I *know* that."

"No, you don't. You *don't* know that. How could you?"

"Because my mother told me."

"But did she tell you *how* I knew your father?"

"No," James admits, staring sideways at him. "Just that you knew him. You couldn't have known him all that well, though. I don't recall seeing you at his funeral, and I never heard him speak of you."

"Watch the road and listen," Martin instructs. "Your father and I met when I was drafted to war in the 60s. He'd already been there a year before I joined and he quickly made an impression with the upper crust. Anyway, we were the first ground troops to break into the Vietnamese jungle and he was one of the leaders." Martin pauses briefly as he reflects. "We grew up together quite quickly during those first few weeks, Jimmy. It was a war that none of us understood, but nevertheless, we had a job to do and we needed to get it done. Yes, your father could be incredibly callous, but most of the time he had my back. Before he became Staff Sergeant and moved to another operation, he introduced me to my best friend and new comrade, Frank Kenney. I'll always be grateful to him for that."

James is pulling into the University of Chicago grounds. He winds his way over to the Oriental Museum area and sees that the place is dead quiet. "You said *that he had your back most of the time*. What do you mean by that?"

"Let's just say that at first your dad wasn't a big fan of the black man," Martin says wryly.

James chortles and shakes his head in disapproval. "Man, I am *so* not surprised."

Martin waves it off. "I eventually won him over. We had plenty of time together in Vietnam. We used to talk about world issues, history, politics … all that good stuff. He used to call me Webster—you know, like the dictionary."

James is incredulous. "So *you're* Webster?"

"I suppose I am."

"Why didn't you come to his funeral?"

"We kept in touch for a long time, Jimmy. But honestly, it was always hit and miss with Aaron. Besides, my brother died the same month so I was kind of tied up. But I *am* sorry I missed it." Martin pauses, momentarily lost in thought. "We did talk about a year before he died, though. He told me all about his family's hospital in Chicago. That's how I knew to register there when I got word about my cancer."

James shifts uncomfortably. Talk of his father or of cancer always makes him antsy.

Martin says his next words cautiously. "He told me back then that his son was having trouble. He said he wanted some advice. It was a long time ago, but I always wondered what became of you. When I got sick, I knew I'd be coming here to Chicago and that you'd be here."

James is stunned. "He talked to you about *me*? Fuck!" He slams his hands on the steering wheel. "Listen, Martin," he says, seething, "I don't want to hear any more about this, okay? Now can we please go?" The words are grinding through his teeth. He starts to feel the panic emerging.

Martin hands James an envelope. "Not quite. First I want you to look at this."

James looks at the brown envelope with confusion.

"Go on," Martin quips. "Open it. Then maybe we can get on with it."

James is too exhausted to fight. He pulls out the documents and starts scanning them. His heart starts to beat rapidly when he sees the date, and even harder when he reads the report title. He flips through the pages, his eyes wide as they scan the information. He is frantically trying to digest the words that are jumping off the page at him. *Stephen Pike ... pedestrian killed ...* He's panting now. "What—what is this? What *is* this?" Panic sears his heart. He pulls out the National Transportation Safety Board report and it feels like he will suffocate. "What the hell, Martin? What is this? Why are you giving me this?" He can barely catch enough breath to force out the words.

"Jimmy, look into your mind and see it. See Stephen that night, on the tracks. What happened? Let yourself see the truth." Martin's voice is low and monotone.

"Goddamn it, Martin! I already *know* what happened, and I sure as hell don't need you and these fucking pieces of paper to tell me anything about it!"

"Yes you do, Jimmy. Look at the information. Look at it! What happened that night?"

James opens the car door with such force that he spills out onto the pavement, landing on his knees. He's heaving, trying desperately to catch his breath. Martin opens his door and comes around the car to kneel in front of James.

"He was there with his headphones on, Jimmy. Sure he was. But look at what the national report says, Jimmy. Look at it!"

James is sitting on the cold ground with the report in his lap. Pain pierces his stomach. His head is swimming. "I can't breathe," he whimpers.

Martin hobbles over to his side. "Oh yes you can."

"I don't want to see this, Martin. Please stop!"

"It says right *there* in the report that Stephen was walking *west* on the tracks." Martin stabs at the pieces of paper as he makes his accusation.

"Shut up!" James screams. He cups his hands over his ears but he can still hear Martin talking.

"Tell me what happened, Jimmy. Tell *yourself* what really happened."

James leaps onto his feet. The pages scatter everywhere. "You want to know

167

what happened, Martin? I killed him! It was all my fault. I couldn't do it!'"

"Do *what*, Jimmy? Save him?" Martin throws his arms up in the air. His cane drops to his side.

"No!" James yells. He wraps his arms around his waist and hugs himself. His guts are betraying him. "No," he repeats, his voice calmer now. "Love him like that."

Martin approaches him slowly. He is nodding. "That's okay, boy. Go back there and remember what happened. Tell yourself the truth and then let it go. The most important thing is to realize that it's not your fault. There was nothing you could have done to change the situation."

James can barely even think. "Aaron ... Aaron always thought that Stephen and I ... that we ..." he trails off. He cannot finish the thought.

"I know," Martin says. "He told me."

Martin is standing next to him with his hand on James's shoulder. The air is turning cold and James is suddenly feeling the effects of the wind and the emotional strain. He barely realizes that he is sobbing, but with each wrenching motion, his memories unravel piece by piece. He sees it all clearly now—sees what he's made himself forget for almost twenty years. *Freight train travelling eastward ... pedestrian walking westward ...*

★★★

The night's warm breeze flows across the fields near Princeville's West Hillock Cemetery, carrying the smell of fresh tobacco up into the country air and over to North Rice Road. James and Stephen are walking back from a bonfire party to celebrate their last week of summer vacation together. As they stagger along towards the town of Edelstein, they enjoy their unique brand of playful banter. James can't help but think about a young girl he was eyeing all night. He can't stop talking about her sweeping dark hair, smoky eyes, and large sumptuous breasts.

Stephen takes off his black and white Bob Dylan t-shirt and dangles it over his head to simulate the girl's long hair. He starts winking and smacking his lips at James, and then mocks a young woman's walk and talk.

James falls to the ground, rolling with laughter. When he stills, he lies on his back and stares up at the clear night sky. Stephen staggers over and lies down beside him. He puts his headphones on and starts singing along to his favorite Beatles song, which is playing on his new walkman—a graduation present from his parents.

James has his eyes closed and his arms crossed behind his head. He can't stop thinking of the girl. Stephen takes off his headphones and places them over James's ears, then turns up the volume. The song fills the night for James, but he can faintly

hear Stephen's voice speaking through the music. Without removing the headphones or opening his eyes, James turns his attention to registering what Stephen
is saying. At first he is confused and thinks he is misunderstanding his best friend's
words. But soon there is no doubt in James's mind: Stephen is confessing his love
for him. James doesn't know how to react, so he pretends that the music is too loud
for him to understand what Stephen's saying.

Deep in his heart, James has always known how deeply Stephen loved him,
and as much as Stephen's poorly veiled affections were at times uncomfortable for
James, they were also very reassuring. He was loved by at least one man in his life,
even if it wasn't his father. And James felt that Stephen understood him more than
anyone else on the planet. They were bonded in mind, heart, and spirit. He closes
his eyes tightly and wonders what he should do. He knows that Stephen indulged
in a lot of booze and pot at the bonfire, which is usual for him, but it also makes
him unruly if things don't go his way. James knows his friend well, and knows that
he must tread carefully.

Tonight is likely their last night together in Edelstein. They've come here every
summer over the last six years to visit Stephen's aunt and uncle. Soon, they will be
travelling down their separate paths to attend college in different cities. James thinks
that perhaps their imminent parting is the reason for his best friend's behavior
tonight. They have less than two months left together, and maybe Stephen's getting his feelings confused after a night of hard partying. James dismisses his friend's
words as passing prattle.

He starts to drift deeper into his thoughts when he realizes that Stephen is caressing his hair. James feels a disturbing warm glow in his groin area, and an unexpected
feeling of shame shadows over him. He's not prepared to open his eyes and acknowledge that Stephen's fingers are rubbing his crotch and making their way towards his
pants button. For a split second James considers caving into Stephen's power, but he
instinctively pushes his friend's hand away. He opens his eyes and meets Stephen's
gaze. He's not sure he'll be able to resist if Stephen makes another advance.

Stephen moves in closer. He places his hand up James's shirt and starts caressing
his pectorals. James feels his nipples hardening and the glow in his crotch persists.
Before James can respond, he feels Stephen's tongue swimming inside his mouth.
Stephen's body presses harder against him, and he is unable to control his own response. He feels the small of Stephen's back with his hands and accepts the lustful
exchange for a few seconds before pushing him off.

"I'm sorry," says James, unable to think of anything else to say.

"I'm not," Stephen calmly replies.

James feels like his world is about to cave in. His heart is racing and he can barely move his mouth to speak. "I'm sorry, Stevie, but I can't."

"Can't, or won't?" Stephen asks.

James can't stop the blood from rushing below his belt. He jumps onto his feet to shake off the situation. He starts to pace around in a circle, rubbing his hands on his head to redirect the blood flow.

"I don't know what's going on here, man, but I'm not comfortable with this," he says. He feels frightened. Everything that's happened over the last seven years of his life now feels foreign, tainted.

Stephen sits up. "I just thought … I've always sort of thought that you … And now that we're going to be so far away …" he begins, then trails off. A look of pain slowly passes over his face, then is suppressed. His face hardens.

James can see the demon in his friend's eyes trying to escape and feels terrified. Something has changed between them. Their perfect past together is erased, and all he can see is a future spent as distant strangers. He is suddenly startled by a maniacal fit of laughter that echoes past him into the distance.

Stephen has thrown back his head and is laughing a laugh that sounds more like the howl of a snared animal. James checks Stephen's face to try to gage whether or not this is all some kind of a twisted joke. Stephen laughs even harder, like a crazy person.

James finally decides to believe the supposed gag and sits back down on the ground across from his friend. He throws the headphones at Stephen. "You little bastard!" he says, beyond relieved. "Oh, thank God! I thought that you … that you—!" He rolls over onto his stomach, smashing the ground with his fist, unable to control his own spastic laughter. He stops just as he hears the sound of a train in the distance.

By the time he sits up and opens his eyes, he sees that Stephen is fast approaching the train tracks. Just before he reaches them, Stephen turns and faces James with no expression. The wind tosses his long blond locks around his jaw and tangles them in his black headphones. From across the field, Stephen is bellowing along with the tune in his ears. "I'd love to turn … you … on …"

He turns his back on James again and jumps onto one of the track rails, simulating a balancing act. James nervously jumps up from the ground and starts to walk towards the tracks, grabbing Stephen's discarded t-shirt along the way. "Hey, man, come on! Don't you want your Dylan shirt?" The sound of the train is amplifying, and the vibration is numbing the soles of his feet. "Steve!" he calls, but there's no response. "Steve, come on, man! Stop fucking around!"

Stephen is still teetering on the tracks, headphones over his ears. The sound of the train horn repeats over and over, exasperating James's growing panic. James starts to run with all his might towards the tracks, screaming Stephen's name until his voice leaves him. His heart is pumping blood through his veins at a rapid speed. The train comes around the corner and soon it is in full view, its whistle blowing frantically. Its headlight seems to find Stephen's back like a giant spotlight. James is running as fast as he can towards the tracks, but it's clear the train will reach him first. The engine's brakes begin to squeal, but the hurtling steel and iron doesn't seem to slow at all.

"Stephen!" James wails, but the last syllable is choked out in a sob. Just then, Stephen turns around to face the oncoming train, and in the headlight James can see that his best friend's face is covered in tears. Stephen spreads his arms open wide and tips his head up towards the sky. His long locks are flowing around his naked shoulders in a way that reminds James of Jesus on the cross. A peaceful acceptance suddenly replaces Stephen's defeatist demeanor.

James stops short of the tracks and shouts out his friend's name one last time, but his voice is small and winded. "Stephen …"

The train is desperate to stop, but it can't. The metal wheels grind, trying with all their might to resist the brakes. James thinks his eardrums will burst from the sound. The piercing whine is replaced by a terrifying hiss, and then everything becomes silent for James as the freight cars speed along before his eyes.

The emotional impact shocks James into a vacant state. Officially broken, he falls to his knees.

SIXTEEN

"How is he?" Lynn whispers.

Stan is sitting on the edge of his bed, adjusting his television set. "I reckon he's doin' all right, ma'am, on account of everythin' he's been through over the last few days."

Lynn feels anxious. "I'm just so worried … and so angry with myself for allowing him to go through with his crazy plan."

Stan stands up and walks over to her. "Ma'am, you can't blame yourself. Hell, I *live* with the dude, and there was nothin' he wanted to do more—and he was gonna do it whether you wanted him to or not."

"In my heart I know that, Stan, but now he's so ill … The stress of it all almost killed him!" She looks across the room. To her, Martin seems to be as tiny as a church mouse. "Look at him!"

Stan reaches for her hand. "I'm tellin' you, I don't know much, but I do know somethin' about being a solider. And helpin' out yer fellow comrades is ingrained in yer blood. He never forgot what his buddy Aaron said to him before he died, and when he came here and met y'all … Well, how could he not do what needed to be done?"

Martin stirs in his bed. "Is that you, Lynn?" His voice is weak and unrecognizable.

Lynn rushes over to his side. "Yes, dear, I'm right here."

"Oh, good," he says in a weak voice. "Give me some lovin'." He reaches out a thin hand to grab her behind.

"Martin Diggs, you dirty ol' fool! Lord, even in the worst of times you manage to think about the unthinkable."

Stan laughs. "Okay, well, I guess that's my cue to leave. I'm gonna go find Julie

173

and ask her for some decent grub."

"There's some leftover lasagna in the small fridge, dear. Just help yourself," replies Lynn.

"Much obliged, ma'am. Thank you."

Martin's eyes are closed again and his breathing is shallow. Lynn strokes his hair as she looks up at the morphine drip hanging by the side of his bed. Her eyes brim with tears. She and Martin have become exceptionally close over the past few months and she can't bear to see him in so much pain. She has been looking for a way to accept the idea that he won't be with her forever. When the answer doesn't arrive, she can only pray. *Please, God, not now. Please give us more time.*

Dr. Lewis arrives with a nurse she doesn't recognize. "Hi, Lynn. How are you holding up?"

Lynn doesn't say a word and just shrugs her shoulders.

"Can we have a few minutes to check our patient?" the doctor asks gently.

"Oh, of course. I'll be right outside." Lynn leaves the room and finds a corner of the hallway to rest her shoulder on. She recounts the events that transpired only a few days before Martin's decline.

Martin called Lynn from a cellphone Kendra had purchased for him for emergencies. He was in the parking lot of the Oriental Museum at the University of Chicago. He told her that he was there with James, and that James was in bad shape—possibly suffering from a PTSD flashback—and he asked if she and Janice could come pick them up. Someone needed to look after James to make sure he was going to be all right. Lynn managed to reach Janice at the hospital, and of course she dropped everything to be there for her son.

When the two women arrived, they found James huddled in the back seat of his car. Martin was standing beside the hood, not saying a word. Janice looked through the window at her damaged son and began to cry.

"What happened?" she gasped, opening the rear door and reaching for James.

"Mom, I'm okay," Lynn heard him say. "Please. Stop."

"All right, honey. That's fine. Come on, let me take you home." James glanced through the rear window at Martin. It was like he was a traumatized child looking for permission.

"You're going to be okay, son," Martin said. "Go on. It's all over now. You're okay," he said softly.

Janice walked around the vehicle and stood beside the driver's door. "Did he hurt himself? Should I take him to the hospital?" she asked Martin.

Martin shook his head no.

"Was it one of his panic attacks?" she asked quietly.

"Just take him home," was all Martin said.

Reluctantly, Janice nodded and then looked at Lynn. "I'll call you later." Then she got in her son's car and slowly began to reverse.

Lynn and Martin stood together in the parking lot, shivering. Lynn could see that Martin was becoming pale and was in pain. "Okay, mister, let's get you home, too."

Martin lowered his face to the cold pavement. "It had to be done," he murmured as he shuffled around to the passenger door of Lynn's Buick. She had no idea what he was talking about, and she wasn't sure she wanted to find out.

"Lynn?" Dr. Lewis calls from down the hallway.

Lynn snaps out of her thoughts. "Oh?" she replies, quickly making her way back towards Martin's room. She stops nervously in front of the doctor.

"It looks like Martin has pneumonia," the doctor tells her. "His latest scans show a mass in his lungs, and we think that's what it is given his fever and cough. However, his white count is also up, which makes us a little concerned about what his scans are showing. But we won't know anything for sure until he's strong enough to do a biopsy. In the meantime, we're going to put him on a course of strong antibiotics to see if his immune system gets a boost. If the mass doesn't go down and his symptoms don't dissipate, it may be that the cancer has spread."

Lynn's heart sinks to the bottom of her soul. "But he said the cancer in his leg and hip was under control … He said his surgery last year made it almost certain that the cancer wouldn't spread …" her voice trails off. Even to her own ears, her statements sound like pleas.

The doctor rubs Lynn's arm. "Because he refused the chemotherapy before, there's a real chance that it could return."

Lynn's head bows. She can hear Martin's voice in her mind, recounting why he believes it useless for a man his age to undergo such a course of treatment when it would probably only buy him a year or two at most. "But let's not even think about crossing that bridge until we have to, okay, Lynn?" the doctor continues. "For now, let's just assume that it's a bad case of pneumonia—which is nothing we can't handle. Okay?"

She nods, and the doctor leaves her to her thoughts. Once again terror overtakes her at the idea of life without Martin. Even though she's only known him for a few months, it was as though she's had as much history with him as she did with Dean, her husband of twenty-seven years.

She peers inside the room and sees that Mark is changing Martin's intravenous bag and scribbling down information into his chart. Lynn knows she has the daunting task of calling Kendra to give her an update on her uncle's condition. She wishes things were different.

★★★

Despite Janice's pleading, James is boarding a plane for Southeast Asia just forty-eight hours after his traumatic discovery. He has been the warden of his own secret for years, and yet Martin, a complete stranger, has held the skeleton key all this time. James is both amused and disturbed by this newfound reality.

He sits on the Chicago O'Hare International Airport tarmac along with the other two hundred and seventy-five passengers aboard the Boeing 747 that is scheduled to take off any minute. He has so many thoughts and feelings rumbling around inside his head that he can't seem to nail any of them down for long enough to get a clearer picture. All he knows is that he wants to examine his present being, find his future path, and finally put his past to rest. As the plane takes off down the runway, James closes his eyes. The pull of gravity inside of his ribs instantly reminds him of Rebecca.

★★★

While James ascends into the early morning air, Martin is grounded in a deep drug-induced sleep. The morphine continues to provide him with the luxury of experiencing three-dimensional dreams and vivid apparitions. This time, he is submerged in dark and murky waters of the Mekong River Delta, fully clothed in his combat gear and struggling against something that he can't make out. He frantically claws at his own skin and kicks his legs wildly. Just when he is sure he's about to drown, a strong arm reaches down into the muddy waters, grabs hold of his collar, and pulls him up for air. He crawls onto the grass and anxiously starts to pull off his wet shirt. Large brownish black leeches are sucking his blood through the skin of his arms, legs, back, and chest.

"Holy shite!" Frank shouts when he sees the large black parasites.

Martin is breathing heavily, trying not to panic.

"'Ere, buddy, just close yer eyes and stay calm. I'm gonna take care of this, by."

Martin starts to take deep breaths, despite the fact that he can feel the leeches pulsating on his legs and buttocks. In a moment, all of his calm has evaporated. "Jesus!" he cries hysterically, then starts to peel off his pants.

Frank grabs a hold of him. "Lard di'en' dumpin' by'! Take it easy now. Just calm yerself and stay still now."

Martin goes back into his mind and attempts to slow his heart rate through meditation again. Little points of pressure release about ten seconds apart. Martin feels his body relax. When he opens his eyes, he sees Frank burning the leeches off one by one with his cigarette. He finishes clearing Martin's torso and moves down to his lower body, working with precision. Martin can feel the pinching dissipate from his quads, hamstrings, and shins.

When it's all over and done, Frank pats him on the shoulder. He snaps open Martin's underwear to check for any more of the water slugs in his 'nether regions' and starts laughing hysterically.

Martin extends his hands upwards. "What?"

"I'm not sure what's sadder," Frank snorts. "Dem der leeches or yer measly hog, by!" He's laughing so hard now that tears are squirting out the corners of his eyes.

Martin walks over to their camp area and grabs a blanket to dry himself. He turns to Frank, who is still wiping away tears, and recites his usual second-hand wisdom. "A gentle tongue is a tree of life, but perverseness in it breaks the spirit."

Frank looks puzzled. "What in hell does that mean, by?"

"No point in doing something kind if you add a bit of nastiness to it," Martin replies.

"Ay," says Frank thoughtfully, and then a dash of fun comes into his eyes. "I shoulda left ya writhin', then, till I could think up somethin' nice to say 'bout yer bits."

Both men laugh. Martin is grateful to his friend. "Seriously, thanks buddy."

"Ah, na, 'twas nothin' you wouldn't've done fer me, by," Franks says, throwing a smoke over to Martin.

"That's true," Martin replies. "You're right, I'd do anything for you, brother."

Martin awakens to see Dr. Lewis hovering over him. "Good afternoon, Martin," he says, smiling. "I'm happy to see some improvement here in your cold and fever."

"Can I have some water, please?" Martin's voice comes out dry and feeble.

Dr. Lewis pours him some water. "How do you feel right now? Do you still have pain in your chest?"

Martin puts the straw in his mouth while Dr. Lewis assists in propping him up. "It … doesn't seem to be … too bad," he manages between clenched teeth. The room appears to be unusually bright this morning. Martin's eyes are having difficulty adjusting.

"What day is it?" he asks, completely disoriented.

"It's Monday, around four o'clock in the afternoon."

Dr. Lewis has a serious look about him and Martin understands why. He knows that the disease is progressing because he can feel the cancer crawling through his bloodstream like a devilish snake. Sometimes it bites his hipbone just to remind him of its overbearing presence.

The doctor drags a chair over to Martin's bedside for what looks to be a heart to heart with him. He's right. "Martin, we have to check your lung to see if the cancer is spreading," Dr. Lewis says.

177

Martin has been waiting for this. He says nothing.

"If the biopsy from your lung comes back conclusive for pneumonia only, then there's a chance you can kick the cancer in your bone," the doctor continues. "You're still reasonably fit, and your brain is incredibly healthy and strong. You could add three to five years to your life."

"You've been talking to Lynn." Martin doesn't need to wait for a response to know he's correct.

"Yes, I have. I've also consulted the other doctors here, and you'd be an excellent candidate for remission."

"Why, Dr. Lewis? Why now? I'm seventy years old, and I've lived one hell of a life. I don't believe in toxic cocktails. Unless we're talkin' Jack Daniel's," he tries to joke.

The doctor smiles humorlessly. "What if I told you that you could have a few more years to enjoy your Jack Daniel's, not to mention more time with a certain beautiful woman?"

Martin's eyes look downward at the mention of Lynn. "I know, doc, I know," he says, feeling fatigued.

"Look, we're going to schedule your biopsy for tomorrow. Your fever has broken, and the quicker we get in there, the faster we get the results. Are you game to start with that for now?"

Martin lets out a heavy sigh. He sees Rebecca standing in the doorway. "Oh, boy. The cavalry is here I see," he says.

"Yep, and there's not a darn thing you can do about it," answers Dr. Lewis as he heads towards the doorway. "In the meantime, continue to rest as much as possible."

Martin winces as a sharp pain takes hold of his hip.

Rebecca grimaces in the doorway. "I've got something to take your mind off the pain, Martin. I just got word that Kendra's on her way."

"Kendra's coming?" Martin's heart lifts. "That *is* good news."

"And she's bringing some of your favorite Thai food for dinner," Rebecca adds.

Martin redirects the conversation. "Speaking of Thailand, I understand that Jimmy left for his trip to Asia."

Rebecca walks over to his bedside and resets his fluid drip. "Honestly, Martin, I can't think about it right now."

"You mean you didn't hear what happened?" Martin asks.

"Yes, I heard. I just don't have the time or energy to talk about it right now, Martin. I've got to leave shortly to get Miesha, and I need to be in a decent frame of mind."

Martin prods. "Because you haven't been, then?"

"No," Rebecca answers shortly. "No, as you can imagine, my frame of mind has been terrible. I feel devastated for James, and horrible about anything I might have done to exasperate his issues."

Martin signals for more water. "You mean being a beautiful, caring, intelligent, warm woman who is the potential willing recipient of a good and decent young man?"

Rebecca blushes and picks up the water jug. "Stop," she says, giving him a love tap. "You of all people know what I'm talking about."

"You only helped open the doors to where he's been hiding ever since he was a young man, Rebecca. How in the world is that a bad thing? What he does with that awakening is truly his own business. Let's just hope he doesn't cave into his self-wallowing and sees this as an opportunity to get to know himself again, whoever that may be."

Rebecca plops down on the edge of his bed, looking exhausted from the day. "Martin, remember that thing you said about Neil?"

"Yes."

"Well, you were right."

"Damn straight I was, girl! Who you tryin' to fool around here?" Martin jokes.

"Hey now, keep it down in here!" booms a voice from the doorway. They look up to see that Stan has just entered the room. He comes around to Martin's side of the bed.

"My man!" he says happily, holding out his downturned fist.

"Howdy, southern boy," Martin replies, bumping Stan's knuckles with his own.

"I'm outta here for the night, guys," says Rebecca, gathering up the garbage. "Aw, what's a party without a purdy gal?" teases Stan.

"Oh, don't worry," Rebecca shoots back. "You'll still be here."

SEVENTEEN

James is cocooning inside the crisp white sheets of his hotel bed in Bangkok. It was a long journey across the Pacific, and he was not prepared for the strain brought on by the tediousness associated with travelling so far. He hates airports and flying at the best of times, and the experience of being confined inside a plane for over twenty-four hours of transpacific travel was a real challenge for James. Xanax soon became his best ally. Luckily, he managed to bypass a substantial layover in Tokyo, a city he has no desire to discover. In his opinion, there are far too many people in that corner of the universe to endure.

By the time his flight touched down in Thailand, James had maxed out his tolerance for anything other than his own self, and even that was waning. He had far too much to think about and all the time in the world to do it. When he finally reached his destination, he wanted nothing more than to rest. He booked himself into a lovely room at the Mandarin Oriental Bangkok for two days and nights of undisturbed tranquility. When he reached his room he downed a few nightcaps from the minibar, then collapsed on the bed and fell into a bottomless sleep.

Now, opening his eyes, James has no clue as to his whereabouts. After a moment of confusion, it dawns on him: *I'm here. Thailand.* He looks over at the bedside table and sees that the clock reads 4:42 p.m. He closes his eyes again and sleep immediately tries to pull him back under. It succeeds. He eventually wakes from another two and a half hours of slumber feeling slightly better, but it's too soon to tell if the jet lag is wearing off. He stretches his body until he feels the kinks iron out and his blood start to circulate. The fog seems to be lifting from his mind, and he has an intense craving for coffee.

When he sits up in bed, his head starts to swim and a slight feeling of nausea comes over him. He notices a small travel-sized bottle of scotch beside his bed and realizes that it must be the perpetrator. He takes in a deep breath to clear his head. The air smells different to him—a combination of sea salt, musk, and flowers.

He scans the room to get his bearings. There is a little bit of sunlight peering in through the pulled curtains. The room's decor is based on lovely hues of gold and yellow. The bedding consists of cream-colored designer sheets with silver and burgundy accents on the duvet and throw pillows. A stunning Asian floral design marks the tightly woven carpet, reflecting the warm colors of the room and matching the texture of the drapes. The sleek cherrywood furniture pulls the entire scheme together. As an architect, James is impressed with the suite's style and ambiance. He instantly feels at home despite the distance.

It's the second wave of nausea that makes James decide he needs to get up and eat something. He slowly rises from the bed and pulls open the drapes. The view is beyond any pictures he's ever seen. The Chao Phraya River is laid out in full technicolor below him, full of boats and ships of all sizes. The sun is closing in on the horizon and he can't wait to see the sunset. A sudden thought attacks his psyche. *Stephen would have loved this.* He pushes the sentiment aside and walks into the bathroom.

It's been at least a day since he last thought about his ordeal, including Stephen and Rebecca, and he wants to keep it that way—at least for now. His slate needs to be cleaned, and he wants to rediscover his identity with a clear mind and open heart. After everything he's been through to get to this point, he won't allow himself to be distracted. In the bathroom he sees his near-naked form looking back at him in the mirror. He has no idea who the person looking back at him is, or what he's doing there. The only thing he knows for sure is that he needs to get to a point where he is able to identify who he used to be. Maybe then he'll be able to resemble the person he was always meant to become.

A hot shower relaxes him as he anticipates his journey forward. He's anxious to meet up with his personal travel guide, Ted B., tomorrow. Ted came highly recommended by Jade, whose brother Jackson made a similar trip across Southeast Asia a few years ago. Even Jackson never learned Ted's last name.

At first James was reluctant to even consider hiring a personal guide, given his lack of social competence, but Jade and Jackson reassured him that Ted would be the perfect guide for just that reason. "He doesn't stick to your side unless you want him to," Jackson told him. "He travels the same route alongside you, shows you the general dos and don'ts, and is basically just on your peripheral to assist you with stuff, including translation. The guy knows a shitload of languages."

James was intrigued enough to research Ted and communicate with him via email. He seemed knowledgeable enough and the price was reasonable. Most importantly, James trusted Jade's opinion, and that alone was enough to seal the deal.

James shuts off the shower and steam hangs in the air. It's been hours since he last ate something and he's feeling weak from lack of nourishment. Room service seems like the ideal solution prior to checking out Bangkok's nightlife. He orders a spicy chili and basil beef noodle soup and a curried eggplant and shrimp rice dish. He checks the bar fridge and, although he emptied it of hard liquor upon check-in, there's still some alcohol left, including a few cans of Singha and Chang beer.

"Excellent," he says, grabbing a cold one.

Room service arrives when James is on his second beer, and the aroma of the food makes him salivate. He rushes to grab some money out of his pocket to tip the hotel server. The teenage boy nods with a grand smile and says thank you in broken English. James puts the food on the coffee table next to his itinerary. He plans to map out his route while he eats. The flavor of the rice dish is so delicious it almost makes him weepy. He samples the noodle soup. The crispness of the vegetables and sweet tang of the basil instantly fills his body with warmth.

His itinerary is full, and he has just over seven weeks to accomplish everything. The first two weeks will be focused inside Thailand. The following two will take him across Laos and Vietnam, and the final two weeks will be filled with the Mekong Delta and Cambodia. He has given himself a week of contingency time in between scheduled stops to accommodate any stumbling blocks he may run into along the way.

He pulls out a large map of the area and spreads it out on the table, tracing his route with a finger. Much of his travel will be by local transportation—bus, bicycle, car, or small plane—and other times he'll be hiking. He tries to write down the details of his travels in the margin of the map, but the exquisite taste of the beef and noodles interrupts his focus. He catches himself digressing and heads towards the fridge for another beer.

Happiness sneaks up on him, making him feel slightly uncomfortable in the moment. He pushes the feeling aside with a swig of his Chang. He reaches for his duffel bag in search of his art books to cross-reference the museums and specific pieces of work he wants to see. On his way back to the table he takes another long gulp of his beer. The cool, bitter ale rolls back on his tongue, accentuating the taste of lemon grass from the soup.

The stack of books fans out in front of him, covering the map. One volume surprises him. It's not one of his books, but it looks vaguely familiar. He remembers that it was one of Martin's books by an American poet. He looks around the room, searching for an explanation. Did he accidently pick it up? He mindlessly flips through the pages and a folded piece of paper falls out. He unfolds a note that is meant for him. *James—Where are you headed? Martin.*

James feels a stab in his chest. He can't believe that Martin has managed to follow him all the way around to the other side of the universe with his little riddles. "Okay, Marty, what's the game now?" he asks across the Pacific. Surprisingly, he finds himself ready and willing to join in.

★★★

A dark haze floats around James's half-opened eyes as he tries to focus. He rolls over and sees that he's fully clothed. It's 6:52 a.m. Several beer cans are scattered around the bed and dining area. He counts them. *Six? Seriously, I know how to party by myself,* he thinks, amused. *I guess I never made it out to investigate Bangkok at night.*

He stumbles out of bed, still half asleep, and sees the book of poems on a pile of pillows. Now he remembers. He became so enthralled with Martin's riddle that he neglected his travel preparations and evening plans in order to solve it. Of course, it didn't take much coercion to entice James into the poems. Books are where he feels the least vulnerable.

There's a subtle knock at the door. When he opens it, an athletic-looking man in his early thirties is standing in front of him. His blondish hair is cropped to the ears, and his scraggly half-shaven beard juxtaposes his piercing blue eyes. His nose is long and crooked, but it suits his face. James is immediately taken with the visitor's friendly and somewhat familiar aura.

"Hey. Ted B. here. Are you James?" He extends his hand. His smile is enchanting.

James takes note of his attire: a white Dave Matthews t-shirt, hemp cargo shorts, and a brown leather belt with a brass snakehead buckle.

"Uh … hi," James says. He's still stunned with sleep. He barely manages to shake Ted's hand.

"Yeah, we were supposed to meet this morning at seven to go over your travel plans?" James is still staring.

"Uh, I can come back later if you want," Ted offers uncomfortably. "It's just that you said seven in your email."

James opens the door wider. "No, no … Um, please excuse me. I'm just … well, I guess I'm still a bit messed up with the time change."

Ted shrugs his shoulders. "It's totally cool, man. You can expect to feel a little upside down for about five days or so."

"Yeah, sure," James agrees, his voice still groggy. "Hey, would you mind waiting for me in the restaurant downstairs? Then we can talk over breakfast. It'll be on me.

I'm just going to grab a quick shower and I'll be right down."

"Not a problem," says Ted. "See you down there."

Now the excitement is setting in. James can't wait to get going on his excursion. He quickly showers and shaves, then digs through his duffel bag for clean clothes. It only takes him a few minutes to dress, brush his teeth and hair, and grab his belongings before rushing towards the elevator and down to the lobby where the restaurant is located.

The hotel lobby is spectacular. Wall-to-wall windows frame the modern gray sofas and lounge chairs that are overlooking the patio on the other side of the solarium. Large bamboo plants and other greenery fill the space, and gold, lantern-shaped chandeliers dangle from the ceiling, making the room feel spacious and palatial. James crosses the foyer to where white pillars join together to form a massive archway over the golden staircase. Extravagant wicker chairs are strategically placed on the landing below, which is framed with palms and flowering yellow bushes. James thinks he may be in heaven.

He asks one of the hotel's pretty desk clerks where the restaurant is and she points him in the right direction with a dazzling smile. He marvels at how well she speaks English as she wishes him a pleasant breakfast. He heads towards the restaurant and is about to approach the hostess desk when he hears a voice calling his name.

James turns to see Ted standing against a pillar. Ted waves him over.

"Thought you might prefer a more traditional Thai breakfast," says Ted. "They're delicious—and cheaper, too."

James doesn't mind this idea at all. "Sure, sounds good."

The two men step outside the air-conditioned hotel into the warm morning air. At first James feels as though he's stepping into a wet blanket, and it nearly knocks the wind out of his lungs. He takes a few deep breaths, attempting to adjust.

James is soon distracted from the air quality by the sights around him. He can't believe his eyes. He's walking the streets of Bangkok, Thailand. Everything seems so pristine and colorful.

As they head towards the river, the unspoiled surroundings seem to take a turn for the worse. They walk through the side streets until they encounter a market made up of rows of farmers and their fresh produce. From a distance they appear dirty and disorganized, but the smell of fresh seafood and herbs draws James in.

"It's a really different space over here," Ted says.

James can only nod.

All around them, men and women are talking quickly in Thai. Hands are busy placing food in appropriate rows and corners. Behind a food stand an old woman is yelling at what appears to be her grandson. Ted turns to James and explains, "She's telling him that customers are already arriving and he's moving like he's got a stick up his ass."

James can't help but laugh. "Grandmothers sound the same in Thai as in English, I guess," he jokes.

Ted smiles. "She's actually speaking in one of the older dialects, Phuan."

The two men walk up to the stand a few seconds after the old lady whips her grandson over the head with a bundle of fresh coriander leaves. She smiles at them and says something cheerful in Phuan. The lines on her face have taken over her features, and her dark gray and black hair is mostly covered by a red handkerchief. Her hands look arthritic, but they deceive as she moves with speed and accuracy.

With ease, Ted places their order in Thai—two chicken broths with rice, noodle, and egg. The young man scurries towards some pots, and a mousy-looking teenage girl with big eyes and plump lips emerges from a narrow doorway to feverishly chop herbs at a rustic chopping block under the weathered grandmother's super-vision. James is enthralled. Moments later the soup comes out in two large plastic soup bowls with spoons. The old woman nods at them to take it, so they carry their bowls to a small table near a low-lying wall.

James stirs his soup and looks curiously at Ted. "So, the initial B in your name. What's it stand for?"

Ted doesn't look up from his soup. "Burthogge," he says casually.

There is a brief silence between them.

"Stick with the B," James advises.

★★★

"You mean dad *knew* that Stephen was gay?" Kitty is sitting comfortably across from Martin's bed as she crochets A.J. a navy blue and white sweater for Christmas.

Martin takes a sip of his hot tea to moisten his dry mouth. "He never came out and actually told me that, but I'm certain that's what he was getting at."

Martin is propped up in his bed, wrapped in warm blankets. Kitty tries hard not to notice how different he looks without his beautiful thick hair. She understands that this is a normal side effect of chemotherapy and focuses on the tradeoff—less hair for more life. She knows that accepting chemotherapy was a difficult decision for Martin to make, but in the end, Lynn was the catalyst. She wanted more time with him, and he could not refuse her. When his decision was made, he surprised Lynn by shaving his head to signify the initiation of treatment. It was a happy occa-sion for everyone. Stan particularly enjoyed the act of shaving his friend bald. Gerry and Max stood by Martin's side, raising the flask of his trusty Jack Daniel's.

"What do you suppose Dad wanted you to do about it, though?" Kitty asks now. "I mean, you didn't know my brother or anything about his relationship with Stephen."

"Oh, but I did. You're forgetting that I spent a good year with your father in Vietnam," he replies before taking another sip of tea. "By the end of our tour together, we ended up good friends. He trusted me more than any other soldier in his platoon. "Then many years later, we reconnected at a United Nations peacekeeping conference in France. We stayed up all night long drinking and talking and of course I found out all about you and your brother. We made a point of keeping in touch more frequently after that. He eventually told me what happened to Stephen and how Jimmy was never the same. He wanted my advice and more importantly, he wanted me to intervene." Martin stops to take a deep breath before continuing. "He was a smart man, your father, and more intuitive then he let on. He knew that I experienced what it's like to carry the blame of the death of a true loved one in your heart. The problem was, I didn't feel I could help at the time, because I too, was still suffering from my own guilt."

Kitty contemplates this as she systematically wraps the yarn around her needles. "So Jimmy's been blaming himself all of these years for the reason *why* Stephen died?" Martin nods his head to acknowledge this fact. "Yes, but without ever knowing the facts about exactly *how* he died."

Kitty scrunches up her face. She contemplates this as she continues to work her needles with precision. "I guess you're right. I mean, we've all been assuming that he just *misses* Stephen and that he's having a hard time getting over watching him get hit by a train. I didn't know there was anything more to it than that." She puts her needles down momentarily. "Dad used to always bark about how *unnatural* their relationship was—God, he was such a Neanderthal! But honestly, Martin, I didn't think of it as homosexuality—not that it would have mattered to me one bit if it was. I just saw two boys like brothers who loved to hang around each other. They were so much in sync, it used to make me jealous. I wanted that kind of bond with someone—especially with my brother. Nobody understood them the way they understood each other. It was like they had their own secret code that nobody on the outside could crack."

Martin takes a swallow of his tea and sets the cup on the bedside table. It lands unevenly and nearly rolls off the table. Kitty reaches out and sets it upright just before it falls to the floor, then resumes her crocheting.

"I suppose James also felt like he'd been abandoned when Stephen died," she says thoughtfully. "It was like ... like half of him went AWOL or something. He was so *lonely*. It was hard to watch all that pain manifest itself like a giant mass slowly filling up the empty space where Stephen used to be."

Martin puts his hands protectively over his ribs and Kitty immediately curses herself for putting her foot in her mouth. *Way to use a* cancer *metaphor with a cancer patient*, she chides herself. But Martin is nodding his head in agreement. "Yes, and it'll be difficult for him to let go of that invisible mass. Trust me."

"How did *you* piece it all together?" asks Kitty.

"It was a series of events and a lot of self-discovery," Martin tells her cryptically.

"Well, I'm glad you came into our lives," she says. "Finally, I feel like someone might actually be able to *help*."

"I promised your dad before he died that I would check in on Jimmy. Your brother and I have a lot in common. Nothing and everything about his behavior makes sense to me. You tend to see things that you know, after all."

"It's been a week now since he left. I wonder how he's doing. It's not like he's going to contact me to let me know or anything like that," huffs Kitty.

"You might be surprised," Martin says, winking. "I had your mom slip a little present into his bag before he left to jog his memory about the people back home."

Gerry comes into the room whistling. "Hey, old man. You wanna join the hockey pool, or are you too much of a pussy?" He suddenly sees Kitty and straightens. "Oh hey, Miss Kitty. How are you feeling, love?"

Kitty smiles. "Fine, Gerry. And you're obviously feeling very well—look at you!"

Gerry blushes. "Thanks. I feel fantastic. So good they're looking to kick me outta here," he says proudly before qualifying himself. "Er ... uh ... not that I want to go."

"To improve is to change; to be perfect is to change often," recites Martin.

The words immediately trip a memory in Kitty's mind. "Oh, wait! I know this one!" She jumps up and snaps her fingers. "Winston Churchill!" She holds her breath and waits for Martin's assurance.

"Young lady, I am impressed," Martin says happily.

"Ha!" Kitty punches the air. "Yes! I guess having a know-it-all brother all these years has finally paid off."

Martin and Gerry laugh together.

"I think you've been spending too much time with Donna," Gerry says to Kitty, smiling.

"Oh, I love a woman who can speak her mind," Martin adds.

"Speaking of lovin' a woman who speaks her mind, when's the big wedding day?" Gerry asks.

Kitty looks at Martin with a blank face. "You're getting married?" she asks, surprised.

"Gerry, my friend, you sure know how to knock the wind out of an ol' ship's sails," sighs Martin.

"What? What did I say? You *are* gonna ask her, aren't ya? That's what Stan said!"

Gerry is embarrassed now.

"That sneaky little dirty southern bird," mumbles Martin. "It's a good thing he's having dialysis right now—otherwise I might be cooking up his kidneys with a few fava beans to have with a nice Chianti tonight."

"Martin Diggs!" Kitty chides. "You watch your tongue, young man!"

All three enjoy a hearty laugh.

"Are you really asking Lynn to marry you?" Kitty prods.

Suddenly a voice interrupts the laughter.

"Who's getting married?" Rebecca gasps, trotting into the room.

Kitty looks at Martin, and Martin glares hard at Gerry.

"Looks like the cat just let itself out of the bag," Gerry says, shrugging.

Rebecca's eyes widen as she stares in disbelief at Martin. "You're going to ask Lynn to marry you?"

Martin's eyes shift in his head. "Alright! Yes, yes I am, and don't *any* of you speak about this again until it's done. I want to surprise her."

"Despite the fact that we want details now, it'll have to wait. We're late for your x-ray appointment," says Rebecca mindfully. She walks over to Martin's bed and gently helps him up. "I have a wheelchair at the door."

"My dear nurse, I'm quite capable of making my way by foot."

"Whatever you say, Forrest Gump," replies Rebecca.

Kitty and Gerry stifle a laugh.

"That Gump kid had a point," Stan pipes in, coming through the door. He starts to imitate the character's voice. "Life is like a box of chocolates …" He stops and points his finger at Martin. "Except this one over here actually *does* know what he's gonna get."

★★★

Lynn is busy in the small kitchen unloading the food she's just prepared for her dinner tonight with Martin. Roasted potatoes with garlic, shrimp and beef in a spicy satay sauce, and broccoli grilled with sesame oil and sea salt. She wants him to be well fed before he starts his treatment tomorrow. There will be many weeks of chemotherapy ahead, and she knows that his appetite and energy levels will likely suffer as a result. She places the chocolate mousse pie in the kitchenette fridge with a note on it saying *Please do not touch* in order to secure the precious dessert for Martin.

She has never been happier than she is in this moment. Martin has made a choice, and his decision will provide them with more time together. She feels like she is in love for the first time in her life.

She leans against the counter and thinks about what a roundabout path life can take sometimes. Before meeting Martin, love and passion were things she had only read about. She'd never really experienced romantic love—at least, not in the way she had always dreamed. When she and Dean met in college, they were naive and had no experience with relationships. After being with Dean for two and a half years, they married—not because they couldn't live without each other, but because that was the next step they both figured they had to take. A few years later, she found herself trapped in a sterile marriage with no clue how to resolve it.

It wasn't that she didn't love Dean; on the contrary, she loved him very much. They were able to manage a solid partnership and they held the utmost respect and admiration for one another. However, something was missing. She felt that they lacked that invisible wire that binds lovers together, and their souls simply didn't have the ability to speak to each another. And when Stephen died, they were able to stick together—which Lynn knows is something that most other couples fail to do under such awful circumstances. Lynn recalls the words of her psychologist. *When two people are passionate about each other, that passion can be fierce in a positive or negative way. It can create good and bad friction all in the same momentum and become the driver to make or break things. If passion isn't a driver in a relationship then there's less potential for individual egos to rebel and for conflicts to occur. Therefore, you and Dean are more likely to stabilize.*

But now she's sick of stabilizing. Martin throws her off kilter—challenges her in ways she's never been challenged before. She is in love with his intellect and the wealth of his soulful experience. She adores him. And now, for the first time in the months since they met, she dares to hope that there might be a future for that love.

★★★

Martin is returning from his outing with Kendra. He is exhausted from the few hours they spent looking for the perfect ring. He finally found it in an antique shop downtown. He loves the idea of vintage jewelry; every piece comes with a history. In this case, his choice is fitting. The shop owner told him that the Art Deco-style ring was worn by the American wife of Benoit Degochest, a twentieth-century French poet and later professor of art and culture at the University of Chicago. The fact that the ring is a brilliantly clear yellow stone surrounded with clusters of diamonds layered in platinum didn't hurt either. There is no question—this is the ring.

Feeling exhausted, Martin decides to lie down for an hour before getting ready for dinner with Lynn. Stan is nowhere in sight, and Martin assumes he's watching the game with the other men in the television room. He shuffles over to his bed and, just as he is about to climb in, he notices a few bumps underneath the covers. He rolls back the bedding and finds a can of fava beans and a bottle of Chianti with a note stuck on it. *Figured you'd prefer Lynn's cooking to my kidneys, but thought these might be a nice addition to the grub tonight. Stan.*

Martin clutches the note in his hand. He is laughing so hard he's finding it hard to breathe.

Lynn is suddenly in the doorway. "Good grief, Martin, what's going on?" She rushes over, worried that Martin is in pain.

"It's nothing, dear. I'm fine. Let's just say I have the best friends in the world," Martin replies, wiping tears of laughter from the corners of his eyes. "I sometimes think Frank is in every single one of these fools."

Lynn smiles and hugs him. "You look tired, Martin." She pulls the can of beans from his bed and looks at them, puzzled. "I won't ask, but the wine is a nice touch."

"Yes, it is," Martin agrees. "I'm just going to lie down for an hour before we eat. I hope you don't mind."

"Of course not," Lynn assures him. "I have some rounds to do anyway. Janice is with A.J. today because Kitty isn't feeling well." Martin is immediately concerned and Lynn reads his expression. "It's nothing to worry about. She just overdid it yesterday, as usual." She gently caresses his bald head. "Do you need anything before I go?"

"I've got everything I need right here, darling." Martin pats her hand and kisses her softly on the lips, then climbs into bed. She helps to arrange the blankets around him. Sleep drags him downward instantly.

An hour and a half later, Martin wakes to find Stan looking out his window. Martin clears his throat from its thickness, which gets Stan's attention.

"Well, ol' man, I never thought you'd get up," Stan teases. "You were done as dirt there."

"How're you feeling these days, boy?" Martin asks, still trying to shake off his grogginess.

"Me? Heck, not much can bring me down, Corporal," replies Stan. "Besides, every day I'm here is like a blessin' from God."

"Which one?" scoffs Martin.

"Any of 'em. Heck, I'll take *all* of 'em," Stan replies offhandedly. "Now let's get movin', my friend. I got orders to get you to the lounge by seven o'clock, and you ain't even bathed or nothing. And trust me, unless you got a couple of farm cats in heat hiding in yer shorts, it's *you* that's stankin' up this place."

Martin looks at Stan and sees Frank's face flash before him.

"Come on, ol' man, what you lookin' at?" Stan's smile is big and bright. It's like

191

the sunshine lives there. The only other person Martin has ever known to have this type of aura was Frank.

"You remind me of someone, that's all," says Martin.

Stan takes his arm and helps him out of bed. His eyes connect with Martin's. "Yeah. I know," he replies, matter of fact.

"How do you know?" asks Martin.

"Because I know, man, I know. Now come on, we got no time to be dwellin' on no black magic. I gotta get you all cleaned up."

"Okay, okay, I'm going!" Martin grabs his housecoat and manages to shuffle towards the bathroom on his own. "You're worse than Donna," he mutters just before he closes the bathroom door behind him.

"Hey! I heard that!" Stan calls after him. "And use some actual soap, y'hear? Not that oatmeal-based shit yer niece gave you. Your days of attractin' sheep are over and done with. Here," he says, cracking open the door just enough to get his hand through to pass Martin a green bar of masculine-smelling soap.

Martin takes the soap without a word. He sniffs it and nods his head to no one. "Not too bad," he says out loud.

Stan raps on the door. "Hey! Don't forget to wash your private parts," he jokes.

Martin rolls his eyes, but he can't help but smile at his roommate's attentiveness and sense of humor. *It's like I have Gomer Pyle as a den mother,* he thinks fondly.

Ten minutes later, Martin opens the door and emerges from the bathroom in his robe. His bald head is gleaming along with his perfectly white teeth. "Now you can stop your bellyachin', boy," he grumbles. "I'm clean."

Stan expresses his approval. "Whoo wee, yes! Well, knock me down and call me Susan. That there standin' before me is one mighty fine-lookin' beast of a man."

"Watch yourself, Chachi," Martin says, smiling and pushing his friend gently out of his path. He starts towards his side of the room and stops in his tracks. A tuxedo is lying on his bed. "What's all this?"

"Yer attire for the evening, sir," answers Stan. He is grinning from ear to ear.

Martin is dumbfounded. "What … But how … ?"

"I took yer uniform to the tailor's last week when you were out and I got yer size," Stan says proudly, blushing. "But don't spill on it. It's just rented and I want my deposit back."

Martin turns towards Stan and grabs his shoulders. "You're a good friend, Stan," he whispers. "A good friend."

"Now don't go gettin' all Liberace on me," jokes Stan.

"Maybe it'll be you one of these days," says Martin, thinking of Stan's sweet young girlfriend Cody Ann. "She'll be done her teacher's schoolin' soon. Ever think about walkin' down the aisle yourself?"

Stan says nothing, just smiles a hugely goofy grin that tells Martin he thinks of that a lot. "Come on, now," he prods, changing the subject. "We only got like ... ten minutes to get you to the lounge on time." Stan shuts the main door to the room while Martin undresses. As Martin pulls on the perfectly tailored white shirt, Stan rummages through his bag for something. "Catch," he says, tossing Martin a bottle of cologne.

"Really?" Martin says doubtfully. He's never been sold on the idea of men smelling strongly of fragrances.

"For cryin' out Christmas, just do what you're told tonight and everythin' will be fine!" As Martin pats some on his neck and scrunches up his nose, Stan runs over to his bedside table and fishes out a pair of cufflinks. He walks over to Martin and helps him with his shirt. "I ain't touchin' yer pants though, man."

"Please don't," Martin retorts. He kicks off his slippers and sits on the edge of the bed. He pulls the trousers over his thin legs, then stands up and fastens them at the waistband.

"Yer fly, man," reminds Stan.

Martin groans and does up the zipper. He grabs the black tie and starts to maneuver it around his collar, but his hands don't manage to work in tandem. Nervousness is blooming in the pit of his stomach.

"Oh, fer Pete's sake! Let me," Stan grumbles and starts to work on Martin's tie. He grabs the jacket off the bed and holds it up for Martin's arms then quickly does up the buttons and smooths the shoulders. He lets out a large sigh as he stands back to take a look at his final masterpiece.

Martin sneaks a glance in the mirror and knows he looks dapper. Even he can see the transformation.

"Ain't no way yer gettin' turned down tonight, ol' man!" Stan heckles.

"I guess it's time then," states Martin.

"Yep," replies Stan. "I'll take you upstairs. And don't forget, you gotta be back before the clock strikes midnight, Cinderella."

When they reach the lounge, Martin sees candlelight flickering through the entrance. A young female hospital volunteer is standing by the door in a nice black cocktail dress with embroidered jewels around the waistline. Her long dark hair flows over her shoulders. Stan lets out a low whistle as they approach.

The young woman flashes Martin a beautiful smile. "Welcome to the lounge, sir," she says sweetly. "My name is Arianne, and I'll be your hostess and server for the night."

Stan chuckles. "Well, I guess I'll leave you here. It looks like you're in good hands." He starts down the hall, then turns. "And hey, Martin?"

"Huh?"

"Knock 'em dead," says Stan. "You deserve the best, buddy."

Martin can only nod. He is overwhelmed by all the love he's feeling tonight. Arianne takes Martin's arm and brings him towards a round table in the middle of the dimly lit room. A cream-colored tablecloth flows over it, setting off the delicate white china plates, shining sterling cutlery, and cut crystal glasses.

Lynn is already sitting there looking like an elegant queen. She stands up to greet him and he is reminded of just how much he adores her. Her long emerald taffeta dress hugs her delicious curves and accentuates her ample bust. A subtle silver and pearl belt defines her small waistline and elongates her slim torso. Her hair is tied up in a lose bun with a simple diamond and pearl comb holding it together, and a hint of cranberry red covers her perfectly formed lips. She is exquisite.

Her eyes shine brightly as they watch Martin approach the table. Arianne releases Martin into Lynn's arms and then disappears into the kitchen. Martin and Lynn stand breathless together in the moment, not speaking. He cannot take his eyes off her, and she doesn't break his gaze. *Finally*, he thinks. *I'm out of the jungle at last.*

EIGHTEEN

James is staring out the window of what he thinks is an old school bus. He wants to sleep for a week after his time in Thailand, but he's got two more legs of his journey to go. He experienced the famous landmarks of a few of the larger Thai cities, and he immersed himself in the colorful culture of the small towns and fishing villages en route to Vientiane, the capital city of Laos.

As the bus drives along the humid countryside, James wonders if he hasn't pushed himself too far. He has travelled halfway around the world to escape the weight of his life in Chicago, only to realize that the heaviness he's been carrying around is indeed *himself.* There are times when he craves the sound of Jade's familiar voice, but perhaps that's because he is used to having her organize his days. Out here in the vast foreign countryside there is little organization—unless Ted has something planned exceptionally well, and even then anything could happen. He spends most days trying to make sense of the unexpected, like the unpredictable weather and road conditions. Somehow all of this disorganization has made him miss home, although being home-sick is ironically making him feel safe and more complete.

Ted is managing to do what Jackson promised he would do—keep his distance. But James is discovering that he doesn't mind the times when Ted makes himself present, because his nonplussed nature brings James a sense of security, especially in times of chaos. As James adjusts himself on the rickety seat of the bus, he recalls their chaotic crossing of the Friendship Bridge from Thailand into Laos. They had managed to hook up with a last-minute tour bus filled with a bunch of young German tourists, some of whom had not applied for their visas in advance and hence held up the group's passage into the country considerably. He wished wholeheartedly that they had opted to bike the long way around instead. As they waited in the stifling heat

195

in a crowded border shack that smelled of vomit, James was sure that an anxiety attack was going to overtake him. Only Ted's casual reassurances kept him calm.

Now back on the road, James watches the shores of the Mekong River pass by through the dirty pane of scratched glass. As he follows the flow of the muddy brown current with his eyes, his mind settles on his Martin, who spent much time along the banks of this river with his comrades including Aaron. He wonders how they ever made it through those months and years. He closes his eyes, struggling to breathe in the muffled hot air that only barely flows through the bus. A memory of Aaron showing him how to cut wood at the cottage comes to mind. It was a good day for father and son, James recalls. When he opens his eyes, he sees Stephen laughing by the side of the road. He gasps.

Ted is sitting beside him, reading. "Hey. You okay?" he asks, closing his book.

James is perspiring and can feel the beads of sweat trickling down his forehead. "Uh, yeah. I guess I'm just tired."

Ted digs into his backpack and pulls out a few disposable body wipes and a bottle of water. "Here, take these."

"Thanks," James says, feeling automatically comforted. Once again he silently thanks Jade and Jackson for putting him in touch with the tour guide.

"Listen, man, I know it's none of my business," begins Ted, "but I've been travelling with you for almost two weeks now and I gotta say, you look like you're carrying around some heavy shit."

"What do you mean?" James asks, knowing exactly what he means.

"Well, like you don't ever sleep through the night. And when you do sleep, you're yelling to someone or you're tossing and turning. A few times I've actually had to go over to you and check your temperature just to make sure you didn't have typhoid or malaria or some other random disease."

The bus hits a big bump and everyone lets out a holler. James groans. Ted has no reaction.

"We've got a half hour or so till we reach the camp," Ted tells him. "Wanna spill?"

James looks out the window, unsure of how to respond. "I … I've gone through something pretty tough, and I'm not sure I'm going to find my way out of it." He is surprised at the candidness of his words.

There is a long pause between them before Ted responds. "I've been through some tough shit too, man. When I was sixteen, I lost my baby sister Mallory to muscular dystrophy," Ted says quietly, his pain evident. "I watched my parents die inside every day for years afterwards. I might as well have lost them too—at least, that's how it felt at the time. I was truly alone. Sure, I had my aunts and uncles and friends from school, but it just wasn't the same."

196

James feels stupid now. He can't imagine losing Kitty. He's instantly reminded of the part he played in her collapse that day in the parking lot and is disgusted with himself. He feels sick to his stomach. "I'm really sorry but maybe we shouldn't talk about this," he says, feeling a surge of panic.

Ted adjusts his tone. "It's okay. You don't have to tell me anything. I'll talk and you just listen." There is gentle wisdom in his voice.

James senses that Ted is aware of more than he lets on. He can't take his eyes off the road as he concentrates on Ted's words.

"I ended up finding out something about myself," Ted explains. "I found out that I was capable of doing *anything* after Mallory died because I had *nothing* left to lose. It was like all of this incredible darkness that hung around me lifted and I could breathe again. I knew that it was actually Mallory's energy roaming freely inside of me. She wanted to be free from my terrible feelings."

These words sink into James's psyche on a deep level.

"She wanted me to live my dreams and aspirations," Ted continues. "I wasn't going to fail her, so I decided to live every day. I pushed myself to do things and go places I would never have imagined doing or going before because she wanted to live, too. She *had* to live through me. It was the only way." Ted takes a minute before continuing. "Once I started to explore my life like this, my parents started to come to life again, too. They started to feel her presence in me—like *through* me, you know? It was a win-win. I let go of her only to get her back. And I got my parents back, too." He taps his left shoulder. "She's this little angel on my shoulder, man, and I take her with me everywhere now. And that makes me feel good."

James is breathing normally again and is genuinely caught up in Ted's story. It feels good to hear him speak—just like listening to the veterans in the hospital. Their stories always soothe him, and so does Ted's.

The bus slows. They pull off the road and approach a complex of large bamboo huts surrounded in lush Laotian countryside. The leader of the university tour begins rhyming off where they are all going to meet for dinner.

"You don't want to lodge here with the gang, right?" Ted asks, making the assumption.

James gives a small laugh. "Um, I could smell some decent pot off some of those students. Not sure I want to end up in a Laos prison, you know?"

Ted shakes his head and grins. "Very insightful of you. Ok, well I've got a better spot for us to hang our hats, anyways. I already had it booked for myself because I wasn't sure what you wanted to do, but there's plenty of room for the two of us. I'll go tell the others not to expect us."

They step off onto the Laotian soil and marvel at their surroundings. The eco-lodge can accommodate up to 22 people—perfect for the tour but not for James.

Its large bamboo hut shape stands out amongst the lush green bushes deep in the beautiful Laos countryside. Ted walks over to Mike the group guide as they chat quietly about their plans to relocate and says something that James can't hear. Mike gives Ted a business card and the two men shake hands before parting.

"Come on," says Ted as he walks towards James. "Grab your pack. I've got someone waiting to take us downriver."

As they walk up the path towards the entrance of the complex, they wave goodbye to all the students who are busy trying to sort out their luggage and other belongings. James feels glad that he packed lightly and has only a duffel bag to carry around.

Suddenly, a giant thorny tree catches James's attention and he walks towards it in awe. He's never seen any living thing like it before. James reaches down inside of his pack to get his camera and notices a strange little Gecko perched on the base of the trunk. Its small eyes are black and bulging. It has cream-colored skin and a swirly khaki tattoo on its back. With its pink nose and open mouth it looks as though it is smiling. James snaps a few quick photos. He knows he's only on a different continent, but at once he has this incredible sense that he's on a different planet altogether.

Ted begins to walk towards him with a small local man in tow. "Hey, James!" Ted calls out. James gathers up his camera and backpack and meets the two men halfway down the path. Ted introduces them. "James, this is Kelii. Kelii, this is James."

The two men size each other up quickly and extend hands to shake.

"Kelii means 'chief,' so that's my nickname for him," Ted tells James. He turns to Kelii. "I haven't thought of a nickname for this guy yet, but I'll let you know when I get one, Chief."

"Call me Jimmy," James says, surprising himself for the second time today.

"Ha-ha, Jimmy. Uh, like—a Jimmy Dean!" Kelii proudly says, bringing a cigarette to his mouth and lighting it.

James is bemused but tries not to show it. "Yeah, that's it."

They walk back up towards the dirt road where a dark green Land Rover sits, looking completely out of context with the landscape.

"Nice car, yes?" says Kelii, beaming. "Mine."

James calculates that Kelii is approximately five feet two inches tall and weighs no more than a hundred and thirty-five pounds. He appears to be a jovial man in his late forties and obviously enjoys smoking, given that he's on his third cigarette in less than ten minutes.

The trio climbs into the Land Rover. It takes them twenty minutes to drive over to the two-bed bungalow that Ted had reserved. For the next ten days, James and Ted will use this place as a landing pad between excursions. The small house is located on an ancient temple site near the banks of the Nam Ngum River, approximately twenty miles outside of Vientiane. Kelii lives in a nearby bungalow with his wife and three daughters, and he will be their driver for the duration of the Laos leg of their trip. James is impressed. Ted is not only extremely well organized, he is also very thorough in his planning and thinks of every little detail. *Just like Jade,* James muses.

James and Ted bid goodbye to Kelii for the afternoon and throw their packs down inside the house. On the outside, their rented bungalow is made primarily of large wood planks and bamboo. Inside, an open concept captures all the light from the large exterior windows. The main floor holds a small kitchen area, a dining table, two twin beds, and a bathroom. The bathroom is a fair size and holds a regular-sized tub and a small, basic shower. The decor is neat, clean, and made out of native materials such as benzoin bark, bamboo, copra, and kapok. A dark cocoa stain covers the shiny wood floor and the light bounces off it to illuminate the surrounding room with warmth and bright colors. Yellow and white bedding cover the narrow beds, and matching drapes fall down to the shiny floor. Local carvings colored with vivid greens, reds, and oranges accentuate the main seating area.

James and Ted realize their hunger at the same time and decide to venture out to the local floating restaurant on the river. Although he knows they're both feeling tired, James is sure that quick, cool showers will rejuvenate them enough to enjoy their meal. He offers the shower to his roommate first and lies down on one of the beds while he waits for the bathroom. He can smell rain somewhere off in the distance and hopes that it will come their way to alleviate the stickiness he has endured over the last seven hours. In the quiet house he hears only a faint wind rushing through the palm trees and the sprinkling sound of the water from the shower. He rolls over onto his side and stares at a painting of a gorgeous young woman. Her eyes and hair are dark and her lips are a soft plum red. His heart melts as the thought of Rebecca pulls him towards her from the other side of the world.

★★★

The floating restaurant is like nothing James has ever seen before. Situated at the bank of the Nam Ngum River, the entire open structure is built out of bamboo rafts and tarps made out of wood and grass. There are five large rectangular tables, each accommodating approximately a dozen people. When James and Ted arrive, plenty of seats are available. The two men sit down in the center of one of the tables. The sun is not far from setting; Ted advises that they will have to eat fast before the mosquitoes come out looking for their own meal.

A stunning young girl comes over to their table to take their order. She is wearing traditional Lao garb. Her head barely peers out from underneath a large, cylindrical beaded hat with yellow and green butterfly designs around it. She is wearing a peach-colored checkered shirt underneath a black kimono that has a white and gold floral print. A bright pink sash wraps around her tiny waist, and brass coin medallions dangle from the rose-colored silk. She says hello in both English and Lao.

Ted says hello back in her native tongue and orders two *beerlao* beers, two shots of *lau-lao*, the local whiskey, and two appetizers of *seen savahn*, a sweet, thinly sliced beef jerky covered with sesame seeds. The girl nods her head and goes off to fetch the drinks.

"Is there anything that turns you off, food-wise?" Ted asks.

"No, not really," James replies. Just then a fair-sized bug with a deep black shell and spiked legs starts crawling along the back of Ted's chair. "Probably nothing that resembles that, though," he says, pointing over Ted's shoulder.

Ted turns around, snatches the bug up in his hand, and pops it in his mouth. The crunching sound makes James gag out loud. "Jesus, Ted!" he whimpers in disgust.

"Ha!" Ted laughs, then opens his mouth wide. The bug's remains are still stuck to his tongue.

The waitress comes back with the drinks. "Just in time, my lovely one!" Ted announces, grabbing one of the shots of whiskey and quickly washing the rest of the bug down. The waitress smiles.

James shakes his head and downs his own whiskey in one shot. "A little warning next time, please," he says, smacking his lips.

Ted goes on to order their main course: *ping pa*, grilled fish with fresh spices and herbs; *mok gai*, chicken steamed in banana leaf; *khua khao*, Lao-style fried rice; *pad Lao*, stir-fried noodles in sweet sauce; and *tam mak hoong*, spicy green papaya salad.

The two men talk about their upcoming adventure to Vietnam, which will take them further along the Mekong River until they finally end up in Cambodia. When the meal arrives, James is overwhelmed by the scent of fresh oils and herbs. The first bite of food lights up all five of his senses. Every bite following the first amplifies the meal's texture and flavor, stimulating the jovial mood and the light conversation—not to mention the beer consumption.

By the time they are halfway through the meal, the mosquitoes are hovering and biting at every chance. James doesn't notice them at first, as he is so engrossed in Ted's descriptions of his life experiences and his expectations for the road ahead. After another hour, however, both James and Ted simultaneously decide they've had enough to eat and that the bugs have too. They leave the barge happy and full.

The bungalow is very warm and Ted immediately starts to secure the netting around the open windows to limit the number of mosquitoes that can slip in overnight. James is eager to help out, and as they work the two men continue their conversation.

"Pass me one of those tacks over there, won't you?" Ted asks, pointing to a small wicker basket on the kitchen table.

James does and takes a few extras to start pinning another net down. "It's amazing the number of the vaccines you need to get before you come to a country like this, and yet here we are, still using the basics—mosquito nets," James remarks.

"You ever had dengue fever?" Ted asks. Before James can answer no, Ted goes on to explain. "It's brutal. I had it one year—I think it was my second year as a guide—and anyway, it totally *nailed* me, man. I was down for at least ten days, and it took *weeks* for me to really feel like myself again."

The two men take another half hour to cover up the windows as best they can. Ted passes James some natural mosquito repellent cream that smells like lemon with a hint of oregano. "Since I have to cover myself all day with the hard stuff, I like to use a more holistic approach for nighttime," Ted explains as James slathers some on to his face and neck. "We won't be using that on the Mekong, though."

The two men get ready for bed. Ted grabs a bottle of whiskey from the pantry and offers James a nightcap.

"Sure," James says, knowing it will help him get to sleep. Ted passes him a few good ounces in a cup and James downs it in a second. They climb into their respective beds. A gust of wind blows through the open windows.

"Oh, I'm liking that sound," whispers Ted in the dark. "Totally worth the work of netting the windows."

"Shouldn't it be cooler this time of the year?" James asks wearily, recalling what some of his travel books said.

"Yeah, the mugginess is sort of unseasonal for this time of year," admits Ted. "But you know—global warming and all that."

"I'd welcome some rain," says James.

"Be careful what you wish for," Ted responds seriously. "When it comes down, it comes down hard."

James is tired of being careful. "Bring on the rain," he says under his breath.

★★★

Rebecca's busy sipping a glass of merlot in her kitchen while preparing spaghetti and meatballs for dinner. As she stirs the sauce, her mind flashes to James. She hasn't heard from him since their encounter in the library, and she doubts she will. She knows he's overseas now, and surely the thought of her hasn't even entered his mind.

"So give it up already," she quietly nags herself.

Her self-reflection is suddenly interrupted. "Mom, can Nicole and I have a sleepover this weekend?" Miesha asks, prancing into the kitchen and grabbing a piece of cheese from the fridge.

"Here?" Rebecca asks, seeking clarification.

"No, at her place," Miesha replies. "She wants me and Kassandra to stay over. We're going to watch the DVD of *Wizards of Waverly*."

"Uh—" Rebecca begins.

"And I haven't had a sleepover since before Thanksgiving," Miesha adds to tip the scales.

"Oh, well, I suppose it's okay, but—" Before she can continue, Miesha runs out of the kitchen. "—but I need to get permission from her mom and dad, okay?" Rebecca calls out. She sees a bigger and more mature version of her daughter flashing her a thumbs up before bolting up the stairs.

Heaviness hangs over her heart. Her daughter is becoming more independent, and she is both happy and sad at the realization all in the same breath. Miesha will be nine in just a few short months, and that means Rebecca is getting older, too. Twelve years ago, things were so different for her. She and Ben were engaged and she had a whole happily-ever-after life in front of her. She never dreamed that she would find herself divorced and living as a single mother, and yet here she was, standing in her three-bedroom townhouse kitchen stirring spaghetti—alone and wondering about her future prospects. She looks out the window and sees that it's snowing lightly. *The first snow of the year,* she thinks with a sad smile.

She can hear her cellphone ringing on the table in the dining area. She wipes her hands on her apron and grabs the phone before the last ring. "Hello?" she says, waiting to hear the voice on the other end.

"Hi, Rebecca, it's Kitty. Sorry to catch you at the dinner hour. Do you have a second?"

"Oh sure, no problem. What's up?" Rebecca asks, her heart pounding at the sound of James's sister's voice.

"Mom and I are planning a surprise engagement party for Martin and Lynn. We want to hold it next week because Christmas is coming fast and then, before you know it, it's New Year's Eve and the wedding will be here!" Kitty's voice is animated. She seems to get off on planning for special events.

"Of course I'll be there!" Rebecca tells her. "I wouldn't miss it for anything. What can I do?"

Kitty jumps in. "Offer to drive them to the staff Christmas party. You live near the hospital so it'll be easy for you to swing by."

"So you're holding the engagement party at the hospital?" Rebecca is trying not to show her disapproval.

"No, woman!" Kitty shoots back. "You'll pick both of them up *at* the hospital. Kendra is renting out the party room in her fabulous condo building for our supposed staff Christmas party, which is officially their engagement party. I've already seen the room and it's perfect!"

"Okay ... but why would *I* be picking them up? Isn't that kind of weird? Wouldn't Lynn just drive them herself?" Rebecca asks, trying to point out a potential gap in the plan.

"I knew you'd ask that!" Kitty goes on to explain. "She was actually contemplating take a cab to the Christmas party so that she can enjoy some cocktails. Tomorrow I'll just suggest that you could probably pick them both up instead, since you live kind of close. Meanwhile, Mom and I and some of the other girls will decorate the party room and everyone will be there waiting to surprise them when you get there!"

"Cool," Rebecca says.

"Great," Kitty answers. "I'll email you all the details." There's some muffled shouting on Kitty's end. "Uh, Rebecca? I've got to go because A.J. just threw up all over Jake. It never ends, I tell you!"

"Been there," Rebecca says, laughing. "I'll talk to you later."

"Okay. But oh, before I go—I've gotten a couple of emails from James."

There is silence. Rebecca reaches for her glass of wine.

"It's hard for him to get on a computer there, as you can imagine. But he asked how everyone was doing," Kitty says slyly.

"So? I'm supposed to be happy that I'm lumped in with 'everyone' now?" Rebecca's voice is trembling.

Kitty ignores her comment. "I said everyone was fine, and then I kind of told him that you were single again and forwarded him your email address." Before Rebecca can get mad, Kitty continues. "He wrote back and said to say hello."

Rebecca doesn't know what to say. She has no idea what this means or what to do with it.

"Hun, I gotta run. Jacob is having a nervous breakdown with this puke situation. Men!" Kitty huffs. "I'll call you tomorrow. Love you!" Kitty hangs up, leaving Rebecca feeling hung out to dry.

Unsure of what else to do, she takes a mouthful of merlot.

"Mom, is dinner ready?" Miesha calls as she comes bouncing down the stairs. "I'm so hungry."

Rebecca refocuses. "Uh, yes, it's ready." She notices Miesha rubbing the back of her right calf for the fourth time today. "What's wrong with your leg? You keep rubbing it."

"I dunno. I have, like, this weird cut here," she says.

"Let me see it," Rebecca demands in her nurse voice.

Miesha pulls up her light gray leggings and shows her. A thin pink cut graces the middle of her calf.

"Hmm. How'd you get that?" Rebecca asks, examining her daughter's skin.

"I think I scratched it on the ballet bar when I was doing my stretches."

"Let's put some Polysporin on it after bath, okay?" she says, stroking her daughter's long hair.

"Whatever," Miesha agrees. Rebecca retreats into the kitchen to prepare the final touches for dinner and Miesha pops a piece of garlic bread into her mouth.

Bedtime finally arrives. Miesha has managed to read one last chapter of her book for tomorrow's class discussion and Rebecca is finishing up the last load of laundry. Just before lights out, she kisses her daughter on the forehead and tells her she loves her. The response is always the same: "I love you too, Scooby Doo."

Exhausted, Rebecca grabs a cup of chamomile tea from the kitchen before climbing into her own bed. Her thin laptop is sitting on the bedside table and she debates whether or not she has the energy to check her email tonight. Sipping her tea, she decides to unfold her machine and log in for the first time that day.

Her email account has ten new messages, half of which are spam mail. There is a joke from her brother, a long note from her mother saying how good it was to see her at Thanksgiving, one from Kitty with the details of Lynn's planned shower, and one with an unfamiliar name and reply-to address but the word 'Hello' in the subject line.

She hesitates before opening the last. Likely it's spam. When she does open it, the words literally pop off the screen, forcing and a wave of anticipation to wash over her. It crashes down hard in the pit of her stomach.

Hello Rebecca. I'm in Laos now, gearing up to head out in a few days to Vietnam, up along the Mekong and then into Cambodia. The landscape is spectacular and the buildings in this part of the world have given me such a great appreciation for Asian art and architecture. The people here are so beautiful and peaceful that it's easy to forget that Laos had such a brutal civil war once. Still, unlike most of us, their past does not seem to haunt them. I recently saw a painting that reminded me of you. Kitty tells me you are doing well. I'm pleased to hear that. James.

Rebecca puts her computer aside. A huge feeling of relief takes over her physical and emotional being. The ice has finally broken, and it seems like a channel between them may finally be opening up.

NINETEEN

It is the first day of December and Martin is marking the date on his calendar, as it is the end of his second cycle of chemotherapy. So far the side effects of the treatment are bearable, thanks mostly to his preoccupation with his pending marriage to Lynn. He always hoped that if he found the right woman to spend the rest of his life with, he would marry her on New Year's Eve. Now the time has come and he is well on his way toward realizing that dream.

He wishes for Lynn's sake that they could be in a normal situation, where age and disease were not part of the equation. His dream was always to have a house constructed by his own hands, and now he would give anything to build Lynn a home specifically tailored to her wishes. However, Martin now lives in a sea of pragmatism, and tries to be comforted by the fact that he will have this time with Lynn, however long and wherever that may be.

He rests his head on the pillow and stares at the empty bed beside him. Stan is at Mercy Hospital waiting for a kidney donor and transplant. He is at the top of the list now, and the next time a kidney is available he'll go under the knife. Martin wishes that he could be the one to help his friend. Stan is filled with so much light that it hardly seems fair that he should have to endure all this at such a young age.

Thinking of Stan makes Martin remember how Frank's aura used to tower over everyone else's mortal existence. It was something that always fascinated and perplexed him. Of all the people that have come and gone in his lifetime, Frank is the one Martin misses the most. He tries hard to push away the image of Frank collapsing beside him on the jungle floor.

Instead, he focuses on thoughts of James, his very own shadow. How strange it is that James is about to set foot on the same soil that forever altered his own person.

205

Martin hopes that his young friend will find the balance of acceptance and forgiveness the way he mostly did through Sloan's letter so many years ago. *Finding that balance is the only way James will be able to escape the madness spawned by guilt and regret*, Martin thinks. *Our destiny is something that we can only partially control, and the sooner we all realize that life will unfold as it should, the better off we'll be.*

The silence in the room is broken by Rebecca's voice. "Hello, Martin. How are you feeling today?"

Martin is tired and feels like he might be sick. He's been feeling this way all week. "Truth be told, I can't wait to have these sessions over and done with," he says, feeling discouraged.

"I know it's hard, but it has to be done. Try to take it one day at a time," Rebecca says with encouragement.

"Humph. Easy for you to say," Martin mumbles.

"I have some good news that might take your mind off things," Rebecca says sweetly, changing the subject. "I got word this morning from Mercy that Stan will be having his operation later on today. A donor came through this morning."

Martin's spirits lift immediately. "That's great!" he says, smiling his first genuine smile of the day.

Rebecca sits on the edge of Martin's bed. "I know, isn't it? Stan is such a special person. He has this incredible energy about him, doesn't he?"

"I'm not surprised that you see it too," Martin says, reflecting on his personal philosophy about those who can find their souls much easier than others.

Martin takes her hand and smiles. "Any news from our travelling friend?" He's referring to James, and knows that she knows it. Rebecca is silent, so Martin tries to coax her out of her shell. "Have you heard anything from him?"

Rebecca's face blushes. "Um, yes, actually, I did. Last night. He sent me an email."

Martin isn't surprised. "And?"

She shrugs her shoulders. "It was a cryptic note about Laos and its people and buildings and landscapes . . ."

"Anything personal in it?" Martin doesn't mind prodding.

"Well, he signed off by telling me that he saw a painting that reminded him of me." Her cheeks take on an even deeper rose color.

"My, my, my. Perhaps our boy is finally finding himself," Martin says softly.

"I wasn't really sure what to make of it," Rebecca remarks. "All I know is that I wasn't expecting to hear anything from him."

"Did you reply?" Martin asks.

"I did," she says sheepishly. "I told him that it was nice to hear from him and that I was doing all right. I told him about you and Lynn, too, but he probably already knows that from Kitty and Janice. Regardless, I'm not sure if he'll get my message before he leaves for Vietnam and Cambodia."

"In due time, my dear," Martin says, shifting his eyebrows.

Rebecca sighs. "I've been feeling like time is running short these days. I wonder why?"

Martin tries to reassure her. "Dear, you're a busy single mother who has a full-time job. Just do what I do and pretend that time isn't a factor. It doesn't really exist. You can't run out of something you don't have, right?"

Rebecca seems to appreciate this philosophy. She walks over to hug him. "I'll be back soon with your lunch—a western sandwich with tomato soup. Try to eat some of it, okay?"

Martin hangs his tongue out in disgust. "Is there any of Lynn's lasagna left?"

She shakes her head. "Sorry. Max and Gerry ate it last night."

"Damn fools," Martin says, shifting down underneath his sheets.

"Oh, and by the way, I'm picking you up on Saturday night for the Christmas party."

"Sure, you can pick us up for our surprise engagement party if you want," Martin says, grabbing his book and trying to hide his smile behind its pages.

"Oh my God! Is there *anything* we can get past you?" Rebecca asks, exasperated.

Martin gives her his most devilish grin. "If you want to secretly clean the land, the noise of the axe will give you away."

"Let me guess—Chinese proverb?"

"African, my dear," Martin corrects, happy to share something he's learned with her.

"Shall I pretend you don't know?"

Martin shrugs his shoulders. "Yes, I think we can still manage to get Lynn."

Rebecca puts her hand on her hip. "You are one crafty cat."

"Why, thank you, Miss Rebecca," Martin says, winking.

Rebecca leaves the room in an exaggerated huff. A moment later Martin can hear her saying hello to another patient in the next room. Her voice is kind and gentle as always. He thinks to himself, *She's a genuine soul, and for that, she will find her way.*

★★★

The road to Vinh, Vietnam, is treacherous, but James finds himself dozing off anyways as a result of the heat and lack of air circulation in the crowded bus. Crates of squawking chickens and boxes of perishable food fill any spare space between passengers. That, combined with the overpowering smell of body odor, is enough to make James want to be sick to his stomach any time he stirs from his sleep. When he is jolted awake, he is thankful for his anti-anxiety prescription. Still, he knows he can't complain to Ted. After all, it's his fault that they're on this bus in the first place.

"Explain to me again why you can't take a train?" Ted asks, trying to push a box of chicken beaks and feet to the side with his ankle.

"I told you, I'm not comfortable in trains," James retorts, half-dazed.

"And this is your epitome of comfort?" Ted asks, chugging back some bottled water.

"We've got to be pretty close now to Vinh now, right? We've been on the road all night."

"We haven't even crossed the border yet, and then it's at least another hour. Anyways, better get your passport ready because it'll be mayhem," Ted says, shuffling around in his seat to retrieve his from the back pocket of his cargo shorts.

"What do you mean? Aren't our papers in good order?" James asks, suddenly feeling even more anxious. He remembers the scene with the German students at the last border crossing and his heart rate accelerates. *Relax*, he tries to coach himself. *There's no reason to think there'll be any problems.* This bus is primarily filled with Asian passengers. Ted and James are two of the five North Americans on board.

"They don't necessarily know the concept of order," Ted explains, sounding like he's speaking from experience. James decides not to ask any more questions.

Within minutes, he understands. The bus pulls up to the border shack and the Asian passengers rush to disembark and start randomly throwing their passports on the ground at the customs officers' feet. Luckily for James, Ted has been through this crossing several times. They stay in their seats and an officer in uniform comes up to them. He seems to recognize Ted from one of his previous trips. Ted slips him a tip along with their documents, and their papers are processed on the spot. *See? That wasn't so bad*, James tells himself.

Still, sensing the chaos being generated by his fellow travelers who are congregated at the front of the bus, James is finding it hard to breathe. Ted looks over and seems to notice this. He hands James a bottle of warm water from his duffel bag. "So, you're looking forward to our bike excursion, then?" he asks, obviously trying to distract James. "No chickens on a bike trip," he jokes.

"I'm looking forward to getting off this fucking bus," replies James, his eyes darting around. He recognizes this as a symptom of his panic disorder.

"All right, all right," says Ted, raising his arms in surrender. "Take a deep breath, man. You were the one who wanted to do this. The train would have been—"

James suddenly cuts him off. "I told you! The train is *not* an option for me!" he barks furiously. Even amid the chaos, people turn around to see what the problem is.

"Okay, buddy, chill. It's okay." Ted's voice is smooth and calming. "So, who's Rebecca?"

James wishes he was back in Thailand, where Ted stayed in his peripheral most of the time. He sighs deeply. "She's someone back home," he says with deliberate vagueness.

"Wow. Someone back home, huh? Well, that *someone* must be someone pretty special, because you called her name out last night—more than once."

James feels like a prodded bear. He looks over at Ted, prepared to erupt, but instead he finds himself saying something completely unexpected. "She's a girl that I ... well, I ... think I might really like. Maybe." He knows he sounds ridiculous even as the words leave his mouth.

Ted bursts out laughing. "*A girl you think you might really like?*" he mocks gently, then laughs some more. "Okay, dude, look—last time I checked we weren't in puberty anymore. Are you telling me you don't know when you're into a woman or not?"

"Fine. I like her," James says definitively. "I like her a lot. I actually think I might like her too much."

"No such thing, man. Not if she's a good woman—which, from the way you've been hit by the bullet, she must be." Ted rummages through his bag and emerges with two miniature bottles of whiskey. He hands one to James.

James downs his in one shot. "I guess I've been a broken-down mess for most of my life. I planned this trip thinking I could just keep running away from myself, but that hasn't happened. I'm right where I always have been." He's looking out the smeared bus window as he speaks openly for what feels like the first time in years.

Ted finishes off his bottle and grabs two more. James reaches for one, snaps the lid open, and downs the liquid. The hot burning sensation feels cool in his veins.

"We all are, man. We all are," Ted says. There's a pause. "But you know what I think? I think you've gotta go after her when you get home."

At that moment, the rest of the passengers begin to flood back onto the bus and mayhem ensues as they find their seats and holler about this and that and everything in between. James focuses on the passing scenery and the fact that he's in Vietnam. An hour and a half later, Ted elbows him and says that they're entering Vinh. After passing through the outskirts of the city, the driver announces something through a megaphone. James can see the bus terminal up ahead and the city of Vinh wrapped around the tiny structure. The terminal appears almost abandoned, with little sign of activity except for a few pickup trucks and food vendors. When the bus comes to a stop, Ted pushes open the bus's back hatch and pulls on James's arm for him to follow. They jump onto the dusty ground, thereby avoiding the madness playing out at the front of the bus.

As they walk away from the terminal, a small local man in his early twenties walks up to Ted and says something that James cannot comprehend. Ted responds in the man's native tongue, and the man nods. As they follow the man across the parking lot, Ted explains to James that they've just secured a ride across the city.

Two small boys around the ages of three and five are sitting in the box of the man's light green pickup truck. Their faces are perfectly round and their eyes are a beautiful almond shape. They are watching James and Ted closely through pupils bathed in ebony. The boys are wearing pale blue and yellow golf shirts and dirt-stained Bermuda shorts.

As they approach, James pulls out a pack of gum from his knapsack and holds it out to them. The boys smile gap-toothed grins and the older one takes the pack. He unwraps a piece and hands it to the smaller boy, who immediately puts it in his mouth. They say something in Vietnamese that James takes to mean 'thank you.' He smiles back and asks the father if he can take a picture of the boys. Ted translates the request and the man nods his assent. James removes his camera and the two boys eagerly pose over the side of the pick-up. The older one makes bunny ears over the younger one's head.

"Hop in," Ted calls over to James. They climb into the back of the truck and the boys wriggle with excitement. As they drive into the crux of the small town, Ted explains that the driver's mother runs a small hotel near the central market area. He assured Ted that the place is lice-free and that the hot water runs well. Within minutes they pull up to a drab two-story clay building with a dozen perfectly square windows. A tiny woman that James assumes to be the man's mother is standing outside. The driver walks up to her and she nods her head and points to the building. The air is stifling and there is an odd smell of overcooked rice and some kind of meat lurking about.

The sun is pounding down on James's uncovered head and he feels the need to lie down. He is trying hard not to feel nauseous and is craving a cold beer. He simulates drinking from a bottle and the mother gestures to a grimy-looking restaurant across the road. Ted pays the driver and then he and James cross the street.

The shabby red and green sign over the restaurant has faded but the words *Pho Bo* are still legible. The inside of the small stall is clean and freshly painted with a pale mint color. Four bright red stools sit underneath the worn and weathered wooden bar that overlooks a small kitchen. An old cash register is stationed on the right-hand side of the counter across from the fridge and sink. The place is devoid of any decor with the exception of a Buddha statue that sits in between a few bottles of rice wine on the shelf behind the counter.

A wrinkled old man emerges from the back. Ted holds up four fingers while James unloads his heavy weight on the seat of the barstool. Moments later four bottles of cold beer are set in front of them, covered in condensation. James eagerly chugs down one of the beers while Ted places an array of paper notes on the counter.

"God, this is the best beer I've ever tasted!" James announces, his thirst happily quenched.

The old man smiles at them. "American?"

Ted answers him back in Vietnamese. The man replies and Ted seems to agree.

"What's he saying?" James asks, feeling completely out of sync with the new world around him.

"He says we should come by for dinner later."

James nods his agreement and raises his second beer for a cheers. Before long he and Ted are reminiscing about their experiences throughout Laos. *Funny how distance makes the heart grow fonder*, James thinks in passing. All the anxiety he felt earlier on in the day melts away.

The conversation turns to Laos's beautiful Plaine des Jarres and the fact that no one knows its origins. Nestled within a vast countryside, hundreds and hundreds of stone jars measuring up to ten feet high and weighing up to six tons are literally littered as far as the eye can see. For some unknown reason, this place spoke to James's soul like no other place he'd ever been. It was here that he felt grounded for the first time since Stephen's death. It was like his past and his future decided to call a truce.

Ted says that he was particularly taken by the monks dressed in saffron robes and praying in the Golden City Temple.

"Me too," agrees James. "It was like I could *feel* them meditating. They had such a calm presence. They definitely had an impact on me."

"I could tell," Ted says. "You sat there for, like, an hour without moving, just watching them."

"I think I needed that," James says. "I wanted to talk to one of them, but it didn't seem like a good idea."

"Then I've got the perfect spot for you to go," says Ted. "Wait until we hit Hanoi. Check this out." He lifts up the back of his Andy Warhol t-shirt to reveal a tattoo script in Asian lettering on the small of his back.

"What does it mean?" James asks curiously as the old shopkeeper pushes another beer in front of him.

"Life goes on within you and without you," Ted replies.

James's face freezes. He recognizes the lyrics from a song Stephen used to sing.

Ted pulls his shirt back down. "What's the matter? You don't like the Beatles?" He starts singing the song softy and without inhibition.

James is still staring blankly into space. His shoulders are hunched over the bar as he slowly peals off the label from his bottle.

Ted stops singing and sits quietly for a moment. "I had it tattooed on me after Mallory died," he says.

James looks over at him and gives him a sympathetic smile. He starts humming the tune of the song and then the words begin to form along with the melody. Ted joins in for the chorus and soon both men are singing at the top of their lungs.

The old man is smiling wildly and pours himself a shot of whiskey.

James and Ted sing the chorus again before their voices trail off.

"You lost someone too, brother," Ted says.

"Yes. Yes, I did," James answers. "And it still fucking sucks almost twenty years later."

The old man says something in Vietnamese. Ted laughs. "Poor sod! He wants us to keep singing!"

Ted starts digging for something in his knapsack. He pulls out his iPod and its portable stand. He digs down farther to find a voltage converter and hands all three to the shopkeeper, directing him on how to plug it all in. James is now feeling the full effects of the three beers and starts laughing hard.

Music starts to blare from the tiny machine. The old man pours himself another shot of whiskey. A heavy baseline kicks in with some funky rhythmic beat and soon James and Ted are on their feet belting out a song by the Talking Heads. A young local couple walks in and orders take-out food. They smile and laugh at James and Ted, complete outcasts in their neighborhood watering hole.

The young couple starts to dance along with the music. The hotel proprietor and her son come across from their building with the keys for a rental apartment. They smile with a pleasantly surprised look on their faces. The old woman goes behind the counter to help out with the cooking. The driver's two young boys come running into the place and join in the dancing. Another customer that the others seem to know walks into the stall, scrunches up his face in a confused expression, and walks right back out. Everyone laughs. The young woman stops her dancing, runs after him, and drags him back into the tiny area where everyone now is collectively bobbing and weaving. He stops resisting and joins in. Beer bottles are accumulating on the bar and the smell of fresh coriander and chicken fills the air.

After a few more songs, the heat inside the small restaurant becomes unbearable for James. He picks up his beer and steps outside. He sees a red kite fly out a window, and a young child and her mother wave at it from the alley. A small hole in the haze opens up. James watches the kite pass through it.

"Goodbye," he says under his breath.

Suddenly Ted is next to him. He wraps his arm around James's neck and pulls him close in a brotherly hug. Both men watch the sky, and for once James's mind and heart are free from everything other than the power of their connection.

TWENTY

"You ready to do this?" Ted asks.

"Yeah, sure," James says, panting. He closes his eyes and recalls their last night in Vinh. They stayed up all night exchanging stories about themselves. They were drunk and emotional, but it was a night that James would never forget. It was the first time he ever told the complete story of Stephen's death and admitted out loud how the event had completely altered his life. The booze also loosened his tongue enough to make him admit that anxiety had been running the show for him for almost two decades and that he didn't want to carry it around any longer.

The sound system blurts out something in Vietnamese, startling James out of his reminiscence. The only word he recognized was 'Hanoi.'

"It's time to move forward, buddy," Ted says, giving him a pat on the back. "Let's go."

With Ted leading the way, James steps onto the platform. The long, sleek train looks fairly modern. Ted steps up onto the movable steps, ready to board. He gives James a gentle look. "It's okay, man. I'm going to be here the entire time."

"This seemed like a better idea last night," James mutters. "I just don't know if I can ..."

Ted digs for some ammunition. "Listen, man, do you really want to climb back on that shithole of a bus again?"

No, James thinks, but he doesn't say anything.

"Well, do you?" Ted prods.

James shakes his head no.

"Okay, then. Come on," Ted says firmly, extending his hand.

James grabs his hand and lets himself be pulled onto the train steps. "Oh God," he says, breathing heavily. His hands are shaking and his vision is tunneling.

Ted grabs James by the shoulders. "We're going to be okay. I promise you, man. I'm not leaving you, you hear me? I'm not leaving you."

James inhales deeply and takes the final two steps onto the train. His heart pumps more adrenaline through his body than he can manage. He feels like he might actually jump right out of his own skin. People are pushing past him to board the train, anxious to find their seats.

"Did you take your Xanax?" Ted asks.

"No," James tells him. "I wanted to try and do this myself."

"Good for you, man," Ted says. "Come on, let's sit over here."

James follows Ted inside a tiny cabin with four berth sleepers. It looks much more comfortable than what he was expecting. "What the hell is this?" he asks.

"Hell, Jimmy, we've been up all night so I figured we could just stretch out for the duration of the trip," Ted tells him, bouncing on one of the cabin berths.

"I'm not so sure I'll be able to sleep," James says.

"We can just hang out and talk, then. Let the world pass us by," Ted replies as he lies down on the narrow bed. He folds his arms behind his head and crosses his legs to achieve an imitation of a comfortable position for the journey.

James lowers his knapsack to the floor as the train starts to slowly pull out of the station. He tries to remain calm while he lies down on the berth across from Ted. He closes his eyes and tries not to think. Then, so gradually that he doesn't even notice it, the swaying motion of the slow-moving train cradles him into a state of unfamiliar calmness.

"Ted?" he says quietly after what feels like an hour.

"Yeah?" Ted's voice is only half-awake.

"Thanks."

"It's all good, my main man. It's all good."

The train starts to hustle down the track and the whistle blows. Startled, James opens his eyes wide. It's a sound that haunts his nightmares.

"It's time to move on, man. Let it go. It's time to reclaim your life," Ted says without looking at him.

James closes his eyes again and starts to breathe deeply. The warm air surrounds his body and the sound of the train forging ahead eventually rocks him to sleep.

In his dream, he and Stephen are young boys running through the aisles of the train. They have gap-toothed grins and he is carrying a pack of gum. Rice fields are rolling by out the windows, and moss-covered hills look like giants standing in the skyline beneath the hazy sky. James jumps onto a seat, smiling and waving at the workers in the fields. Their pointed hats lift up from their crouched positions as they wave back.

In the distance, shots fire out and the train comes to a sudden grinding stop. The force of the brakes being applied jolts everything inside. People start floating around in air that is suddenly devoid of gravity. Pieces of metal and cargo hover aimlessly in between the bodies. James can feel himself tumbling around like a wispy feather. He calls for Stephen, but he can only hear his laugh. Martin floats by and grabs onto James, pulling him down to the floor. James is no longer a boy, but a man. He and Martin stand with firm feet, looking at each other. Martin is bleeding from one side of his head but he doesn't seem to notice.

"Where are you going?" he asks James with a smile.

James looks around and calls for Stephen again. Martin takes his hand and pulls him away from a pile of rubble anchored to the train's floor. A Vietnamese man climbs over the heap and says something in his native tongue to Martin. Martin leads James towards a doorway. As they stand together holding hands, they watch their fellow passengers float off the train—dozens of weightless bodies bouncing lightly in the air. Some are injured and some are dead. A little girl in pink ballet slippers floats by James. Her eyes are closed and she looks peaceful. Martin takes his hand and leads him to another doorway where new passengers are cheerfully boarding the train with their bags and children in tow. The Vietnamese man goes into the engine room and starts the train. Martin and James move to a window and watch as the train starts to speed away.

James spins around, anxiously calling out for Stephen one more time. Martin whispers something in his ear that makes him look out the window. Stephen is standing there, waving. A large man in army fatigues is standing next to him and giving a salute. Both men look perfectly healthy and unscathed by the train accident. The little girl is running with all of her might alongside the train trying to catch up to it—her slippers now torn and tattered.

James feels Martin's arm around him. He watches as the figures fade into the distance. James buries his face in Martin's chest and cries hard. The strength of Martin's courage wraps around him like a warm blanket. "It's their stop," Martin tells him gently. "Not ours."

The sound of the cabin rattling jostles James from his sleep. He wakes up feeling brighter. Ted is snoring in his berth. James is happy to have this moment to himself. He thinks about his dream for a moment and then suddenly realizes the answer to Martin's riddle. He grabs his backpack and starts to fish around for the book.

His fingers fumble through the pages. He finds the poem written by Carl Sandburg, bookmarked and ready for him. He reads each word carefully and then reflects on the words. He reads the last line out loud again to solidify his own interpretation. "...I ask a man in the smoker where he is going and he answers: 'Omaha.'"

James releases the pages of the book. "I get it," he says quietly under his breath. "We are all on this great journey together until we reach our collective destination and whenever that may be is the only thing that varies."

James rests his arms on his knees and watches the Vietnamese landscape pass by. He begins to understand the significance of his dream and of Martin's last riddle: Where are you going? Finally, like the man in the smoker, he reveals the answer.

"I'm going home," he says quietly to himself.

★★★

It's been a week since Rebecca received the email from James, and every day she checks her messages for another one. She tells herself that it must be difficult for him to find a computer, and even if he did, he has other more important people to check in with, like his mother and sister and possibly even co-workers. She tries to comfort herself with this thought as she heads out for the last rounds of her shift. She passes Gerry and Max and two new patients in the television room.

"Hey, sports fans. How's it going? Did you have fun at the engagement party?"

Gerry pipes up first. "Max sure did! He found himself a date."

Max raises his fist and punches Gerry in the shoulder. "Shut up."

"Aha!" says Rebecca, truly pleased. "I saw you getting cozy over there with Kendra's friend Shelly. She's lovely!"

Max smiles. "Yeah, she is." The way he says it tells her that he prefers to keep his personal news to himself.

"Hey, have you guys gone to see Stan? I hear he's allowed visitors now that he's stabilized."

"Sure have," Gerry says. "He's looking real good. Says he'll be back here in a week or so to be monitored for the next few months. He's got that pretty little thing looking after him, you know."

"Who? A nurse?" Rebecca asks.

"No, that young girl that was hanging out here all of the time."

"Cody Ann? Yes, she is cute, isn't she," Rebecca remarks. "Well, I'm off to make my rounds before heading home. You guys need anything?"

"Nah, but thanks." Max winks at her and waves.

She passes the reception desk where Donna's looking at a chart. She tries unsuccessfully to slip past, unnoticed.

"Oh, Rebecca!" Donna calls.

Rebecca groans and backtracks to reception. "The afterschool program just called looking for you. Miesha isn't feeling well. They said she has a slight fever."

Rebecca thanks her for the message and walks over to the staff phone to place the call. "Hi, Amanda? It's Rebecca Doyle. Miesha's sick?"

"Oh, hi, Rebecca. Yeah, she was complaining of aches and pains so we took her temperature and it's slightly elevated—a hundred point four," the caregiver says into the line.

"I'll be there within a half hour. Thanks for calling." Worry gnaws at Rebecca's gut as she picks up her purse from behind the staff station. "Donna, I've got to take off a bit early to pick up Miesha. She's not feeling well and she's running a bit of a temperature. I might not be in tomorrow depending on how she's doing. Can you put Julie on standby?"

"I'm on it," Donna says. "And I'll even check up on the rest of your patients for you."

"Thanks," Rebecca says, already heading towards the exit.

"Hope the wee one feels better," Donna hollers down the hall.

"Thanks!" Rebecca shouts back as she steps in the elevator. *I hope so, too,* she thinks to herself.

★★★

Martin comes around the corner just as the elevator doors close to see what all the fuss is about.

"Where's the fire?" he asks with a twinkle in his eye.

"I'd say it just walked in," Donna says.

Is she flirting with me? Martin wonders. *Well I'll be darned. There's a first time for everything, I guess.* "Ha! You sure know how to charm the pants off a fellow, Donna. Where's Rebecca going in such a hurry?"

"Miesha isn't feeling well. She's got a bit of a temperature," Donna remarks.

Martin sighs. "I suppose it's that time of year, isn't it?"

"Mm-hm," she agrees. "Oh, and speaking of time of year, I can't believe you're getting married on New Year's Eve!"

"Yes, I'm a lucky old sea dog," Martin says proudly.

"I have to say, Martin, your niece is an exceptional young lady," Donna says as she puts her files in order. "I had a nice long chat with her at the engagement party."

"Yes, she's incredible. I'm very lucky to have her in my life, too." A wave of fatigue suddenly washes over him.

Donna looks at him closely and narrows her eyes. "Martin, you don't look so good. Is it the meds again? Here, let me help you back to your bed." Donna gets up and moves towards him, then gently takes his arm. "Speaking of temperatures, you feel warm yourself," she says with concern.

"I'm not enjoying this chemotherapy, Donna."

"Well, don't forget that you had a nasty chest cold not that long ago, so your body's still recovering from that strain, too. I'm about to leave for the day, but let's get you checked out by the doctor first. And I'm going to see about getting you something decent to eat. I'm pretty sure there's something left over from Lynn's care package for you."

Donna helps him down onto his bed and takes his temperature. Sure enough, he's running a slight fever as well. Donna presses down the crisp sheets until they are just above his waist. "I'll have the doctor over here in a jiffy."

"Thanks, Donna." As Donna leaves, Martin's cellphone starts to ring. He turns over the various books on his side table looking for it. "Gotcha," he says when he locates it. "Hello, this is Martin."

"Hey, Uncle Marty, it's me. How are you?" Kendra's voice is always pleasing to his ear.

"I'm fine, dear. Are you well?"

"I am, Uncle. I just wanted to let you know that some guy named Ty ended up getting my phone number somehow. He asked me to let you know that James wants to pass along a message, but he doesn't have your email address."

"Of course he doesn't. I don't have one," Martin says, rebelling against the idea.

"I *know* that, Uncle Marty. And James figured that out too, which is why he asked his friend Ty to track me down to give you the message."

"Who is Ty?" Martin asks, feeling a bit overprotective.

Kendra sighs. "Uncle Marty, chill. He actually seems super nice. He works with James and they're apparently good friends. I guess you must have told James where I worked, because he told Ty where to find me. Anyway, do you want the message over the phone? It's only a sentence or two. It looks like the answer to one of your riddles."

Martin's lips curl into a grin. "Give it to me over the phone, love."

She articulates the words carefully. "He says, 'Although I have no plans in the immediate future to ride the last train to Omaha, when my turn comes to board, I will take comfort in knowing that I won't be alone. I owe you one. Thanks, Jimmy. P.S. Get into this century and get on email.'"

"I have no idea what he's talking about, Uncle, but I agree with him on the whole email point," Kendra says firmly.

"All right, angel, I get it. Maybe you can take me shopping for a computer."

"Now you're talking! I gotta run. See you for lunch this weekend?" she asks sweetly.

"You bet," he answers, feeling his chest swell with love for his niece.

They both sign off with big goodbyes.

"Well, I'll be damned!" Martin exclaims happily after he hangs up.

Lynn comes into the room with dinner wrapped in aluminum foil. "What on earth are you swearing about now, Martin?"

"My dear, I do believe a spell has been broken."

"Well, your fever has yet to," Dr. Lewis says, entering the room not far behind Lynn.

"Hello, Doctor," Lynn and Martin say in unison.

Dr. Lewis walks over to his patient and asks to listen to his chest. "Sounds good. But I'm assuming you're either overexerting yourself or you're fighting off the remainder of that nasty chest bug you had. Either way, you need to rest. Here's some Tylenol." He pours Martin a glass of water and watches him swallow the pills. "I think I've already explained that the immune system becomes very compromised during chemotherapy, and even though in your case I believe everything is going well, we all want to keep it that way. So I recommend that, for the next week, you don't go on any outings, and no one with even so much as a sniffle should enter this room. Okay?"

"Ack," Martin huffs, turning away from the doctor. It was hard enough for him to agree to chemotherapy in the first place. He likes the idea of adjusting his routine even less.

"You know how important this is," says the doctor, addressing Lynn now. "Make sure you talk some sense into him and get him to eat." He winks at her and exits the room.

"Did you hear him, darling?" Lynn asks, moving closer to his bedside. "I couldn't bear to watch you get sick."

"I *am* sick," Martin scoffs.

"You know what I mean!" she exclaims. "I'm going to go into the kitchen to heat this up. You'd better behave yourself while I'm gone." She kisses him on the cheek and is out the door before Martin can think of a response.

"Humph." He crosses his arms, feeling agitated. He hears a voice of reason in his head, thick with a Newfoundland accent. *Don't be biniky. Yer a chucklehead. Long may yer Jib draw.* "So you're nagging me from the grave now, Frank?" Martin asks under his breath. Then he laughs softly and agrees. "All right, by, all right."

★★★

Miesha has gone to bed early. Since she isn't going to school tomorrow, Rebecca decides to take advantage of not having to prepare lunch and laundry tonight and relaxes instead. She called the doctor as soon as they got home and luckily was able to get an appointment first thing in the morning. She peeks into her daughter's room again to feel her forehead. It seems a little cooler now that she's been on a

219

rotation of fever-reducing medication.

Rebecca decides that a cup of tea is just what she needs now that Miesha is sound asleep. She heads downstairs to fix one before she heads to bed herself. It seems odd how quiet the house is, and she has an uneasy feeling in the pit of her stomach. She pours the boiled water over the tea bag and tries to distract herself by thinking about the last time she and James made love. She never felt like that before and she aches for that feeling to return.

She carries her mug upstairs. The bedrooms are warm and cozy from the heat coming off the gas fireplace in the master bedroom. She makes sure that Miesha isn't too heavily covered so that her fever won't spike. Rebecca kisses her daughter on the forehead and moves into her own bedroom where she sits down on the bed, feeling drained from the day's events. Her laptop is already on her bed and she settles into her warm blankets before checking her e-mails.. There are twelve new messages—one of which is from James Milligan. Her stomach drops to her pelvic area. She double clicks on it.

Hello from North Vietnam. Hanoi is a fabulous city with so much to do and see. We could have spent an entire week there except we're too eager to hit more sites along the Mekong Delta. There are so many beautiful things to see in this part of the world. I feel as though my eyes have been opened for the first time. I wanted to let you know that I'm thinking about you. James.

Her heart is racing as she writes him back.

Hi! It's so good to hear from you. Are you able to send some pictures? Things here are pretty much the same. Martin is slowly getting through his chemotherapy, and both he and Lynn are excited for the wedding on New Year's Eve. Do you think you'll be back for it? Your sister is doing amazing, and so is your nephew. He's a little firecracker just like his mom. Janice is busy, making things happen as usual. Everyone misses you. You are very much loved here, James. Come back safely. Rebecca. xoxo

★★★

The next morning, Rebecca opens her eyes to find Miesha standing over her bed, trying to wake her. Her daughter has been crying. Rebecca jumps up immediately.

"Honey, what's wrong?" she gasps, clutching her little girl in her arms. Her thin eight-year-old skin feels warm again.

"My tummy hurts," says Miesha. "I just threw up."

Rebecca can smell it on her hair. "We're going to see the doctor in a bit. Let's get you in a bath and wash up in the meantime."

"I'm thirsty and my head hurts," Miesha moans.

"Then let's get you some water and see if you can keep down some pills, okay?"

Rebecca leads Miesha into the bathroom. She grabs the thermometer and reads her daughter's temperature. The digital stick reads a hundred and two degrees.

"Oh boy," Rebecca says nervously.

"What, mommy?"

"Nothing, baby. Let's take off your nightgown and get you into a bath. It's not going to be very warm though, okay?"

"Okay," Miesha says, whimpering.

Rebecca pulls the nightgown over Miesha's head and helps remove her underwear. She notices that the small scratch on her daughter's calf has manifested into a blister. The area is red and inflamed. Rebecca's heart starts to race.

"Honey, is this boo-boo still hurting you?"

"My whole leg hurts, Mom," Miesha says, starting to cry.

Rebecca turns off the taps. As a nurse she knows full well the signs and symptoms of a staph infection. She grabs a brush out of the drawer and quickly brushes Miesha's hair. She finds the few strands at the front that were grazed by vomit and rubs a wet cloth with soap on them to try and get most of it out.

"Come on, baby, we're going to see the doctor now, okay? Let's get you dressed."

"I just want to go to bed, Mommy," Miesha whines. She hasn't referred to her as Mommy in years.

"Go pick out your clothes, okay sweetie? I'm just going to call them to let them know we're coming now."

As Miesha does what she's asked, Rebecca sneaks off into her bedroom and calls the pediatrician's office. She explains the situation and the receptionist instructs her to take Miesha directly to Children's Memorial Hospital.

Rebecca is now shaking and trying hard not to cry. She's alone and terrified. She dials her mother and then realizes that her parents are out of the country. She can no longer hold back her tears.

Miesha is calling her from the other room. Rebecca tries hard to pull herself together. "Coming, love." She wipes her eyes and heads into her daughter's bedroom.

"Is this okay?" Miesha is wearing loose leggings and a long-sleeved t-shirt.

"That's great, hun. Now listen up, okay? I called Dr. Zue and she said we should go to the hospital instead of to her office."

"Why?" Miesha is confused.

"Well, baby girl, I think it's this bump on your leg that's making you sick, and the hospital will be able to take care of it much faster than Dr. Zue can."

Miesha starts to cry. "I'm sorry, Mommy."

Rebecca grabs her and holds her tightly in her arms. "No! None of this is your fault! Don't be sorry, okay? Don't be." She kisses Miesha all over her face.

Miesha sees that Rebecca is crying, too. "Mommy, am I going to die?"

Rebecca almost faints at the sound of those words. "No! Absolutely not. Nobody's dying around here, okay? We still have way too many flavors of ice cream left to try!"

They both start giggling. Rebecca feels Miesha's forehead and it feels the same. *This is good. No spike yet*, she thinks to herself. She decides to call a cab. It's rush hour and her nerves are already shot. She dials the number for the cab company and requests one urgently. Miesha is lying on the floor with her doll while Rebecca phones the hospital. Janice answers.

"Hello, Veterans' Hospital nurses' station. How can I help you?"

Rebecca starts to cry again. She can't get out any words.

"Hello? Who is this?" Janice demands.

"Janice?" Rebecca is trying hard to keep herself from breaking down. "It's … it's Rebecca." She manages to explain the situation to Janice, who tells her not to worry and that Julie is covering her shift.

"I'm coming to be with you at the hospital, dear," she says. "I'll be there in half an hour. Don't worry, okay?"

"Okay." It's Rebecca's turn to whimper now. "Thank you."

Before she can hang up, Miesha is standing at the door. "Mommy, the taxi is here!"

"Okay, let's get your jacket. And oh—bring your dolly, okay? And where's my purse? I have my phone. Insurance? Where is it?" She looks in her wallet. It's there. "Oh God—Ben! I have to call him." Rebecca can't keep from talking to herself. She dials Ben's number, but there's no answer.

"Mom, I feel sick again," Miesha groans.

"Oh, shoot." She runs into the kitchen and grabs a few plastic bags. "Let's go!" She rushes her daughter out the door.

Once in the taxi Miesha rests her head on Rebecca's shoulder. Rebecca goes into her soul and prays hard that Miesha's illness is treatable.

Her phone rings. "Hello?" Rebecca answers, panicked.

"Hi, it's Ben. What's up?"

"I'm on my way to Children's Memorial with Miesha."

"What? Why? What's wrong?"

"I'm not sure, but you need to meet me there," Rebecca says quietly. She looks down at Miesha, who is now asleep on her shoulder.

"Rebecca, what's going on?"

"I don't really know, and Miesha is with me so I can't really … Can you please just meet us there?"

"I'm on my way," Ben says, then hangs up without a goodbye.

Rebecca calls her mom's cellphone. Her mother picks up after one ring. "Hello, dear!"

"Mom? I'm on my way to the hospital with Miesha." She's unable to control her tears now. The cab driver can hear the angst in Rebecca's voice and meets her eyes in his rear view mirror. He immediately speeds up and begins weaving through the traffic.

"Oh, my. What's wrong?"

"I think it's bad. I think she has a staph infection, and if that's what it is, she's had it for a week now and that's not good." The tears are running down Rebecca's neck now.

"Your father and I are on the next flight out, all right?" Her mother sounds frantic. Rebecca can hear her father in the background, asking questions. "We'll be there in a few hours, okay dear? Let's just all pray really hard."

"Okay, Mom. Thanks." Rebecca is choking on her words.

Miesha's cheeks are a fiery red now. The fear that gripped Rebecca's chest only moments ago has started to rage throughout her entire body. "Are we almost there?" She asks the cab driver.

His heavy-lidded eyes show concern. "Yes, ma'am. We'll be there in five minutes."

She closes her eyes and starts to pray. Within five minutes the cab pulls up to the emergency doors. He rushes out of the driver's seat and helps Rebecca out with Miesha, who is out cold. He picks up the girl and drapes her over his chest. Rebecca tries to pay him but he refuses any money.

"I'll pay you back one day," she says. "Thank you so much."

The driver rushes in with Miesha in his arms. Rebecca is right at his side. They run up to the counter. There are at least twenty other children and their parents in the emergency room waiting to see a doctor.

"Please, ma'am," the driver begs the receptionist before Rebecca can open her mouth. "I just bring in this lady with her girl. She is very, very sick. Please, she needs help." Rebecca is thankful that the cab driver is speaking on her behalf; she's not sure if she'd be able to get the words out otherwise.

The emergency nurse comes out from behind the counter and rests the back of her hand on Miesha's forehead. It's clear that the girl is in need of immediate medical attention.

Miesha whimpers from her fever-induced slumber. "Mommy ..."

"It's okay, baby, Mommy's here. I'm right here, okay?"

"Come this way, please," the nurse tells them. The driver carries Miesha into a small examining room with Rebecca on his heels. The nurse motions to the driver to put Miesha down on the bed. When he does, Miesha starts to vomit.

"Oh, my God!" Rebecca runs over to her little girl and holds her shoulders tightly. The nurse ushers the driver out of the room and comes back right away.

"Miss, I need you to stay calm," the nurse insists, wiping Miesha's face and neck with a moist towelette that she's taken from near the examining room sink. "Here, help me get her clothes off." Rebecca follows the order.

Another nurse rushes in with a few tubes and several intravenous bags.

"How old is she?"

"She's going to be nine next month."

"Does she have any allergies?"

"No, no allergies."

"How long has she had the fever?"

Rebecca explains the entire situation. The nurse looks down and Miesha's leg and examines the red blister and surrounding area.

"You say she's had this for about a week?"

"Yes, but it was just a small scrape before. She said she got it from her ballet bar." As she speaks, Rebecca is twisting Miesha's doll in her hands. She realizes that Miesha is no longer sleeping—she is now unconscious.

Just then an emergency doctor rushes into the room. The nurse and doctor start to talk. They're speaking quickly. Another nurse and an attending physician rush in. Rebecca stands completely still from shock.

"What's going on?" she asks, panicked. Nobody answers.

They continue talking amongst themselves. The doctor is ordering the nurses around. They scatter in action. He's looking at Miesha's pupils.

"What's happening?" Rebecca's voice is wavering. She starts to cry. "Please tell me what's happening to my baby!" She's wailing now at the top of her lungs.

The doctor turns and speaks to her directly. "Miss, your daughter is very sick and we need to take her to the operating room right now."

As he says the words, Ben comes barreling into the room. "What the hell is going on?"

The doctor looks at his attending for help. The attending pulls Rebecca and Ben out of the room. "My name is Dr. Belford," she says. "We're going to take really good care of your daughter, okay? But she's very sick right now and we need to focus on getting her stabilized."

"*Stabilized?* What the hell does that mean?" Ben shouts. His eyes are red. Rebecca instantly recalls that he is not good under stress.

"She's going into shock," the doctor explains. "She's showing classic signs of sepsis caused by the staph infection that has been brewing on her leg and has now likely entered her blood stream. We need to get the infection out before it takes over her entire system."

Rebecca is on her knees, sobbing on the hospital floor. Anxious parents are holding their children. Two nurses rush over. The doctor prescribes a sedative. Ben is standing next to her in a state of complete bewilderment.

The nurses pick Rebecca up off the floor and take her to a quiet stall in the emergency section. One of them speaks kindly to her. "We're going to allow you upstairs to where the procedure will be done, but we need Mom to remain calm, okay? Do you have any allergies to medication?"

Rebecca shakes her head to signal no. The nurse holds out a pill. "Here, take this. It will help."

Rebecca takes the pill and washes it down with a sip of water from a plastic cup that the nurse hands to her. Her voice is strained. "Please don't let her die."

The nurse puts her arm around Rebecca's waist. They walk together, with Ben trailing behind. "We won't let her die," the nurse promises.

How many times have I said those very same words to family members? Rebecca wonders, trying not to think of how many times those words were empty.

★★★

The day becomes a relentless nightmare for Rebecca. The infection in Miesha's leg went deep into the layers of her skin. The emergency operation has removed the damaged layers of tissue, and now the doctors are waiting to see if the antibiotics will stop the infection before they have to consider a last resort—leg amputation. They are concerned about the possibility of the infection spreading into her organs. Miesha is heavily sedated and not conscious of her surroundings.

Janice is there to offer some comfort to Rebecca until Rebecca's parents arrive. After Janice leaves, Rebecca, Ben, and Rebecca's parents keep vigil by Miesha's bedside long into the evening. Rebecca finally sends her parents home, knowing that the strain of the last-minute travel and lack of sleep is hard on them. They promise to return in the morning. Janice manages to come and sit with Rebecca through most of the night and Rebecca is glad for her company, as Ben has basically broken down and isn't able to offer her any comfort.

After Janice leaves, Rebecca wonders how she could have let this happen. She blames herself for not taking the scrape on her daughter's leg seriously. She is a nurse, after all, and she should have known the signs. Although Ben hasn't said anything, she knows he blames her, too. Rebecca can see it in his eyes and hear it in his tone of voice, but she doesn't care about his forgiveness. Why would she? She could never forgive herself if Miesha dies; in fact, she would welcome being condemned to death herself. Nothing matters without her daughter, not even her own life.

These thoughts cycle through Rebecca's mind ceaselessly as Miesha lies motionless on the narrow hospital bed. Machines and tubes run through and across her delicate body. Her tiny chest is heaving up and down. Rebecca refuses to take her eyes off her for fear that her breathing will stop. She looks at her daughter and wonders if she's dreaming. She strokes her dark, tangled hair. "I hope you're having sweet dreams, baby. Mommy is here. I'll protect you."

"Really?" a voice says sarcastically from the corner of the room. Ben is slouched down in a chair, looking haggard.

Rebecca turns around to face him, her eyes glaring with hatred. "I will *not* get into this with you now, Ben. Leave it to you, Mr. No Class, to want to pick a fight with me in this situation," she growls.

The doctors come into the room, involuntarily interrupting the standoff. Ben jumps off his chair. The attending Dr. Belford checks Miesha's vitals while Rebecca and Ben gather close to Dr. Siam, the surgeon. "Miesha seems to be holding her own right now," Dr. Siam says. "We managed to scrape out all of the infected tissue …"

Rebecca interjects. "Oh, thank God," Rebecca sighs, clutching her breast. Her knees feel weak with the relief.

"However," Dr. Siam continues, "Miesha's skin and nose swabs came back positive for staphylococcus, which means her blood stream is being compromised right now. We're going to have to switch her to a stronger antibiotic. We're currently feeding her through tubes so that her body can receive the nutrition it needs to keep her body strong."

"You mean she has *another* infection?" Ben asks, trying to understand. He looks lost in all the medical talk, but Rebecca feels painfully aware of what the doctor could be referring to.

"Oh my God, is it MRSA?" she gasps.

Ben turns to her, confused and frustrated. "What the hell is MRSA? How long will she be sick?"

Before Rebecca can ask another question, the doctor places one hand on each of their shoulders. "What she is referring to is methicillin-resistant *Staphylococcus aureus*, a potentially lethal strain of this kind of staph infection. It needs to be treated with strong antibiotics."

Ben is glaring at Rebecca. She can feel his hatred.

"Listen, we're doing everything that we can to ensure she comes out of this all right," the doctor assures them. "She's a strong girl and has a history of being extremely healthy." He leads them to the chairs in the back corner of the room and urges them to sit down before he continues. "What we need to determine is whether or not the bacteria will spread to other places, such as the lungs. It's rare, but it does happen—especially if the bacterium is in her blood stream, which might be the case. We're still waiting on the test results to rule this out. In the meantime, her fever isn't getting any worse, but she'll stay on a very strong dose of antibiotics. We have to give this time right now. I'm going to have to ask that anyone entering into this room over the next while wear a fresh clean hospital gown, mask, and gloves to prevent the risk of spreading. No one with a compromised immune system should come anywhere near this room. Understand?"

Rebecca and Ben stand there, dumfounded.

"As I said, we're doing everything possible to make sure she gets better," the doctor says. "I'll be back this afternoon to check up on her. In the meantime, the nurses will be by on a steady rotation every fifteen minutes."

"Thank you, doctor," Rebecca says softly.

As soon as the doctor leaves the room, Ben starts in on Rebecca. "What kind of a mother—who, by the way, happens to be a *nurse*, for Christ's sake!—can't tell when her own child has a potentially fatal infection?" He is seething. "What the hell is wrong with you, Rebecca? She's an eight-year-old girl and she relies on *you* to know when something is wrong with her!"

Rebecca cannot dispute anything that he is saying. In her mind he is right, and she deserves this emotional assault. Her body shakes more and more with every blow he delivers.

Suddenly another voice interrupts. "Stop it, Ben. Stop it right now!" Kitty is suddenly there, a foot away from Ben, yelling in his face. She's got an undone hospital gown hastily hanging off her body, and she's holding a mask over her mouth. "What's the matter with you? Your daughter is gravely ill, and you have the nerve to take out your personal feelings on the one person she adores most in life. How *dare* you think of yourself at a time like this? Shame on you! I suggest you go home and cool off. This is *not* good for Miesha—who, by the way, has lived the *best* life an eight-year-old could live thanks to her mother!" Kitty is spewing her wrath through gritted teeth. She points to the door and Ben walks through it, following her orders like a wounded dog.

Rebecca doesn't know what to do or say. Instead she begins to cry again. Kitty grabs her in her arms. "He's right. He's right," Rebecca sobs. "I should have known …" She's slipping through Kitty's arms now towards the floor. "I should have known."

"Stop it, Rebecca. Stop it," Kitty orders her. She lowers her own body into a crouching position so she can look Rebecca right in the eye. "This could have happened to any parent. This is *not* your fault. I've seen staph infections like this a million times in my career so far, and they're nobody's fault. Do you hear me?"

Rebecca nods weakly. In her head she knows that Kitty is right, but her heart refuses to release the blame. Still, she allows Kitty to help her to her feet and lead her to a chair in the corner.

A nurse in her late fifties bounces through the door, oblivious to the drama that has just dissipated from the room. "Hello, ladies," she chimes, light and cheery. Her red hair is freshly dyed and cut just above the shoulders. She has vibrant green eyes that sparkle in the sunlight coming in through the window. She is wearing gloves and a clean hospital gown over her blue scrubs. A disposable mask hangs around her neck. Rebecca can't help but notice how strong she seems for such a short and petite woman. "My name is Mary," she says. "How's our girl doing now?" She hovers over Miesha, checking her fever and affixing a new bag onto her intravenous pole. She stops for a moment and strokes Miesha's cheek. "Lovely girl," she says quietly. She unfolds the bedding. "I'll have to give her a quick sponge bath just to keep her body cool and to wipe the germs off her skin."

"Can I help you?" asks Rebecca, wiping her eyes and nose with her sleeves. She desperately wants to help her daughter in any way she can.

"Not with those germs you've been collecting, Mum," she answers, taking a Kleenex and holding it out to Rebecca. Her eyes are like deep hypnotic emeralds. "Now you listen to me, young lady. Your daughter will be fine. But you have to believe this in your heart of hearts." Rebecca notices an Irish accent as Mary continues speaking. "By the grace of God that child will come through this just fine, I just know it. She's a fighter. Look at her. She's got Irish in her blood."

"How do you know that?" Rebecca asks.

"I can tell by her spirit," Mary replies with a wink.

Kitty pipes up from where she's been sitting quietly in the corner. "It wouldn't have anything to do with the name Doyle-Cahley written over her bed, now would it?" Rebecca can't help but give her a wry smile. Skepticism is just part of who Kitty is.

"Ah, she's a Doyle, is she? I have cousins who are Doyles. Where are you from?" Mary asks Rebecca.

The personal question takes her off guard. "I, uh … I'm from Woodstock, Illinois, but I live here in Chicago," Rebecca answers.

"Do you know a Bobby and Siobhan Doyle?" Mary asks.

"Can't say that I do," replies Rebecca with a slight smile. She can see what Mary is doing and realizes she's a very good nurse. Distraction is always a good emotional diversion in times of crisis.

"Crazy bunch they are. Can't imagine how they go on making a living, you know. They're always boozin' away their money at the local watering hole. O'Brian's,

I think they call it. Do you know that place? Anyway, it's a bit of a dive I'd say, but they like it there, yes they do. My Jeffery used to go there too in his healthier days, but now he's gotten himself the gout. Can't say I'm sorry he doesn't frequent that hole any more, though." Mary's laugh is a soft cackle. "Now listen. Why don't you and your friend over here go and get something to eat? You're all skin and bones, love." She winks at Kitty and nods her head towards the door. "Oh, and be sure to wash up good and come back with a clean hospital gown and gloves."

"No. No, I can't leave," Rebecca whimpers, looking at Miesha.

"Becky, listen to me," Kitty directs from behind the mask she's holding against her mouth. "You need to eat something, otherwise you'll collapse. And you can't do that, because Miesha needs you."

Rebecca knows she's right. "Okay, fine. But I want to be back in fifteen minutes," she says firmly.

"Go on now, girls, we'll be fine here," Mary says, adjusting her face mask before beginning Miesha's sponge bath.

Rebecca reluctantly leaves the room in Kitty's wake, feeling completely empty and lost. Her insides feel like they have all caved in, and she can't tell whether or not her feet are touching the floor. Tears start to flow down her face again and her jaw won't stop quivering.

She floats above her body and looks down at the scene where her daughter lies limp, her delicate body fighting death. *This is not my life*, she thinks to herself.

TWENTY-ONE

James wakes up early after a rough night's sleep. He has an uneasy hunch about something—the kind of feeling that usually escalates him into a state of anxiety. He tries to rationalize it away by thinking about all the ground he and Ted have covered over the past four weeks. They travelled from northern to southern Vietnam in the span of four days, and now both men are exhibiting signs of fatigue and irritability.

Lying in bed and staring at a cracked and water-stained ceiling, James tries to distract himself from his growing unease by recalling the past few days. Hanoi was an exceptional rush. James and Ted found themselves touring across the city and surrounding area on little to no sleep. James was mesmerized by the city's Old Quarter, which holds the original street layout along with its famous jewelry and silk merchants and spectacular architecture. And with the nearby scenic lakes and abundance of historical museums, the two of them barely stopped to even eat. When they did, they gorged themselves on exotic foods prepared by the most recommended restaurants and food stalls.

James smiles when he recalls the cuisine they indulged in at a famous restaurant in Khuong Thuong village. It wasn't until they finished the first delicious course that Ted explained the origin of the delicacies—insects and larva. Immediately afterwards, James found himself vomiting in a coconut planter by the rest rooms while Ted laughed so hard that the owners of the place seemed to fear he might die if he didn't catch his breath.

Turtle Tower was the structure that James found most interesting. Situated in central Hanoi on lake Hoan Kiem, it is a pagoda-like shrine that resembles a tiny tiered castle perched on a little island. As James stared at its beautiful design, Ted recounted the sixteenth-century legend surrounding it—that here, a golden sword was stolen from the mighty emperor Le Thai To by a giant lake turtle. Some believe that the turtle was only returning the sword to the lake where it belonged, while others believe that the turtle lent the sword to the emperor so he could smite his enemies, and when that job was done, the turtle reclaimed the weapon.

James gets up from his tiny bunk to make tea on the small stove in the corner. He's careful not to wake Ted. As he steeps the tea leaves, he thinks about the Temple of Literature. It was the place James fell in love with the most. Famous for being a temple for Confucius, it was also home to the Imperial Academy, Vietnam's first national university. Surprisingly, this stop hadn't been on his original list of things to see, and it was Ted who steered him in the direction of this enormous temple. Its giant gates open onto three distinct pathways: one for the monarchy, one for the administration, and the third for the military. The interior courtyards are filled with plenty of greenery and flowers, making it a soothing and peaceful spot for thinking. The names of over a thousand learned graduates are immortalized in stone tablets, and as he traced the characters with his fingers, he thought of all the knowledge that was shared within the temple's gates. The history and wisdom lurking through-out the various rooms and hallways made it the perfect place for James to release his thoughts and emotions. He was getting better and better at that ever since his train trip a few days before.

It was at the Temple of Literature that he and Ted met up with a group of Australian university students. Their youthfulness and eagerness to learn excited him. As he trailed their tour through the various rooms and courtyards, he found himself butting in with answers regarding the country's architecture and the general history of the era that the temple was constructed. He loved taking on the teaching role. He hadn't felt that comfortable in his own skin since he landed in Thailand almost four weeks before.

"Hey," Ted says, groggy from sleep. "You look pretty deep in thought for six o'clock in the morning."

James smiles. "I was just thinking about Hanoi."

"Quite the city, eh?" Ted throws the sheets off his body and rolls out of bed. "How's your arm, mate?" he asks, throwing an Australian accent at James.

James looks down at the dark script wrapped around his forearm in a perfect circle. "Ah, good as gold, mate," he says, sounding just like an Aussie.

"I wonder how those kids are feeling tonight," Ted says, referring to the rounds of draft, cat apple wine, and whiskey consumed by the students at a local pub in the downtown area.

James hands a cup of tea to his friend. "All I know is that I'm glad we didn't stick around all night to suffer the same consequences."

"Cheers," Ted says, raising his cup. "Listen, man, you'd better cover up that tattoo before we leave. It's not exactly pristine in the jungle, and you wouldn't want to get an infection—especially out there."

"Yeah, good point," James says, looking at his body art again.

Ted swigs back the last of his lotus tea and heads into the cramped washroom. "Gonna grab a quick shower," he calls over his shoulder.

James grabs a few rice dumplings with mung beans, pork, and shrimp out of the minibar for a quick breakfast. The taste of cold rice, coriander, and salty meat swirls around his mouth, lighting up his taste buds. As he chews, his gaze drifts to his arm again. He still can't help but feel that it's someone *else's* arm he's staring at. The sight of it makes him think of the person he came across just twenty-four hours before on the streets in the Soc Son, near the Temple of Buddhism.

Ted and James were coming out of the temple after a short tour when they came across the old man, who was relaxing under a tree near where Ted and James had parked their bikes. He wore a black robe and matching pants. He was balding slightly, though his small features made him look much younger than the lines of his skin revealed him to be. The old man gave them a happy smile as he ate from a small lunchbox perched on his lap. As James bent down to unlock his bike, the old man pushed his lunch to the side and looked him straight in the eyes. He spoke to James in an unrecognizable language that sounded something like Vietnamese.

Puzzled, James looked to Ted. "Cambodian," Ted said. "Khmer."

The man repeated himself and pulled James down to his knees. James could see that the old man's eyes were clear and bright, despite the hauntingly dark circles surrounding them. He touched James's face and repeated his words.

"He claims to see sadness and fear in your aura, man," Ted explained. "He says that in order for a man to be free, he must bind himself to his own destiny. I think it's a proverb or something."

The words hit James with their enormity and truth. He looked inside the man's soul then. They exchanged mutual understanding and respect before resuming their respective business. Now, this man's wisdom graces his skin permanently—and marks a significant passage in his personal journey towards self-peace.

"Blast it, man!" Ted exclaims in a somewhat ridiculous British accent. "Did you save me some dumplings?" He is bent down rummaging through the fridge for last night's leftovers. He's wearing only a towel around his waist and James notices how well his skin has bronzed over the past few weeks.

Ted grabs a beer and chases the last dumpling with it.

"I don't know how you can even think of beer after what we witnessed last night," James says, his mind thinking back to the young Aussies. "The only thing on my mind is hydration."

"Ah, you might be happy with your tea, but I need something a little stronger. We're like bookends that way—the same … only different."

James's heart trips. "Bookends. That's what Lynn and Mom used to call me and Stephen," he says quietly.

"Well, that's a good thing, isn't it, buddy? We've been through a lot together in the last few weeks." Ted wraps his arm around James's neck and points to his new ink. "And right now, *we're* each other's destiny. So let's roll with it."

James smirks and pushes him off. "Speaking of *rolling* with it, let's get this show on the road."

"You sure you're ready for the jungle, man?"

James nods, ready to take on whatever comes next. "Let's do this."

A half hour later, Ted and James commence their journey into the heart of the Mekong Delta. They decide to make their first stop about a hundred miles outside of Ho Chi Minh City to visit the Great Temple of Caodaism in Tay Ninh. The temple is built on nine levels and represents nine steps to heaven. They arrive just in time to experience a prayer session at noon. The participants believe in one God, the existence of the soul, and the ability to communicate with the spiritual world— a theory that both James and Ted can easily digest.

By early evening they arrive at the Ben Dinh tunnel. It's one of many sections of the over hundred-mile-long Cu Chi tunnel, which took over twenty years to build and was used as an army base for the Viet Cong during the Vietnam War. He heard many stories from his father and other veterans about this tunnel, which they referred to as the Black Echo.

At first James cannot enter the narrow space. Just the thought of it makes him claustrophobic. Finally, after some extensive coaxing from Ted, he is able to explore the entire system that includes trap doors, various storage and living areas, a weapons facility, a command center, a hospital, and even a small movie theater. He emerges feeling liberated from his anxiety and excited by the absorption of more history.

"I'm getting hungry," says Ted, his mind clearly on less lofty subjects. "Let's catch a bite to eat on the way to My Tho."

The night's sky is slowly creeping in and both men are trying to find stable ground as their motorbike passes over the unpaved road. James holds onto the hand grip at the back of the seat, free to watch the scenery pass as Ted drives. They stop and ask a young man for directions to the main highway leading to the city of My Tho and a place to eat. The stranger speaks too quickly for Ted to understand at first, but after several attempts he manages to get the idea. Approximately fifteen minutes later they find themselves on a paved road and continue on. The sky is turning orange and reminds James of a few paintings that hang in Rebecca's house. He closes his eyes to feel the warm breeze brush across his hair and face.

Another motorbike passes them on the highway. The young driver has a large mesh sack filled with live dogs strapped onto the back of his seat. A billy club is stuck in his boot. The dogs' collective white and beige fur blends together into one big furball. James cannot help but stare at the pink and beige tongues poking through the netting. A small black eye darts to one side and watches James longingly. James has to look away. He knows that these dogs are strays and are on their way to be slaughtered. The motorbike changes lanes and accelerates to pass James and Ted. James is relieved.

A few minutes later they approach a small cafe along the roadside. A few old junker cars and some motorbikes are lined up in front, and James can see a floating market on the river not far beyond. He catches a glimpse of the dog hunter walking down the path towards the market. He's left his bag of dogs strapped to the seat of his parked motorbike. At that moment, Ted pulls over onto the side of the road and parks their bike as close to the bush as possible.

"We're not going there to eat, are we?" James asks. He doesn't want to be anywhere near the dog hunter.

"Nope." Ted is looking through his knapsack. He pulls out a Swiss Army knife and a pair of small travel scissors. "Come on, we have to do this in a hurry."

James is breathing heavier now. He feels anxious and sick all at the same time. "You're not actually going to try to rescue those dogs, are you? We could go to prison for life!"

"Come on," Ted directs, ignoring James completely.

"Oh, sure thing. If I don't hurl first, that is," James quips.

"Are you in or what?" Ted asks.

"Are you fucking kidding me right now?" asks James, panicked. But he finds himself nodding anyways.

Ted hunches over. "Let's go!" He rushes up the street in a crouched position and James follows. A few cars drive by on the highway, making James even more terrified. Ted creeps over to the parked motorbike and James reluctantly mirrors his motions.

The sound of whimpering coming from inside the heavy mesh sack unleashes emotions inside of James that he's only felt once before—on the night of Stephen's death. The dogs' bodies are twisted up so close together that James cannot make out which dog owns which body part. He sees their dark eyes following him, silently begging him for help. The sharp nylon rope presses up against their faces, making tufts of fur squeeze out every opening. He cannot bear to watch the suffering, and yet finds himself unable to avert his eyes.

Ted whispers urgent directions. "While I cut the mesh with these, you take the knife and cut the ropes binding their feet." Ted tosses the Swiss Army knife over to James and keeps the small scissors for himself. "But you gotta be fast."

Ted starts to cut the mesh and the dogs begin to tumble out of the scrum one by one, whimpering and squirming as they land on top of each other on the gravel. "Hurry!" he grunts under his breath.

The dogs are squirming to get away, but James is fast in grabbing them to cut the twine binding their legs. The first one he frees bolts into the night like a rocket. The next one tears down the pavement and runs deep into the bush. By now Ted is working to cut the dogs' legs free too. One of the larger dogs lies dead on the pavement, and another ruddy mutt looks like death is not far off. The last dog they release is a small white shepherd mix. It appears to be the runt of the litter and stays right beside Ted, seemingly unscathed by the whole ordeal.

"Go on, git!" Ted says, trying to push the white dog away. But the dog won't go. He stands whining over his injured, rusty-colored pal. "Shit! He's not leaving without this guy," he says, pointing to the injured dog on the ground.

James scoops up the maimed mutt in his arms. "Let's get the hell out of here!" he pants. "Come on, the other one will follow."

Ted jumps up and starts running towards the bike. James is right on his tail, jostling the limp dog in his arms. The runt is following them so closely that James nearly trips over him.

Ted helps James get his balance on the seat. Then he hops on the bike, kick-starts it, and speeds down the highway. James just barely manages to hold himself and the dying canine throughout the ride. The mutt's ruddy fur is matted with grease and dirt. Its smell is enough to make James choke for breath. Soon Ted pulls into a forested area alongside the river.

James lays the sick dog down on to the ground and stares into its eyes. It is struggling for breath and its eyes have a milky film over them. James can see the bones on its front paws where it tried to chew through the restraints. James wants to be sick, and Ted can't stop pacing back and forth, swearing through quiet sobs. Minutes later, the small shepherd mix comes barreling through the trees. Within seconds of its arrival, its ruddy pal is dead. The white shepherd whimpers, circling its deceased companion and licking its face in an attempt to revive him.

James strokes its small white head. "It's okay, Shep. It's okay." He knows exactly how the small dog feels.

The dog moves over towards where Ted has lain on the ground. He circles three times and then lies down beside him, resting his chin on Ted's thigh. The white shepherd pants steadily from his ordeal and the heat. Ted strokes his ears.

Finally Ted breaks the silence. "Thanks," he says to James, wiping his eyes with the back of his hands. "We tried."

"We did pretty well," remarks James. "We saved a few, and at least the two that died didn't end up being butchered." James knows that Ty would call him hypocritical; he is aware that in some cultures, dog is a form of meat. *But Ty didn't have to see their big brown eyes begging to be saved, either,* James reminds himself.

The white dog licks his lips and whimpers. James gets out his flask of water and pours some into his cupped hand. The dog drinks feverishly.

Ted gives a small smile. "Hey, why did you call him Shep?" he asks James.

"Because he looks like a mini version of a shepherd, don't you think?" James replies.

Ted nods. "I like that. Shep." The little white dog looks up as he says the word. "Hey, he even knows his name!" Ted exclaims.

James suddenly misses home. He thinks about Martin and Robert and Hans. He misses his conversations with them all. "They call me 'The Shepherd' back home at the hospital," James says, looking up into the dusk through the bush.

"Why is that?" Ted asks, rubbing the ears of their new pet.

"Because I could talk them through their journey towards the end, I guess. Lead them in the right direction for some reason. I think mainly because I read so much, and they just had an appreciation for all the stuff, you know?" James neglects to mention that he, too, sought solace in the presence of these dying veterans. They were the only ones he could feel close to without having to emotionally invest. He understands now how different things will have to be from now on.

As James reflects on this, Ted searches in his bag for his own flask. He offers it to James first, who happily takes a mouthful of whiskey.

"Ah, I get it now," says Ted. "Shep One and Shep Two." His eyes point towards James and then the dog as he says the words.

Within the hour the mosquitoes are out in full force and both Ted and James have cigarettes burning around them to deter the pesky bugs. They spray bug repellent over themselves and the dog, though it doesn't make any noticeable difference. When they finally decide that the coast is clear for them to move on, they cover up the deceased animal with a mound of soft leaves. Shep cries at the pile until they wrap him in a blanket. They prop him up between their two bodies on the motorbike, then slowly drive the three miles south towards My Tho.

★★★

Martin and Lynn are sitting on Martin's bed looking at books filled with different styles, shapes, and flavors of wedding cakes. After an hour of fussing, Martin decides to let Lynn have her way.

"It's only fair because you picked out the flowers, too," he says with an undertone of sarcasm.

Lynn's laugh is lost in a sea of commotion that overtakes the entrance of the room. They look up to see that Stan has just arrived back from Mercy after being away for a few weeks. He is being wheeled in by Mark. Both Lynn and Martin fumble to their feet to greet their good friend.

"Howdy, gang!" Stan says, turning on the gurney while the nurse tries to line it up with his bed.

"Okay, Geronimo," says Mark. "On the count of three, I need you to shift your butt over onto the bed. Hang on to me, now."

After the transfer is complete, Lynn doesn't waste a second before she embraces Stan. "Oh, Stan, we're so happy you're back!" She grabs onto Stan's neck and wraps her arms around it.

Stan's smile is as wide as ever. "Thank you, ma'am. You know I've gone and done all this just so I can have a pretty lady like you fuss over me, right?"

"Watch it, boy," Martin warns with his largest grin. He is immediately by Stan's side, high-fiving him. "Damn, we missed you around here." Martin's voice cracks with emotion.

"I gotta say, as kind as they were to me at Mercy, I sure as hell missed you guys, too—heck, like a baby bear misses his mama out in the woods." He looks at the couple standing in front of him now. "Well, lookie here. You're all grown up now and getting ready to be married."

"That's right," agrees Lynn. "And I was hoping you'd walk me down the aisle, Stan."

Stan's eyes take on a moist look. "I'd be proud and honored, ma'am," he replies, smiling from ear to ear.

Martin grabs Stan's arm. "And I was hoping you'd be my best man, too."

Stan sits up straighter on his bed. His face is bright and his eyes wide. "You bet I will!" They shake hands and Stan claps Martin on the back. "So, Mark over here tells me it's on New Year's Eve? Boy, that'll be quite the humdinger of a party!"

Mark is busy preparing Stan's intravenous. When he's done, Mark hands Stan the push button to the nurses' station. "Now don't forget to use this if you need me, okay? You're out of the woods, but we want to make sure you stay that way, okay?"

"Fine," huffs Stan. "But tell you the truth, I'd be more inclined to call for you if you were pretty as Rebecca. Where is she, anyways?"

Mark shakes his head. "She's off today, bud." He pats Stan on the shoulder and looks nervously at Lynn and Martin before he leaves the room. Martin feels his face drop at the mention of Rebecca.

"Okay, I might just be a slow southern boy, but what in Sam Hill is goin' on here? I can tell somethin's wrong, so just tell me already. Are Gerry and Max all right?"

Martin sits down on the bed next to his best friend. "It's Rebecca. Her daughter is ill. In fact, we just received word today that she may be dying."

Stan doesn't say anything. His eyes brim up with water for the second time in as many minutes. "What's the matter with her?" he asks.

Lynn takes his hand and caresses it gently. "She has a bad staph infection. They've tried her on various antibiotics, but nothing appears to be working. Her fever spiked earlier today. Rebecca's been at the hospital all week. Her family's with her, and Kitty's also been spending a lot of time there helping out."

Martin can tell that Stan is taking the news badly.

"What can I do?" Stan asks. "There must be somethin' I can do for her."

"All we can do is pray hard and pray often," Lynn says.

Martin is angry inside. He is sick with disgust that any type of God would take away such a precious child. But for Lynn's sake, he keeps his views silent on the whole prayer idea.

"Is Jimmy with her?" Stan asks.

"No. He's been away for weeks. He's in Southeast Asia," Martin explains.

Stan is suddenly annoyed. "Well, somebody's gotta get him on the line and get him back here, right now. He should be there for Rebecca and her little girl."

Martin tries to calm Stan down. "Apparently Kitty has tried to email him, but it's not easy for him to access a computer over there. Kendra's asked his friend at work to try to get his tour guide's cellphone number, though. It's all under control."

Stan starts to get up from his bed. "We need to be there for her, too."

"Whoa! Wait a minute. Calm down, my friend," Martin says, trying to keep Stan in his bed. "You and I can't be there because of our immune systems, and don't say you don't care because I already tried that and all it did was upset Rebecca. You know the way she cares about us!"

Stan just stares at the wall. After a minute or so of silence he says, "Lynn, I reckon I'd like to go over to the chapel and pray if that's all right with you."

"Certainly, dear. I'll get a wheelchair and be right back."

Martin turns towards the window and looks out into the afternoon sky. Shades of blue and gray are mixed together, and the clouds seem to be rushing towards the building from the north. He thinks hard about James. He hopes James will receive the message in time—and even more than that, he hopes he will do the right thing.

TWENTY-TWO

"**H**ey, buddy, wake up. James!" Ted is shaking him out of his sleep while Shep licks his face.

"What the … Hey, what's wrong?" James is pushing the dog out of the way, trying to see what's straight in front of him. When his field of vision clears he sees the worried look on Ted's face.

"You—you gotta go home, man," Ted says reluctantly.

James sits up on his flimsy cot. "What are you talking about?"

"Look, I just got a text from Jackson. Apparently his sister Jade got a message from someone named Kendra …"

"Kendra?" James interjects.

"Yeah. She said her uncle is a friend of yours?"

James scratches his head. "Uh, yeah. Martin."

Ted sits down beside his friend and it feels to James like the cot might collapse. "Buddy, something's wrong with Rebecca's kid. They say she's dying."

"Jesus … How? What happened?" James feels as if his whole body has been blown away. He starts to breathe faster as panic surges throughout his body.

"Stay calm, James. Just stay calm," Ted tries to reassure him. "All I know is that she got real sick, real fast. Listen, get your stuff packed and I'll take you to the airport."

"What?" James is stunned and confused. "I can't leave. I can't just leave like this." *I've come so far*, he thinks. *What if things just go back to the way they were once I get home?* The terrifying thought consumes his mind.

"Yes, you can just leave. And more importantly, yes, you *will*," Ted insists. He's already stuffing things into his duffel bag.

James pushes himself up. "What is my leaving going to do for anybody?"

Looking irritated, Ted turns to face James again. Shep runs over to a corner and lies down and James marvels at how the animal can sense the anxiety filling up the room. "Have you learned nothing during this trip? Nothing at all? About life, love, trust, pain, loss—about how none of these things can run their course if you keep intercepting them?" He tosses James's bag onto his bed, then sinks down onto his cot and places his head in his hands.

James knows his friend is right, but he suddenly gets the feeling that something more is going on here. "What's really bothering you, Ted?" he asks.

Ted takes a few deep breaths. "I don't want you to go, either," he confesses. "But the fact is that you love this girl, and her baby is about to die. So you need to be there not only for their sake, but for our sake, too. You have to be there, because if you choose not to be, then you're putting yourself right back to square one—and that'll kind of put me back at square one too, you know?"

James suddenly understands. This odyssey has been about Ted just as much as it's been about him. "Okay, I'll go," James says, knowing in his gut that it's the only choice he has. "God, how am I supposed to do this?" He can hear the fear and desperation in his own voice.

Ted folds his arms as if to hug himself. "You've done it before. Many times, for all those veterans who needed you."

"Not that," James whispers. "I mean, how am I supposed to leave *you*?"

The silence between them is like a heavy cloak. Shep comes over and starts licking Ted's hand.

"You're not leaving me, Jimmy, just like you didn't leave Stephen. You have to follow your instincts here and stop fighting them. I'll see you again, buddy. I promise you. You're the best friend I've ever had. Shit, you're my *only* friend next to this guy," Ted replies, rubbing Shep's head. "Maybe I'll come to Chicago and …" he trails off.

They get up and embrace each other. James is so overwhelmed that he can barely speak. He looks down at his arm and his script encourages him to try. "I can't thank you enough for giving me back my destiny, man. I never imagined coming across another brother again after losing Stephen."

Ted's eyes are red with tears he won't let fall. "I'm lucky too, you know. Now come on." He turns and points to all the gear lying on the floor. "Let's do this!"

While Ted gets on the phone with the airline, James steps into the shower. His mind and heart float over the ocean towards Rebecca. What he feels for her is more real than ever, and it fuels his determination not to let her and Miesha down.

He closes his eyes. As the warm water rushes down his back, he talks to Stephen out loud. "I know you're there because you're the one who put me together with Ted and you're the one who's going to get me back home. And if you have any pull up there at all, please be there for Miesha."

There's a bang on the bathroom door. "Who are you talking to in there, man? Come on, we gotta go! Your flight leaves in a few hours from Ho Chi Minh!"

James trembles as he steps out of the shower. The fear of the unknown grips his heart with every breath he takes in. Flashes of his dream sequence on the train appear before his eyes. Stephen was standing there with a man in combat fatigues. Who was that man, and why was he there? His mind flashes to Martin's words: This is not our stop. He pictures the people floating in the air. He recalls seeing a little girl with ballet slippers, but he can't remember whether she was boarding the train or leaving it. The harder he tries to focus on it, the more distant the vision becomes in his mind.

The relentless uncertainty of the situation makes the ride to Ho Chi Minh feel long. Ted drives the rented motorbike as quickly as he can back to the main city with James on the back. They left Shep at the hotel to wait for Ted's return. James can only hope that he won't bark and give himself away.

When they finally reach the airport, Ted has to practically pry James off his seat. James feels like he is becoming paralyzed, which is a symptom of the earlier version of himself—and a version someone he does not wish to see return. James can't speak; he simply takes his backpack off the back seat and organizes his identification. When he's got his documents in order, he follows Ted towards the entrance of the busy airport.

"You're all right," Ted says calmly. "And, for the record, I'm going to be fine too."

Twenty minutes after he checks in, James finds himself in the security lineup. He is scheduled to be back in Chicago early tomorrow afternoon. Everything seems so surreal. Unlike the last time he boarded a plane, he is not escaping from his life; rather, he is rushing towards a hard face-to-face meeting with it.

He turns to say goodbye to Ted before he heads into the waiting area for his flight—United Airlines Flight 9716 to Chicago via Tokyo. Ted pulls him into his arms for a final bear hug. "I'll be seeing you, bro," he says quietly.

James tries hard to hold back the fear in his heart.

★★★

By the time the plane takes off from its brief stop in Tokyo, James is already fed up with the tedious routine of flying. The time in Tokyo is just past four o'clock in the afternoon. He calculates the time difference and figures he'll be home by approximately five o'clock Chicago time on Thursday afternoon.

The thought of another thirteen hours in the air is almost impossible to stomach without several ounces of scotch and plenty of books to consume. Although he's never been one to sleep on planes, the stress from the situation back home allows his fatigue to take over for a good portion of the trip. Luckily, there are quite a few empty seats on the jumbo 747 and James happens to be sitting next to two of them, leaving him plenty of room to stretch out. He manages to doze in and out for what seems to be three-hour intervals.

After the third time he falls asleep, he is awakened by a little boy in the seat in front of him. The boy is standing on his seat, holding onto the headrest. He is looking at James's tattoo and reaches out to touch it. His mother reprimands him in what sounds like Cambodian.

"I am so sorry, sir," the woman says sincerely to James. She is a beautiful young Asian woman with a tiny boyish figure. Her short-cropped black hair has copper highlights.

"No problem," James replies, still half asleep.

"We've been away visiting my mother and father and he's getting very excited to be back home with his father and sister," she explains. "I guess he's getting a little antsy."

"I don't blame you," James tells the child kindly.

He is a small boy of around seven years old. His black and red Chicago Black-hawks baseball cap frames his perfectly oval face. He points to a specific character on James's arm. "Look, Mom!"

The mother leans over to read the script wrapped around James's bicep. She smiles. "He very much likes your tattoo," she says. "He recognizes a word in it that is the meaning behind his sister's name. My brother painted it in Khmer characters for her as a gift, and she has it hanging on the wall in her room."

James raises his eyebrows with surprise. "Cool! What's the word?"

The boy grabs his arm and pushes his finger right onto the word. "It says 'bind'."

"Hey, that's really impressive."

The boy is rolling his toy car over the back of the seat. "Yeah," he replies, launching his car off of an imaginary ramp. "Her name's Rebecca."

James feels stunned and a sudden surge of blood rushes to his face. The woman notices the sudden change and gently removes her son from the seat. "I'm sorry to disturb you, sir."

James looks at her without seeing her. "No, no, it's fine. He's a very nice boy. Very smart."

The flight attendant is walking towards James just in time. He discretely motions her over. "Excuse me, but could I have a Johnny Walker Red on ice?"

"Certainly," she replies, batting her beautiful dark eyelashes. "Is there anything else I can do for you, Mister?" Her question is suggestive.

"Yes," James says, turning his eyes towards the window. "You can make it a double."

Landing in Chicago feels strange to James, but he knows it is the final act of his long and overdrawn personal discord. So much has changed for him during his brief absence from home, and he knows that much of this is thanks to Ted. Martin, too, has been a player in the theater that has really set his life in motion.

As his plane touches down in Chicago, he tries hard not to question his life and decides to capitalize on his capacity for growth and fortitude. Dedication, trust, and love are the things he now wants to possess and exercise the most. Thinking back, he knows that he was too desperate to be able to uncover any purpose to his life. Instead, he subconsciously exposed himself to the deaths of those whose lives had been full and plentiful. The veterans were not only his heroes; they were his own personal sanctuary.

He thinks of Rick Miesner, and of Anna McBain and Hans Webber and the countless others whose journeys had provided him with a significant piece of his safety net. Each represented an outlet he could tap into to unload his pent-up energy. How odd it was that their deaths allowed him to release his secrets without fear or shame. Nonetheless, he vows not to disappoint them in his quest to find peace and live honorably, as they did.

After clearing customs and exiting the arrivals area of the airport, James hails a cab and climbs in for the twenty-five minute trip. The change in temperature has him feeling like he's been freeze-dried and turned inside out. Still, the snow has yet to arrive for the holidays, and although he is pleased, it doesn't leave much of an atmosphere for Christmas, which is less than a week away.

The taxi pulls up to the front entrance of the Children's Hospital. James pays the driver and tells him to keep the change, but instead of getting out of the vehicle, he finds himself unable to move.

The cab driver waits a few seconds before breaking the silence. "Sir? Are you all right?"

James looks down at his feet. "Yeah, sorry. I just need a second."

The cab driver's voice becomes sympathetic. "I hope that whatever it is, it's gonna be fine."

"Huh?" James asks, not sure what the cabbie's getting at.

"No child should be here," the cabbie elucidates. He looks in his rear view mirror, and James meets his soft hazel eyes.

James's worries are suddenly put into perspective. "Thanks," he says as he pushes himself out the door.

The hospital appears to be quiet this evening. He makes his way up the elevator to the Intensive Care Wing. When the doors open, he's hit with a sterile scent and blinding florescent lights that amplify the white floors surrounding the large reception desk. Christmas decorations grace the hallways and a giant Christmas tree stands tall and proud in the center of the main foyer. Several nurses are coming in and out of rooms and a doctor is speaking to a couple in the main waiting room.

A nurse is standing behind the reception area. James approaches her nervously, still feeling unsure of how he fits into this picture. She looks somewhat unfriendly, but James figures it's just from the stress of the job. Her shoulder-length black hair is a mess of curls and her mascara is smudged around her squinty dark eyes.

"Can I help you?" she asks, sounding somewhat uninterested.

James's voice is quavering and he suddenly realizes that he never knew Ben's last name. "Uh, yes. I'm here to see Miesha. Her mother's name is Rebecca Doyle."

The nurse looks at him suspiciously. "Are you immediate family?"

James doesn't know what to say. "Yes, I'm … her uncle."

"What's your name?" the nurse asks, checking the chart for the list of names.

James has to reach deep into his memory bank for the names of Rebecca's brothers. He picks the name of the one in Australia. Given that her other brother, Kane, is a pediatrician in Toronto, he is likely here already. "Eric," he replies. His voice is not overly convincing, even to his own ears.

She looks at him doubtfully. "You're not immediate family, are you?"

Another nurse, this one with lively red hair and sparkling green eyes, comes around the corner just in time to witness the interrogation. "Oh, come now, Maggie, it's all right. Let him through. I'll bring him myself."

Maggie gives James the evil eye and gets back to work while the redhead loops her arm through his. "Now who would you be, lad?" she asks with a slight Irish brogue, walking him down the corridor.

"My name's James Milligan, ma'am. I'm a … a good friend of Rebecca's." "Milligan, huh? By golly, are you related to that little firecracker, Kitty? I tell you, I wouldn't want to be growin' up beside that one without wearin' footgear."

James smiles and is overcome with a pang of love for Kitty. "Yes, she's my little sister."

"Well, God bless her heart. She's here every day makin' sure that young girl comes out of it and that her mom stays alive herself. She's an absolute wreck you know, poor thing. I've threatened her with my cookin' if she doesn't start to eat somethin' more than half a piece of toast. I says, Mary's gonna bring you her cookin'. She's wastin' away to nothin', poor lass."

James feels his heart sinking. He doesn't like to think of Rebecca suffering. "How is Miesha?"

"Well, dear, she needs our prayers right now. The doctors just tried her on some new medication—a stronger cocktail of antibiotics. We're hopin' this might bring her back to us. Such a sweet child she is." Mary shakes her head. They turn into another hallway and stop. "It's right there," she says, pointing to the room on the right. "It's a private room. Try to be quiet, though. Last time I checked, Mum was asleep on a cot beside the bed."

James nods. "Is her father in there, too?"

Mary sighs and lets go of his arm. "I'm afraid Dad isn't managin' too well, dear. He's not able to be here without makin' a fuss. He's mad and he's gunnin' for somebody—anybody!"

James feels a sudden urge to track Ben down and knock some sense into him.

Mary seems to be reading James's mind. "It's guilt, that's what it is. And guilt is a nasty thing, boy. Don't let it ever take you."

James likes her insightfulness. "All right."

She leaves his side momentarily to rifle through a closet on the other side of the hall. She returns with a hospital gown, a paper mask, and gloves. "Here, put these on," she instructs. As he pulls on the sterile smock she adds, "I'm here for another hour, so don't be shy to come and get me if you need anythin'. Just ask for Mary." She pats his shoulder gently before heading back down the hallway.

James stares down at his new garb and takes three deep breaths before entering the room. The air is stifling and he can feel his lungs struggling to breathe. He closes his eyes and, thinking of Ted, he tries to channel his courage. When his eyes open he sees Miesha lying on a bed, hooked up to many tubes and machines. Her tiny body seems almost doll-like. Her long black eyelashes look like they've been sealed shut for an eternity, and her skin is a translucent mixture of olive and peach.

He scans the room and finds Rebecca curled up on a cot two times too small for even her frail frame. A long burgundy shawl is draped over her hospital gown. James places his hand over his mouth in order to suppress his gasp. To his eyes she appears almost emaciated. His impulse is to rush over to her side and take care of her. Even though he knows in his heart that he would have come anyways, he silently thanks Ted for forcing him onto the first flight out.

The room is dim and the curtains are closed. There are several flower bouquets and baskets with stuffed animals and candy lying around the room. Cards from Miesha's school classmates and friends decorate the bedside table. The sound of the respirator pumping rhythmically is the only sound in the room aside from Rebecca's raspy, erratic breathing.

James quietly pulls up a chair and sits by Miesha's side. He takes her perfect little warm hand and strokes her sunken cheek while he whispers to her. "I know you can hear me, doll face. I want you to know that I'm here for you and your mom now, so you don't have to worry about anything. I see the way you watch how your mom works so hard for you every day. You're such a smart and brave girl. I like that about you. I was never that smart or brave when I was your age. You get that from your mom, too. Next to you, she's the bravest girl I know."

James glances over at Rebecca's unmoving form. As he says the words, he realizes just how true they are. He suddenly feels Martin's influence in his heart. "When I was younger, I was so scared that I disappeared. I wasted a lot of years being afraid to live. But I *know* you're not afraid to live, Miesha. And because of that, I know you're not afraid to die, either. But please, do us all a favor and choose to stay here. That's what I've chosen. And as tempting as it might be to disappear and fly up there to whatever it is that's waiting for you, you can't go yet. It's not your turn. This *isn't* your stop, you hear me?"

"James?" comes Rebecca's half-conscious murmur from the cot.

James releases Miesha's hand and moves over to crouch by Rebecca's side. He grabs her shoulders with all of his strength and holds her to his chest. She clutches at him, sobbing. "James, I can't live without her. I can't."

James rocks her in his arms. "Rebecca, I'm here," he says over and over. It is the only thing he can think to say. The two of them hold each other on the cot for what seems like an hour. Finally, Rebecca lays her head in James's lap and they both succumb to the luxury of sleep.

A few hours later the sound of a man's voice stirs them. James is the first to open his eyes and the first thing his eyes land on is the bedside clock. It reads 1:37 a.m. and James feels like he might crash from extreme sleep deprivation. He looks over to Miesha's bed and sees a man standing over it with a night nurse by his side.

Rebecca rises quickly. "Kane? What is it?" She jumps up and stumbles to the head of Miesha's bed. James follows. "What's going on, Kane?" Panic has seized her voice.

"Becky, calm down. It's good news. Her fever is going down, and—" Kane's words are interrupted by Rebecca's cries of relief.

"Oh my God!" She falls to her knees and James quickly stands her back onto her feet. She moves towards Miesha, unable to control her emotions.

Kane happily updates them on her condition. "She seems to have responded well to the newest cocktail we gave her," he says. "Her fever is down to just under a hundred and one degrees, which is good news. It should be back to normal in twenty-four hours. If her lungs continue to clear, we'll be able to gradually take her off the ventilation machine to gauge her ability to breathe on her own again."

Rebecca hugs her brother. "I knew you'd fix it," she weeps.

"Well, I'm thinking *she* had more to do with it," he replies, looking at Miesha. "She's a pretty determined little girl. It's a good thing she's a Doyle," he chuckles before turning his eyes on James. "So, Maggie tells me that you're my brother, Eric."

Rebecca looks at him curiously and James silently curses himself for trying something so foolish. He extends his hand. "James Milligan, actually."

Kane shakes his hand and gives a brotherly nod of approval. "Alright, then. Nice to meet you."

The nurse excuses them by explaining that she needs to do an anti-bacterial sweep of the place. Rebecca reluctantly agrees to leave her daughter's side for a few minutes and Kane heads off to talk to the doctor on staff. James and Rebecca stand across from each other outside the room. She puts her hand on his face and smiles. After a week of being in the depths of desolation, her prayers are finally being heard.

"You look different," she tells him.

James takes her hand and pulls her in closer. "I'm not different. I'm finally myself." He hugs her tightly. "I'm so sorry for everything, Becky."

She likes hearing him call her that. "How did you find out?" she asks. Before he can explain, she answers for him. "Kitty."

James laughs. "Yeah, well, you know her. Where there's a will … well, let's just say she's the force behind it."

The nurse comes out of Miesha's room to let them know they can go back in.

Rebecca takes a closer look at James. "You should go home to bed," she says, concerned. "You look exhausted."

"I'm not going anywhere," he replies. They re-enter the room holding hands and go to stand over Miesha's bed.

James watches the little girl's chest move up and down with the aid of the ventilator and reflects on the past six months of his life. The evolution of time launched him towards the solution to his most challenging and complex issues—and landed him right back into a brand new series of events. It's a perfect circle, he realizes. One that represents the theory of cause and effect which, it turns out, is something he knows quite a bit about.

TWENTY-THREE

"I'm sorry I can't be there with you, pumpkin," Martin says sweetly over the phone to Miesha. "But you know there's no place I'd rather be on Christmas Day. I promise that as soon as we're both better, we're going to watch *The Polar Express* together and eat a lot of popcorn and junk food. Just don't tell your mom, okay?" Martin is gushing into the receiver. He can't remember feeling so happy to be talking on the phone before. "I'll see you at the wedding!" he says before he hangs up.

"Oh, you're a soft old cat," Stan teases, but he's grinning from ear to ear.

"There's nothing better for the soul than a child's voice on Christmas Day," Martin says, his voice boisterous. "Especially that one's."

"It's a miracle, man. God works in mysterious ways," Stan replies.

"Which one?" Martin asks sarcastically.

"Okay, you two. We're not getting into that again, okay?" Lynn scolds, but there's a smile on her face. "And speaking of God—Stan, are you taking me to mass in a half hour?"

"I reckon I am, and with pleasure, ma'am," Stan replies gallantly.

Martin rolls his eyes. "Well, I'm going to the lounge. I hear they're playing *It's a Wonderful Life*."

"I love that movie," says Lynn, stacking up the Christmas lunch dishes.

Martin stands up to grab his wife-to-be. "So does God, and he says he's going to be there, too. So why don't you join me?"

Lynn has no response other than a hardy laugh and a kiss for her fiancé. "Never you mind, Mr. Diggs. Stan, I'll be back to get you in a few minutes."

Stan gives her a friendly farewell wave. "Thanks for a delicious lunch. You really know how to treat a fella well." After she passes out the doorway, he turns to Martin. "Speaking of, you're lookin' mighty good these days, Marty."

"I know," Martin says with a grin. "But not as good as you. So when are you leaving, anyways? I'm surprised you're still hangin' around, now that you've got your fancy-ass kidneys and all."

"I reckon it'll be sometime during the next month," Stan says. "They just want to make sure no infection creeps in over the holidays."

"Is your girl coming for the family dinner tonight?" Martin asks.

"Oh sure, and so is my ma. She ain't been up here since I went into the hospital. She wasn't well enough to travel then, and when she got stronger was when I had my surgery and couldn't be exposed to no germs."

Martin is happy that his friend will have his loved ones around him for the holidays. "I can't wait to meet her."

"I know you're gonna love her, Marty. She's full of catfight and moonshine."

Martin holds his belly while he laughs. "Stan, I sure am gonna miss your special language when you leave here."

Just then Lynn comes back into the room "Okay, Stan, you ready?"

"You betcha," he tells her.

She walks over to Martin and gives him a kiss on the lips before heading back out the door pushing Stan's wheelchair.

"Maybe we'll catch the tail end of the flick," Stan says.

"Have fun with God and all that," Martin replies, knowing full well that Lynn will shoot him a look of disapproval for his blasphemy. She doesn't disappoint.

They leave the room and Martin slowly makes his way back to his bed. The pain in his lower back is excruciating, and he's tired from trying to hide it from Lynn and his friends. He reaches underneath his bed and feels around for the flask of whiskey in his duffel bag. He finds it, and a sense of relief washes over him. When all is clear, he takes a mouthful of the malt liquor. It burns on the way down, but it's a good feeling. He holds the flask up in the air and raises a toast to his family—to Moe Carter, his dear brother, as well as to his folks, Ester and Joseph. He misses them all terribly today.

He takes another big swig and feels the buzz of the alcohol relaxing his sore muscles. "And here's to you, Frank. I'll be seeing you soon," he says to the empty room. "I sure as hell hope you're there to pull me over to the other side."

Martin lowers his flask and feels his fear washing away. It isn't the fear of death per se that has him worried; rather, it's the fear of leaving Lynn behind. He knows that she will be devastated at first, but, like the soldier she is, she will march on without him. Still, his heart is pained at the thought of having to lie to her about how well his treatment is going.

At first the chemotherapy seemed to show progress in killing the cancer cells, but now the disease is retaliating and becoming even more relentless during this third session of treatment. The doctors have found another mass at the base of his spine, and the cancer is proving to be the demon antagonist in his story. Martin has decided that the fight is finally over—or rather, his body has made the decision for him. He is just too tired. Despite the pleas and advice from his medical team, he has decided not to say anything to Lynn—or to anybody else for that matter—and has begged them to keep quiet as well.

Selfishly, perhaps, he wants to marry Lynn despite his imminent absence from her life here on earth. But in his mind, their past together *would* have been their future at one point in time, and therefore time really isn't a factor. Lynn even said so much herself on the very day they discovered they had feelings for one another. How could she dispute her own philosophy? Yet he finds himself doing just that in the moment.

Martin's eyes feel heavy from the whiskey and his body releases all of its tension under the warmth of his blankets. The room is spinning and he turns on his side to grip the pillows for stability. Blackness fills his mind and his breathing becomes deep and shallow.

Voices are speaking to him in the dark, but he can barely hear them. "Speak up, I can't hear you. Or at least light a damn match, Aaron, so I can see where you are," Martin says from where he is lying on the bottom of the south side of Ap Bia Mountain, otherwise known to the men as Hill 937.

"Relax, Webster. I'm here," comes a voice from behind a large bolder.

"Piss off, Aaron, I know you're there. I asked you to speak up because I can't make out a single word of what you're saying." Martin is irritable because he's tired and hungry. He and Aaron have been on watch for the Viet Cong for twenty-four hours now.

"I love you too, buddy," Aaron snaps back.

"Hey, did anyone ever tell you that you mumble all the time? Martin asks while stating a fact. "There isn't a single damn enunciated syllable that comes out of your trap. It's just one big long run-on drone. God, Janice must go out of her mind when—"

"Shhh!" Aaron interjects.

Silence fills the gap between them. "They should be coming out from the northeast slopes," Aaron whispers, clearly this time.

They wait motionless for a few minutes before Martin speaks up. "I don't see a thing. We've been here for days and we haven't come across anything except for a shit load of dead bodies and booby traps," Martin grumbles.

"Remember Webster, we're here because they want to conquer the south, that's why. We have the opportunity to intercept the spread of communism! Shit, you're the history expert you should know," Aaron huffs. "Besides, we could be saving the lives of a few thousand American soldiers."

"Yes, I know—and compromise the lives of thousands of innocent Vietnamese and Lao women and children while we're at it," Martin replies, annoyed.

"Webster, you're just like my cousin John—a big ol' pussy who's got more brains than balls," Aaron says, disappointed.

"Well, then, I think I just might like to meet *her* one day," Martin snaps back.

Two clear shots ring out and they hear men shouting in the distance. There's more gunfire. Aaron radios down to the men stationed below the foothills. A barrage of machine gun fire consumes the night air.

"We gotta move uphill, Webster!" Aaron yells. "I sure hope you brought a change of undies!"

"I borrowed your mama's," Martin shouts back, jumping up behind him.

Running through the night, Martin can hear nothing but his own heavy breathing and Aaron's footsteps in front of him. He curses the shortage of night-vision goggles that left him and Aaron basically sightless.

Bullets rattle past Martin's helmet and he goes down with massive ringing in his ears. When he opens his eyes he sees Aaron's mouth wide open with spit flying out of it. He can tell he's yelling, but he can't hear anything except for the bells in his head. He bounces back up instinctively and both men start running upward again, shooting at anything that moves. Enemy fire is tracking their progress towards from the north and more bullets come flying their way. Aaron ducks behind a large bush and covers Martin as he runs along the hillshide where several other American soldiers are signaling him.

When his hearing begins to return, Martin can make out Aaron yelling to one of his subordinates. "Man down, man down!"

"Shit," Martin hisses under his breath. His heart is pumping blood like wildfire through his temples. He looks back out into the clearing and sees that Private Jona Bert is down.

Martin doesn't stop to think. He lunges back out into the open. "Bertie! Come on, I got you," he says to Jona, as he pulls him further into the bush. Aaron comes barreling towards them, hot on Martin's heels.

"Bertie, man, hang in there," Martin begs. Jona is coughing up blood. His left quadricep is blown wide open.

"Goddamn medic! Where are you?" Aaron's voice is blasting out into the night air, competing with the thunder of gunfire coming from both sides.

Martin pipes up. "Aaron! Shut the fuck up! He *is* the medic!" he cries, pointing to the injured solider.

"Well, shit," Aaron groans as realization dawns on his face. "Now you're the goddamn medic, Webster," he orders before taking off again.

Martin is in a state of panic. "Bertie, tell me what to do!" he begs.

Jona is breathing quickly, which makes the blood spurt out of his mouth in a crimson spray. "You gotta grab my pack and get me my tool kit," he wheezes.

Martin immediately wrenches the pack off his comrade's back and rips the zipper open. A hard case falls out. "Okay, got it!"

"There's a vile of morphine in there. Jab the needle into my hip." He's struggling to get the words out. He coughs again; this time there's no blood.

That's a good sign, Martin thinks. *Please, oh please let that be a good sign.* He jabs the short needle through Jona's dirty fatigues. The needle bounces back slightly as Martin hits a bone.

"Argh!" Jona seethes. "Good, good. Now grab anything you can find to bind up my leg. But you gotta disinfect it first with the peroxide."

"Got it," Martin says as he grabs the bottle of disinfectant from the kit. *Where the hell's Aaron?* he thinks desperately, even though he knows full well that Aaron is down below gathering up what's left of their battalion.

"Just pour some on," the medic wheezes.

Systematically, Martin does what he's told.

"Christ almighty!" Jona cries out in pain as the peroxide bubbles in his wound.

"You're going to be fine, right, Bertie?" Martin pants as he ties a handkerchief tightly around his friend's leg.

Jona's eyes begin to glaze over from the morphine. "I am, Marty, thanks to you," he breathes shallowly. "But you're not."

Martin feels a dull ache in his backside. Blood starts to seep through his white t-shirt. He winces with pain and feels his body falling backwards. Jona tries to break his fall by grabbing onto his dog tags, but the chain breaks under his weight.

Martin calls out to him. "Bertie!"

Martin's eyes pop open wide from the pain in his backside. He looks around the room and sees familiar surroundings—his robe, his favorite books, the Chicago skyline through the window. He feels cold and sticky. He pulls his bedcovers down to see what's transpired. His pajamas are completely saturated with sweat and urine mixed with blood. Humiliation sets in fast. He pulls his bedding down quickly and tries to maneuver his body to the other side of the bed so that he can make a beeline to the shower. But as he turns he finds Stan sitting directly across from him.

Stan's expression is filled with dejection. Martin can see in his eyes that he knows. "You're not okay, are you, roomie?" Stan asks. His voice is somber.

Martin doesn't reply right away, but Stan's surmise is on the mark and he feels that he owes his best friend the truth. "I'm dying, Stan."

Stan folds his arms across his chest. "So yer gonna take this truth away from all of us?"

Martin is taken back by Stan's words. "I'm not trying to take anything away from anybody," he explains weakly. "I'm merely trying to exonerate Lynn from having to deal with my suffering right now."

"Not telling her is *not* the right thing to do, Marty. It's dishonest."

Martin is agitated by his insight. "Do you mind, son? I'm sitting here in my own piss and I would like to get into the shower."

"Well, at least let me help ya," Stan says, sounding irked at being dismissed. He raises from his chair, takes his friend's arm and gingerly helps him off the bed and across the room.

"I'm gonna find some clean sheets for your bed," Stan tells Martin as the bathroom door closes. "And a clean pair of jammies." Martin can't be sure, but it sounds like Stan's voice is cracking with emotion.

Martin feels his heart weakening with sadness and fear. He needs to distract his friend from feeling the same. "Listen, buddy, how about putting some music on in here? And try to find a station that's not playing Christmas music!"

"Can do," Stan replies. After a pause, Dave Matthews comes over the airwaves.

"Say, Marty, is that loud enough?" Stan calls through the closed door. "Can you hear it?"

"Yeah. It's great. Thanks, buddy." Martin steps into the shower and feels the warm water rush over him. He thinks about how it will be to not exist, to no longer feel the simplest things that living entails—like warm showers and the love of a friend.

He pushes his noxious thoughts away and concentrates on the music. He decides that he has no choice but to keep his secret—at least for now.

★★★

On Christmas Day, James is overcome with eagerness and enthusiasm. Although Miesha is still in the hospital, she's alive and well—and as a result, Rebecca is healing too. He spends his day by her bedside with her entire family, watching both mother and daughter open up presents and eating their favorite foods, like shortbread cookies and chicken nuggets with plum sauce.

By the end of the day, however, exhaustion overtakes him and he can make only a brief appearance at Janice's Christmas dinner. When he meets little A.J. for the first time, however, he receives a short second wind and feels a rush of hope for the future—for both his own and his nephew's.

Kitty decides to drive his car home for him to make sure he arrives safely. Jacob will follow soon after with A.J. to pick her up to take her back to their house. The roads are completely clear, which makes Kitty feel more relaxed about the drive. Christmas lights dazzle the houses along the streets and the cold air carries the scent of wood fires burning from many of the chimneys they pass.

As they pick up speed on the highway, James watches the lit-up skyline whiz by and focuses on the moon peering out from behind the dark clouds. He flashes back to when he and Stephen were young and used to sit in the back seat of his parents' car and pretend they were captive spies, and that the moon was actually their ally coming in for a big rescue. He finds himself laughing.

Kitty takes her eyes away from the road for a second. "What's so funny?" she asks, and is soon smiling herself.

"Remember when Stephen and I used to pretend we were secret agents when we were coming back from the cottage at night?"

Kitty bursts into a cackle. "Oh, yeah! You guys scared the daylights out of me! I was afraid to even look out the window." Her voice softens. "Stephen used to try and make it even worse, though. He'd talk about aliens wanting to chop our heads off and scoop out our brains for food."

James looks at the sky again. "God, his imagination was incredible."

Kitty sighs. "Then, when he dozed off, you'd whisper in my ear to tell me that it wasn't real and that I shouldn't worry—there were no such things as Martians."

James smiles. The memory warms his insides. "I didn't want you to be scared."

Kitty places her hand on her brother's. Her voice wavers with emotion. "Jimmy, I'm so glad you're back. I can't tell you how much I missed you. I'm so happy."

James squeezes her hand. "I'm getting closer every minute," he says quietly.

"Closer to what?" she asks.

"To that eleven-year-old boy again. You know, the one sitting in the back seat with his baby sister, feeling happy and at peace with my life."

Kitty smiles. Her eyes are glistening. "It only took you two decades," she scoffs.

James yawns and leans his head against the window. He feels exhaustion gripping him and his breathing slows.

Right before he falls asleep, he thinks he hears Kitty murmur quietly, "Thank you, Stephen, for finally releasing him."

★★★

When James wakes up in his own bed, he is unable to move. The force of gravity pulls him into the mattress, and his body is not responding to its habitual demand for coffee. He closes his eyes and decides to wait another minute before a second attempt. In the meantime, he recaps the last few days until his internal GPS sets him back on course.

The days following Christmas were clusters of time spent between the Children's Hospital, Kitty's place, and Rebecca's townhouse. He had conversations with Rebecca, Janice, and Kitty about his revelations, and he asked each of them for their forgiveness and continued patience throughout his transition towards a more conclusive wellbeing. He spoke with them about his commitment to building their trust and about the importance of allowing him to flounder through the process without judgment. He still needs time, he realizes, to digest his liberation and to fully understand the expectations of those he deemed to be most valuable to his life. His most pertinent objective now is to find a way to re-enter their lives with a greater presence—one that he still felt comfortable with. He knows that achieving this and finding the balance he needs to sustain his own individual path in life will require effort, but he is ready to work towards being whole again, and he isn't afraid to ask for the help of his loved ones.

The gravity pulling at his core slowly absolves him and his feet finally hit the floor. Today is New Year's Eve—Martin and Lynn's wedding day. He promised Miesha that he would help her prepare for the occasion, and he has some running around to do before heading over to see her and Rebecca. He walks into the bathroom and looks at himself in the mirror for what feels like the first time in weeks. Not at all happy with his rugged, shaggy look, he decides that a shower is priority number one. When he's fully groomed he heads into the kitchen to make some coffee. On his way past he stops to check on Thatcher, who's swimming around at the top of a freshly cleaned tank.

"You must have been a pit bull in your last life," he says as he drops some flakes on the surface. He makes a mental note to thank his neighbor for looking after Thatcher so well.

The doorbell buzzes loudly, startling James.

"Hello?" he says into the intercom.

"Did you miss me?"

James grins at the familiar voice. "Like a foul smell," he professes sarcastically before pressing the button to unlock the main entrance. A minute later he opens the door in response to Ty's knock. They touch knuckles and share a quick but honest embrace.

"Wowee, your fine ass is lookin' mighty thin," Ty says, sizing him up. "You catch Ebola over there or something?"

James laughs and slaps his gut with his right hand. "I'm working on it, man." He can sense how happy Ty is to see him and the feeling is mutual.

"Hey, nice tat," Ty says, referring to James's arm band. "Bet that hurt like a son of a bitch."

"Sure did," agrees James. "Coffee?"

"You know it." Ty goes into the kitchen to help himself. "We have some catching up to do, brother. You can't even imagine what's been going down at work. Did Jade fill you in on anything?"

"I only opened my work email for the first time yesterday," James replies. "Just long enough to see that you got the rapid transit project all bundled up and ready to go. Good work, man."

"Yeah, thanks," acknowledges Ty proudly. "Turns out I did okay without Papa Bear around for once."

"Yeah, sorry I've been so out of touch. I've been preoccupied with more important matters."

"Shit, I know," Ty says sympathetically. "I'm sorry about Becky's girl. I hear she's good now, though. I mean, she's at home, right?"

"Yeah, she's doing fine. Hey, thanks again for helping Jade get the message to me while I was overseas. I can't imagine all this transpiring without me knowing."

"No prob. But next time, bring your cellphone, bro," Ty quips.

James goes for more coffee. "So I hear you've been seeing Kendra?" he asks when he returns with the pot.

Ty's face is gleaming. "Yes sir, and thank you for hooking me up with that fine woman. Had you not sent the answer to that riddle to Marty … well, who knows, right?"

James laughs. "I'm happy for you, man. She's a nice girl."

Ty bounces his eyebrows up and down. "Oh, you have no idea …"

"Hold it right there, Don Juan!" James says, putting up his hand. He doesn't want to picture Ty with his good friend's niece; it somehow feels disloyal to Martin. He quickly changes the subject. "So, you coming to the wedding tonight?"

"Oh, yeah," Ty says. "Apparently the uncle wants to meet me."

"Nice." James shoots him a smile. "Off to get the blessing of the *pater familias*, huh?"

"What?" asks Ty, clueless.

"Aw, nothin'," James says, then chuckles. *You have no idea what you're in for, buddy,* he thinks.

★★★

Later on that afternoon, Lynn, Janice, and Kitty are at a downtown spa getting their hair, nails, and makeup done. Champagne flutes are being topped up by one of the stylist's assistants, and although Janice and Lynn decline, Kitty eagerly accepts. "I'm officially off mommy duty tonight," she says gleefully. "I've pumped enough to last two days, and I've already told Jake I'm sleeping in tomorrow."

The women look beautiful. Lynn is finding it hard to believe that she's a bride again after almost forty-five years. Last-minute touches to her makeup keep her focused on her reflection in the mirror—and keep her mind from jumping ahead into the future.

Kitty gulps down her glass of bubbly and emerges from her chair. "You look gorgeous, Auntie Lynn," she exclaims.

Janice agrees. "You really do, dear," she says, getting up to give her best friend a hug.

Kitty snaps a photo with her cellphone before grabbing her winter jacket. "I just saw Jake pull up," she tells them. "He probably can't find anywhere to park, so I'd better skedaddle. I'll see you two at the Art Center at six?"

"Will do," replies Janice.

Lynn waves goodbye as the stylist inserts a beautiful crystal comb into her hair. It's the final touch to her wedding makeover. She thinks that her face might crack from smiling so hard. She and Janice thank the stylist for her outstanding job and give her a generous tip. After the young woman leaves to tend to her next client, Lynn and Janice sit quietly in front of the mirror.

"I know," Lynn says. "I mean, about Martin. I know."

Janice is struggling to find words. "Oh, sweetie. I feel so terrible for not being able to say anything … but as a member of the hospital staff, I had no choice but to respect patient confidentiality—"

"It's all right, Janice. I understand."

Janice reaches over to take Lynn's hand and Lynn holds on tightly.

"At first, I just wanted to curl up and die," Lynn says, trying hard not to cry and failing. "I thought, 'Why is this happening to me—again? Why is God punishing me this way?'" She blots away a tear so that it won't ruin her makeup. "But then I found myself being thankful to God for bringing Martin into my life at all. I mean, he could have passed before I even had a chance to meet him, and *that* would have been the bigger tragedy."

Janice nods, never breaking Lynn's gaze through the mirror.

"Martin isn't the first person on earth to die, and he won't be the last," Lynn says plainly. "I know it must seem ridiculously evident to you, working in the Veterans' Hospital and all, but somehow if I just focus on the obvious, I feel more at peace with it. Do you know what I mean? Our turn is coming, too. There's no escaping it."

Janice nods. "To everything there is a season …"

"Exactly. I can't feel bad about something that's taking its natural course, can I? I spent years of my life resenting God for taking Stephen when he was so young. Losing your child isn't supposed to be the natural order of things, you know? And I hated God for it. I really did. I mean, Stephen was *so* young." Lynn takes a deep breath. "But I think I've come to learn that we need to accept that there is no natural order to life and death. Each person has their own life cycle, whatever that entails. And I'm just happy that mine includes Martin—even for a short time."

"Let's drink to that," says Janice. She raises her empty flute to the assistant, signaling for more champagne. In a moment, two fresh glasses are placed on the counter before them.

Lynn raises her flute into the air. "Time itself isn't relative—but what you do with it most certainly is."

Janice clinks her glass. "Here here. You're a wise woman, Lynn. Wise and *brave.*"

Just then the stylist walks over and catches sight of the women's wet faces. "Ladies! Your makeup!" she cries, grabbing her sponges to touch up their powder. "We girls are such softies on these happy days, aren't we?"

"Yes, we are. Especially on these happy days," Lynn agrees. And she truly does feel happy, in spite of everything.

★★★

"It looks like a magical palace, Mom," gushes Miesha, grabbing onto Rebecca's arm with her frail hand as they enter the Art Center. "Like in Swan Lake or something."

Rebecca and James can only nod in agreement. Large white pillars line up perfectly down the aisle towards a small, quaint altar framed by translucent white curtains embossed with gold embroidery. Cream-colored linen covers the chairs, which are set in a few semi-circular rows in front of the altar, and large arrangements of fresh-cut yellow and white orchids sit at either end. A second-floor balcony overlooks the scene, and a bar has been set up there to offer cocktails to the guests. Beautiful twinkle lights hang from the ceiling beams, setting the perfect mood for the evening.

It's expected to be a small gathering tonight for Martin and Lynn. Only fifty people or so have been invited, mostly friends from the Veterans' Hospital and some of Lynn and Martin's distant relatives.

"Save me a seat," James tells Rebecca as he gives her a kiss on the cheek. He goes off to man the front entrance in order to usher guests towards the wedding site. As he takes his post he feels his BlackBerry go off, signaling an incoming message, and is reminded to shut it off before the ceremony begins. Before he does, he glances at his notifications. He's got one text and one email. The text is from Ty.

Ty: Where r u? I'm upstairs at the bar alone. I came with Kendra but she's off with Lynn and your mom. Still haven't met the uncle. Come save me!!!

James smiles. *Maybe waiting on a woman will do Ty some good*, he thinks with satisfaction. He opens the email. He is filled with happiness when he sees that it's from Ted.

Hey Jimmy. Just checking in. Jackson says things are cool with Rebecca's kid. Fantastic. The weather is crazy wet here in Cambodia, and there are tons of tsunami warnings back in Thailand. So I'm thinking of heading back to California to sort some things out. I'll bring Shep Two with me. Maybe I'll hit up Chicago beforehand and this time you can be the tour guide. Cheers buddy. Ted.

The message lights up James from the inside. He misses Ted a lot. He writes back immediately.

Ted! So good to hear from you. Rebecca's daughter is on the mend. Thanks for everything, especially getting me back home to her and Rebecca. Glad Shep is still around. You should definitely come to Chicago. You and the mutt have got a place to stay for as long as you like. Take it easy bro. Jimmy.

"What are you smiling at?" Rebecca asks. She is suddenly standing behind him with her arms around his waist.

James can't help but smile at her easy touch. "I just got an email from Ted. He's making his way to Chicago," he says, flushed with excitement.

"That's great news!" Rebecca exclaims. "I can't wait to meet the guy."

"Mom, look!" cries Miesha.

Stan breezes through the entrance with Gerry and Max following behind. "There's my girl!" he calls out to Miesha. She walks gingerly over to Stan and swirls her skirt around, trying to snag a compliment.

Stan bends down to give her tiny frame a gentle hug. "Why, you're the prettiest thing I've seen since pink cotton candy on a stick," he remarks with mock seriousness. "And that was a long time ago."

Miesha smiles and saunters over to Max to ask for a ride on his wheelchair. Rebecca promptly follows her.

"You seen Marty yet, Jimmy?" Gerry asks, scouting out the place. He looks better than ever, and at least ten years younger than the first time James saw him.

"No, not yet," James says. Something clicks inside his head. "Wasn't Stan supposed to pick him up?"

Gerry looks confused. "He called Stan earlier today to say that Rebecca offered to drive him and that he'd meet us here."

Now it's James's turn to be confused. "Rebecca and I came here together with Miesha. And as far as I know, Rebecca hasn't heard from Martin all day."

Rebecca steps into the conversation. "I haven't heard what?"

James has no idea how to answer, and Gerry offers no help.

Rebecca looks over at Stan with a worried expression. "Didn't Martin come with you?"

"No, he called and said he was coming with *you*. He said to meet him here."

Gerry clears his throat. "He didn't get a ride with them, Stan."

"Well, where's Kendra?" Rebecca asks. "He must be with her."

"No, Kendra's with Lynn and Mom," James says quietly. "Ty drove her. Martin wasn't with them."

Rebecca turns her beautiful, worried eyes on him. "They're about to open up the doors for dinner and Lynn is going to wonder what's going on. God, I hope he's okay."

Stan runs his hands through his hair nervously, then starts to head towards the door. "Um, I gotta go."

James steps in front of him. "What's going on, Stan?"

Stan doesn't say anything, which only worries James more.

"Stan, if you know something about Martin that the rest of us don't, you really need to tell us," urges James.

"I don't know anything for sure ... but I think I should go find him," Stan says definitively. "If only I knew where to look," he adds under his breath.

James suggests that Rebecca bring Miesha, Max, and Gerry into the reception area. "Everything'll be fine," he reassures her. "Just keep things normal. Do it for Lynn," he adds. He turns to Stan. "I think I know where he might be," he whispers.

"How do you know?" Stan questions.

"Let's just say we have this odd insight into each other's lives," he replies. Without further question, Stan follows James into the cold night to find the missing groom. Their breath comes out in visible puffs as James scans the parking lot for his car. "Are you going to tell me what you know?" he asks Stan.

Stan is struggling to keep up with James's pace so James slows his step. When they reach the car, James unlocks the doors with the press of a button on his keychain. He sits down on the chilly leather and Stan follows suit. James is about to repeat the question when it suddenly dawns on him.

"He's dying, isn't he?"

Stan looks down at his scuffed black Italian leather shoes. "Yes."

James tries to ignore the sting in his chest as he drives off towards the university. He's glad when Stan doesn't ask any questions. As he drives he studies the city's bright Christmas lights. He is reminded that every year brings a celebration of hope towards a change for the better.

After a few blocks Stan breaks the silence. "Last year, when I was stationed in Iraq, me and my buddy Billy Kilroy were spendin' New Year's Eve in Mustafar, patrolling. And let me tell you somethin'—it don't feel nothin' like no celebration there. Anyway, we'd heard that the President was plannin' to send the troops home for the holidays, and some of them did get to go, but heck, we just figured we weren't lucky. Well, earlier that day our battalion caught these two little Iraqi boys tryin' to sneak into one of the armored vehicles to steal a big ol' box of candy—M&Ms, to be precise. They got about a foot away when one of the other soldiers on duty shooed them away. A real Grinch, that one. Anyways, later on, it was just me and Kilroy on watch with nothin' but time to think about home, you know? I was thinking 'bout what I wouldn't give to be home at my ma's place, eatin' her sweet home cookin'. Then suddenly this old man comes over to us with this long shirt and funky hat—"

"A *kurta* and a *kufi*," James cuts in.

Stan rolls his eyes. "Yeah, whatever. As I was sayin', he was comin' over carryin' this bundle of somethin' in his arms. Kilroy went ballistic on him, as if he was carryin' somethin' like maybe a bomb or a grenade. But I had this way of knowin' who were the bad guys and who were the good guys, you know? And this wasn't no bad guy. So I turned around and told Kilroy point blank to chill out. I walked over to the old man, and he's sayin' somethin' to me in his language, and he's pushin' the bundle up in my face. Kilroy is screamin' at me to move outta the way, but you know what, Jimmy? Right under my nose was the smell of fresh baked bread. Yep, I opened up the bundle real careful like, and there it was. The prettiest loaf of bread I ever saw."

James finds himself smiling. "What about the boys?"

"We pulled out that jumbo box of M&Ms and gestured for him to take it, to take it to the boys. The next day, they came runnin' over to us with chocolate spread over their faces from ear to ear." Stan is laughing hard at the memory, and James can't help but chuckle too. "Hot dog! The younger boy came runnin' up to us and he kept sayin' 'goodbye, goodbye.' We had no idea what he was talkin' about until we got word that Obama was sendin' us home." Stan shakes his head in disbelief. "Them two little fellas got wind of our homecomin' before we did, and they wanted to be the ones to give us the good news."

James puts on his blinker to signal that he's about to pull into the university parking lot across from the Oriental Institute.

"You sure about this?" Stan asks.

James nods. In his heart, he knows that Martin is here.

Stan begins to say a prayer out loud. "Dear Lord, please let this night turn out all right."

James turns off the ignition and they sit in silence for a minute before James lays out the plan. "This is one of his favorite places in the city, so I'm thinking he's here somewhere. Come on."

The men exit the car and head across the parking lot across towards the institute. The surrounding streets are busy but the university appears to have less traffic. The icy wind whips around their necks and faces as they brace the collars of their coats to shield themselves from the cold. Stan is shivering.

James is concerned for his health. "Listen, man, why don't you go wait in the car?" he suggests. "It's just about closing time, so if he's here, he'll be out any second."

"No, I ain't budgin'. But thanks, Jimmy."

The sound of a cellphone makes them both jump. James realizes it's his and fishes it out of his pants pocket. "Hello?"

It's Kendra. "Jimmy, Lynn is freaking out. Where is my uncle? Is he okay?"

"We're …" James trails off. Stan nudges him. He looks across the street and sees Martin hobbling out of the institute. He is looking incredibly frail.

"Kendra, we just spotted him. I'll have to call you back, okay?"

James and Stan jut through the traffic towards the entrance of the university building. As they approach, they see a cab pulling up.

"Hey!" Stan yells, running faster.

The cab comes to a stop and they see Martin reach for the rear door.

"Marty!" Stan yells, louder this time.

Martin looks up and an expression of surprise crosses his face. He watches as his two friends sprint towards him.

"Jesus, Marty, what's going on?" James asks. "You've got an entire room full of people worried sick about you, especially Kendra and Lynn."

Stan says nothing. He is trying to catch his breath, bending down to rest his arms on his legs.

Martin looks tired and impatient. "I'm just trying to get some perspective, that's all."

Stan has regained his breath. "Well, can you try to get some of that while we get you to your weddin'? Come on, Marty, it can't be all that bad. You got a beautiful woman waiting for you, wantin' you to spend the rest of your …"

Martin is suddenly on the attack. "Rest of my what, Stan? The rest of my chemo treatments that aren't working? The rest of my excruciating pain? The rest of shitting and pissing myself?" His voice cracks with the fear of his looming death, overriding his ability to reason. Martin wobbles closer to his friends, his cane his sole support. Stan is at a loss for words.

The wind picks up speed and changes direction so that James's eyes begin to water. He knows that it is his turn to take over the situation. He can see Martin lost for the first time and understands his role in the search to reclaim him. "Stan, buddy, go bring the car around, will ya?" he instructs, tossing over the keys.

They tinkle like bells before Stan snatches them out of the air. "It's just 'cause I care, Marty, that's all," Stan whimpers before turning to head back to the parking lot.

James fixes his eyes on Martin's as they stand toe to toe.

The cab driver rolls down his window. "Excuse me, sir, but will you be needing a ride or not? It's very, very busy tonight."

James turns around and reaches into his coat pocket. He hands the driver a twenty through the window. "You're free to go," he says. "Thanks."

As the cab pulls away, Martin snaps his cane against the cold ground. "I'm not going to stand here, Jimmy, and listen to you lecture me. I'm an old man and I've lived a lot longer and harder than you. Time isn't a factor for me anymore. In fact, time is just a figment of our imaginations, and it continues to taunt and tease us with its supposed abundance. But just like the codfish in the ocean, Jimmy, what once was plentiful is now running out. And the reality is, the more time we have to harvest, the less of it we actually have to live by. I'm sick of it all. I have a right to choose not to play this game anymore."

"You selfish old man," James scoffs.

"Now listen, boy, don't you talk to me in that tone of voice," Martin growls. "I knew your dad and—"

James cuts him off. He feels himself glaring now. "How dare you be such a hypocrite!"

Martin's eyes are wide. "It's essential that we remain within the order of things Jimmy. Please do *not* disrespect me."

"Or what? You're going to turn your back on me?" James retorts.

Martin's mouth trips over words.

"Well, that's great, Martin," James continues. "And while you're at it, you'll turn your back on Lynn, too?"

The wind threatens to catch Martin off balance, but his thin figure withstands the buffeting.

"Your fiancée is waiting for you, Martin! She's waiting to marry you at the stroke of midnight. This isn't about *you* anymore, Martin—it's about *her*. It's also about Kendra and Rebecca and Miesha and Stan, and Gerry and Max and Kitty … Shall I go on?"

A security guard walks out of the university building to assess the situation. "Is everything okay here, sir?" he asks Martin, concerned.

James is suddenly awash with anger that the patrolman thinks he's harassing an old man. "Everything's fine," he seethes.

The guard looks to Martin for confirmation. "Sir?"

"It's fine, thank you," Martin responds.

Just then Stan pulls up to the curb. James motions for him to stay in the car.

"Martin, do you remember that a few months ago we were standing in this very place, only it was *me* who was too afraid to live my life, and it was *you* who was talking sense into me? I might as well have been dead back then myself, Martin, for all that I was living. But you gave me back my life. You gave me the courage I needed to take the first steps towards living again. Well, it may be your turn to go sooner rather than later, but if you give up now, you'll be letting everyone who loves you down—just like I was." James is breathing heavily now, but he can't stop himself from charging on. "You showed me how to face up to the hard parts of life, Martin. You taught me that I had no other choice, because I was hurting too many people by living with my head in the sand. And if you refuse to live your life now, with Lynn, well, you'll be just as bad as I was. Worse, even."

Martin starts to hunch over his cane. He suddenly looks totally dejected to James. "I can't give her anything, boy. I'm *dying*, don't you understand? Your situation was far different from mine, and you're too smart to even try and establish some type of comparison, because we both know there is none." Martin leans on the waiting car for support. "I can't be the man they need me to be, so I would like to die alone and with honor."

"Martin, you are not Frank," James blurts out before he even knows he's going to say it.

"Of course I'm not Frank, Jimmy. Do you actually think I would compare my death to his?"

"Isn't that what you're doing?" James accuses, suddenly more sure of himself. "Is this what Frank would tell you to do? Die alone and with honor by leaving your bride-to-be at the altar and abandoning your niece, who's been like a daughter to you? What was it that Frank said in his letter to his brother again?"

Martin's glare is gripping. "How do you know about that?" he asks, the anger in his voice obvious.

The words run out of James's mouth. "I came by one night after Anna died to talk to you. I needed to talk to somebody, and for whatever reason, that night I wanted it to be you. Your room was empty so I thought I'd wait for a few minutes. There was a book on your bedside table—the same book you snuck into my bag when I left for Southeast Asia. Anyways, the title intrigued me so I opened the book and the letter was inside. I read it. I'm sorry. It was unethical of me and wrong, but I read it."

"You-you had no right, boy," Martin stammers.

"Frank told Sloan how bad things were there, but that he shouldn't worry because he had you and there wasn't anything that you guys didn't do for each other. He said that Sloan shouldn't be frightened for him because he was all right—"

Martin begins to reflect on this point. "Yes son, that's what he said," he says, his voice softening.

"I remember what he said too, Martin. I remember because it had a profound impact on me. Frank's display of compassion for his family was so honest and honorable," James explains. "He *wanted* to engage his family in everything that was happening to him in Vietnam, no matter how horrible it was, because he completely understood the importance of sharing his experience with them. In the end, they found comfort in knowing that they were with him all along, even when he died."

Martin looks the other way.

James can't tell if he's still listening or not, but he continues to make his point regardless. "I realized when I was away that I had done an utter disservice to my mother and sister by *not* allowing them to participate in my life—and in my pain. What I didn't realize was that they, too, needed to grieve throughout the process of my healing. Instead of giving them the comfort of being there for me, though, I decided to literally check out. And I won't let you do the same thing to Lynn, Martin. I won't."

Stan rolls down the window. "Jimmy, we should get Marty into where it's warm."

"What do you say, Martin?" James asks.

Martin reluctantly nods, no doubt caving into the idea of being warm and comfortable. Stan gets out of the vehicle and helps guide Martin into his seat while James calls Kendra. She's frantic when she answers. "He's okay," James tells her. "We're on our way. I'll explain later."

The ride back to the Art Center is somber and awkward, although Stan scans through the stations and finds the music of Procol Harum, which offers a much-appreciated break.

"You were right, Jimmy," Martin says quietly from the back seat. "I was being selfish. The pain … it just gets to be too much sometimes. But I wasn't thinking of them—I was thinking of *me*. I certainly don't want to punish anyone. It's just … it's just that death's closing in on me. I can feel it, and I can't be as courageous as I wish I were." He grabs his chest and starts to weep quietly.

"Marty, you're *not* gonna die today," Stan's sturdy voice assures him. "And you're not gonna die tomorrow or the next day or the next day either. You got that? You got to use your mind to get through the pain, Marty. It's the strongest body part you got, and it's tougher than anyone else's I know."

Through the rear view mirror James can see Martin smile and wipe his tears with his handkerchief. Somehow, Stan knows just how to speak the truest of all truths.

★★★

As the evening unfolds, Martin and Lynn's presence fills the room with happiness. Dinner comes and goes, and the simple marriage ceremony takes place only minutes before midnight, making the anticipation of a new year even more electric. After the vows are exchanged, champagne bottles crack open and the music ramps up for an hour or so of dancing before the event is scheduled to end.

James hasn't been able to take his eyes off Rebecca all night. By the time one o'clock in the morning rolls around, Miesha has fallen asleep, cradled in her mother's arms. James smiles at the sight. He has come to adore Miesha in ways that he cannot explain to anyone, let alone himself. Kitty interrupts his thoughts to kiss her brother goodnight before heading out. James watches her leave on Jacob's arm, then goes back to leaning against a pillar with a whiskey in hand, happily observing the room.

Gerry and Max are leading the dance floor in La Bamba. Stan has his arm wrapped around Cody Ann's waist as he's chatting up the bartender, making them both laugh. Martin is sitting beside Kendra, completely engrossed in a conversation that is clearly hovering miles above Ty's head. James laughs out loud at this visual before catching Rebecca's cue that it's time to take Miesha home. He signals back that he will fetch the car.

On his way to the parking garage, James can't help but think about Martin's wedding speech. He recalls it word for word so as to etch it into his long-term memory. *I've been blessed my whole life to have had the privilege of being in the presence of such grandiose personas. Each of you has helped me pave my way to where I am today. Tonight, I would like to thank you all from the bottom of my heart and soul for your love, loyalty, friendship, and patience. I have learned much about the meaning of my journey here on Earth through my interactions with you, as you've graciously endured my sagacious questions and conversations and general avaricious need to be right in my opinions. Looking out at all of your faces only deems confirmation that we all make up a part of this eclectic epicycle—an unbroken chain of time and events linked together forever. I am honored and privileged to be a part of this magnificent circle. Today, I continue my way along my mortal path with my beloved new wife, Lynn. I truly believe that I am the luckiest man alive at this moment. Now, before we*

269

leave here tonight, I would like to share a poem with you. One inspired by Lynn and all of you – my dearest and closest allies.

James pats his breast pocket to confirm that the piece of paper is still there. It is the thought that Martin went on to share, and then later slipped to James in a handshake. James starts the engine and sits back to let the windshield defrost. He turns on the interior light and unfolds the piece of paper. As he rereads it now, he can't help but think that Martin wasn't just inspired by poetry—he *is* a poet in his own right.

He reads, *Love is larger than life. Perhaps this is why so many of us fear its presence or find it too difficult. But if people could only see things from love's point of view. It requires patience, understanding, sacrifice and hard work. It is not something that is easily dispensed and digested without keen will and desire, nor can it be sustained without the acceptance of its obvious weaknesses and challenges. Although it is most powerful, love lacks perfection. It is true that it can be cruel and unkind. However, we, the perpetuators of love can evolve through the necessary experiences we must face. Whether they be good or bad, their significance is essential to the outcome of our journey here on earth. In the end, love remains the only immortal part of our existence, with which we should all be compelled to make our mark.*

TWENTY-FOUR

"Frank?"

"Yeah."

"Is that you?"

"Yeah, by."

"What time is it?"

"It doesn't matter none. Come on now, let me help you."

"Are you all right, Frank? I can't see you."

"Yes, by, I'm fine. Just fine.

"Is there anyone else with you?"

"Diggers ..."

"Yeah?"

"Not to worry. I'm here. Just ... let go."

★★★

It is an unusually warm and clear day for early May. Martin Joseph Diggs's coffin is perched in front of the altar of St. Thomas Church in the south end of the city. An American flag lies over the silver-plated coffin and James can't help but stare intently at the abundance of colorful flowers perched alongside it. He smiles, shaking his head at the irony. As far as James knew, Martin was—not unlike himself—skeptical of God's existence, yet here Martin lay in a place of God's worship. James looks across the pews and catches Lynn's face. She appears content and proud to be celebrating her late husband's life here. *He did it for her,* he thinks to himself.

Veterans fill up the front pews; their faces are grim with the loss of yet another comrade and friend. A local children's choir starts singing a powerful rendition of "Oh Happy Day," heightening the already sweeping emotions of all two hundred attendees as their voices echo and bounce off the marble walls of the cathedral.

The remaining members of Martin's battalion are saluting his coffin. Local policemen and firemen line up along the outside aisles in honor of Martin's many contributions to their community charity events over the years, as well as for the bravery he showed during his time at war.

Lynn is sitting in the front pew in between Kendra and Janice. She is smiling and weeping at the same time. Kendra is singing along with the choir as Ty sits beside her, holding her hand. Behind them sit two of Martin's cousins, as well as Lynn's former sister-in-law and her two children. Next to them, James has his arms around Rebecca and Miesha, who are trying to manage their heartfelt grief discretely. Kitty is holding A.J. in her arms and praying at the opposite end of the pew, while Jacob dozes off from extreme sleep deprivation. James looks over to catch Kitty poking her husband hard in the ribs, startling him awake. James catches himself smiling and welcomes the momentary reprieve from sadness.

After the choir finishes the gospel hymn, Kendra gets up to speak about her uncle. "I've always had this connection with my Uncle Martin, even when my own father was alive and well. We seemed to be more like each other than anyone else in the family, and I'm so happy that I can truly attest to the fact that he does and will continue to live through me. I thank you, my sweet uncle, for giving me the gift of unconditional love and courage, and for showing me the importance of learning for the joy of discovery …"

After a few more minutes Kendra finishes her eulogy and takes her seat. Ty squeezes her hand and she buries her face in his neck for comfort. The pastor moves back towards the altar and asks everyone to stand for the Lord's Prayer. The mantra murmurs from pew to pew. A military friend is asked to come up to the front to say a few words on behalf of the United States Navy. Laughter fills the church as he tells a story about Martin during his service overseas.

"We hadn't had much to eat for days, and Martin started talking about this famous macaroni and cheese that his mama used to make. He described each ingredient in detail, and by the end of it, he had us all drooling. He painted the most beautiful picture of cheese pasta that anyone could ever imagine—especially this South Vietnamese officer, who was trying so hard to decipher what Martin was saying that he forgot all about the gaping wound on his head. He was fascinated by Martin's description. I'd never seen eyes so wide…"

When the story finishes, the choir starts to play another one of Martin's favorite hymns. This particular song is James's cue to stand up and head to the front. Stan,

Gerry, and Max start to make their way to the coffin as well. The four men assemble around it and prepare to chauffeur Martin on his final journey.

James chokes back his emotions as he lays a hand on Martin's casket. "You changed my life for the better, Martin," he says quietly. "You'll always be a true friend and mentor."

Max pulls out Martin's flask from behind his back and commences a toast. "Godspeed, Marty!" He takes a swig and passes it to Stan.

"I know you're where the sun burns bright, buddy!" Stan says. He winces at the taste of the warm whiskey.

Gerry takes the flask next. "Wait for me in the big bunker, Marty!" He passes the flask to James.

James lifts the flask. Tears sting his eyes and turn the stained glass windows into floating orbs of color. "I'll see you again, Martin. This won't be the last shot of whiskey we toast to you." Jack Daniel's has never tasted so good to James as it does in that moment.

The last chords of the hymn fade away and the pastor asks everyone to stand for the procession. A soldier starts to play "Taps" on a shiny bugle. The four men and two additional military officers prepare to perform their responsibilities as pallbearers. James rests his hand on the coffin's back left side. It feels almost weightless as they roll the casket down the aisle.

Suddenly a quotation comes into James's head. *To improve is to change; to be perfect is to change often.* "That's an easy one, Martin," James murmurs. "Winston Churchill."

And he smiles.

TWENTY-FIVE

It's a beautiful late spring day, and it's warm despite a slightly damp wind that has come down from Canada. Today is the day of Martin's final departure from Chicago; his remains are set to travel by train to Nebraska where he was born and raised. At his request, Lynn and Kendra will travel by train to his hometown Omaha with the majority of his ashes and place them alongside the graves of his mother, father, and brother. The rest he asked that Stan scatter into the north Atlantic, off the coast of Newfoundland, in honor of his best friend, Frank Kenney.

Lynn walks into the dining room to clear away the breakfast plates. Today she is feeling good. It hasn't been easy since Martin passed away—she'll be the first to admit that—but today she's beginning to feel like herself again. "Ted dear," she says, distracting her houseguest from the morning newspaper. "Can you go fetch Jimmy for me? He's just in the backyard with Miesha. I need him to help me with a few things before we head to the station."

"Sure thing," says Ted, as amiable as ever. "Is there anything I can do for you, Lynn?"

"Oh no, thank you, dear," she says, shuffling off to the kitchen with dirty plates piled up in her arms.

Ted jumps up to help her put the dishes in the dishwasher. She looks at him with a smile. His presence has been a blessing in disguise, in more ways than one. "I'm so grateful that you came to Chicago, Ted. You and my husband had quite a bit in common with Jimmy's recovery, you know."

"I'm happy to be here," he says. And he is so gracious and sincere that she knows it's the truth. Her womanly intuition tells her that being in Chicago is just as good for Ted as it is for James.

She watches him pull on a light windbreaker in preparation for heading out the back door to get James. "My word … it's uncanny how much you remind me of Stephen," she tells him.

Ted grins. "So I've been told."

Lynn rests her hip up against the dishwasher and crosses her arms. She looks out the kitchen window and watches Miesha, who is running around with James just as though she'd never had a close brush with death only six months ago.

"Because of you, Ted, that little girl and her mom have a good man in their lives. You know, James was lost for most of his life, and now I'm watching him and thinking, God, he's that same little boy I used to watch play in my backyard all those years ago."

"He certainly has come a long way over the last few months," Ted agrees.

"Yes, and now look at him. He's got a woman in his life, an adorable little girl, and a baby on the way!"

"Well, I shouldn't let him have all the fun," jokes Ted. "I'll go take over for him out there while he gets his butt in here and helps you get ready for your trip."

"Thanks, Ted," she says meaningfully. "For everything."

"Come on, Shep!" Ted calls. The little white shepherd perks up from where he's lying on his bed in the corner and comes skidding towards Ted, adoration in his eyes and his pink tongue hanging out. Ted gives Lynn a quick wave and then ushers the dog outside. He closes the door behind him, careful not to slam the screen door on his way out.

Lynn watches through the window as he walks across the new grass towards James. *Just like two bookends*, she thinks.

★★★

"Hey, Jimmy!"

James takes his eyes off Miesha and sees Ted coming across the back yard towards him. "Hey, bro. Is Lynn ready to head out?" He turns his gaze back to Miesha, who is trying to catch tadpoles in the small pond.

"Soon, I think," replies Ted as Shep licks his hand. "Lynn asked me to come out and get you. She said she needs your help with something."

"Um, sure thing. Can you—"

"Watch Miesha for you? Yeah, of course. Go ahead. We'll be fine out here."

"Don't let her go in the pond—"

"Dude, I can handle it. It's all good." Ted rests his hand on James's shoulder to reassure him. "You don't need to worry, my friend. Uncle Ted is on patrol."

James is grateful for the reminder to keep his anxiety under wraps. "Okay, okay. I know." As he strides towards the house he hears Ted calling out to Miesha.

"Hey Miesha, wanna jump in the pond with our clothes on?" James spins around, shocked, only to find Ted holding his stomach in laughter. "I'm just joking, bro. Seriously, relax."

James rolls his eyes. He immediately thinks about Stephen and feels his presence in the yard.

"Oh good, you're here," Lynn says when he pulls open the screen door. She waves him into the den. In the corner of the room stands a large cherry armoire with bulky gothic-style brass handles. James remembers how he and Stephen used to rummage around in there when they were preteens, looking for Halloween costumes. The smell of Lynn's perfume still lingers among the wool jackets and old fur coats draped in cellophane.

"Please, sit down, love," she says, pointing to the old red tartan wing-tipped chair. *This is odd,* James thinks. He sits down nervously, anticipating the unknown. "I haven't been in this room for years," he remarks, trying to break the ice.

Lynn looks softly at James. "I know, dear. And it's so good to have you back." She places her hand on his cheek as she says it. A large box full of books sits on the computer table next to them. Lynn gestures to it with her eyes. "This is something that Martin asked me to give to you."

James finds himself holding his breath at the mention of Martin's name.

"He said that you'd be the only one to understand them," she says, laughing. Her eyes start to brim with tears. "He also wanted me to give you this letter." She hands him a white envelope with writing on the outside.

James looks down to read the words. *To the one and only true Shepherd of the Aaron Milligan Veterans' Hospital.* James smiles as his emotions rear themselves too quickly. "Thank you," he says, his voice cracking under pressure and his eyes growing moist.

"It's okay to cry," Lynn says, easing his embarrassment. "I'll leave you for a few minutes so you can read it in privacy. I've got a few more things to pack before I'll be ready to leave, anyways."

She kisses him on the cheek and leaves him alone with the box of books from Martin and memories of Stephen lurking about. After a few minutes James collects his composure and opens the envelope. Martin's handwriting is well crafted, with strong strokes and elaborate flourishes.

Dear Jimmy,

I want to thank you for everything you have done for me and for all of my comrades at the hospital over the years. Mostly, I want you to know how much your friendship has meant to me. You're the only other person in the world that understands what it means to be feverishly erudite, and you were the only other person who ever figured out my insufferable riddles. If ever you feel the void of unhappiness and darkness, turn around to the other side of the room and you will find me there, in the form of one of my books, and I bet you'll find the answer. I may no longer be a person of flesh, but I will be all that is inside your mind and heart.

Until we see each other again, my friend and brother. Martin

James can barely feel his legs as his heart bears down on his entire body. He gently folds the letter back up and places it in his pocket. A heavy feeling in his chest makes it hard for him to breathe. He pushes the feeling away with his mind and reaches for the box of books on the desk. He carefully pulls out a few and scans the titles through his tears.

Miesha comes barreling through the door. "Jimmy! We have to go or else Lynn and Kendra are going to miss Uncle Martin's train!" She leaps onto his lap and one of the books catches her eye. "What's this?"

He checks out the title and smiles in recognition. "It's one of Martin's favorite books of poems."

She takes it from him and flips through the pages. "Can we bring it to the train station with us?"

"Sure."

Suddenly her brow knits pensively and James gets a glimpse of the serious and intelligent woman she will one day become. "Why did Uncle Martin ask to ride on a train to Omaha?"

James looks out the window. The sun is peeking through the tree buds and shadows reflect whimsical forms on the new grass and flowerbeds. Life is blooming everywhere, where months ago there was only stillness and death. He wonders how Martin would respond to that question, then finds himself answering in the simplest way he knows.

"Because, sweet girl, it's his turn."

The End

PERSONAL THANKS

To my exceptionally brilliant and patient husband Doug Gillen, who not only helped me with endless preliminary and final edits, but who continues to march with me throughout my journey in life as my true ally and comrade.

To my precious children – Cody Ann, Ava, Arianne and Eric, who continue to be my light and life's true blessings.

To my sisters Dawn, Theresa, and Bridget Whitely and to my stepfather, Gerrit Voskamp, for their unconditional love and for always having my back.

To my incredible extended family members and all of my loyal and trusted friends who have stuck with me through thick and thin and believed in this book.

SPECIAL THANKS

Thank you Elizabeth Bond, of Bond Writing Services (www.bondwritingservices. ca), my wonderful editor who helped me bring this story to life with her insight into the characters and her impeccable precision and expertise.

Thank you Thierry Black for your expedited and excellent work on the final edits.

Thank you Lynda Kanelakos from WildElement for taking charge of this project and for your boundless energy and wealth of knowledge.

Thank you Ray MacDonald for your legal advice and for always being there.

Thank you Neena Singhal of Phredd Grafix (phreddgfx@sympatico.ca) for your enthusiasm, patience and amazing cover designs.

Thanks to Beth Martin (Very Good Marketing) for her fabulous marketing strategy.

ACKNOWLEDGEMENTS

"Thatcher" appears courtesy of Laurie MacDonald (thank you my friend!).

Author's photograph by Alan Dean Photography. Make-up by Susan Kealey. Hair by Saly Mak Sayaphet.

Ann Whitely-Gillen *is a freelance writer, musician, and communications advisor. She happily lives with her husband and four children in Ottawa, Ontario, Canada.*

WWW.ANNGILLENBOOKS.COM